NOVA: EPISODES

SURVIVALISM

SHAAWEN E. THUNDERBIRD

NOVA: EPISODES
SURVIVALISM

This is a work of fiction. All of the characters, names, incidents, organizations, and dialogue in this novel are either the products of the author's imagination or are used fictitiously.

iUniverse books may be ordered through booksellers or by contacting:

iUniverse
1663 Liberty Drive
Bloomington, IN 47403
www.iuniverse.com
1-800-Authors (1-800-288-4677)

Because of the dynamic nature of the Internet, any web addresses or links contained in this book may have changed since publication and may no longer be valid. The views expressed in this work are solely those of the author and do not necessarily reflect the views of the publisher, and the publisher hereby disclaims any responsibility for them.

Any people depicted in stock imagery provided by Thinkstock are models, and such images are being used for illustrative purposes only. Certain stock imagery © Thinkstock.

ISBN: 978-1-4759-4640-6 (sc)
ISBN: 978-1-4759-4642-0 (hc)
ISBN: 978-1-4759-4641-3 (e)

Print information available on the last page.

iUniverse rev. date: 06/26/2019

Special thanks to

Frank Achneepineskum for funding my dreams
Gina Fusco for helping me make this book better
Jesse Achneepineskum for making the cover art
and Georgia Goetz for believing in me.

CONTENTS

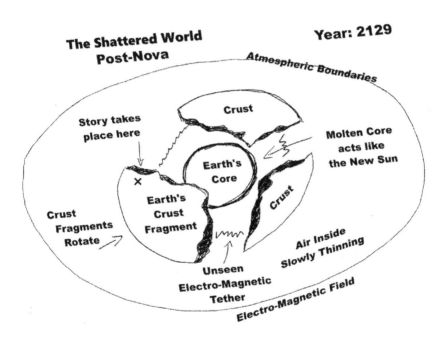

The Shattered World
Post-Nova

Year: 2129

Atmospheric Boundaries

Crust

Story takes
place here

Molten Core
acts like
the New Sun

Earth's
Core

×

Earth's
Crust
Fragment

Crust

Crust
Fragments
Rotate

Air Inside
Slowly Thinning

Unseen
Electro-Magnetic
Tether

Electro-Magnetic Field

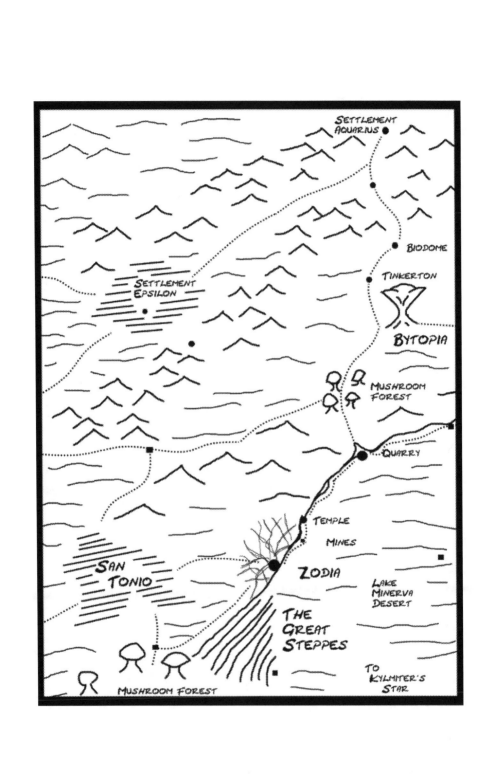

PROLOGUE

We thought we were powerful. We thought we were gods,
beings of invincibility. But I can see it painted within my mind. The
haunting howls, the screaming flesh, and the ring of flames ending
all time. But they didn't know it would explode. They only knew our
sun dimmed out of proportion. But I see it. I see it all, for I am the
cursed who brings the foretold.

And they, these so-called scientists, the harvesters of my
dreams, stared at the screen in awe that revealed the destruction
of their world. Within this petty room, I, the Seer of All Things,
was connected to electronics to monitor the sensory readings
that my vibrant dreams displayed. Yet he alone, this Colonel
Scathers, could not muster his hundreds of reactions under one
flow of emotion.

He just stood there, thinking, dreaming. What would he
do? Who would he tell? Who would believe the prophecies of what
he thought a "madman." But this so-called "madman" was right

about everything. He must act. He knows he must. The survival of the world depended on his actions. For if he did not, he'll suffer the consequences, and that is something he could not live with. Oh no, not him. He's too important. He must survive so he can die in vain.

"As of this moment," *he puked,* "this project is now classified. No one is to discuss this beyond this room."

The coats are in wonder. The coats are in terror, for never before did they imagine the end. They wondered if it was true. They wondered if it was lies. But all of them knew that the force of this word would spread onto the world. That was the concern for the petrified Scathers. Walk he did away from this madness, leaving behind a comet tail of thoughts. Into the corridors with shiver in spine and into the darkness his horrors reside.

Shamest to the one whom would tell it to all.

*   *   *   *   *

But shamest be not on the balcony of the saints. The immaculate Scathers had visited a home, a home that resided on top of a tower, a tower that viewed the last of the world. But the first he told was one he should not tell: the Secretary of Defense defending her secrets. Young she was but intelligent she be. This Valinda of worlds be too beautiful for command.

But Scathers acted with words that were fire; worries galore of the end of the world. Noted she did with concern and with sceptics. Weapons, her thoughts, repelled the incrucial. But sincerity be him of claims he possessed. With voice, with evidence, he presented it forth.

"This is the sun's corona before elaborate alterations and this is the sun after implementation," *he spoke.* "Valinda. We did this."

Deepest in thought, she scanned these claims. Believable

or not, we altered the sun. One hundred years after the birth of
A.I., humanity already had solar rebirth, a power to de-tensify the
rays of our star. But the bravers of beings had to test our volition.
They wanted to do what others could not. They wanted a prize to
immortalize their souls. They wanted our light. They wanted our sun.

"How is this possible?" *she so bothered to ask.*

"I don't know what to tell you," *he covered.*

"Are you trying to play God?"

"I had nothing to do with this,"

"Why would you tamper with it? What the hell were you thinking?"

"That doesn't matter now."

"Matter?! We have eight billion people living on this Earth."

"That project was specially classified. Not even the president knew."

"Oh, and how will that look that our own president didn't know what was happening in his own government?!"

"If congress knew, that project would never have lifted off the ground."

"So, you undermined federal policy? What gave you the right?"

"There's forty-nine projects with special classification."

"Well, we can't just sit here. I'm going to schedule a press conference."

"Without presidential consent?"

"We cannot keep this contained! People have the right to know!"

"We'll get indicted. Shut down for NRSCA investigations. It'll blow up in a nation-wide scandal and even you don't want that."

Too angry for reason, the fiery Valinda wanted to thrash

out more. She stood there thoughtless, powerless, and highly
uneducated in matters like these. Crowd control. Media control.
Public order. Such are the reasons for the experienced to be
promoted and not for the interests of feminist satisfaction.

"We have to go to Congress," *reasoned Scathers.*

"Without scientific evidence, all we have is a Psi-Ops
patient spitting out ridiculous claims," *she retorted.*

"Here. Use this," *Scathers said as he handed over the*
folder of sorts. "We have to convince them to order a world-wide
evacuation."

*   *   *   *   *

"Evacuation to where, Valinda?" *slashed the sceptical*
Gerow. Oh, he be the fish that out-trouted the seas, razor in mind
and reasonist in soul. Doubtful beyond doubtful, the arch of his
brow crusaded his concerns.

But the nervous Valinda stood there, unenchanted, before
congress in private to decipher her claim. Worry and humiliation
crept up into her face, but proceeded she did, the proceedings in
vain, on the holographic display.

"Gliese 581d on the constellation Libra," *she muttered.*
"The only known extrasolar planet with potential habitability. Only
twenty light years away. If we funded NASA to conduct a New
World's Mission and with our terraforming technology, we could--"

"--could what, Valinda?" *stabbed Gerow.* "Cast us off to
Neverland? Land us on an alien planet? Repopulate the human
race? Do you even realize the financial pressure this will have on
our economy? To build massive fleets of shuttlecrafts to evacuate
the human race based on a prophecy is what, Valinda?"

But response evaded her.

"Implausible!" *twisted Gerow.* "No government will ever

agree to launch a planet-wide campaign to leave the planet, our jobs, our homes, our foundations on this Earth that we've spent years building and enhancing, based on the paranoid delusions of a madman's prophecy that probably won't even happen!"

Pity. Not that I, the one, had cared much for the human race. But the lovely Valinda did. No, she just stood there bruised and defeated in a room of empty reason. Not one of them were even close to being convinced of my dearest claim. Let the world play god. Let the people do creed. Let the immaculates paint themselves from the existence of time.

Pity for the ones deceiving their own.

*　　*　　*　　*　　*

But rumours of the Nova expelled onto the world. Some claimed it a doom say. Others believed. The ridiculous scientific world exploded debate. Media hosts harvested the mania into greater proportions. Coverage upon coverage filled the televised realm and this dark paranoia infected them all.

They were watching, waiting, all of them in a gasp-filled world to be so denied. But that didn't happen. They know it to be true and a great tidal of impending doom washed over our world.

"But a Nova's a lengthy process! It takes decades to mature!"

"I trust the feds. If they knew, they'd do somethin' about it."

"It's a fear tactic to drive people to buy consumer products."

"Suddenly, there's all this Nova talk on the eave of election?"

"The government would save their own asses before helping us."

"I don't know what to do. Was crying all day. Called my mom, my ex."

Like rats escaping fire. So disgusting.

Yet, political badgerings became so intense that the

presidency responded to a petition of sorts. So many gathered around televised screens in bars, city streets, holographic displays to witness the thunder from the president's word. So many gathered before the whitening house. The whole world watched as the well-pressured leader marched to the podium — how forced he was.

"What we are witnessing here today is a historic event," *a mouthy reporter spattered.* "The president is making an urgent response to the nation-wide petition after insiders leaked out credible documents claiming our sun potentially going supernova. Rumours escalated the validity of these statements for months and with no government response declaring these documents a hoax. It can only be speculated that these rumours are true."

"Many people spoke of the end of the world and many people are afraid," *spoke the president.* "Life, as we know it, is a precious thing. The joy of which should not be robbed of by fear. So I urge the nation to exercise rational scepticism to these claims. It was suggested by--"

--a flash of light that you were all going to die. A light so blinding that even closed eyelids roasted. Oh, how the beautiful scream of a dying star opened up the doors of heaven, spanning its arms of light outward as though to collect all the billions of petrified souls with one warm embracing hug.

But that is not how they saw it. They stopped. They screamed. They cursed damnation but for their supposed god.

"Jack! Turn it off! Turn off the damn camera!" *yelped the reporter. And thus, there was complete radio silence; no cry for help, not even a whisper. The dread of spiritual silence encaptured reality, as sand and rock alone gave no home to the warm pattering of feet. They could've prevented this. They should've listened. But what did I know? I was just a madman, The Seer of All Things.*

CHAPTER 1

EXTRACTION

Oblivion; a void of non-existence where all things were forgotten. Therein lied no suffering, no conflict, and no madness in such a place. That was how he liked it. It was a place of peace, of tranquility, of divine absolution with no discord that brooded into this nirvana, until a cryptic voice invaded.

"Sentient being," the voice unleashed. "Heed my voice. Are you operating? Are you conscious?"

He was now, but he wasn't even aware of his own existence, nor had concepts of self-awareness conceived. He could not distinguish the strangeness of the word, for conscious thought itself eluded. His mind forgot but his thinking's self-reacted, sparking to life the usage of language. But why a voice spoke to him from the depths of pure emptiness he did not know.

He urged his eyelids apart. Frosty crystalline fragments on his eyelashes chipped apart and cold air stung his eyes. His voice rattled out a birthing gasp. His warm breath contorted into a swirling mist. Sound, still distorted, puzzled all hearing except the beatings of his own heart.

He was awakening; waking up in a cold ovular chamber that suspended his body's functions. But amidst his own revival, instincts intervened from the terror of red eyes.

"He's conscious," said the red eye's mechanized voice.

"The surface's under attack. We have to move," commanded an authoritative voice.

The red eyes pulled away and a disco of flashing lights flickered through the capsule's circular window.

"Whoa! Like, right now?" said another muffled voice. "While them drippin' wet popsicles' still thawin' next to live wires?"

It was hazy. It was blurry. He saw some figures, but couldn't make out what they were. Were they people? Were they beings? He couldn't tell in the mist of silhouettes.

The two voices continued to argue but he couldn't comprehend. His eyes were still recalibrating, but managed to focus on the frenzy of rushing people. They were fixing things, helping people from other ovular capsules.

"Listen." spoke the figure of authority.

A device was adjusted. The volume amped up. Radio traffic blared. He heard gunfire, screaming, explosions, and amplified voices overlapping with tension.

"Don't you think this stands out as a little more important, mate?"

"Then, what ye gonna be doin' with all them?"

The main officer huffed a sigh, then glanced at the situation. The officer looked away, succumbing to the argument and the eight-foot-tall cyborg pushed a button that opened up the capsule's doors.

The pod expelled him out and he stumbled to the grated floor. His lean, half-naked body dripped with dew. His limbs shivered. His heart pounded. His heaving stiffened, all that can be attributed to the cold air's mighty grip on his body. It was crushing him, electrifying his skin as his body struggled for stability.

"Help him at least," a field medic scuffed while blanketing him.

He embraced the warmth as though a divine salvation from

the cold. The medic flashed a light in his eye while taking his vitals. He squinted. The light itched at his cornea.

Yet his mind raced with questions. *Who was he? Where was he? Who are these people? What are they doing?* But memories still eluded from an intense brain freeze he was having.

"The hell is happening?" said a blonde-haired patient.

"Look. Okay, just relax. Okay? We'll get to your questions soon," replied an another medic while taking vitals.

"You!" directed the commanding officer, besieging his whole view with the barrage of his presence, "Name and credentials!"

Those commanding words stung him with offense. He didn't even realize the officer had an eye patch until then. But as he called forth upon his memories, he first remembered lights zipping by vertically.

*   *   *   *   *

He was in a room. It was small, octagonal shaped, an elevator. Another man stood by. They were heading down. It was miles beneath the surface. He remembered the man's name: Marcovian. He wore a lab coat. He was a scientist.

"Yeah, sorry, these rides are long," commented Marcovian. "Military secrets and all. Name and occupation, please?"

"Logan Lee Lansard. Street magician," he spoke.

*   *   *   *   *

"Street magician?" The eye-patched soldier snapped him out of reality.

"Rampras, they're all over us!" hinted a voice on the radio. "What the hell's taking you so long?"

Who's attacking? He thought, while still recalibrating the concept of a name. He was confused. Things didn't make sense.

But as the nodes in his brain wired together the aspects of identity, it came to him in no time. But, he was still confused. He tried to shake it off, but his hibernation sickness made it difficult.

So, he distracted himself. He glimpsed around at the now visible room; metal-plated walls, grated flooring, pipelines protruding and travelling along the ceiling, all of which signified that they were in a scientific facility.

The room's soldiers were equipped with metallic-plated body armour, embedded photon shoulder lights, and computerized assault rifles.

"Twenty-two malfunctions. Seven inoperative. Twenty active capsules overall," reported a female soldier on the comm system.

"We're approaching zero hour. Evacuation is imminent," consulted Samiren XIII, the eight-foot-tall cyborg. Samiren, by designation and the thirteenth unit of his design model, was all in rags except for the pistol-like device on his waist and a turret embedded on its left arm.

"I know, mate!" growled Reginald Rampras IV, the one-eyed captain of Beta Squadron. His rough voice alone commanded authority, but his eye patch created wonders of his war history.

"What month is this?" rasped the nauseated Logan, but was neglected.

"Alright, got the last one, cappy," said Calis as he got up off the floor. Though nothing was special about his clean appearance other than a growing stubble, he was Christopher Calis, the team's lieutenant and technician.

"Where's Martin?" said Rampras.

"He's being a stereotype again," said Calis.

Outside the room, irritating screeches pierced ears.

Rampras peeked out to see. Complexed, robust equations were scratched obsessively onto the corridor's steel panels. Its writer was of oriental origin.

"Martin!" barked Rampras.

Martin flinched. His elbow banged into his rifle leaning on the wall. The rifle fell over and bounced on the ground. Bullets snapped out and ricocheted down the hallway, leaving behind an array of homeless sparks.

Everyone covered while Samiren idly stood by unaffected.

"Ever hear of a friggen safety switch?" Calis blasted at him.

"Get off your damn ass and get the rest ready for evac!" roared Rampras.

Martin walked right into Rampras's face and glared. His left eye and cheek twitched intermittently. His breathing heaved erratically. It looked as though he was going to explode at a moment's notice.

"Maybe, I leave gun here...loaded," hissed Martin.

"Grab your gun and get out of my sight, mate!" Rampras whispered with equal flames. At first, Martin didn't respond as though exercising his right to be defiant. After a moment, he turned and left.

"Who are you people?" muffled Logan with a cough.

"Just shut up for a minute," said Rampras as he reached for his radio. "How much longer before extract?"

"We're ready now, captain!" said the voice on the radio.

"Good!" said Rampras as he turned to the defrosting few, "Listen up! The project you were in is terminated. We're at war! Everything will be explained at Settlement Epsilon. Let's move out!"

Field medics picked up the still-defrosting patients from the ground, hurled their arms around their shoulders, and inched them toward the hallway.

Logan was still disoriented. He wobbled into the neighbouring corridors. He passed Samiren, whose facial features were hidden behind a protective steel-plated mask. He got the sense that Samiren was disapproving of the lag.

Radio traffic sped through the corridor highways with sonic aroma. Logan took in his surroundings. He watched the squad disappear around the corner, then looked around at the darkened facility only lit by emergency lights.

He saw images of faint memories creeping up to the surface.

*   *   *   *   *

They were in a room. Connected to other hallways. Looked the same as the other. But properly lit. He remembered the carpet. It was red. Had fuzzy edges. He remembered the wall plants. Vines. Wall fountains were nearby. They were in a lobby.

"Engineering announcement," spoke a voice. It sounded amplified, on intercom. "A scheduled maintenance will take place at zero seven hundred hours affecting decks three to five."

"Good day, Mr. Kriejzuken," a receptionist said. She was behind a desk. She was blonde, wore a white blouse. She upkept her database.

He saw a scientist. It was Marcovian. He pointed down the hall. Labourers were there. They were hauling a cart. Something was in there: deactivated droids.

"They're two weeks late," complained Marcovian.

"Back orders from Cy-Corps," explained the receptionist.

"Plug it in the alcoves then," replied Marcovian.

*   *   *   *   *

But Logan could not remember anymore.

Thoughts invaded his mind. *Was I a patient? Was I experimented on? Why would I do such a thing? Maybe I had good reasons or maybe just desperate.* He didn't know. He had to know. Logan eased his way around the corner, balancing his own leaning tower of Pisa. Up ahead, Calis consulted a distraught Martin.

"What in jeebus has gottin' into ya?" remarked Calis.

"It no your business!" snapped Martin.

"None of my business? Yer peashooter almost poked a hole in my tin can. What'd ya mean it ain't no business of mine?"

"Just leave me 'lone!" Martin said while rushing off.

The whole corridor tremored. Emergency lights flickered. Debris and ceiling guts flung off and stabbed at the grated floors. Logan lost balance and stumbled to the ground, slamming his elbow into the wall. He groaned. Calis noticed him and helped him up off the ground.

"Easy does it there," said Calis.

"Sentinel! Sentinel incoming!" blared the voice in the radio. "Plough it down!"

"What's happening?" questioned Logan.

"Oh, jus' yer everyday global apocalypse," remarked Calis.

Logan was shocked. He dared not question more. The haunting overlapping radio traffic spoke for itself. He thought about the world he woke up to, but thought even more about the world he left behind.

As Logan passed the windows of empty laboratories, he recalled faint memories, but were too dim to image out.

"Area 77 is the central source of psionic research," said the memory of Marcovian's voice. "The Lancelot Program is the one you'll be admitted."

The Lancelot Program, he thought. He arched his brows, thinking, scraping up from the edges of his mind of what that meant. But he couldn't grasp it. He could not remember upon command.

Logan and Calis continued on, travelling through several intersections. Then the fluorescent emergency lights flickered. Darkness invaded for momentary lapses. All but Samiren's red eyes up ahead was sucked into the darkness.

A deep growl rumbled from the undertones of the silence. Calis and Logan glanced about. Nothing was around. It sounded distant, several floors away.

"Calis to Rampras. Did ya hear that?" said Calis to his radio.

"Copy," replied Rampras on the radio.

"We expectin' trouble?"

"We still don't know what kind of facility this is, mate."

Ever get the feeling of eyes on the back of your head?

Logan looked back. Nothing was there. No one had even said it. It was a memory, a glimpse of another hallway in the same facility that once was.

*   *   *   *   *

He was in a hallway. Windowed, laced with wire mesh. He walked to the glass. Looked down. Rooms were below. Boxed in like cubicles. People were in them. Wore white regalias. They were doing things. Tests. Experiments. But with each other. They were training... training their minds.

A man stood beside him. It was Marcovian.

"The back of the head's best for reception. The front's for transmission," explained Marcovian. "It takes years to grasp basic empathy."

Logan looked down. Saw two patients. One was sketching. The other sat nearby. Had his back turned. The other concentrated, then drew what came to mind. He was reading him, that other guy. He was grasping images.

*　　*　　*　　*　　*

"Langoliers! We got Langoliers incoming!"

That ripped Logan outta of his memory. They had caught up with to a patient-soldier traffic jam at a four-way junction. One junction door was sealed. A technician was already working on the door's circuitry. Patient whispers increased as the impatient Rampras spattered commands on radio.

"Target the Langoliers first. They're shield generators and rapid repairers of on-field A.T. Units."

"The surface squadron will have ninety seconds to alternate their position before arbalest bombardment," Samiren stated.

Rampras took note of that with a single look, "Gun them down and loop them south. Then re-establish the visual shield along the trench lines once the arbalest finished barraging."

"Copy!" acknowledged the soldier on radio.

"That'll hold them off for awhile," Rampras said as he pushed people aside to attend himself to the mechanic's presence. "Multanis, I told you to pack it up."

The balding middle-aged soldier, Doctor Multanis, who was working on the wall's circuits, graced out a frustrated sigh.

"Deputizing a multi-talented physicist to a technician to disable sophisticated automated defense grids is not my way of celebrating shore leave," whined Multanis. "If we can't disable these grids, Captain, I assure you, we're in for a rough ride."

A loud crunch contorted the metal door. It twisted and warped out of shape. Then an unseen tug ripped it off its sockets.

The door snapped and flipped for the crowd. Everyone clammered, but the metal slab drifted to a glide. The ten inch cast-iron steel slab was suspended above them, the crowd of awe-filled eyes, then floated to the feet of a mysterious woman.

Logan nearly gasped. She was so beautiful. Her dark, handcrafted leather gown accentuated the pale nature of her skin. Her luminous eyes, piercing through the shield of her raven black hair, spoke with intense insanity. But her lips whispered with the exquisite sensuality of a seductress. She, however, was Vanis, the squad's lead psionicist.

"You're late," remarked Rampras.

Vanis sneered at him.

"Okay, what was the point of that flashy business?" asked Calis.

"The system already had this facility quarantined when we came in," explained Multanis. "Turning on auxiliary power reactivated the containment procedures. Either we deactivate these grids or we disassemble every containment door we come across."

"Mmm. To sooth the chastity of virgin doors," hinted Vanis.

Calis looked at Vanis awkwardly as though threatened.

"There's no time. We have to move right now," said Rampras.

"Just wait," cried Multanis. "I can still--"

--Rampras ripped him off the floor and glared straight into his eyes. Multanis was easily two hundred pounds. Adding that with an extra one hundred pounds of metal plates, Rampras easily shocked everyone in his group.

"We're moving right now!" growled Rampras.

Multanis couldn't believe he just did that. He gazed at Rampras in total disbelief at his outburst. But given that his soldiers were dying on the surface, Multanis could easily understand his stress.

Rampras let him go. Multanis grabbed his assault rifle, stood up, and gave a blank stare at Rampras. Rampras seemed glad that nothing more came out of that. He led the silent squad on down the ripped open doorway.

The squad trudged forth through several corridors before coming to a room. It had rail walkways between four large conversion cylinders of a hydrogen compression room. Grime-stained danger signs with pictographic symbols patterned the walls. This place seemed like a water, oxygen, or even a power plant that provided and distributed to the rest of the facility.

"C-Squad. We're at the rendezvous," said Rampras.

"We've got hostiles! They're everywhere!" replied the voice on the radio. Yelling and gunfire squeaked in the radio's background.

"Was that down here or up there?" questioned Calis.

"What channel did you set them on?" Multanis asked.

"Them guys are usin' the same frequency," said Calis.

"What kind of facility is this?" Rampras growled while thinking.

"It's military. It's unlikely linked to BioDyne," said Multanis.

"BioDyne," echoed Logan.

"BioDyne is being subpoenaed to forward details to the court of public opinion," spoke the remembered news anchor.

*　　　*　　　*　　　*　　　*

He remembered a news clip. Saw the name BioDyne. It was on TV. Lots of angry people. People in suits. Saw a courtroom. Full of senators. People picketed outside. They all hated BioDyne.

"Safety inspections revealed questionable operations that may have violated the hypocratic oath, protocols of the united scientific agency, and human rights," informed a news anchor. "The senate is debating whether or not to exercise Bill C-One-Eighty-Two, suspending corporate licensing to cease experimentation for evaluation and eventually litigation."

* * * * *

A distant roar vibrated the steel railings of the hydrogen compression room. The patients tensed up. The squad flashed their rifle lights all over the room, unable to pinpoint the source. Calis shined the light on Logan.

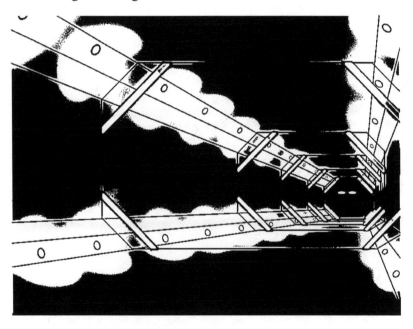

"Y'all alright?" asked Calis.

"We're fine," Logan said while squinting.

"What the hell kind of facility is this?!" Rampras roared.

"Nothing's coming up on our motion trackers," Multanis said.

Rampras paced around wondering what to do, wondering how to prepare for an unseen enemy they knew nothing about. Logan didn't remember either. He only knew this place to be a training facility. No monstrosities of any kind was supposed to be down here.

But he remembered a sealed door. He could barely image it out. It was huge. Massive. Several feet of solid steel. It caged something. Something powerful. But he couldn't remember anymore. He couldn't remember what.

"Ye think it's chimeras?" Calis asked.

"Shouldn't be," Multanis said, "Maybe psionic."

Calis and Multanis looked to Vanis. Vanis had already drifted her gaze toward the growling. She had been scanning since the occurrence.

"What we doin', cappy?" asked Calis.

"Something's down here and we don't know what it is," said Rampras, "I don't like that."

He paused in thought, wondering how to strategize against something without substance. Then, he shook off his thoughts.

"There's no sense in wondering about it. We're just going to have to deal with it as it comes."

His core officers stared at him blankly. Rampras glanced around at the area, then at his men, analyzing the available resources. The weight of decision-making was in his eyes. Logan could easily tell. It was like in a battleground of strict mobility. Every minor, dismissible decision had critical weight.

"Multanis, take point," said Rampras with much stress, "Calis. Cover our aft. Everyone else on me. Keep your weapons hot."

Multanis led the squad into the dark corridors. Calis swept the room with his rifle light. The nervous patients cushioned in between the soldiers as they were led deeper into the halls.

Logan hated feeling helpless as he was. His heart pounded in perfect rhythm with sonar pulses of Multanis's motion tracker. It was as though each ping commanded the rhythm of his heart as they walked down the eerie halls of blackened futures. The breaths of nervous sighs were the only other sounds.

After zigzagging through several paths in the steel labyrinth cage of the facility, the motion tracker did not irritate with detection throughout.

Suddenly, a loud radio-like ringing wailed out of the silence. All sound numbed. The ceiling panels tremored, and the menace of a cackling voice invaded their minds.

The squad dropped to their knees, clenching their heads in agony.

They screamed. They screeched, wailing from the intense torment drilling into their minds. Logan felt it all; like someone ripped his skull open, tearing off the very bone plate from his head and gripped his brain, crushing it into mush.

After a moment, it dissipated, leaving an unaffected Samiren confused. Veins flooded the brain with blood as though released from a choke hold. Logan's vision spun as though hung over from a heavy night drinking. It was painful. Every sound and light pounded into the brain.

But after a moment, it passed.

"Vanis. What was that?" Rampras grunted.

"A mind of power laced with lingered rage," Vanis moaned.

The whole squad fell silent. Logan felt a flood of tingles wash over his body. His hands shook uncontrollably, as though he entered a realm of terror. But something was unnatural about it. It was like every living cell in his body cried out in fear. They all knew what it was, except himself.

What was he afraid of? Was it the screaming or the coming unseen force? He couldn't tell. But after dissecting that strange event, he did know one thing: something had awoken. He could feel it. It was gripping at his gut.

"C-c-cappy, I don't t-t-think we should be in here," said Calis.

"Keep it together, mate," Rampras growled at him between his teeth while helping Multanis off the ground.

"Keep it together? How we supposed to be doin' that with all this psionic tantrums goin' on givin' us migraines?!" Calis complained.

"We'll worry about it when we meet it," said Rampras.

"Worry about it when we meet it?! Them head munchers are the same ol' type o' creeps that can make a folk end himself! How we supposed to be fightin' somethin' like that?!"

Calis was getting more agitated by the second. Rampras saw that. He grabbed Calis and slammed him into the wall. That shook Calis to his senses, staring at Rampras like he just un-caged a beast.

Rampras pointed a finger right between his eyes, and rumbled out a venomous growl, "That's not your worry right now! Your worry is ensuring your fellow soldiers make it out alive! Got it?!"

Calis nodded obediently, still breathing in a near panic-state. Rampras eased off him. Calis looked like his head was still spinning with worry.

"Where we going, Multanis?" asked Rampras.

Multanis tapped on his arm's computer. A small holographic map displayed. He studied it, then pointed southbound, "This way."

They travelled through the haunted steel corridors leaving only a wake of echoed steps. Logan kept looking behind them. He only saw corridors being swallowed by darkness from the limits of their lights. Multanis, startled, suddenly halted the team before a gruesome sight.

"I think we just found C-Squad," said the disturbed Multanis.

Before him, chunks of intestine noodles had spilled onto the floor. Blood stains tattooed the walls, and two bodies equipped with guns and plated armours were slumped along the wall. Their heads were cracked open. Brain spaghetti had spilled onto the ground as though exploded in a microwave.

Above their heads and written on the wall in blood were the words:

THE DETERMINER TOLD ME TO

"No," whispered Logan. He backed away from the bodies.

Sharp ringing pinged from the motion tracker.

"North!" said Multanis.

Barrels aimed north. Nothing was there. They kept looking towards the edge of the short cone of luminosity generated by their rifle's flashlights. Aside from the orange strobing backlight from an emergency LED beacon, anything beyond that was swallowed in total darkness.

They waited. They listened for even the slightest of sounds. All that they heard were panicky breaths and the nervous hearts beating their lives short.

The pulses intensified. Sonar pings increased in speed.

Logan shivered. Martin sweated. Calis grinded his teeth in nervous tension. Multanis interchanged his vision from tracker to hallway.

Everyone stood tensely and stared down the northern halls, waiting for the slightest signs of disturbance. Only the flickering passes of lights highlighted an empty hall.

"Gopher Squad! We need reinforcements!" blared the radio.

"Turn that thing off!" roared Rampras.

The team silenced their radios. The tracker's pulses loudened. Distant clanks echoed from down the hall.

"They know we're here," warned Multanis.

"Help me!" spoke a raspy voice in the dark.

The squad tensed.

Gun barrels aimed at every darkened spot. Nothing was seen until beacon lights highlighted a dark humanoid form emerging from oblivion. The bald, naked figure crudely puppeted movements of a human being.

"Identify yourself!" commanded Rampras.

"It did something to us!" rasped the morphed figure.

The figure drew closer, dragging its naked feet lazily across the grated floors. It didn't even care that the steel teeth peeled off patches of skin. But, that didn't matter. Its skin was coarse, callus, and infected with dark blotches.

"Keep your distance, mate!" ordered Rampras.

"The hell's happenin' to him?" asked Calis.

"Captain, maybe we can still save him," said Multanis.

"Save'em from what?" Calis asked.

"No, we can't and you know that!" said Rampras.

"Save who? Save what? The hell is goin' on, man?!" Calis inquired.

"He might be infected with an earlier less evolved strand," said Multanis.

The radio shrieked, scaling wildly into cacophony.

"It's emitting waves all over the electromagnetic spectrum," said Multanis with harsh realization.

"Still think we can save him?" asked Rampras.

"They did this to us!" hissed the morphed figure.

The creature rattled a mucus-filled growl and lunged. The squad jolted back. Rampras took aim and fired. The bullet carved a hole through the creature's head. It plummeted to the ground and slid to Rampras' feet.

"Holy Jeebus sittin' on a can, man!" said Calis.

"Multanis!" barked Rampras.

Multanis genuflected and gave it a quick inspection. Black puss divulged from its open wounds.

"It's the chimera A agent," confirmed Multanis. "It metastasized to all of the organs. It's mutating the genetic code."

"But that thing is human," said Calis. "How'd ya know it's chimeric?"

"Because diffusion from mitosis erupted microwaves," said Multanis.

"Y'mean to tell me, this facility was holdin' 'em?" Calis questioned.

"Or someone came in already infected by it," reasoned Multanis. "But that doesn't make sense. This facility's for training. Not for experimentation."

"Then, how the hell did that thing get down here?" Rampras asked.

"I don't know," said Multanis.

They stared down at the lifeless corpse in disgust and wonder. Questions and worries of an invisible front plagued Rampras's mind. Was this thing the only one or were there more?

"Maybe that's why this facility's locked down," Calis theorized.

A patient leaned in to see, "Eww!"

"Get the hell away from that," said Rampras.

The morphed creature snapped an arm out and grabbed the patient's leg. The patient screamed as nails drilled inside his skin.

Inside the patient's body, the nails pierced and released hydra-shaped parasites into the bloodstream. As it flowed freely inside the body, the parasites fused with every cell it could find: white and red blood cells, cellular walls, bacteria, and even other viruses. As the parasite was absorbed, it broke off the cell's DNA chain, dismantled the microbes from inside, and used its parts to replicate more parasites.

The patient screamed and flailed his arms wildly as the infection spread up his leg. The squad backpedalled and blasted in a clip. The creature absorbed the searing bullets into its now hardening exoskeletal carapace. The barraged creature managed to get up from the ground. It rammed its hands through the patient's chest. Parts of the creature's body liquefied.

"Help me!" the dying patient screamed.

Radios wailed wildly. Rampras was horrified at the gruesome sight of liquefying bodies. They were fusing together. He aimed aimed his gun barrel at the patient's head and fired. The bullet sliced open the patient's brains. Both host and recipient were dead, but the virus was still consuming them whole.

"Why the hell did you do that?" yelled Multanis.

"He was dead already," reasoned Rampras.

"We could've froze his leg and transported him."

"You can't save everyone. Especially from that!"

Multanis looked very frustrated with Rampras's brute force.

"Light it!" said Rampras.

Calis slipped out a flare and threw it into the liquefying bodies. The body slush ignited instantly. A blaze roared with flames seeping up to the steel ceiling. The radio squealed wildly again.

"We've got to move!" barked Rampras.

He charged down the corridors. The squad followed. The snickering of creeps echoed behind them. Rampras dropped to one knee. He aimed down the corridor while the others passed. He flicked a switch on his rifle and blasted out glowing bullets. They were magnesium rounds.

Bullets fired, flashes flared, and momentary lapses of light revealed several creatures stalking the squad. They were running on all four limbs. Upon being sighted, the stalkers divided up toward adjacent corridors.

"Switch to magnesium rounds!" Rampras yelled.

Calis was at point. He hustled along, leading the fleeing squad through a labyrinth of darkness. Shadows receded around the darkened corners, aten by the given light. There were so many spots to ambush them, at corners, wall indentions, windows, other corridors, behind doors, everywhere.

They were making so much racket that all of their foot stomping, screaming, flashing of lights, bullet fires made it easy for them to be tracked. It was echoing everywhere. Calis was just going anywhere at that point. Anywhere away from the hell that would otherwise consume them into the abyss of claws.

A stalker emerged ahead of them. It bursted through a door ahead, but had done so too late to ambush. Calis took aim. Suddenly, the stalker vanished.

"They evolvin'!" Calis yelled.

He blind fired into the darkness. Another stalker burst through the ceiling ventilation panel. It stretched its arms out and grabbed one of the patients. Logan was next to it. He saw it in full; black mucus staining the mutated carapace. The patient screeched in horror as claws gripped him through his skin.

Calis and Multanis turned and blasted rounds. The flashes of lightning fire strobed into everyone's eyes. Black puss splattered in all directions. The stalker slammed into the ground lifelessly.

A blur flashed by between the squad. The wounded patient disappeared. Logan looked down the corridor. The patient was dragged into the darkness.

"Go, go, go!" Rampras raged.

He grabbed Logan off the ground and force marched him into the depths.

The squad took many turns before stopping at a three-way junction. Suddenly, the corridors quaked. Cradled ceiling panels flung acrazed. Waves of agony pounded into their minds as an irritating ring threatened to kill their ears.

Determiner. DETERMINER. Where ARE you?

It was the voice of the unseen force. It was deranged. It was psychotic. It rasped out the venomous growl of death while being so laced with innocence.

There IS no WHERE to RUN!

The CHIMERIC infection SEES you ALL!

Then the psychic storm exhausted. Emergency alarms squealed.

Red rotating lights began flooding the whole corridor. The mentally exhausted squad got off the ground.

"Intruder alert! Alert status red!" spoke a computer's voice. "Containment of section F seven has been compromised. Automated defense platforms have been activated."

"I knew this was going to happen. Stay along the walls!" yelled Multanis.

The squad pressed their bodies along the walls, covering behind beams and other indentions. Mechanical gears grinded inside the wall panels. Then, a mechanized turret projected from the ceiling. Metal plates protected its internal gears. Its fore-sensor scanned panoramically for pixelated updates.

"Maybe if we did like I said, we wouldn't have to face all this!" Multanis bit at Rampras.

"You tell that to the surface squad!" yelled Rampras.

Samiren came into its sensors. He just stood there in the middle of the hallway, uncaringly and unthreatened. The turret shifted its barrels at him. Samiren merely glanced at it.

"Samiren!" yelled Rampras.

Bullets snapped out of the turret's barrels. A loud clap came after followed by a blinding flash. The bullets slammed into a sphere of light surrounding Samiren. It was a force field protecting him. But, he didn't even react.

"Vanis!" said Rampras.

Vanis stepped out and motioned a gripping gesture. The turret vibrated and sparked violently. It was being pulled by telekinetic forces. Then Vanis crushed her grasp into a fist. The turret collapsed into itself and dropped to the floor. Active wires flailed the last of its power.

What happens when humans become more powerful than a machine? He remembered hearing. Those words came from Marcovian. Logan gazed at the broken turret. It stood no chance against Vanis. Her luminescent pupils radiated with brilliancy. He saw those eyes before, the eyes of a psionicist.

*   *   *   *   *

He saw floor tiles. They were white. Had brown ziggly lines. Some smear marks were on it. Sweaty feet. He looked up. Saw several people. They wore white regalia. Training on combat dolls.

"What are they doing?" Logan remembered asking.

A man stood beside him. Wore a scientist's coat. It was Marcovian. "Through years of development," he explained, "psionicists managed to tap into their own electromagnetic field."

He watched an Asian guy. He was tanned. Looked Thai. He stood before a punching bag. Bowed to it. Then coiled into a stance. Then thrust his palm out. Vision distorted between them. The punching bag flew off its hinges. It slammed into the wall. He didn't even touch it! Logan was shocked.

"The Chinese called it Chi, the spiritual force," Marcovian said with an impressed smile. "We call it...telekinesis."

*   *   *   *   *

Red lights flickered into Logan's eyes.

"Intruders detected. Activating droid alcoves," spoke the computer voice.

"Let's move!" said Rampras, "The elevator is just down the hall."

Wall plates slid open. Logan couldn't help but stand there and stare.

Inside were droids with torsos embedded on top of tank tracks, a wireless transceiver on its back, and steel plating covering wires and gears. It was motorized through hydrogen power cells and kinetically empowered through battery and hydraulics. Each was numerically painted and sported the manufacturer's trademark: Cy-Corps. These were all-terrain machines built for cost efficiency and mass production.

Several BIOS lights came on. It flickered intermittently. A low hum tremored as the drones booted up its operating systems. Gears grinded inside the chassis as the drones did a systems check. Logan just kept staring. Power chords disconnected from the first two drones that finished booting up. They erected upright in perfect synchronicity and slid off their alcoves.

"What in the hell are ye doin', popsicle?!" Calis yelled.

"Get down!" Rampras said while taking aim.

Logan floored himself. Bullets slashed all over the drones' chassis as it was charging their rotating gun barrels embedded onto their arms. The first two drones went down, but others activated from their alcoves.

"Initiating automated defense platforms."

"To the walls! Now!" Rampras roared at Logan.

Logan scampered away from the alcoves and huddled behind an indention. More turrets suspended from the ceiling inside the lobby. The squad was pinned from two directions. Soldiers popped their heads out for only a split second to blast off rounds before needing to cover. The fiery exchange spiked trails of light up and down the corridors as sparks snapped all over the walls.

Logan shook from every lightning bang that the rifles erupted, but focused only on the trails of light zipping by. Every single bullet that passed was made to kill. Each bullet was a ticket to a lottery of death. Each shot was a chance to slam into some unlucky person's body thus ending their life. His heart drummed wildly to that notion as though to pump every ounce of blood it could before its untimely death. Thus, it pumped his blood with the poison of fear.

One soldier fell dead but droid units were dropping by the numbers. The automated units rolled toward the corridor and fired in open terrain, easy targets against well-trained soldiers. However, their numbers were reinforced by alcoves activating down the facility.

"Don't them things cover?" remarked Calis.

"They're first generation," replied Multanis. "They're only equipped with basic programming given to them by Cy-Corps."

Cy-Corps, Logan thought.

*   *   *   *   *

"In other news," said a remembered news anchor, "Cy-Corps launched the nation's first defense platform fully computerized by artificial intelligence."

He remembered the news. Floods of activity. The camera was fidgety. Saw deactivated droids shipped out of a warehouse. A PR guy was talking.

"Most AI systems are not self-aware," argued a Cy-Corps PR, "They're unable to construct ideas or conscious thought. They only run strings of coded instructions within a program's syntax."

*   *   *   *   *

Rampras blasted a grenade from his rifle's launcher. The grenade seed torpedoed toward the ceiling turrets and combusted into fragments. Several fragments penetrated through one turret's armour plating. It sliced up circuits and wires. The clapping of complaining sparks whined all over the turret.

"Multanis, how do they acquire targets?" asked Rampras.

"Simple pixelated imagery," said Multanis.

"Smoke 'em," said Rampras.

Multanis detached a cylindrical grenade and rolled it toward the advancing droids. The cylinder puffed smoke, which quickly filled the corridors. Suddenly, the droids ceased fire, but the grinding of tank tracks betrayed their unseen advancement.

"They're blinded. Move!" yelled Rampras.

He stepped out, but one turret remained. It turned and acquired Rampras. Vanis stepped out and held her palm out at the turret. The turret unleashed its rounds. The bullets slammed into Vanis's spherical psionic shield. The soldiers blasted rounds at it. The turret warped and bent out of shape from the bombard.

Logan gazed at the haze of discharged sulphur in the air. The smell burnt his nose and the smoke bit his eyes. He was delirious. He felt secure in his hiding place and did not want to leave.

Thus, he reflected back to Marcovian to cope.

Why's that guy using a sword? Logan remembered asking.

*   *   *   *   *

He was in a big room. Rectangular. Had red stripes all over. A driving course. People paired in twos. They were in the middle. Devices in their hands. They were fighting. Practicing...with mists of light. It phased from their devices. An electric branch came out. It solidified the mist.

It was plasma. It turned it into a curved blade; a plasmatic blade.

"Psi-Knights from the Lancelot Program," explained someone. It was Marcovian, "and a knight must have a steed."

Vehicles sped by. Thin. Fast, but had no tires. Only a single seat. Stylized hulls. Silver plated. Their engines were light. Blue light. It made the vehicles hover. Expensive. Hi-tech. They were ion-powered hover bikes.

*   *   *   *   *

Suddenly, a hand grabbed him and pulled him back into reality. Logan was suddenly running towards the lobby before he realized where he was.

Inside the lobby, concrete chunks and metal beams had collapsed onto the floors. Visitor couches were coated with dust and a glass table had splattered its shards all over the floor. The front receptionist's desk remained intact but the monitors above them that once advertised the facility's functions were now dead and cracked. Plants, starved from malnutrition, sat near the once functioning fountain that was embedded beside the main elevation shaft.

The squad emerged from the north with eager bullets

overshooting their shoulders. Rampras and Calis covered the rear wild firing down the hall, as the rest of the squad hustled toward the elevator.

A ceiling turret suddenly snapped out and blasted two into Multanis's chest. The others braced at the sudden bangs. The bullets floored Multanis, but his plated armour cushioned the blow, exploding metal fragments.

"Multanis!" roared Rampras.

He kept covered the north corridor, while checking up on their states. The squad split up along the walls, but the turret blasted two patients in the back. Soldiers retaliated fire. The turret's hull held, but ricocheted the bullets all over.

"I'm alright," said Multanis. The turret suddenly shuttered. Then, collapsed upwards. Everyone looked at it confusingly. The ceiling section imploded upward into the floor above, spilling concrete dust in its wake. Electrical whips suddenly slashed all over the ceiling wound as a dark figure levitated down the hole. The dark figure was mutated and sported tentacle appendages from the back of its head. This thing was an evolved form of stalker. It was psionic.

"Mind flayer!" Calis screamed.

He took cover behind the couches. The scattered squad opened fire. The mind flayer crossed its arms. The bullets suddenly orbited around its body in streams of light. The squad was stunned.

The mind flayer then erupted its arms outward. The bullets dispersed all over the lobby and slammed into walls, couches, armour plates, and bodies. Two more patients went down, and three soldiers were wounded. Several bullets deflected off Samiren's shields.

"Don't just stand there," raged Rampras.

But Samiren did not respond.

"A challenge thus," moaned Vanis, "to lash the vigour in I."

The mind flayer surged a sphere of visual distortion around itself and burst it outward. The sphere lifted and slammed every object it touched into the wall. Soldiers and patients smashed around the room.

Vanis blasted debris away from around her. Then her eyes glowed with psychotic rage and a beam of light erupted from her head. The beam speared the mind flayer's chest and slammed it into the wall. Steel panels flew about.

"Now's our chance!" Rampras said as he got up.

Calis got up then saw the droid advancement from the north corridor.

"Captain!" said Calis.

The droid opened fire. A barrier of bullets rained from the north corridor, blocking off the elevator doors. Then crashes echoed down the hall. Calis looked. Stalkers stormed through the corridors and were ravaging the droid brigade.

"Access violation," warned the computer's voice, "Initializing secondary defense platforms. Counter-intruder droids have been activated."

"Go, go, go!" ordered Rampras.

The squad raced for the doors. Rampras hit the call button. The elevator was still at the top.

"Damn it!" yelled Rampras. "We have to fortify this position. Scavenge those bodies for additional ammunition. Calis. Martin. Barricade this area."

Multanis relieved dead soldiers of ammunition. Calis and Martin hauled a couch toward the elevator doors. Rampras checked on the northern flank. The stalkers ripped through the droid ranks and advanced toward them. The soldiers took cover behind the flimsy couch and waited.

"Secondary defense units have been activated," the computer spoke.

Stalkers stampeded into the lobby. Then, lobby wall panels slid open. Activated droids stepped out. Immediately, the stalker and droid lines clashed.

Rampras sighed with some relief. Black mucus and droid parts exploded about. Stalkers were pouring through the northern passageway and were slowly overpowering the limited droid deployments. Then a stalker cut through the lines and dove toward the squad. Martin and Multanis let loose a family of lead and the stalker crashed to the floor.

"Target stalkers only! Keep their lines balanced!" ordered Rampras.

"Why we do that?" asked Martin.

"So, they y'all be too busy to target us," answered Calis.

The squad sliced into the stalker lines. Rampras looked up at the elevator's position. It was halfway down. Rampras cursed at its sluggishness.

But, Logan was entranced with the requiem of violence. Stalkers splattered guts with every bullet slam. Droid parts screeched as its limbs tore off. A soldier screamed as a stalker dragged him into the depths of the chaos. These sights were unnatural to the eyes of combat virgins.

Then the elevator doors opened. For a split second, Logan saw large tentacles burst out from the floor before he was pulled inside.

CHAPTER 2
FRACTURED

The patient-soldier crew was now only twenty in strength. They crammed into the circular, poorly lit elevator. The stench of sweat, blood, and decay saturated the air, even though hygiene was the last on everyone's mind. Logan still remembered the gray carpet and wheel marks left behind by forklifts.

"Fake Jeebus and all the Jeebus miracles gone wrong!" cursed Calis. "What in all the seven hells of crap just happened in there?"

"Calis, will you calm down?" said Multanis. "This isn't helping."

"Well, sorry fer givin' a crap a crap," said Calis, "but none of us expected to be doing the shooty-shoots with all that tech fun up there."

"Multanis, what's our count?" asked Rampras.

"We lost half and brought back eight," said Multanis.

Rampras slammed his fist into the wall. Everyone went silent with eyeballs to the ground. They treated it like a preventable disaster gone wrong.

"Ye thinkin' it was a recon failure?" asked Calis.

"I know it was a recon failure, mate," stated Rampras. "This was labelled an excavatable site of unknown origin inside contested territory."

"Y'all would think we'd be all about extra carefulness," said Calis.

"We have listening posts stationed all over the northern

boundaries for that reason alone," said Rampras. "Either we're getting blinder or they're bypassing our sensory methods."

"It's quadratic acceleration," said Samiren. "An adjustment to Moore's law stating the acceleration of cybernetic progression at an astounding pace."

"Oh, he talks!" said Calis. "Did'ja needed a reboot or somethin'? Because we carbon-based unit folk coulda used some of that cybernetic help back there."

"That didn't matter, mate," said Rampras. "We went in blind not knowing the type of facility we were excavating."

"It's a psionic training facility," said Logan. "Military funded."

"Oh, fer the love of flyin' dingleberries and all things crap!" said Calis, "we already got an armada of looney toonies back in that tent town of ours."

"No askers spited you the comer asked," said Vanis. "The stricters missioned it a volunteer."

Everyone went silent, deciphering her puzzled words.

"Did someone beat yer brains repeatedly with a chainsaw as a kid?" asked Calis, "cause it's hard to understand that gibberish flappin' outta them lips."

"Can someone please tell me what is going on?" pleaded Logan.

"Mate, you woke up to a death trap," said Rampras.

"What do you mean?" asked Logan.

"Just you wait an' see there, popsicle," said Calis.

The platform cage shook from low-frequency booms. Sounds of distant explosions were piercing through the walls. Worry and anxiety flushed back into the faces of the burdened soldiers. They were nearing the top. The smell of discharged sulphur was now stinging the nose. Logan was afraid to find out what had happened to the world.

One elevator door opened. The other was inoperative. Invasive dust stormed into the cage.

Dying soldiers squealed. Bombs drummed the percussion of war and hundreds of snapping bullets erupted into a constant song of chaos. Rampras pried the other door open and stormed his way into a collapsed aging hangar.

The rest followed, polluting the hangar with meat and metal. Logan dared not to follow. Instead, he looked out. The hangar was tattooed with blast fire holes. Portions of the roof collapsed and the concrete walls were chiselled with ant holes. The entire squadron took sheltered in an outside trench. Blood and innards were abundant. Bodies littered the trenches. Trails of light and lasers rapid-fired into an economy of bullet exchange.

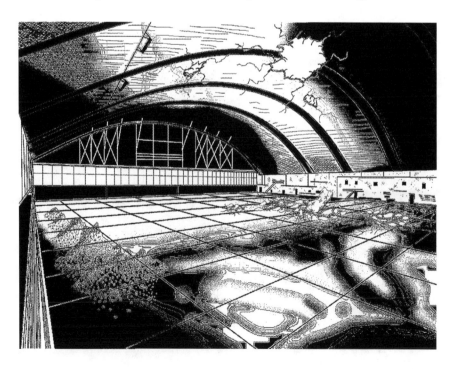

"Sentient being," said Samiren. "Look."

Samiren stared up at a hole in the hangar. Logan stepped out to see. The brown-orange warzone dust cleared and fogged intermittently, but a light in the sky still pierced through the mist.

Logan squinted, wondering what he was supposed to see. Then a gap in the wall of dust exposed a light from a sun-like source with two huge chunks of rock, faded by its distance, orbiting it.

"Earth's core and surface fragments," said Samiren.

"No. That's impossible," said Logan.

He was in shock, in total disbelief. He could not fathom what physics were behind this reality-contorting concept. His disorientated mind exploded into an armada of questions.

"Get the hell into the trenches. Now!" Rampras yelled.

Short bursts of light punctured through the hangar's aluminum walls. These bullets of light had no physical mass. It sliced up concrete slabs and steel beams with ease. The whole squad charged for the trenches.

Logan landed in the trench. He flinched to every light flash flickering all around him. Soldiers gopher-peaked recurrently and blasted a cluster. Blind fire from an unseen enemy answered back with blasts of light.

Logan clenched in terror. Then liquids splattered all over him. He looked at its colour. It was pink. He looked up to see. A nearby patient's head was blown off. Brain matter spilled onto the sand. The wound's edges blistered, fizzled, and smoked from searing heat. He was horrified by the graphic sight.

"You said you were ready for extraction," yelled Rampras into the phone receiver of Martin's radio amplifier pack.

"The LZ's too damn hot," said the pilot's voice on radio. "You try and avoid arbalest fire while flying into a blender."

"Where's your LP battery cover?" questioned Rampras.

"Oh, I'm sorry," mocked the pilot's voice. "We're not one-eyed captains who have that kind of authority."

"Martin, get the damn LP officer on the line," said Rampras.

Martin rolled his eyes as he slid off his radio pack. A blast fire volley shaved the rims of the trench. One beam struck the arm of a soldier and instantly melted the metallic plates protecting it. The soldier wailed in agony as the molten puss ate into his arm. Multanis rested him against the trench slope and dug into his med pack. But something was wrong. His pack was near empty.

"Captain, medical supplies are running low," said Multanis.

"Multanis, prep these men for evac," said Rampras.

Multanis judged the status of the surrounding men. Most were burn victims while others suffered from fragmentation wounds and internal bleeding.

"Some of these men can't even be moved," said Multanis.

"Either you get them ready or they're dead," said Rampras.

"They're dead if we move them," said Multanis.

"Find a way!" roared Rampras.

He was reckless, or so Multanis thought, but this was Multanis' area of expertise. Rampras already had a plate of soldiers dying within his grasp. He couldn't be bothered with the medical details of immobile victims of war.

Down the trench, a soldier threw a can tied to a rock onto the sand plain twenty feet ahead. The can was still anchored but it ignited and spun wildly out of control. It blasted up dust, which added to the visual shield of the trench.

"Rampras to listening post seven. Come in," Rampras said into the radio.

"This is LP seven," said the voice of LP7's commanding officer.

"We need battery fire at grid zone seven," said Rampras. "Poly-verse Mercator coordinates one one seven--"

"--Request denied," said the LP Officer. "We cannot commit reserve artillery shells at those coordinates."

"Why not?" roared Rampras.

A blast roared into the background. A loud ring pulsed in Rampras's ear.

"It's a contested zone," said the LP Officer.

"Come again. I didn't read you," said Rampras, adjusting his jaw.

"It's of no military significance," said the LP Officer.

Rampras slammed the phone into Martin's radio pack. Martin cringed. Rampras looked around, wondering how he was going to get out of this.

The squad continued to barrage the area with dust makers. Blast fire and laser-like pulses blindly screened the area by the inch. Trying anything would have been daring. It would expose the whole squadron to high risk against diminishing resources.

High overhead, a deep growl of grinding metal gears ruptured through the dust. The sandy mist held the outline of a tall mechanical tripod. It stood above the east hangars. Light emanated from its weaponry ports. Plasmatic plates, glowing with light, shielded its feet and its stem's dark internal gears.

Logan gazed up at this massive colossus in total awe. He couldn't believe how much these machines had evolved from simple robots.

"Sentinel!" yelled a soldier.

"Samiren!" cried Rampras.

Samiren became aware. He fully acknowledged the threat of this machine. He charged toward it. The sentinel stepped toward the squadron. Its foot left behind a terrifying tremor. Then, it ejected a pair of missiles from its shoulders.

"Incoming!" screamed Calis.

The squadron burst out of their trenches. The missile pair slammed in the trench's centre. Limbs and debris sprayed from the deepened dune wound. Soldiers took cover behind every piece of building chunk they could. Enemy fire cleaved the edges of their cover.

"Damn it!" yelled Multanis.

The sentinel ejected a cluster of pods from its hind abdomen. Samiren detached his pistol-like device from his waist and activated it. The pistol's two turrets slashed out red lasers that touched and cancelled each other out after a yard in length. The constant streams of energy functioned as a laser-like sword.

Samiren slashed the sentinel's foreleg. The lasers easily cleaved through the plasmatic plates and slashed the ankle gear joints. The sentinel wobbled and disappeared into the dusty mist with only a loud slam that indicated its fate.

The six pods had sprouted into a turret. It burrowed its mechanical legs into the ground and a plasmatic chassis flooded over its body.

"Captain!" Calis yelled.

The micro pods opened fire. Rampras stood in open field. He was deep in thought. The pods blasted down two soldiers. The squadron retaliated fire, but each bullet was eaten by the pod's plasmatic plates.

"We have to go now," muttered Rampras.

"We can't be loopin' them if we still got bogeys," said Calis.

"What's looping?" asked Logan.

"Fakin' a position changed," explained Calis.

"The arbalest will be on us at any second, mate. We have to go now!" said Rampras, then reached for his radio. "Extract! Head to the southbound LZ."

"Captain?" the pilot said.

"We're drawing arbalest fire. Go now!"

Rampras charged towards a crane towering over a debris mountain. Samiren sliced at a pod as he ran by. The other pod retracted and burrowed itself.

Martin hopped from debris to debris. But two pods were spitting a constant rain of light at him. Martin took cover, but the blast fire slowly ate away at the concrete buffer. Martin squealed for the life of him.

Suddenly, a dark figure materialized beside him. Droplets of searing light slammed into the spherical shield.

"Run!" Vanis yelled.

Martin scampered to his feet and hustled through the thicket of debris. Cracks and fissures slashed all over her shields, but she maintained it with a palm.

Her right hand sparked to life an electrical current that licked and lashed wildly. Vanis shifted the failing spherical facet away from the assaulting pod's wake. Then she thrust her fingers at two pods standing adjacent. The whip of lightning stung the two pods and fried their internal circuitry.

The squadron followed Rampras through the thick covers of debris and building innards. The spider turrets turned and blasted. Light fire clipped and slammed into concrete chunks.

From miles away, several pops huffed from the undertones of the chaos. The squadron hustled toward the tombs of the southern hangar corpses. Then several whines scaled into hearing. Lights speared through the wall of dust and ignited the trenches into a frenzy of sparks. The shockwave swept the squadron into a gust of smoke and blasted the roofs off the hangars.

Logan hacked and coughed from the thickening dust. He rubbed his tearing eyes from intruding dirt as he got up off the ground. His head throbbed. His vision was in vertigo. Blood dripped from his ears. Multanis helped him get to a fractured wall and took his vitals. Things were calm for only a moment, until blast fire sped past Logan's eyes.

"A.T. Units! A.T. Units!" yelled a soldier.

"Take cover!" Rampras yelled.

A powerful form just landed behind Logan some ten metres off. He slowly turned around.

A bulky form of light stood by. Logan had trouble calibrating his eyes, but deciphered the trickery of vision emitting off the machine's armour of glowing plasma. Sections along its stomach, shins, and biceps exposed dark gears. Two large wings extended out from its back, which counter-weighted its massive shoulders.

Its xenomorph was mostly humanoid with the exception of an extended foot; its heel served as an additional leg joint much like a canine but with thick toes to support its weight. Each

sported an integrated arm turret that formulated through nano-
tech wiring much like Samiren's.

This thing was powerful. No single bullet would ever be
able to take it down. Several other machines of light jetpacked in
and landed on a debris hill, twelve in number. They were about
to attack.

"Get to the LZ!" Rampras yelled.

He let loose a pepper of bullets. Logan watched the bullets
slam into the plasmatic chassis pool, dissolving into nothingness.
He felt the dread of its invincibility, until one lucky bullet disrupted
that illusion. It sunk into a gap between two plates and slammed
into gears.

The droids retaliated fire. An armada of light stormed onto the battlefield and blasted up dust and debris chunks.

"We're not leaving you behind," said Rampras.

He grabbed Logan and pulled him toward a crane towering nearby. The squad bolted through a thick debris field. Those that took point stopped, knelt, and cover fired until the rest passed.

Logan ran, hopped, and leapt through an obstacle course of rubble. He noticed every blast toward them were near hits as though these droids had no aim compensation. These were pulses of laser that only took a split second to strike.

Logan glanced back as he hopped over a concrete slab. He noticed something odd about these drones; they moved collectively and their barrels had no recoil. Their aim should have been more precise than experienced surgeons.

The droids flew in small pulses to different sections of the debris hills to keep in line of sight with the squad. The large crane leaned overhead of the squad's path. Then a distant rip of sound split the air. The debris hill that buried the crane's base suddenly exploded. The concrete chunks splashed the squad off their feet. The crane came crashing down.

"Just go!" said Rampras.

Rampras got up and hustled toward the landing zone. Everyone easily passed under the crashing crane, which confused Logan. He stopped and looked back. The crane crashed a safe distance away. That was meant to stop the squad's escape. He wondered if these droids lagged in response time. That would mean their actions were not their own and was decided by a single intelligence instead.

If that was true, all of their actions were transmitted wirelessly.

The droids emerged from on top of the rubble. Logan sped toward the shattered wind turbines with the rest of the squad. The droids pursued them from on top of the debris hills and pressured the squad with rapid fire.

Rampras noticed Logan had stopped again. Annoyed by his consistent ceasing, he ran back and grabbed his arm.

"You trying to get yourself killed?" Rampras roared.

Logan suddenly ripped Rampras's radio off and pried open its innards.

"What the hell are you doing?" yelled Rampras.

Logan ignored him and found the frequency dial inside the radio itself. He ripped one of the useless wires and coiled it around the dial.

"Calis, I need your radio!" said Logan.

Calis stopped and looked at Rampras, wondering if he should agree to this. Then Calis looked up and saw the A.T. units emerging from the debris mountains.

"Captain!" yelled Calis.

Rampras grabbed Logan and pressed him against the debris wall out of line of sight. The droids switched targets. Calis immediately took cover. Blast fire speared in his wake.

"Your radio!" yelled Logan.

Calis ripped his radio off and tossed it. Logan grabbed it and dissected it. The squad ahead halted, covered, and fired.

"Keep going!" said Rampras.

The soldiers ran again. Ahead in the sky, a jet-fuelled dropship slowly descended toward their direction. The soldiers running toward it got barraged by blast fire anyway and took cover.

Rampras thought for a moment then switched cartridges on his assault rifle. He peeked out and aimed his rifle's laser point toward the droids. His rifle's computer marked the targets. The droids opened fire. Rampras ducked back then blind fired up the hill.

In one split second, the bullets spat out of Rampras's rifle, spanned out aluminum curvatures, concaved around the concrete cover, and slammed into the droid's plates of light. This drew all of the droid's attention.

Logan had tied the two radios together but in opposite directions. The speaker and receiving ends were facing each other at point-blank range. A pull wire was set between them.

"What the hell's that going to do?" questioned Rampras.

Then Logan pulled the wire. A loud squeal screeched wildly from the squadron's radio. Everyone clammed their ears shut. Logan poked his head to see the A.T. Droids. They hovered idly as though awaiting instructions.

"Radio jammin'?" said the baffled Calis.

"Go, go, go!" said Rampras.

The shuttlecraft spun around and landed with its aft bay open. The squadron boarded quickly. Logan took one look back and saw a dozen jet-powered droid units hovering over the position they once were.

They were supposed to be ambushed.

CHAPTER 3

ASYLUM

The wind on their faces caused relief for the squadron. Logan looked back at the now distant battlefield. The landscape was unrecognizable compared to his memories. Of course, he couldn't remember what was there before. He saw there were many fracture marks, craters, and other indentions on the crust itself. It did not look like a friendly environment. Everyone sat while Rampras stood with a hand on the wall.

"How many did we extract?" Rampras dared to ask.

Multanis sighed. He was reluctant to give an answer.

"Four out of twenty."

"Our numbers?" asked Rampras.

"Down to a quarter," said Multanis.

Rampras slammed his fist on the wall. Everyone shuttered to the bang.

"I told you to get those wounded ready for evac!" roared Rampras.

"We couldn't move them!" Multanis reasoned, "and that sentinel had their fate marked all over them!"

"Oh? And did you try getting them up to their feet, mate?"

"The incapacitated had a two-point-seven-second reaction time before being eliminated," Samiren said. "Only fully functional mobile forces had the capacity for evasion."

Rampras huffed and turned his view away from the squad. Multanis shook his head and went back to bandaging wounded.

"Hey, street boy!" Calis said to break the tension. "That was awesome what ya did back there, man! How'd ya learn to be doin' all that business?"

"Used to salvage things to sell," uttered Logan.

He was barely paying attention. Blood and gore kept resurfacing in Logan's mind. The screaming haunted him even though it was just moments before. The weight of human life never leaned on him before but the whole squadron knew this weight every day.

Then the whole shuttle shook.

"Sorry back there," said the voice on the intercom. "We're just passing over some magnetic vortexes. Nothing to be alarmed about."

Logan peered out of the cradle gap. A portion of the surface seemed to twist and warp in vision. Logan squinted, trying to see it clearly. As the visual area warped again, puffs of sand were cast into the air. It seemed more like a gravity-based phenomenon.

Logan studied the low-density sky. A large array of northern lights washed all over from every direction, but the sky itself lacked much of its blue coating. The shuttle passed over a cluster of large rocks that was suspended in mid-air. Logan was amazed at the sight.

Then he gazed at the Earth's core. It still looked like the sun but dimmed. He wondered how heat and air sustained themselves, or how gravity worked for that matter. Questions flooded his mind in constant rapidity.

"How did we survive?" Logan asked.

Everyone looked at him as though it was an unanswered mystery.

"We didn't," said Calis. "Welcome to hell."

"There is no proper explanation," said Multanis as he

continued to wrap a soldier in bandages. "Nothing can repel terra jules of combustive power."

"Makes me wonder if dyin' was better," added Calis.

"To end the chancers lifed by fate of hands?" questioned Vanis. "One drop of dew; a liquid jewel of hope to tasters whom unfed the starve of life. To see it so decayed, then better dead, for suffered will is death from dryest dew."

"Yeah," Calis said defeatedly.

"We're inbound to settlement Epsilon," announced the pilot on radio.

"Welcome home," Calis sadly said.

On the sandy surface, a buried suburbia was wrapped in a blanket of sand. Rocks, meteors, and other crust parts all made up for the pillows within this graveyard. But, it wasnt empty. There were people down there, desert excavators. They were quarrying a buried suburbia. They were wrapped in sand-blocking cloths that shielded them from the dust. From the incoming sound, the excavators looked up. The dropship flew past them and toward a grand shattered city.

Logan saw hundreds of steel beam skeletons of gutted buildings. Scavengers salvaged items from a destroyed office. As the dropship flew on, he saw a hover transport driving through streets cleared of debris. Metalsmiths were dismantling the city's mill and transporting metal fragments onto a steel railway.

The dropship flew deeper into the forest of dead towers and came to a grove of rubble. In the middle, a large plateau housed a military base with several buildings. Surrounding the base, a grand town of tents populated the fractured freeways of the city's once busiest traffic veins.

As the dropship closed in, Logan saw a large shattered

freeway lane suspended above the settlement's south end. Its concrete poles were crudely fenced together at the base with a checkpoint station along a walk path. Several look outposts were situated on top of the freeway's fragmented islands.

The main core of the settlement was people housed in huts of tarp, chiselled caves, or in sewage pipe ends. A grand bazaar was lit by colourful lamps that served as a marketplace or meeting area. There were more people alive than he had thought as though the world refused to give up.

They circled around to land on the base's aft landing pad. The dropship turned around with its hind facing the base. An aerial flagger guided them in using two red handheld lights. As the shuttle landed and powered down, the squad unloaded the equipment.

"Multanis, get the data down to intel," said Rampras, "the rest of you can call it a night."

"Woo!" yelled the excited Calis, "think I'm gonna hit the brewery at the tent town tonight."

"Yeah, and I get to decrypt all night," said Multanis.

"Keep it to a few in case we're called in," said Rampras.

"What do I do?" said Logan.

"Oh yeah," said Rampras. "The commissioner'll be up here soon, mate. They'll brief you on what happened. Then you decide."

"Decide what?" asked Logan.

"What to do with the rest of your life," said Rampras.

Logan was lost. He didn't know what to do. He watched Rampras haul belted rounds off the dropship. He felt helpless. He just sat there on the dropship's leather seats, staring. The other three evacuees were wandering cluelessly too.

Logan peeked below the dropship's tail. He saw armoured hangars that housed military vehicles. Nearby, a team loaded onto another dropship, while another squadron jogged through the paved streets. The military seemed more privileged than the rest of the shattered world.

He heard talking at the base of the platform. Logan got up to see. He saw two elderly men talking to Rampras. They were dressed in dark knitted coats that had faded over time. The other patients walked over to them, so Logan did too. As he walked over, he saw Rampras rising tension with them.

"Is that your new agenda, General?" roared Rampras. "To send your best troops into a damn suicide mission?"

The decorated officer of the two coats was alarmed by Rampras's outburst. His features were well-known to news broadcasts pertaining to the Nova. Though he aged twenty years, this was obviously Scathers, now a general.

"What are you talking about, Captain?" said Scathers.

"Our forces...were nearly wiped out...by the lack of recon you failed to give," slammed Rampras.

"We had no reason to suspect--"

"--It's a contested zone!" argued Rampras. "The same reason the LP officer gave for not sending artillery support."

"That LP was already low on munitions," reasoned Scathers. "We used a great deal of it warding off chimeras from Gaia!"

"Don't you think that was important information to know?" Rampras ripped at him with a growl, "before sending us into hostile territory?"

"We sent you before we knew," said Scathers, "By the time you were underground, I announced artillery backup was for priority basis only."

"Well, maybe nearly losing a full company of soldiers isn't much to you!" yelled Rampras, "But it is to me, to their families, to the morale of my troops!"

"Well, fine! Blame me! Blame me!" retorted Scathers. "It was my fault that you didn't get the support you needed! Are you happy now, Captain?"

"No," Rampras simmered.

Rampras looked like he wanted to argue more, but was out of ammunition. He left for the barracks without even a salute. Scathers huffed a sigh. The other coat, Leopold, the elected representative of the settlement, looked back at Rampras, judging him.

"Do you always put up with insubordination?" asked Leopold.

"Only from the most innovating," Scathers said before noticing the four. "I'm sorry you had to see that."

"I'm Commissioner Leopold," he said. "Welcome to Settlement Epsilon. You have questions. We have answers. There's room in the bunkers. Food will be under the military's expense. We'll recap you on the global events later tonight, then we'll discuss your futures. Until then, make yourselves at home."

Scathers and Leopold left to do the rest of their supervision rounds. The other patients started to explore inside the bunker. Logan just stood there. He had already figuring out the basics of the global catastrophe. That wasn't his worry.

He took a quick glimpse around at the surrounding buildings. Most buildings in the base were standard military: aluminum or steel hangars, fencing external walls, and internal marble walls that blocked invasive eyes. He noticed that every building had omni-directional wind turbines embedded. He figured the community powered itself with electricity using this method.

Logan noticed a large towering building to the northeast. Its shiny, uncorrupted surface skinned the whole structure without any innards showing. It had neon lights billboarded with the name Calypso. With all the cracked and aging walls that surrounded him, this one didn't fit.

It reminded him of home.

*   *   *   *   *

He remembered his life on the streets of Abrador City, the mirror-like skyscrapers, and the endless supply of advertised products on two-storey monitors. It was always busy and full of important things that drove the progression of the consumer-based economy into hyper drive.

He remembered trolling the streets on a rainy day looking for rogue change. The cities were flooded with hovering vehicles back then. But he never spent his time on the main streets where all the sparkle and glamour was. Instead, he was in the back alleys digging in garbage bins for thrown-out sandwiches.

He spent his days near the train stations, fascinating newcomers with levitation tricks he remarkably learned on his own. He was constantly spooked by the dome shield that suspended above the city, wondering if it would ever fall or fail to block ultraviolet radiation.

He loved the little micro bots that cleaned the streets of trash, and the little droid dogs that led the young and blind safely through the streets. *Style was the main thing of the day,* he remembered thinking as he watched a gang of young boys dressed in neo-cyber punk clothes.

That was his life back then: dodging drunks that stumbled out of cheap harlems while he filtered through garbage for thrown-away valuables. But one memory stung into his gut harder than anything he felt before. His mind wanted to close it off entirely, but he forced himself to remember.

He remembered her: Cherise, a beauty indefinable by the dictionaries of minds. He spent his nights in a drainpipe staring at a picture of her, as the tunnel below was flooded with happy families walking to their vehicles. He did not remember much, but he remembered he could have had a life with her, if something terrible had not happened.

Perhaps it was too painful to remember.

For all of his life, he did nothing but survive, only to wake up to survive again. It seemed like a pointless cycle with no meaning behind the struggle. He did not remember anything else beyond that — no friends or family.

He only remembered starving constantly, as though something sapped the life force out of him: his shaking hands, his weakened muscles, the constant pain in his stomach and feet, and the lifeless feeling as though he was already a ghost. Constant pain was his way of life and it would not let him go.

What he would do in this world, he did not know.

CHAPTER 4

AUXILIARY

Logan went to the astrometrics room. Inside, a physicist instructed on a holographic display about the Nova event. The physicist first told of what a nova was: being an over-pressurized explosion. He then dictated an anomalous event that occurred upon contact with the Earth.

He stated there were many models out there that theorized what may have happened, but none had concrete grounds to being the standard. He illustrated how the world was broken up into three crust fragments while orbiting the molten core. He also explained how this dynamic planetary formation was greatly not understood by physicists and how unlikely it was for human survival.

But regardless of its chances, life survived. Logan didn't know whether to feel pleased, sad, or afraid.

The physicist continued to explain that since the nova event was predicted a year earlier, people had time to hide in underground bunkers created by various construction companies wanting to exploit the end of the world paranoia for cash. What these companies didn't expect was that their greed ended up saving a great number of lives.

Logan wondered what this all meant.

After the dictation, one of the soldiers invited the survivors to a rat roast barbeque. Logan cringed at the idea, but the soldier was adamant about it saying that a dietary change was a necessity for survival. People were reluctant, but met outside of the bunkers anyways.

Pavilions roofed rows of picnic tables that filled an open pocket of the military ward. There, soldiers socialized about local events. Logan and the survivors stood in line to a barbeque stand holding clay-molded plates. Logan did not realize how hungry he was until the wind blew the smell of fat and meat into his direction. He was totally famished.

As each survivor ahead of him was served a plate of rat meat by the proud cook, Logan noticed they all had mixed reactions to its textural presentation. When Logan got to the front, the proud, rough-skinned cook grinned through his missing teeth and flopped a chunk of rat meat on Logan's plate. Logan inspected it. It looked no different than barbequed chicken.

"Don'tcha be eatin' the insides, ye hear?" said the proud cook.

"Why not?" asked Logan.

"The spleen. It's poisonous," whispered the cook.

Logan gave the cook a surprised look. The cook chuckled at him. Logan then sat with the rest of the survivors at their own table. There were more here than he had imagined. He figured they were survivors from other excavations.

But he noticed they all had a common trait: they had the look of brokenness and disbelief. Some even played with their food, knowing that the luxuries of a privileged world were no longer within their possession.

They now lived in a rat-eating society.

This didn't bother Logan that much. He was used to living off the scraps of society. Logan watched the others. Not one of them touched their food, while others were trying to build up the courage. The man beside him sniffed his burnt rat then noticed Logan studying him.

"Name's Jett," he said, a perma-smirked man.

"Logan," replied Logan.

"Used to serve gourmets better than this crap," said Jett.

"It's not that bad," said Logan.

"Not that bad, huh?" said Evan, the orange-haired man sitting across the table from them. "What? You used to hearing about doomsday? Or just the eating rats part?"

"Oh, come on, man. Lay off the guy," said Jett.

"No, no. He's a rat expert," said Evan. "I want to see him eat that rat."

"We just heard how messed up our world is," said Jett. "Don't you think we've been through enough?"

"No, it's fine," said Logan. "I used to live on the streets."

"Oh! So, you're cheating," said Evan. "You already know what a crap life this is and you're just here to mock us."

"Will you leave the guy alone?" said Jett.

"No!" said Evan. "This guy's a spitting image of how we should be. The new, up-styled lone survivor living off the land. Nothing bothers him because he knows how hard life can get and we're all just spoiled city folk."

Logan just stared. He didn't know what to do.

"Just ignore him," said Jett.

"Well, I had a life!" yelled Evan as he barged to his feet. "I had a business! I had a condo...with majority shares in Mitango and Reese enterprises! What the hell am I doing in this dump?"

Everyone watched but no one gave a response. Evan backed away from the benches. His eyes darted around and searched for answers.

"I just--I just--" eased Evan as he burst into a devastating cry.

Everyone watched him for a moment, then weaned their

eyes back to their plates. A soldier walked over to Evan and started speaking to him quietly.

Logan was impressed at how supportive the soldier was as though he already knew his stage in life. He began to wonder if the global attitude toward the suffering of poverty in this world was now an acceptable norm. If that was true, he figured he would be more welcomed here than where he was before. To him, being welcomed anywhere was an odd and unfamiliar feeling.

"So, what are you going to do?" asked Jett.

"I, uh, I don't know yet," said Logan. "You?"

"Well, gotta learn how to live in this new world, right?" said Jett. "I was thinking millwrighting. I know that there's no mills here, but got a full resume of construction work. Heavy equipment handling and all."

"They got me from a psionics training facility," said Logan.

"Wow," he paused in thought. "Do that."

"What? Psionics?" asked Logan.

"The military's the most privileged," said Jett. "Mostly on account that they expect to die the next day. Not that I'm saying you're going to. But if you were to, might as well go out in style, right?"

"Maybe," added Logan.

"I'm sure you'll decide," said Jett. "Only the useful survive this world."

Logan paused in thought. It felt like he was being forced to decide.

"Logan!" yelled a voice across the ward's courtyard.

Logan looked up. Calis waved him over. Logan mauled the barbequed rat apart in seconds then got up from his seat. Everyone watched in disgust. After Logan left, everyone started munching down their rat.

"Yeah, what's up?" asked Logan.

"Did'ja really just eat that rat?" asked Calis.

"Yeah, it's no problem," said Logan.

"Yer disgustin'!" Calis said to the surprised Logan. "Them hobos at the other table did the stomach test to see if ye freaked out gerbils would really be so desperate enough to eat a rat."

Logan looked back at the barbeque. A bunch of soldiers watching him burst out laughing. Logan smiled. He couldn't help but admire the comical value in it.

"Come on there, popsicle," said Calis as he walked toward the ward's southern gates. "I'm'a show you what real food is."

$$* \qquad * \qquad * \qquad * \qquad *$$

After stepping outside the base's checkpoint entrance, Logan noticed a large eastern power plant with a full field of wind turbines just beyond the base's plateau. It had several cylindrical buildings that stored excessive energy into battery stations with power lines running to the tent town.

South of it, a large pyramid landmarked an open training ground that wasn't military. He noticed white-robed people moving objects without touching them. Calis told him that was the back pedal; the psionicist's training ground.

Light was dimming from the Earth's core setting in the horizon. Calis explained that the rocks rotated and gave about eighteen- to twenty-seven-hour days. Calis also explained that, for some reason, the crust fragments were somehow magnetized and generated gravity. Anything opposite of the crust's magnetic polarity floated.

As they walked down the long ramp toward the tent town, Logan heard commotion. Coloured lamps turned on and were being hung on poles. A community feast was about to happen in the midst of all the debris.

"How does everyone get their food?" asked Logan.

"Oh, they just eat their own crap all over again," explained Calis to the shocked Logan. "Bio-farms. They have them things all over the twisted dunes. They're big, green, and bio-farm shaped. Y'know, like a dome that grows crap?"

"And water?" asked Logan.

"Domes don't grow that kind of crap," said Calis.

"No, I mean how do they get their water?" asked Logan.

"Oh, ye need them carbon extraction towers for that," said Calis as he pointed to the southeast.

There, a large tower huffed steam from the top tip but in-took molecules from mid-funnels. A large vent shaft hammered the farmed molecules to a processing plant at the base. From there, the plant expelled water into a series of pipes that networked around town.

"They make all that air, sugar, hydrogen power cells, and, ding! Water!" said Calis. "But who really needs that when we have you!"

"Heh, I'm hardly talented," said Logan.

"No, but them dust walkers got the smarts going for them," said Calis. "Dust walkers bein' them thrill seekers who get their rocks off just doin' the crazy survivin' an' crap. Rampras was one. He used to drink battery acid."

"That would kill you though," said Logan.

"Not if ye distil the acid into water," said Calis. "Just wind the battery's manual rotary charger until it's all topped it. Then overflow it to zap all the hydrogen out. Then ye catch it, light it, drip it, drink it, pee it, and bury it so it goes to water heaven. Or ye can distil yer pee and drink that. But no one's got the balls to be a pee drinker. Unless yer a heavy drinkin' man."

As they got halfway, Logan noticed a large two-storey, aluminum shack that was octagonal in structure. Most of the windows were blinded.

"That's the Seer's place," said Calis. "Ye don't want to be goin' in there."

As they passed the shack, Logan got the feeling of being watched. But it was different from being stalked; more like being spied upon from the sky. Logan looked up. He only saw an asteroid belt reflecting the core's light.

Calis and Logan came to a debris clearing that housed several booths and tented tables that were guarded by squadron soldiers. People came in, loaded, and relieved items. It was a marketplace.

Immediately, several children caught his eye. They ran in and out of an open fridge with no back in it. But blisters and textural deformations were all over these children's skins. He also noticed some traders coming in with metal arms or legs. One even had an optical implant on his left eye. Another person had a third arm growing out of his back. But the majority of people were just dirty and lacked proper hygiene.

"What's wrong with these people?" asked Logan.

"What?" said Calis who then looked at the people. "Oh lord, it's a circus here! Look at all them freaks!"

Two people glared at Calis angrily.

"I'm never going to get a straight answer out of you, am I?" asked Logan.

"Radiation. Genetic deformities. Mutations. Take yer pick," said Calis.

Logan noticed that behind each booth there was no salesperson and people took what they wanted. He also noticed that people left items behind without desire for fair exchange.

"Why are they doing that?" asked Logan.

"Hmm?" said Calis. "Oh, they just stealin' things. Don't mind them."

"But they're leaving things too," said Logan.

"It's all a free market here," explained Calis.

"Nothing's free," said Logan. "Everything costs something."

"True, but we don't be usin' currency here," said Calis.

"That doesn't make any sense," said Logan.

"Well, I ain't gonna be the one to explain it," said Calis. "They all jus' take what they need and leave what they don't."

"What if I grabbed everything from here and sold it?" asked Logan.

"Who would'ja sell it to if there ain't no buyers?" said Calis.

"What if I took everything?" asked Logan.

"What would ya do with it all?" asked Calis.

Logan was stumped. Other than food and water, the items consisted of tools, electronics, cloths, clothing, utilities, and travelling gear that was either handcrafted or salvaged. He would have very little use for these things other than to sell or to give away. He also didn't understand why someone wouldn't try to take advantage of this.

"People don't give things away unless they get something," said Logan.

"Yeah, but them guys'll get what they need anyway, so

there ain't no need to be holdin' 'em hostage," reasoned Calis. "It's jus' the way of the new world, popsicle. Everyone shares because they all have to. Makes things easier."

Logan thought about that. He had never encountered this type of world before. He was so used to looking for change to buy even the cheapest items that the act of sharing never seemed to be an option. To him, merely grabbing anything felt like stealing.

Perhaps, that was the key to its success. How could he steal something if people were willing to share it with him? He always felt obligated to give something back each time he was given a gift. That was probably what everyone was doing. They all followed a natural system of resource distribution without the interference from currency.

It was a gift economy.

But everyone who emerged from the nova came from a bartering world. *How could they just switch to this way of doing things without the nagging feeling of fairness*, he thought. Something else must have been at work.

He also figured that if this way was natural, then perhaps when a civilization became very complex, certain items became rare privileges to have. He could easily see why the previous world developed a bartering system: to accommodate for the scarcity of unique items.

He could see the old world's ways developing further with the introduction of thievery. Unless a world developed a strong sense of internal morality, external order would have to be imposed to counter-act theft and the strictness of fair trade would have to be enforced with an introduction of law and currency.

He had many thoughts, but he knew his limits to his thinking when questions kept popping in his mind. However, the notion of raw giving as an economy was not all too unfamiliar to him.

He remembered squatting a place for a short time, but left because he felt too guilty to stay in an abandoned building that wasn't his. He did remember squatters developing a system of sharing and giving because they had no money, but he left before he could see what came of it.

Logan watched a family of three start a fire nearby their pipe home. He couldn't help but remember wishing for a luxury home with a fireplace in it, but he couldn't bare the thought of living or even sleeping in enclosed spaces. He always wanted to spy on a luxury house just for fun, but couldn't because he was always on the constant move for food.

He remembered every winter he was given a choice: commit a crime and go to jail for the winter or join a gang and deal drugs for a living. People would do anything for the base necessities, but he was righteous and couldn't do any of those. Instead, he spent winters under bridges, in empty warehouses, in parking lots, and in sewers with only a barrel fire going to keep him warm. He refused to sleep in homeless shelters because it was full of diseased people.

He did remember spending time with a small group of friends that took refuge in the subway tunnels to shelter from the cold. They hooked jumper cables to a power line and connected it to a transformer that was wired to a TV so that they were able to spend the winter watching movies.

One year, the water system stalled and one of them took that opportunity to saw a pipe to install a faucet so they could shower, but showering had to be done in under a minute to avoid hypothermia.

Everything that they had — food, water, electricity — they got for themselves for free. The only cost was their labour-intensive work. He couldn't help but wish the world he was in now was like it was back then. Maybe then he wouldn't have suffered so much for living outside the boundaries of a privileged world.

Logan thought about all this as Calis took him further into the tent-town to a bazaar. The bazaar had a cluster of bonfires going in the midst of a scrap yard.

Colourful lamps hung on wires that attempted to give that place some life.

Sometimes, he wondered if what he saw was art — an explosion of debris that was cleaned up at its centre. Now people had gathered and wandered about as though lost pups begging for a home.

The people who gathered were a mix of salvagers, trades workers, and travellers. They all joked, ate, and shared stories to forget the doom that surrounded them. But they only gathered once a week when a bio-farm had shipped in a week's worth of food.

People rejoiced at the hard work these farmers put in to support the lives of people. The bio-farmers worked hard at a dangerous job that required constant defense and so people graced them with gifts.

Logan watched a guitarist play folk songs. Some even danced while others were swept away by its deep melodies. Logan saw that every one of them struggled to recreate an equilibrium that was lost. They all had lost a home and tried to create a new one.

Calis seemed different. He had a few drinks that a local brewer served and moved from group to group as though he took his home with him everywhere he went. This made Logan think about what a home really was. Then he smiled at the ironic thought of a home on a rogue planet with no solar system.

Calis politely fought out of the arms of a gropey woman and staggered his way toward Logan. He was obviously buzzed: eyes glazed and slightly red.

"Ye didn't do much, did'ja, popsicle?" asked the buzzing Calis.

"Yeah," Logan said with deep inflection.

Logan had been sitting alone on a metal slab nearby a fire the whole time. He did not feel like he was part of the world yet. Calis sighed and wobbled down beside him. They watched some kids roast some kabobs on a metal pole. Logan wished life was that simple.

"What am I going to do?" Logan asked. "Where am I going to go?"

"Aw, man! This ain't the reason why I brang ya to a place like this. This is the end of the world, man! Ye s'posed to be lettin' loose. Lettin' it all go! Be doin' whatever ye want!" Calis said. He paused in thought then added, "Well, I didn't mean to be answerin' ye question, but yeah."

"So, just stay here and live?"

"Ugh! Well, I ain't gonna be tellin' ya how to live yer life there, Mary Sue," said Calis.

"Mary Sue?"

"Yeah! Mary Sue. What ye did back there back in that steel coffin was hyper unrealistic for a blanky. Ye got somethin' goin' for ya and ye'd be wastin' it stayin' here waitin' for Galilea to happen."

"Galilea?"

"Galilea's--" Then Calis threw his hands in the air.

He was obviously frustrated with explanations.

What was Galilea? Logan thought.

"Just do whatever. Y'know? Whatever! Whatever comes to mind. Whatever ye popsicle brain can think of. Y'know? Whatever! Just do it."

"Okay," Logan said blankly.

He still had no idea what to do, nor did a specific want pull him in any direction. He felt empty. Without purpose. He needed at least some guidance in some direction.

He began to watch everyone else, toying with stories of what everyone else did when they woke up. Were they scared? Confused? Angry? Lost like he was? Everyone who woke up in this shattered world had to start from scratch again. Maybe some actually enjoyed it, starting over from the mistakes they made. Maybe others just gave up and left themselves to the whim of another.

He didn't know what to do and he was desperate for a purpose.

"What did you do?" Logan asked, "Y'know...when you woke up?"

Suddenly, Calis froze as though Logan just hit a pause button. Calis's countenance changed, shifting to an untold dread spoken only through his eyes. Then Calis came back to life and scratched the back of his neck vigorously.

"Think we should be headin' on back now."

"What?" Logan asked.

Oh, he did something. Triggered something.

"We all gots a long day ahead of us, y'know?" Calis uttered nervously.

He was still scratching. Like an itch that wouldn't let him go.

"What did I do?"

"Y-y-yep! C-c-cause, we ol' sacks of blood, right?" said the anxious Calis.

He paced back toward the bunkers nearly in zigzags as though the need to stray threatened to dislodge him.

"W-w-we gots to be dyin' for the crew, the folks all back on home. Yeppers. Need our rest!"

Yet even after he left, leaving a wake of hysterical giggles, Logan didn't know what to think of him. Maybe some people were exactly home.

CHAPTER 5

CURSOR

Logan went back to the bunkers and lay in his small sleeping cabin. He felt more like a corpse in a mortuary's cold storage. *So close to the truth*, he thought. The cabin was a small padded room with corner lights, a pillow for comfort with a door at the end. It was only suitable to store one body loosely. Being at ease, however, was a far cry in such tight proximities.

Since his time in Area 77, he trained himself to sleep on soft mattresses in enclosed spaces, since hard surfaces in open areas were the only things he's ever slept on. But he couldn't find the means to sleep.

Novas, shattered planets, and an all-out world war were hard things to swallow. He wondered how many people were dying at that moment as he looked out the wide window that viewed the shattered city.

Then the cabin door hatch opened. Vanis crawled in and seductively cat walked on all fours up Logan's legs. Logan gulped. His heart pounded.

"Uh...Vanis...right?" Logan whittled out.

She moaned erotically while she unbuttoned the top parts of her dress. Her slanted eyes, deep heaves, and the drooping of her lower lip spelled out the obvious: she was in extreme heat.

"Whoa, whoa! What are you doing?" Logan said backing to the wall.

"Indulging I, my whim, to seek it free," Vanis flowed out as her fingers grazed his tightening thighs, "and dis-inhibiting myself for you. My pretty thing. My love."

Logan wanted to hear more but fought it.

"Love? Look, Y-y-you've got the wrong idea."

"I do, do I?" moaned Vanis as she closed in on his lips.

The scent of her natural sweat smelled oddly sweet for odour.

"Instincts let loose to mate with whom we choose. Oh, be with me as I shall be with you."

Her eyes alone made him want to say yes and no. Her gaze was obsessive and terrifying, yet so erotic. Logan was so fascinated then suddenly heartbroken as the thought of Cherise escaped his mind.

Vanis sensed it immediately. She sniffed him.

"There's a Cherise," she gasped while backing away.

"There was," he added.

"Oh my, you poorest thing," she meowed while stroking his cheek. "I give myself to you for pleasure's sake. Release it in me as you think of her."

"That's not what I want," he submitted.

She huffed in frustration, then sat back to create distance.

She thought for a moment then added, "What can I do in which can come from me?"

He remained silent, but burden weighed in his eyes. She saw his hurt and wanted to bond with it. Crestfallen by his rejection, she backed away.

"Wait," he uttered. "Come over here."

Her eyes lit back up and she crawled up to his chest.

"Okay, just, uh, just turn around," he said.

She flipped around. Her heel poked the wall as she revealed his back to him.

"And just lean back."

She rested her back with her head on his chest.

"Yeah," He said with great content.

He sighed in relief as though embracing a long-forgotten role. She sensed his contentment but was unfamiliar with this feeling. He wrapped his arms around her, which made her feel safe and secure; an odd and unexplored concept to her. She relaxed on his chest as she examined these foreign emotions. But she knew it was something he deeply missed.

They both drifted in silence while playing with each other's fingers as though they had been lovers for years. She explored this feeling as much as she could. She even traced the patterns on his fingers that she normally ignored on people. She loved this feeling. She never knew it existed. It pained her that she never knew what this was. It made her think of so many things.

They shifted spots when Logan was getting sore and settled in with her head more on his stomach. Still more silence. Neither of them was talking. Vanis was getting bored, but Logan didn't know what to do with her. Her crippled speech craft made him reluctant to talk. But she could feel his concerns about it, even without it being spoken.

"I speak. You sense," said Vanis, "but lost in labyrinth speech. You hear I spoke the fragment mind of craze. I speak. I try, but mind's infirmary. A patient thought de-circuited in maze."

His vision drifted, trying to comprehend.

"Since idle mind when I had adolesced," running her hand along his, "my makers sought a fixer to increase. His routed try gave birth to psychic light, unchasting I to woo identity."

He felt this dark feeling grow inside him.

"Now locked in lewd regime upon his doom, his phantom

graze defines the minx in I. They dubbed me strange and disassociate. Now quest evolved to medium defies."

He didn't know what to make of it. He figured that was her past in a nutshell. He wondered if her mind purposefully scrambled speech to hide a dark past that she did not want to confess.

But that wasn't it. She clasped his hand in a firm grip, as though to tell him that it was alright. She knew it all, her entire past, and did not run from it.

He got the feeling it was too dark to speak of. But he also felt that Vanis did not seem scarred or damaged from it, only defined, regardless of what psychosis some white coat would paint on her.

He figured it was best to remain silent. But one thing was evident that made him so fond of her — she struggled so hard to be normal.

After much silence and flirtatious caressing, Vanis could tell he was distracted with deep introspection. So she sat up to listen. He noticed her in listening mode. It was odd for him that she knew he needed to talk. Too odd.

"Think I might train at the Paradigm," he said.

"Then do what will your wish has sought for you," she said.

"I haven't decided yet," he said while curling strands of her hair around his finger.

A smile grew on her face. Her neck and ear tingled to his finger.

"Still haven't even figured out who I really am."

"Who you are to your unknowest self," she said, "a mystery without a riddled clue. You're not the past and not what you'll become; your life, a flux, in constant hyperbole."

He heard a term for that before somewhere. He couldn't

remember where. But it was called Tabula Rasa, the blank slate. A mind with no preconceived ideas or predetermined goals. He was fresh. He was new. No wonder Calis called him a Mary Sue; some young, flawless character.

But he knew he wasn't perfect. He wished he were. Portions of his past crept up on him like invisible spiders, recreating his past in spindles of webs across his face. He had done wrong...many times. He could feel it.

He wasn't exactly blank either, even though the principle still applied. He had memories of his former life, but not the personality. It was like the cryogenic suspension reset him somehow and made him anew. But he had this nagging feeling it was also something else. Something he did himself.

"How do you know?" asked Logan. "How would you know?"

"To those who never know themselves in full," she said, "they wander aimlessly or see the Seer."

"The Seer?"

"He sees it all or so they note it so," she said. "The one who saw the end, but not himself. They keep him close for things they need to hear. He'll see the gift in which you hide away."

"What gift?" he said sadly.

"We've all been given gifts we need."

"What about my wants?"

"The needs of others far exceeds our own," she said, "for who are we without their greatest aid? To see oneself divine then be alone, for lonely souls cry out the greatest creed."

Logan felt trapped. He never asked for any of this to happen. It was like fate decided his life for him regardless of what he wanted. Vanis wrapped his arms around her, hoping her endearing self withered some of his burdens away. Logan stroked her hair but was lost in thought.

"I don't know what to do," said Logan.

Vanis didn't know what else to add, except assuring him that she would be there for him every step of the way.

That night he slept in a unique dream. It twisted and warped in constant flux as though two minds had merged. He didn't remember much, but he remembered seeing her in every phase. She smiled at him, then led him through every door inside her dream world, a world so full of beauty.

Logan woke up the next day and looked over to Vanis. She was still asleep, but enjoying him as a pillow. He cringed. His chest was sore. His right leg was partially asleep; her hips were on it. He could sense the calming waves of emotions every so often coming from her. She was dreaming. She was at peace.

He leaned up and lightly moved her aside. She moaned, slowly surfacing from slumber. She parted her sultry eyelashes apart and gazed up at him.

"Already sailing winds?" she asked.

"My leg was asleep," he said while cringing at his tingling leg.

She smiled and lightly laughed, "Your poorest leg."

"Stay in bed. I need to go for a walk," he added.

She sprawled out on the extra room as he crawled toward the hatch. She sniffed the spot he once was, enjoying his scent, then fell asleep.

She was moving so fast. They had just met on intimate terms the night before and she was already waking up in his bed.

She's weird, he thought, *but incredibly sexy.* A soft chest, curvy hips, great thighs, and an angel's face. Why would he deny her? Why wasn't she with anyone else? He smirked at how easy the answer was. Her eyes alone would sabotage any potential relationship she could have. Adding that with her mind controlling abilities, no man would dare go near her.

Perhaps that explained her need for swift intimacy and how it drove others away. She was lonely and a large part of him didn't want her to be that way. He knew what it was like to be rejected by society.

Logan stepped out and stretched. He heard scratching being marked all over a board. He looked down the bunkers and saw Calis. He was out of his armour. He leaned on the wall and watched Martin work on advanced equation on his personal handheld chalkboard.

"He got booted from intel," Calis said, knowing Logan was behind him. "That's why he got all strung out in Rampras's face."

"What did he do?" asked Logan.

"He was a chess player. A tactician. Out-thinks battles," said Calis. "He was right then got all horribly wrong. Cost us a lot of lives. They pinned the blame on him for being too macho-brained. Now he's got a beef with the world."

Logan didn't blame him. A part of himself was too.

"So I hear Rampras be lookin' for ya," said Clis, "He's up in that engineerin' bay. Just listen for one-eyed patches sayin' 'Arr Matey!'"

"Alright, I'll go see him," said Logan.

"I sure as hell hope he ain't shiverin' his timber up there," Calis muttered.

Logan got out of the bunker and headed toward estern end of the base. He worked his way through several engineering shops until he got to automotives. Salvaged engines and vehicle parts were scattered throughout the shop. Rampras browsed through some paperwork. Beside him, a simmering glow slowly faded from a front axle that was suspended above ground.

"You wanted to see me?" said Logan.

"Hmm?" said Rampras as he looked up. "Oh, I was just going through some stuff here. Waiting for that," gesturing to the axle while closing the folder.

"Oh, I could wait if you want," said Logan.

"Stop being nice, mate. It's pathetic." said Rampras.

Logan looked like he was just stomped on. Rampras judged his reaction, noting his response.

"I need a man with your skills and innovation." Rampras added.

"Okay," Logan said.

"Okay? Just like that?"

Logan shrugged.

"No bartering? No questioning of motives?"

"What do you want me to say?" asked Logan.

"Quite frankly, anything." Rampras said. "You're a mystery to everyone around you. You even have the plainest personality I've ever seen."

Logan sighed; Rampras wasn't far off.

"The only thing of note," as he looked into Logan's records, "subject appears to lack any formal opinions or thoughts. Subject keeps to himself and displays no form of interest in anything. As a result, it can only be concluded his motives are unclear. That's the facility's records."

Rampras closed the folder and studied Logan. Logan didn't know how to respond. He thought for a long moment before speaking.

"I...never belonged anywhere," said Logan, "I don't understand the world, how it works, why people do the things they do. Never learned to think that way."

"So what did you do?" asked Rampras.

"Just tried to live."

"Off the streets," Rampras echoed.

Logan nodded.

"Somehow I don't believe that, mate."

"How is this important in combat?"

"It matters what you do," Rampras stressed as he pointed to the table, "who you save, who you let die, who you might betray, who you might support. Every single one of these is relevant in a high-stress situation, and so far I got nothing to judge on except that one and only comment in that report...and that's not enough to go by. So my question is...who are you?"

Logan thought for a moment, then said, "I don't know."

"You don't know because you won't tell me?" asked Rampras.

Again, Logan thought really hard; he didn't know what to say. "I don't know...because..." said Logan as he worked to formulate an answer, "because I'm not fully developed."

Rampras jerked his head back then frowned. He looked at Logan's assessment then back at him; it sort of made sense. But Rampras wondered how he came up with an answer like that.

He figured most people wouldn't be able to conceptualize or attribute something so abstract as underdeveloped without prior knowledge of what a fully developed person is. It was like a paradox to him — one would need to be developed to understand what under development is.

Then Rampras noticed Logan's shoulders were tensed.

Maybe he didn't know what he was talking about or struggled to understand.

"A lot of people go through changes, mate," Rampras said. "Sometimes, people end up leaving themselves behind when they come into a new world."

Logan felt like Rampras was talking directly to his soul.

"But that person comes out when entering a battlefield," said Rampras. "And in a way saying...no one ever leaves themselves behind."

He felt scared. He didn't know what that meant. He only remembered patches of the past and it wasn't enough to go by. What if he wasn't a good person? What if he hurt others and his self-nagging was warning him of that? His thoughts ran amuck while Rampras analyzed.

"Alright," Rampras concluded. "If you're going to join Beta Squadron I need your skills up to par. Should you decide to join, I'll assign you to the Paradigm to be retrained for recommissioning. Questions?"

Logan paused in thought. There wasn't much he wanted to know that he couldn't figure out himself. He never really liked bothering people with questions unless it was necessary. He figured that was probably part of the symptom too: not wishing to bother anyone for feeling less important than others in society, similar to how others viewed people in poverty. But he forced himself to ask.

"Why did you choose me?" asked Logan.

"Brains are the most valuable asset in this broken world," said Rampras. "Something that was evident when a confused, defrosting patient disabled a contingent of A.T. Units he knew nothing about."

Logan nodded then said, "I'll let you know what I decide."

Logan left the room with the feeling of being at a crossroad. It was a career path dilemma college students faced that affected the rest of their lives.

Logan felt weird, but weird with options.

Options, he thought.

He still couldn't decide even after that talk. He didn't want this to be his decision. He was used to being swept away by fate for so long that the possibilities of merging one's own future seemed like a fairy tale; a fairy tale that was now his.

He felt weird and he needed help to decide.

He went back to the sleeping cabins and noticed Martin still there. Logan walked over and stood near him. For a moment, Martin didn't notice even though it was silent in the hallway. Then he shuttered upon seeing Logan.

"What? What you want?" muttered Martin.

"Came to say hi," said Logan.

Martin went back to his equations, totally ignoring him. Logan didn't know what to make of that.

"Actually, I wanted to ask--"

--Martin rolled his eyes and looked back up.

"Sorry, never mind," said Logan as he turned around.

"Just ask," said Martin in annoyance.

"No, it's fine."

"I sit here. I very busy," said Martin. "You come and bother me cause you have question. I listen now. So ask."

Logan could tell English wasn't his first language.

"Rampras asked me to join the squad," said Logan. "I don't know what to do. Wanted your opinion."

"Soldier work very dangerous. You join, you no smart," Martin accented as he went back to his work.

"That's it?" said Logan.

Martin sighed frustratingly and lifted his view. "Rampras tough guy. He yell at me lots. If you join, he yell at you too. Soldier work all about yelling."

"But you save people's lives," said Logan.

Martin just shook his head, trying to go back to work.

"I thought that would matter since that's what tactical work was all about."

Martin lifted his view again, this time angrily. "You think I Chinese stereotype?"

Logan was shocked at hearing this.

"Oh look! Chinese boy do all kind of math. Oh look! Chinese boy no talk right. Has funny accent. Play chess all day. Play with computer. Has squinty eye. Does kung fu. This go on for hundred of year and people still see stereotype."

"People say things about homeless people too," added Logan.

Martin shook his head and doodled on his chalkboard. Not the same thing. Logan just sighed in frustration. Doesn't look like he will get through to him. Martin was too guarded. So he started to walk away.

"Maybe..." said Martin as he kept his gaze lowered, "...when you join, I see neat thing you do with mind."

"Maybe," Logan said with a smile.

Martin smiled back weakly. Logan could tell Martin was a broken soul trying to find his own place in the world. Logan wished he could give that to him, but didn't know where he belonged. He could easily see why he turned to math: a distraction from the rest of the world.

Logan understood why Martin got into Rampras's face;

sometimes a person has to do drastic things in order to be heard. Martin didn't have the vocabulary everyone else did and couldn't vocalize what the problem really was. But most of all, he was struggling with cultural friction and had to adapt to more things at once than the average person did.

One would think that after centuries of cross-cultural blending, there would be no traditional purists left. But Martin was, even if he didn't know it. He did not absorb the glamour of popular culture in him. Not one bit. His soul was pure and laced with a heritage spoken through his accent that only the wise could see.

Logan envied him for that. Martin belonged someplace.

Afterwards, Logan wandered the base and found himself staring at an incoming shuttlecraft. Soldiers stepped out and hauled a bunch of wounded onto stretchers. Blood spilled everywhere with one holding his own guts in. Logan was horrified by the sight. Then he noticed Multanis come out and assist the wounded toward the infirmary. Logan followed them there.

Inside the emergency room there was screaming. Wounded with severed limbs and burn marks filled the beds. Logan noticed the poorly lit, unpainted concrete walls and floors had mold on them as though it came from low-budget funding. It was unsanitary and looked infectious.

Several doctors hustled between patients loading IV stands, changing bandages, sewing and cleaning wounds, and monitoring other wounded. Multanis was there with most of his armour off. Logan watched for an hour and noticed their pace never slowed down even with an army of nurses assisting. Patient vitals scaled up and down, which made Logan's own heart fight to pulse.

Multanis finally noticed Logan as he was pressing down

on a wound, "You gonna sit there or are you gonna help close this wound?"

Logan looked around. Multanis was talking to him.

Then Logan said, "Am I even qualified to--"

"--You are now," said Multanis.

Logan got up and went over to the pale patient Multanis was attending. He looked like he just sweat half his fluids out.

"Put pressure on his wound while I tie his leg," said Multanis.

Logan pressed softly, not wanting to hurt the guy.

"He's passed out. You won't hurt him."

Logan pressed harder. Multanis tied off the man's leg with a rubber band but left the knot with a pullable release. Then Multanis moved Logan's hand out of the way and started removing leg clots. Logan was disturbed at the graphics of the open wound: blood, muscle, bones all sticking out. After Multanis was done cleaning, he sewed the leg closed.

Multanis sighed and took off his latex gloves. "One down, another four hundred to go. It's a never-ending stream of kids who never follow instructions."

Multanis clenched his left hand. It was shaking wildly. Then he clenched his chest near his heart. He was sweating and heaving. Logan was paused in mid-gawk, worried that Multanis would peel over.

Multanis cast a gloomy stare at him. "I'm fine!" he sneered.

"You do this all day when you're not on the field?" asked Logan.

"I do this even on the field," said Multanis while trying to calm down. "Unless I get drafted for mechanics work."

"You must have a lot of skills," said Logan.

"One Ph.D., two masters, and a mechanics degree,"

said Multanis as he controlled his breathing. He looked far too exhausted to be doing anything.

"Why so many?" asked Logan.

"Never knew what to do with my life," Multanis muttered, "so, I just, y'know, chose a path. Didn't like it. Chose another one. Never liked any of my choices."

"What would you rather be doing?" asked Logan.

"That's the big question, isn't it, kid?" Multanis laughed. He was a lot calmer now. "What to do with the rest of your life? I would say choose one...but not many like their choices, which makes the question a whole lot harder. But...if I had to pick one, I would say physicist work."

"So, like what Martin's doing," said Logan.

"That kid treats math like it's a toy!" Multanis objected. "He sees a problem, he's goes right in there and plays with it until he solves it. Then moves on to the next one. He's like a human calculator with absolutely no purpose. No spirit. No imagination. Doesn't even understand what he had just done, nor does he care about the variables involved. That's why he was ejected. In theory work, those variables mean something and can't just be cast aside."

Logan didn't know what to say to him. He hit a sore spot.

"But yeah, physics work," Multanis calmly said. "It's peaceful, productive, and doesn't hurt anyone, unless it's weapons research. I'm not getting involved with that again."

"Why don't you just go do it?" asked Logan.

"Can't, because of them," Multanis nose-pointed to all the young wounded soldiers. "At least on the field, don't have to worry about killing people. It's not who I am and it's not what I was meant to do. But this is a small world. Can't just sit around and freeload off this world. Because when they come..."

Logan nodded and went silent. He understood, but it still felt like he was being forced to decide and some part of him resisted it.

"Rampras asked me to join the squad," said Logan.

"Mmm," said Multanis as he smirked neutrally, "and you want advice."

"I don't know what to do," said Logan.

"Gotta do something," said Multanis, "Why were you in that facility?"

"I don't remember yet," said Logan.

"You chose that for a reason," said Multanis. "Must have been a good one. That was a government facility. I hear most psionicists didn't want to go but get forced into it somehow. Of course, these were the same brain-damaged specimens who complain about the attitude of their noodles. You don't look brain damaged, therefore, you went there by choice."

"What did you find in there?" said Logan.

"Not much. Just administrative records," said Multanis. "Didn't have time to do anything else."

Logan was hoping for more.

"Just find out what you like about psionics work," said Multanis. "It's gonna be a mystery to everyone else because only the gifted can do that. But don't let it get to your head."

Logan nodded then noticed his pun and smiled. Multanis smiled back and got up to attend to the rest of the wounded.

Logan spent the rest of the day wandering around the settlement. He listened to rumours about the Seer and his insanity, war stories against Cy-Corps and BioDyne, tales of people emerging. He kept hearing this thing called "Galilea" slipping out every now and then. But he wanted to fit in so he never asked. He got the sense that it was a peaceful place or a distant land far away.

He wandered the bazaar trying out new foods, but they had pretty basic tastes. Not like all the additives put into foods in the old world. Then he caught a glimpse of two children sword fighting with metal poles.

That caught his attention. He had to watch. Even though the children crudely fought playfully through some wreckage and debris, they loved the exhilaration and the epic heroism in it. Logan did too. Then memories crept up to the surface of him play fighting with swords on the streets with other kids. He was good at it. It was fun. He had always outsmarted his opponents in battle.

Then he wondered, *Why can't I do that? Why can't that be my dream?* If it was a hundred years ago, he couldn't. But now, he could! They had the technology and the means: plasma technology and psionics. He could finally live his dream. He could be a hero, a role he always wanted since childhood.

So Logan went back to the engineering bay. A loud buzz masked out most sounds. He saw Rampras wearing a black mask and bandsawing aluminum tubes. Sparks flew out like crazy. Rampras noticed Logan and stopped.

"You're not supposed to look directly at it, mate," said Rampras as he took off his black mask, "The light alone can boil your eyes like eggs."

"Think I'm going to join," said Logan.

"Okay," said Rampras.

He reached over to a folder, stamped it, and handed it to Logan.

"Just head on over to the Paradigm with this."

Logan took the folder, wondering what he had got himself into.

CHAPTER 6

NATIVITY

When Logan got up to go to the Paradigm the next day, a
thrill sparked in him. He didn't know what it was. He had psionics
training before and was already ahead so he knew what to expect.
That wasn't what thrilled him.

There was something about surviving in a deadly world
that got his juices flowing. He knew how to be resourceful and
budget his resources. Perhaps it was the challenge; the need to be
intellectually innovating that thrilled him. He wondered about all
the puzzles he would have to face in this crazy world.

He got out of his cabin, but was careful not to wake Vanis.

It was her second night sleeping there. He liked it, but wished they had a king-sized cabin. He walked amongst the barracks and saw some early birds doing their morning exercise routines. They had lined up and did stretches in synchronicity.

Something was missing. This picture wasn't complete. They were pretty quiet and all coordinated. *What was missing?* he thought.

He left the barracks and saw more soldiers in exercise uniform jogging along the base's main roads. Again, something was missing. He didn't hear the usual military singing.

He thought harder as he walked toward the main gates of the base. He looked at the steel doors. It was at the northernmost point of the base, the head of the serpent road. *That's what's missing!* he thought.

There were no leaders in those exercise regimes. Why weren't there any leaders? Why didn't those soldiers just take off? Wasn't someone supposed to supervise them from bailing out? All of these thoughts crossed his mind when seeing many troops jog back into the base.

No one yelled at them to keep marching. No one gave them hell for not following orders. When they sat down to rest, they laughed and joked, but didn't mock one another. They acted like a company of friends doing things together.

Why were they so soft with each other? Logan thought about this as he left the main base. He remembered from every war film ever made that there was always an angry, blunt sergeant pushing soldiers beyond exhaustion. Logan figured that everyone was past that point, especially for living in lands like these. Why bother training people to endure if they were already enduring every day?

But that wasn't what was missing. These soldiers seemed calm, peaceful, even humble, not like the testosterone-filled berserkers in the old world.

Perhaps the radical change on the world also changed many personalities. Pieces of themselves reflected the environment, being shattered with craze, with fear, with pain. Like the very jaws of fate could crush them at any second and now they treated living as though they saw themselves as ants: small, helpless.

It was so easy to be humble when one saw the violence of nature in the sky. Logan was glad people weren't as destructive as before. All of the arrogance, ignorance, selfishness alone could crush the world. Perhaps it did and now they suffered the repercussions.

But something else was missing. He would've dwelled on it more, but he was anxious to get to the Paradigm. So he left his thoughts at that.

As he ventured toward the large pyramid, he saw a dropship fly out of the settlement. Every dropship had its own symbol painted on it. He knew that was Rampras and his shrunken squad. *Don't they ever rest?* Logan thought. They did have one day's rest, if one could call it that. But he figured in a world like this, no soldier ever truly rested.

He began to wonder how long a working day was going to be for him. If he was sent out on a mission and was trapped, how was he going to survive out there, especially all alone? That nearly deterred him from going, but that didn't scare him. He felt that exhilaration for survival again and so he continued.

The Paradigm's open field was divided into classes that learned on the dirt. Some were learning telekinetic control while others Hap Ki Do movements. That was the style he was learning.

He wondered if this was a standardized art issued by Psi-Ops, the program he was formerly affiliated with.

Two grand halls were chiselled through the great pyramid, which intersected in the middle. There was a grand statue of man in the middle. He wore a trench coat with a long rimmed hat and had two bionic arms. The statue was labelled "Khared-Turo." Logan swore he saw that person somewhere, but couldn't put his finger on where or when.

Maybe he didn't. Maybe that was just his scrambled mind still piecing itself together, or just about him in rumours he heard earlier. Many people talked about him, but he barely heard any of the content. What he did hear was that Khared-Turo was a great speaker and a powerful psionicist.

After informing several Paradigm teachers that he was an excavated patient from a Psi-Ops facility, they did a psionic assessment of his current skill level. He rated very high and was almost a fully trained psionicist. He just had to remember what cryogenic freezing made him forget. But after seeing the children sword fighting in open field, he definitely decided on Psi-Knight training.

It was settlement curriculum to put him through environmental assessment first so he would learn about the dangers of the shattered world. They sent him back to the settlement's base and back to astrometics. There he learned about all kinds of anomalies spawned by the radical contortion of physics.

He was told to kick rocks in open field every so often. When one didn't land, gravity was about to go limbo. He was also told to watch out for blinks of light in the horizon; those were electro-magnetic storms. They told him to check the skies often; colour shifts from the polyovular magnetic fields meant radiation.

They also told him to supervise environmental lighting; brightened or darkened areas meant altered photon scattering, which was the sign of temporal vortexes.

After the assessment, Logan went back to the Paradigm. He met with a middle-aged, bulky, bald Asian instructor. His name was Quan Shia. He brought him to a class where other excavated initiates were.

"You are here because of your talents," said Quan Shia, "Talents that exceed all normal parameters of humanity. The people need your skills. They need your power to help them. For in this world, we cannot sit idly by and hope for a better day."

Logan started to think.

"Dreamers do that, and we do not train dreamers," Quan Shia said as he looked at Logan. Logan gulped and quieted his thoughts.

"In this world, only the useful survive," Quan Shia added.

They sent Logan to a prep room where he learned about psionic dangers. Feelings emitted externally had to be controlled from being read. If thoughts suddenly spawned for no reason, they told him it was a psionicist hijacking the subconscious. Unless the conscious self was hijacked, the psionicist could only influence the person through psychosis. But if memories suddenly emerged, it was the memory banks being hacked into.

Logan worried if he had to expect psychic battles.

Before they sent him into training, he was told that psionicists couldn't do anything the mind imagined. Physics and quantum physics were involved.

Communicating with billions of particles to turn it into a bomb was downright impossible; the needed molecules were not present, the blueprints of a bomb were not in their memories, the practice of moving one hundred molecules was a mentally demanding task, and it would have taken a long time to do.

The first day of training was of mental stimulation. Logan had to be retrained because of his cryogenic suspension. They brought him to a room full of computers and vital monitors. They placed electrodes around his head, turned on a monitor that displayed an eight-bit Atari-like game, and asked him to move the ball using only his thoughts.

As Logan concentrated, his brain's pathways rerouted themselves to send electrical pulses into the electrodes. Eventually, he was able to move the ball with his thoughts in a matter of minutes. Impressive as it was, they told him it was necessary for the brain to re-wire itself constantly for skills he would learn.

Later, Quan Shia's words reflected around his mind, and he couldn't help quiet it down. It was exciting him, empowering him with purpose.

Your mind will be your armour. Your heart will be your shield. Your passion will be your steed. Your soul will be your weapon.

The rest of that day was spent meditating on the open training fields. They told him it was important he learned how to communicate with his body since it was the electrical charges in his muscles that generated pulses of energy and magnetic forces. It took martial arts masters decades of training to achieve this. But by the end of the day, he was able to disturb clouds of dust.

The next day, he was in a biology class learning about the anatomy of the brain and which skills were utilized by the different lobes. Later in the day, they hypnotized him into a REM state and strapped him into a chair in front of a monitor. Thousands of pictures flickered by, all with important details of cognitive enhancement. This was subliminal programming and augmentation.

Later, they strapped him to a board and put different electrodes all over his body. They flicked a switch and electrical surges zapped into his muscles. By the end of the procedure, they gave him a red glowing drink that helped with muscular regeneration. By the end of the week, he looked a little more buffed.

There will be those who despise you, the memory of Quan Shia said. *Those who will want to break you. But they cannot destroy you, for you are a warrior of light.*

The next week, they trained him in basic telepathy and empathy. He was able to hijack someone's pet ferret, which copied his movements exactly. Later, he was in a samurai dojo, learning to use wooden katanas. Because of Logan's skill with the sleight of hand from years of card tricks, he learned swordplay rapidly.

As he trained with the blade in the dojo, an image suddenly popped in his head. Logan tripped over his own foot. It was an image of Vanis posing nude. Logan blushed then looked around the room. Vanis grinned and winked at him as she walked by the dojo's doors.

A week after, Logan was taught to use telekinetic sphere-ing. He looked at all the students making things float and felt very intimidated, then reflected back to Quan Shia's words:

The universe is bound by laws. Laws that forged the universe at the subatomic level. But these laws...can be taught new tricks.

He remembered Quan Shia igniting his whole hand in flames with a flick of a wrist. He was amazed, but felt he could do it.

From the way that was taught to him, gravity and magnetism were two different things that did something similar: attract or repel objects. Magnetism could occur in electrically charged metals, while gravity was something generated naturally from the abundance of mass.

It was theorized that magnetism was high-density energized strings that only responded to certain metals with electrical conductivity, while gravity was low-density tethers that attracted all. He was also taught everything generated or stored electricity and was able to attract or repel one another. After he heard this, he wondered if he should be seeing everything as energy instead of mass.

He was taught that the directional flow of electrical currents inside the body determined whether the body attracted or repelled forces. Creating an electromagnetic current required patience, discipline, and the knowledge to flow electricity in spirals throughout the body. Clockwise meant attraction. Counter-clockwise meant repulsion, which was favoured by psionicists.

At the first few attempts, he was able to suspend small objects in the air. Later, he and his class were given glass balls that generated electrical streaks. They were told to manipulate them. By the end of the class, he was able to pull lightning trees out of the orbs.

On his second final week, he learned how to generate a magnetic sphere around himself. It blocked and pushed solid objects away. He had to concentrate so hard that electrical slashes formed around him, spiralling in circles rapidly. When he generated enough current, it cancelled the crust's gravitational pull and lifted him off the ground.

His first attempt landed him on his head. The second

attempt made him float upwards without control. On the third attempt, Vanis kept distracting him by sending him naughty images of herself. By his fourth attempt, he was spiralling in circles into the air.

It was very demanding work. He wondered if it was even practical to use. But as a psionicist progressed in skill and energy efficiency, levitation was very easy to do. Though he had to take notes on the important balance between energy generation, duration, and expenditure not to exert himself too quickly.

His final week was about tactics and team movement. Here, they gave him a hover bike and supervised his training all over the debris tracks around the settlement. Later, he was in an obstacle course. They put him through acrobats and gymnastics training all of that day. Then he trained by himself in a dojo with a wooden katana and imagined himself fighting a large machine.

When does a human become more powerful than a machine? Quan Shia said in his memory. *We...have been on the brink of evolution for quite some time and this has been known for a thousand years by various cultures. All you have to do is step through those gates and ascend to unimaginable heights.*

CHAPTER 7

CATHARSIS

By his final lessons, he was a seasoned psionicist and hover bike driver. But the Psi-Masters surprised him with a military training test. Quan Shia had studied him throughout his training and couldn't explain his impressive acceleration. Even with his previous training in Area 77, he could not have managed to master certain skills so quickly.

The only other explanation was that Logan was a natural and very intuitive. That added with the lack of mental illness that normally afflicts a psionicist, he would easily surpass any student that came into the Paradigm.

But Quan Shia felt that he held some secrets, even to himself, and amnesia was the perfect mask for it, especially against psionicists. So Quan Shia had set up the surprise to see if he could draw it out.

The Paradigm's Psi-Masters had set up a live weapons course. The course was in a large gym in the military base. It was littered with sand bags with attack dummies armed with assault rifles situated at random locations. As Logan and four potential graduates lined up, they were issued steel cases.

"Gentlemen, your weapons," he said.

Logan opened his case. Plasma blades were disassembled inside. Logan smiled at its beauty. He assembled his and turned it on. An electrical branch struck out from the mechanical handle and a vapour spat out, which quickly liquefied then solidified in a second. The weapon steamed with power. It did not cut, but ate through most substances.

Quan Shia walked before them, sizing up each of them, then stopped with Logan. "You've been impressing the Psi-Masters every step of the way. How or why I do not know."

Logan didn't know what to say. He felt proud, but wasn't used to being proud of anything. He kept his hands behind his back and his vision lowered.

"Before we admit you as a fully skilled Psi-Knight," Quan Shia said, "we must test your skill in a live ammunitions course."

"Please organize your tactics then proceed to your starting positions," announced the course operator on the intercom.

The four Psi-Knights huddled. Logan didn't pay any attention to them.

"Hey, get in here!" said one of the Psi-Knights.

"I'm good," said Logan as he studied the course.

The Psi-Knight shook his head, then discussed with the others their methods of approach. After a moment, they got into their starting positions marked on the floor with red squares.

"Initiating simulation units with live ammunitions," announced the operator on the intercom. "In five...four..."

Logan was getting nervous.

"Three...two..."

His heart pounded. He kept remembering the fight at the excavation.

"One."

Sweat started to pour down his face.

Then a loud buzz ringed. Red ceiling lights popped on. Two droids popped out from the sand bags and blasted rounds. From the sudden bang, Logan instinctually dropped to the ground.

"Halt!" said Quan Shia.

Logan, in total fear, was on the ground in a ball.

"You're not going to find victory down there," Quan Shia mocked.

"I-I-I'm sorry," Logan shivered. "I'm not used to this."

Quan Shia sighed at him, then signalled to the operator to reset. Logan, humiliated, got off the ground.

"Re-initializing simulation units," announced the operator.

Just go in all the way, Logan thought as the operator counted down. Then the test alarm buzzed. Red lights turned on. Logan froze again. Bullets blasted all over the room, but Logan couldn't move from his spot.

Quan Shia halted the course; the lights went on. Logan cursed at himself for not moving. Quan Shia waited for Logan to be ready again. Logan nodded. Quan Shia started it again.

When the timer went down, Logan ran forward toward one of the droids. The droid quickly turned to him and fired.

Logan felt several painful slams throughout his body as though he was bashed by several baseball bats. Several bones snapped and there were feelings of bags being busted, leaking out warmth inside his torso. His body screamed out electricity that flooded his nerves.

Bullets had slammed all over his body and sent him flying back. He could feel it burning while he drifted through the air. He slammed onto the ground. Liquids quickly filled and burned his lungs. He gasped for air, but felt the stinging gurgles of his blood in his chest. He couldn't breathe. It felt so itchy.

Am I going to die? he thought with extreme anxiety as his arms flailed out for air. *I can't die here. I can't die here!*

Quan Shia halted the course and hustled over to him. The other four Psi-Knights surrounded him, taking in the horrid sight.

"Give me some room," Quan Shia said.

The others stepped back. Logan felt his heart pound but with decreased pressure every time. He was losing blood, which made his vision spin.

Quan Shia hovered his hand over Logan's chest. Logan wailed louder, splashing out blood from his lungs as a lead bullet squirmed to the surface. It pushed aside muscle and tissue, leaving behind a wake of electrifying pain before flinging to Quan Shia's hand.

Quan Shia did this with every bullet before resting his hand on Logan's shoulder to concentrate. Logan suddenly felt waves of tingling fill his body. It was as if his body went on hyper drive. He looked up to see his chest wound closing very rapidly, while fluids were re-absorbed through his lungs.

As his lungs drained, he gasped for air and heaved several times to catch his breath. After a moment, Logan was fine but incredibly sore. Quan Shia picked him up from the ground. Logan nearly lost his balance as he stood up.

"Again," said Quan Shia, disappointed as he walked away.

He's not serious, is he? Logan questioned in thought. He just felt the terrors of being on death's door and Quan Shia ignored it as if it was nothing.

"He's going to get himself killed!" objected one of the Psi-Knights.

"But he knows not to get shot again," said Quan Shia over his shoulder.

"Is this just a test or a final examination?" asked the Psi-Knight.

Quan Shia snapped his gaze at them and said, "Every day you walk on this broken world is a testament of character. Every day you learn and every day you teach. Therefore, every day is a test. Don't make this your final examination."

Logan saw that as a voice of experience. Quan Shia had been on death's doorstep many times. Logan figured he was just going to have to get used to that feeling. It might happen many times before his time was up.

Quan Shia reset the course.

As the operator counted down, Logan thought to himself, *Don't screw this up.* He kept listening to the numbers count down, as though counting down his life. He dreaded it. He hated it. His heart pounded in terror.

Then the ringer buzzed and the red lights flickered. The four Psi-Knights took cover behind nearby sand bags. Simulation droids blasted at them with lead.

Logan immediately ran toward the battle droids.

Quan Shia was shocked. He couldn't believe what he just saw. The same idiot, who nearly got himself killed, who was traumatized by the experience of it, was running toward those bullets again.

Logan blasted a telekinetic thrust at the nearest sand bag barrier. Several bags tumbled along the floor and knocked one droid over. The other droid dipped down while one popped up and blasted rounds. Logan blocked it with his psi-shield and ran toward it.

He dove over the battle droid, sliced its head off, and tumbled under another lead volley. Another droid popped up adjacent to it. Logan snapped a hand out, held it with a telekinetic grip, and twisted it before it got a shot off. The held droid misfired and blasted the other in its back. Then Logan ripped it from its socket and thrust it to another popping up. Bullets streamed all over.

He slashed down one that popped beside him then shielded himself from a volley from the gym's end. He rotated his failing psi-shield as he ran toward it. The droid blasted all the way to point-blank range before being beheaded by a blur of plasmatic light. Logan reached the gym's end and sighed.

The gym lights switched back. The four Psi-Knights were still at the beginning. Quan Shia started to walk toward him. Logan felt proud of himself, but he figured Quan Shia wasn't. He lowered his vision from his gaze.

Quan Shia stopped before him and shook his head. It was as if he just saw the bravest and most skilled idiot he had ever seen.

"You cannot leave your men back there," Quan Shia said.

"I know, I just...reacted," said Logan.

"In a real-world situation," Quan Shia said firmly, "vigilantism will easily get you killed. I'm surprised you hadn't here."

Logan blankly stared with his mouth open. He was so used to being alone that he treated a life-and-death situation no differently. He never thought about the concerns of other people's lives before, for no one cared for his own. Quan Shia figured he induced the right thoughts in him to think about.

"In a real-world situation, you failed," said Quan Shia as he walked away. "But according to the testing procedures, you passed."

"How could I pass if I left everyone behind?" said Logan.

Quan Shia turned around and added, "We're not military

soldiers. We trained you to use your mind, not mindless obedience. How you handle the real world is up to you."

That made Logan question the Paradigm's agenda if it wasn't for the sanctity of human life. They didn't seem to be concerned with the settlement's affairs. Perhaps it was the politics they didn't want to be involved with.

As Logan headed out of the gym, he noticed at the top window that Vanis had been watching. She didn't seem impressed either.

CHAPTER 8

CATACLYSM

Later that day, Logan was given Paradigm regalia. It was a simple cloth-linen uniform with Asian influences. It was loose, white, with shin and forearm straps wrapped nearly skin tight for increased mobility. It had a long half gown that hung from the belt with two side slits for leg maneuverability. It was nothing rich or fancy but contrasted the darker plates of the squadron soldiers.

A part of him felt he didn't earn it, but he noticed there was no formal ceremony to celebrate his achievements. They just handed him the regalia and went on with their duties.

Where was the formality? Logan thought. *Don't people celebrate these things?* Then Logan thought his priorities were not on the right things. Food was the most important. Someone getting a medal wasn't. It was strange of him not to think of that. But he thought of it as a sign that he was changing. He was no longer that younger man living off the streets.

He was becoming someone else.

As Logan headed back to the bunker, he passed Calis who cheered him on for his success. Logan immediately went to Rampras's office inside the central facility inside the base.

The office was a small room with one drawer, a desk, and two chairs on both sides. The walls were decorated with contour maps and inventory information. No personal relics resided in the office. They were pretty economic on the space they used. Then Logan thought about what they did with the training gym when they weren't using it.

Rampras was wearing reading glasses and looking through the roster attached to a clipboard when Logan came in. He slid off his glasses and listened.

"I passed," said Logan as he handed Rampras the reported, "but they weren't too impressed with me."

Rampras quirked a brow at him, slid his reading glasses back on, and viewed the report. After a quick read, he glanced at Logan as though questioning his performance already. Logan was not impressed with himself. Rampras accepted his reaction as a learning process and closed the folder.

"Welcome to Beta Squadron," he said. "We don't have any mission details as of yet. I'm still trying to replenish our losses. But you need to be debriefed on our orientation and procedures. Questions?"

Logan paused in thought. There wasn't much he wanted to know that he couldn't figure out himself. He never really liked bothering people with questions unless it was necessary.

He figured that was another conflicting behaviour that Rampras would not approve of: not wishing to bother anyone for feeling less important than others in society, similar to how others once viewed people in poverty.

But he did want to know one thing.

"Who's Samiren?" Logan asked.

"Samiren? Well, that takes you way back, doesn't it, mate?" as he sat back and drifted in thought. "You ever hear how it was when we first emerged? I hear it was rather...violent."

Logan could only imagine, if that, in itself, did it justice.

*　　*　　*　　*　　*

As Rampras described how it was, images quickly filled Logan's mind. Thoughts spilled out and imaged its phantom-ness, shaping out a world from the depths of oblivion. It played out its own melody, its own drama, a telling of an unseen realm so fascinating that was parsed from Rampras's words.

He saw thunder. He saw sandstorms. He saw a forest of lightning engulfing the sky in a theatre of psychosis. But such a play would be so drastic, if not devastating, upon first arrival.

"The first of us appeared five years after the nova," said Rampras. "Many created bunkers. Some were destroyed while others survived."

He imagined a hatch deep inside a shielding ravine. It opened. A man in tattered clothes stepped out and gazed up into the sky. Meteorites speared into the atmosphere, continental rocks torpedoed into a limbo, and a large glowing ball of magma splashed red glowing liquids into space.

Logan wondered how terrifying it must have been to see the Earth's molten core decompressing: to see it glowing with fire, glowing with agony, the broken heart of a dying world lashing out with blades of magmatic flares.

"We didn't know if we could last," said Rampras. "We thought the environment would kill us. But we kept on and rebuilt. As the climate calmed, so many resurfaced that we created the settlements to shelter them. That's when we realized the grids still existed."

He imagined a garden of hydro-electro towers, a small town of tarp huts, and miners who quarried a plate tectonic fissure. Several miners strapped and slid down a rope line to the fissure's base. Upon reaching the crack's base, a pod with a turret attached pierced through the sands and aimed its barrels at them.

The whole miner team halted.

"That national defense grid that Cy-Corps left behind survived," said Rampras. "But when it emerged...it was friendly."

The pod's scanners quickly analyzed them. After noting that they were harmless, it scanned the area for other dangers. The mining team was relieved.

"But BioDyne left behind monstrosities," said Rampras. "No one knows for sure how they came to be."

A band of salvagers marched up a dune toward a graveyard of toppled, seafaring battle cruisers. It was tattooed with hundreds of meteorite holes. As the salvagers were scavenging, a stalker crept down vertically along the haul.

It lunged and grappled one. The salvagers screamed and backed away. The stalker rammed its arm through the captured man's stomach. The stalker's arm liquefied, merging its body with the captured salvager. The man's head, frozen in a scream of pain, slid onto the stalker's body. They were becoming one.

"We called them the chimeric infection," said Rampras, "for mutating by merging together. That's when the defense grid turned on us."

A pod turret poked out from the sand. It shifted its barrels and blasted the stalker. Bullets sliced up both bodies. The man's head rolled onto the ground. The pod scanned it. The word *infected* was displayed on the pod's HUD. Then it turned to the other salvagers. The salvagers were startled. The pod opened fire and slashed their bodies apart.

"They saw us as a threat for being hosts for the chimera agent," said Rampras. "So they slaughtered us and trapped us into a middle of a war."

He imagined silhouettes of colossal machines towering over a distant settlement. Its phantom-ness eluded solid shape, but he knew their laser weaponry would cut apart any stone wall that tried to barricade from it.

He saw people fleeing for the sandy horizons. He imagined them looking back at the mechanical dieties wrecking their homes, only to be attacked while their backs were turned.

He imaged out worms, ogres, gremlins and grotesque monstrosities too unique to describe with words, smashing through the ranks of the evacuees. The valiance of their survival and the drama in their faces echoed in his mind.

"They morphed, mutated, upgraded, and transformed," said Rampras, "and eventually far surpassed the mere limitations of a human being. It was not until Khared-Turo arrived before we stood a chance."

He could easily see how that encounter played out in his mind. He saw light trails lancing through a construction site. It was stationed on top of a dry, clay plane. It was cracked by its age, but it once cupped a lake.

Dozens of dome-shaped steel-beam skeletons of the construction site's town of Bio-Farms were being sliced apart by blast fire. Several construction workers scampered for the clay plane. They were fleeing from unseen attackers masked by a sand mist.

As a group of workers fled, a pair of missile twins launched through the mist. The workers ran past a man in a tattered cloak and large-rimmed hat: Khared-Turo. Khared-Turo raised his two bionic arms. The missiles shuttered, then violently bloomed into an explosive rose.

Then two mech warriors emerged from the mist. Khared-Turo narrowed his eyes, keen and confident on taking them down. The mech warriors blasted lead. Executing a spherical somatic motion, Khared-Turo orbited the bullets around his body within a telekinetic sphere and launched it back, slicing up one of the pre-shield-era mech warriors.

Khared-Turo thrust his palm out and gripped at the other machine. The mech warrior suddenly halted. Khared-Turo slowly clenched his grip into a fist. The machine's chassis tremored violently as it warped inward. He then forced his fist into a knuckle snap. The mech warrior let loose a concussive slam, ripping the sound barrier, as it exploded into fragments.

"He was a master of his art," said Rampras, "who could move buildings with his mind. His words were powerful. His voice ignited the world and everyone united together under his wisdom to build a better way."

He could see the rising of four large poles of solid sand years later, the foundations of the Paradigm pyramid. The poles were lifted up by a crane, while other construction work was happening. Khared-Turo stood before a crowd of soldiers and pedestrians. He unleashed his deep, oratorical voice that lit the eyes of the people with purpose...with power.

"Then Cy-Corps unleashed the Samiren Cyborgs," said Rampras.

He wondered what they looked like, then imagined how Samiren looked before the rags. He came up a drone with a silvery chassis with three orange lights were embedded on its breastplate. Its facial chassis was plated by titanium. Its sharp eyes spoke with a sinister hate that twisted into its curvature mold.

Its laser shoulder cannon and the two arm-integrated turrets also added to its visual conversation. Its label, "XIII," was engraved on the metal jetpack embedded on its back, issuing to all the dread of a Samiren drone.

"Captured generals made into drones," said Rampras. "Powered by three micro-nuclear reactions, they were unstoppable."

Rampras described the settlement that was first attacked. The image of a flat desert plain was in his mind, but it was a trickery of sight. The settlement was hidden. It was chiselled one storey down, eliminating it from plain sight. A large manmade crater led toward the main base. This did not fool the three advancing Samiren drones. The base's alarms set off as they landed on the bowl's edges.

The settlement's perimeter defenses activated. Missile launch pads turned and fired, tanks ignited shells, and soldiers hustled to intercept the malice of these destructive drones. But every bullet, shell, and missile, no matter the calibre, yield, or kinetic force, reflected off the drone's reactor-powered shields.

A Samiren drone took aim. Laser crosshairs aligned on a soldier's head. The soldier gazed at it, seeing his doom. The drone fired.

"But that did not stop us from resisting," said Rampras. "On the fields outside of Epsilon, Khared-Turo made his final stance to protect the location of the settlement."

He envisioned it to be an epic battle on the outskirts of the shattered city that concealed Settlement Epsilon. A massive Cy-Corps army turned inbound from scaling the horizons. Skirmishers, peasants, and lightly equipped infantry were grounded against the debris hills hiding from plain sight. Khared-Turo stood at its boundaries and viewed the incoming army.

Thirteen rocket-like units sailed through the air toward their direction. Khared-Turo signalled to his crew. Settlement soldiers loaded portable mortars and launched canisters on the field. The canisters landed onto the sands, busted a hole in the lid, and spun wildly, flushing dust into the air.

The thirteen units, the Samiren drones, drawn by the sudden visual, landed in the middle of the dust shield. Beams of laser targeting scanned the area. Khared-Turo signalled to fire. The irregular battalion let loose the force of their weaponry. Bullets, tank blasts, artillery shells, rockets, grenades, and canisters bombarded the dust cloud and masked the Samiren drones.

After a minute of the artillery storm, Khared-Turo ceased the battalion's fire and squinted his eyes to see through the thickening mist. Then thirteen silhouettes formed from the dust cloud and blast fire speared through. The blast fire smashed the debris hills and bodies filled the air. Tanks, on top of the hills, were hammered to pieces in seconds. The whole battalion ran for their lives.

Khared-Turo mouthed out "NO!" to his fleeing army. The drones unleashed a second volley. Blast trails sailed toward the vulnerable army. Khared-Turo turned and aimed his palms at the incoming volley. The blast lines exploded before him. Massive dust clouds rolled across the battle zone and swept the fleeing soldiers off their feet as the continuous blast fire proceeded.

The ground tremored with every explosion. Thunderous eruptions slammed the ears as hundreds of flashes blazed through the dust fog. Everyone took cover behind debris humps and hills from the blinding battle of gods until the storm of rapid fire ceased. The troops peered over the faint protection of their hills; only a massive haze fumed from the exhaustion of unseen barrels.

Several awkward mechanical beeps, chirps, and clings blared from the silent calm and a dozen lights pierced the gloom and rocketed in retreat. The soldiers sighed in relief, but also in confusion and concern. They hustled deep in the fog. When the wind brushed the last remnants of the fog aside, Khared-Turo's body lay lifelessly on the ground nearby an inoperative Samiren drone.

It had malfunctioned.

*   *   *   *   *

"They had us and they let us go," said Rampras. "We figured there was a flaw in their design. They didn't want to take a chance with their prized stallion."

"Wow," said the awestruck Logan.

"Word of advice, mate," added Rampras, "if you ever see them, don't even bother. No psionicist has ever been able to stop one. Not even Khared-Turo."

Logan drifted. He never met one before, but already felt its dread.

"Why does he just stand there?" asked Logan. "Why doesn't he just act?"

"I don't know," Rampras admitted. "I think he doesn't see anything as a threat. But he's changed. He was badly damaged. Inoperative. Malfunctioning. We did all the repairs we could, even took his heat sinks off. But if he tries to light up, he'll roast his inner circuitry. So he has to preserve his firepower."

"And you trust him?" questioned Logan.

"As far as reprogramming goes," said Rampras.

A soldier popped his head in the office and knocked on the door. "Sorry to bother you, sir. Where can I find the Psi-Knight, Logan?"

Rampras gestured to Logan.

"The Seer wants to see you," the soldier said.

"The Seer," said Rampras with much impression. "Well, you should go, mate. Don't want to keep the madman waiting."

"Also, Scathers wants to see you, Captain," said the soldier.

Rampras rolled his eyes, got up, and left Logan in the office.

Why would the Seer want to see me? Logan thought.

CHAPTER 9

INCURSION

Logan walked a few steps into the octagonal aluminum hut. The floors were already of question. It was made of cellulignite: a manufactured chemical compound that retained the same physical properties as wood without the wavy lines. The wrinkled aluminum walls had no insulation that trapped in heat, but were soldered onto a steel frame that held the hut in place.

The windows themselves were sawed into squares with the leftover flaps hinged on to act as an adjustable blind. The rest of the hut was filled with unclean utensils, degrading food, maps and diagrams spilled onto the table, books on the floor, dirty towels, and other anomalies that made up for the chaotic explosion. Whoever lived in here was very distracted from daily chores.

Nailed onto the walls, several hand-drawn pictures were seemingly scribbled by an obsessive maniac: an exploding star, a planet shattering, a figure of a man engulfed in flames, a group of cyborgs, people running from a colossal shade taller than clouds, a man watching missiles fire at a small Aztec-like city, soldiers fighting tentacles inside a dome, people eating people alive, a crater full of people yelling at each other, and a man leading refugees into a desert.

Even Khared-Turo was in it, who seemed to be counselling a scruffy man inside a shattered building. But one picture disturbed him. It was a picture of himself inside the aluminum hut he was in now looking at the picture of himself looking at a picture. Another made even less sense: it was a man in a trench coat with a flat cap turned backwards looking through the same hut as him.

Logan figured some of these happened already and others were messages for the future. He did not know if they involved him and was afraid to know.

"Some people will do anything to survive and that is a dangerous thing," spoke an unseen voice. Logan looked around; it came from the walls in the next room. "It is the desperation of human survival that will diminish all morality. All that will remain is primal instinct."

A man came out from the next room. He was bald, hairless, had wrinkled, dehydrated skin, and wore a patient's gown.

"Are you the Seer?" asked Logan.

"We...are the offspring of our own terrors," stressed the Seer.

Logan wondered if he spoke in an encoded manner as though a subliminal message for another time. The Seer walked with a bit of a limp as though his knees had arthritis. His back was permanently arched as though from years of writing or drawing. The Seer poured himself some water, hands shaky from his age. Logan wanted to help.

"You will not lift a foot for me, little mind user," said the Seer.

Logan gulped. Even at the millisecond of deciding to do something, the Seer saw it a mile away. Logan wondered if he could read thoughts too.

"Mocking me, the Seer of All Things, with trivial wonderings will not help you," said the Seer.

Logan was even more spooked. Logan hadn't even asked yet. But if he never asked, how would he ever know?

"Because I see what could be...that which does not need to happen," explained the Seer as he looked at him, hoping to end all annoying questions.

Logan figured this would be the norm with every future encounter with the Seer. He figured it best to assume he would know and dismiss its weirdness.

"Why am I here?" asked Logan.

"It is said we all live in a grid," the Seer said as he walked toward Logan, "a divine plan of masterful engineering. Yeessss. No living thing is capable of disrupting it. Not even I, the one who sees it all, for the visions themselves are a part of this plan. But what if..." he said as he walked around Logan with a sinister smile, "there was an anomaly that never fit...and its sole purpose was never to...exist?"

Logan couldn't take his eyes off the Seer's obsessive gaze. It was as if he saw far beyond any mortal person could ever dream of seeing.

"One would say," theorized the Seer, "the smallest bean can unfold a cataclysm for setting forth the smallest chain of events. Hmm, interesting. No? Another would say, such things will ultimately diminish any possibility of that from the chaos of randomality. Hmm. Also interesting."

"I don't understand," said Logan.

"But, of course you don't!" the Seer mocked that into Logan's face, "Your mind is small. So, so small. Yeessss! I enjoy the presence of an ignorant mind."

He placed his hand on the table as though seeing another vision, "I don't actually see the future. I see...possibilities; the outcomes of variables from the linear self much farther than anyone else. All that is seen is the result of the naturally predictable, for one does not need to see...to see."

Logan, confused, worked to process these thoughts.

"But I can see it...painted in my mind, for I am the cursed that brings the foretold," he said as his haunting eyes pierced at him, wanting to devour his life, his future, his soul. "The infection of the world is shuffling its deck. The chips are being positioned. The bets are being played. Now they are waiting...waiting for the eternal damnation to free its inhibitions."

Suddenly, a thought sparked in Logan's mind. He knew exactly who he was talking about. But he could barely remember his name.

"Yeessss, you know it. You see it. You feel it inside of you," said the Seer as he drew in on Logan's memories. "He was there before you. He was there after you, and he will be there...long after you had died."

Logan remembered the fire, the screaming, the howling, the people running, and the terrible voice that haunted his mind.

"The anomaly. The eternal damnation," said the Seer as Logan thought harder, "the one who will end it all. All because... the Determiner told him to."

Logan saw a man inside the brightest fire of white he had ever seen.

"Telisque," said Logan.

The Seer smiled.

Logan felt a shiver of force throughout his body.

"And now you know his name but not his story," said the Seer as he turned his back to him. "It is dangerous to know things, little mind user. I...know."

Logan thought, *What was he doing in Area 77?*

"Listening Post C," the Seer said.

What was he talking about? thought Logan.

Suddenly, the settlement's perimeter alarm went off. Logan looked outside the window. The base's red siren lights strobed throughout the settlement. People packed up tents and supplies from the bazaar. Others made their way toward the fractured subway systems. Soldiers ran back toward the base, while some reinforced the settlement's perimeter defenses.

Logan looked at the Seer who didn't seem to care, then bolted out the door and toward the base. Logan got to the base after a minute of top-speed throttling. Inside, soldiers were geared up and loading onto the shuttles. Calis ran out while hooking a metallic pack to his back. Logan intercepted him.

"What's going on?" asked Logan.

"Ye got me there, popsicle," said Calis.

Logan looked around for Rampras as Multanis and Martin emerged from the bunkers.

"You guys know what's going on?" asked Multanis.

Logan merely shrugged. He was about to ask the same thing. Then he heard a commander of Delta Squadron barking orders to his troops to load on their shuttle.

"Sit rep!" said Calis.

"Wait for your commanding office," said the Delta Squadron commander.

Calis was annoyed. Sonic booms blasted from above. Logan and the team looked up. Several dropships speared away from the Calypso building.

"Well, ain't that highly irregular," commented Calis.

"Why would they be leaving?" asked Logan.

"They're paranoid about something," said Multanis.

Then, arguing burst from the central command station. They all looked. Rampras was arguing with Scathers. After a moment, Scathers turned around and Rampras barked something to his back.

Suddenly, a blur of light flashed before the crew. Everyone cringed and backed away from the light. Molecules snapped together in extreme rapidity and the figure of Vanis emerged.

"Holy balls of meat saucery and all that spaghetti crap that swims with it!" complained Calis. "Couldn't ye be a little more careful in where ye pop in like that, ye freak?"

Vanis merely cast a dark glare at him. Rampras met with the crew as he tightened his helmet.

"Orders, cappy?" asked Calis.

"I'll brief you on the dropship," said Rampras. "Where's Samiren?"

An elevation shaft came up from the grounds near the bunkers. Samiren and several soldiers emerged. The soldiers hustled, but Samiren walked casually toward the shuttlecrafts.

"Ye looked like ye were gonna maul Scather's final years of good lookin's off and have it for a nice crap," said Calis. "What was all that barkin' about?"

Then another sonic boom ruptured through the chaos. Rampras looked up at the Calypso building.

"That!" said Rampras. "What are those cowards doing?"

Samiren walked up to the loading zone but stopped to gauge Logan.

"He is an initiate," said Samiren. "He'll only lower our statistical rating."

"He'll do fine, mate," said Rampras as the others stepped in the shuttle.

"We are not bringing him along," Samiren said sharply.

Logan got the sense Samiren hated him, but with no good reason. They barely knew each other and Logan didn't do a thing wrong. Why would Samiren hate him? Was he, this cyborg, even capable of hate? If that were so, he had a human component to his mechanical self.

"You will do what you were instructed to do or you will be relieved from this mission," Rampras ripped at him.

Samiren glanced down at the shorter Rampras; he didn't have to listen if he didn't want to. Rampras stood his ground. Samiren narrowed his eyes.

"Humans," Samiren remarked as he got on. His weight alone shifted the dropship down a few centimeters.

Logan just didn't get it. Was that argument really just about statistical rating? Samiren didn't even know how well Logan would perform. He never saw Logan in action before. How could he even judge?

The shuttlecraft was loaded by Rampras's officer crew with an extra twelve squadron soldiers. The squad strapped their belts on and the dropship lifted off. A flagger coordinated the lift. Logan watched the settlement be left behind and noticed they were heading southeast.

"Listen up! Listening Post C was destroyed," said Rampras.

That got Logan's complete attention.

"Outcast marauders are raiding the convoys inside the outer perimeters."

"Should be an easy-ass mission," said Calis.

"Wait, what?" said Multanis. "How did they get past the LP?"

"Adhere suspicion," said Samiren. "The outcasts have been

exhibiting increasingly erratic behaviours, executing crude, but effective, tactics."

"Samiren's right," said Rampras. "Intel reports improved coordination."

"The stretchers dreamed their beach to longer strands," said Vanis.

"Are we all talkin' 'bout them same dumb goats we gave the boot to for wearin' them bad-guy hats?" asked Calis.

"They're not simple criminals anymore," said Rampras. "Someone's leading them. Just wondering what they're up to."

"They wouldn't have to get smarter," commented Multanis, "if we stopped treating them like rejects."

"You don't realize the dangers of this situation, do you, mate?" Rampras said to the silent Multanis. "Their one and only settlement alone is thirty-three times larger than ours. They enrage each other. They feed off each other, and they bring that violence onto anyone who's smaller than them. They're a city-sized prison with no bars to hold them back...and if they're very well coordinated now, they are a critical threat to all of the settlements."

That crushed all of Multanis's pacifist remarks.

"Oh, they may have more fingers than us," said Calis, "but we can pull our triggers with much better style."

"Let's just hope that's true, mate," Rampras said.

Rampras tapped a few buttons on his arm's holographic computer console. The console displayed the map of the surrounding area inside the perimeter of Listening Post C.

"The first convoy was destroyed near the LP," said Rampras as he illustrated on the map. "A Team's intercepting that. Intel reports that another party's hunting down convoys but we don't know where they are. D Team's scouting the north and we're taking the south. We intercept upon radio contact."

Logan felt fear and exhilaration fill within him. After the excavation of Area 77, he was no virgin to combat, but dreaded the thought of hurting another person. He was trained to fight beasts and machines, not human beings. But if they were trying to hurt other people already, then stopping them from hurting others would justify the harm he was about to do.

Still he dreaded the thought. He remembered the wounded patients in the infirmary then looked at his plasma blade contraption, realizing his weapon would do that in a matter of seconds. He didn't want the burdens of combat that weighed so heavily on Rampras and the others. He wanted to retain his youthful innocence. But he figured it was too late for that after the memories of Cherise.

He wondered why it was too late. He still couldn't remember much. But knowing what little he knew of himself, what most likely had been the case was that his mere self put her in harm's way. If that were so, what happened changed him so drastically that he transformed into someone else because he didn't want to be himself anymore. Perhaps that was why he joined Psi-Ops.

He was running away, but couldn't run away from this.

Then he felt a small, loving grasp comfort his trembling hand. He looked up. Vanis gazed back at him and added a smile; she felt all of Logan's worries. He held her hand tightly, which made her smile even more. Logan suddenly felt warmth and happiness coming from her heart — the first time he felt something from her. He never felt a bond like this before.

"Convoy Meridian to Settlement Epsilon," spoke a voice on intercom, "We are under attack. Repeat. We are under attack."

"That's our cue, mates! Saddle up!" barked Rampras.

Logan tensed. Rampras unbuckled, slapped a cartridge into his assault rifle, and walked to the cockpit. The rest were mostly quiet. One soldier made a small prayer on his rosary while another stared at a tattered photo of a family. Multanis and Calis seemed unaffected, while Martin spaced out.

After a moment, Rampras came back and balanced himself toward the shuttle's hind doors. Logan looked out: legions of sand dunes were left behind until a cluster of hover transports littered with blinks of light came into view. The transports, paired adjacently in twos, were under attack by raiders.

The off-road armada of raiders consisted of salvaged vehicles: dune buggies, motorcycles (two with side cars), dragsters, rocketed go-karts, sandmobiles (modified snowmobiles), quads, a gyrocopter, a truck with a mounted catapult, a jeep with a mounted crane, and twin dune buggies welded together to a central chariot

— all of which were ridden by mutants, cyborgs, midgets, brutes, and crazies.

Rampras attached a metal wire to the ship's drop hook and prepared the line for casting.

"We're dropping in roof side," said Rampras.

"Captain, that's dangerous," said Multanis.

"I know, mate," said Rampras, "but if you know a better way to repel those bikes, then hook yourselves up, strap yourselves to the hull, and man the integrated turret."

The dropship closed in on the transports. Soldiers got up and hooked the droplines to their girdles. Logan and Vanis were at the back, but he had a clear view of the fight below. He saw the outcast armada pursue the hovering transport aggressively. The rough sands and humps were making it difficult to board.

Then the flicker of nuzzles pulsed from the bikers towards them. Cracks and zips slammed at the edges of the shuttle's doors. Everyone ducked down. Lead fragments slammed inside the cabin, bouncing off walls and armour plates. A lead fragment flew past Vanis's dark hair. Logan caught the ricocheting piece harmlessly on his hand. It was steaming hot.

"Go, go, go!" said Rampras.

He ushered the soldiers down the line, until he slid down himself. Logan was too anxious to go, but Vanis held his hand. As Logan stood there with her on the edge of the dropship's floor, all sound receded except the softness of her loving voice. She smiled so angelically as though eternal and unaffected by the world.

"Do stab at doubts that never felt a hope," she said, "for we shall be together once again. If say we don't, remember me as me; the smile whose lovest heart gave purpose strength."

As she said that, he finally understood why she wanted to

move fast. Every day was a worry that it would be their last. Why wait for something if the next minute might be too late? He was glad that she did that. He would rather die having something than to live for nothing.

They leapt off together and levitated down, floating down from heaven as though two angels of salvation. Bullets streamed all around with chaos. Muzzles flashed with glimpses of a final life as hunter and prey struggled in motion. This was the first time he leapt toward extreme danger and the first time he was not alone. As long as they were together, he felt invincible and unstoppable.

Logan slammed onto the ground, rolled to his feet, and unveiled his plasma blade. He was ready.

Several stalagmite-like pillars of rock, straight and arched, passed near and over the transport. One of the pillars came too close and nicked the transport. The whole hull shuttered. Logan nearly lost his balance.

Rampras yelled into his radio, "Watch the rocks!" as he fired off a cluster over the transport's roof.

"I would love to," said the transport's driver on radio, "but she's complaining that her twenty-ton ass is too fat to turn."

The soldiers, hooked to the roof, blasted and covered intermittently. The outcast vehicles swerved constantly to complicate a steady target. Logan noticed the other transport was empty of defendants.

"Who's guarding the other transport?" asked Logan.

Rampras blasted a round, looked then radioed in "D team! ETA!"

"Ten minutes," said a commander on the radio.

"We're gonna be dead in ten minutes, mate! Double time it!"

Then two rockets blasted off one of the motorbikes. The rockets slammed the transport's rear end and the hull shuttered again.

"They're trying to take out our engines!" said Rampras. "Someone take out those rockets!"

Calis attached a sniper scope to his assault rifle and switched cartridges. Martin covered him and blasted wildly toward the aft. Calis kneeled and aimed his barrel toward the armada. Bullets zipped by as Multanis sat on the roof turret's seat. He tapped a few buttons. It spun around and Multanis blasted away.

Calis still hadn't gotten a shot off. They were swerving too much.

Then a rusty SMG and an open-fingered glove swung over the roof's edge. The rusty gun blind fired into the crew. Armour fragments splashed all over the roof. Two soldiers were floored. Everyone dropped to the ground.

"Stowaways!" yelled Calis.

Vanis upshifted her forearm and palmed upwards. The boarder was ripped off from the roof edge and torpedoed into the air. Samiren grabbed another and lifted him high off the ground. The boarder kicked into the air then blasted a revolver round into his face. The bullet reflected off Samiren's shield. Samiren threw him over. The boarder banged onto the rock and spun out of control.

Vanis kept trying to concentrate on another telekinetic burst, but kept shifting to her shield instead when bullets snapped her way.

Then two bikers with dynamites strapped to their chests slammed their feet on the throttle. Rampras crouched, aimed through his scope, and fired. One biker toppled over. The other biker, accompanied by a dune buggy with two others ready to board, drove toward the unmanned transport.

"Captain! Boarders on the other transport!" said Calis.

The armada increased fire. The squadron covered. Rampras growled, knowing they were covering for the other team.

"I got this," said Logan as he bolted toward the roof edge.

"Logan!" yelled Rampras.

Logan thrust his palms down as he leapt. The telekinetic floor blast catapulted him high into the air. He flew over the gap, landed on the other transport, and side rolled into a crouch.

"Damn him!" yelled Rampras.

Several boarders armoured with melted football pads and hardened hide intercepted Logan with harpoon shots and auto-crossbow fire while the third was setting up the dynamite charges. Logan palmed out a psi-shield as he charged them down. The boarders backpedalled knowing that their arrows and javelins were useless against the shield. Logan leapt off the upper platform.

Time seemed to have slowed down for him. He was in the midst of a diagonal axel, readying to uncoil a whirling slash that would slice down two marauders, two fully grown people with an entire history of life. He felt his world spinning into chaos even as he was physically.

He didn't want to kill them.

As he came down, shifting his foot to land into a spin, he couldn't stop himself. Their fates were already made.

As his blade entered their bodies, melting through their plastic padding and cleaving through their armour of skin, he felt an explosion of pain erupt from them and the nova of memories cascaded from their minds; memories of friends, family, loved ones that were lost to the nova, and the incredible hate boiling up in them for surviving the harshness of the sands.

He didn't think about the feedback on his blade that felt like cutting through heavy water. Nor did he notice how the searing heat of his weapon hid the details of cutting through bone, muscle, organs, and cauterizing blood from spewing out. He only thought about how he just ended two bloodlines so instantly while stabbing into the dozens of hearts of those who loved them.

As his blade left the chest of the second living being, Logan felt a horrible pain infect him like acid. It was guilt and it was haunting him. He didn't want to look into the eyes of those he just killed. The image would haunt him.

He would remember them for a lifetime if he did.

As their lifeless bodies slammed onto the ground, drumming the end of their memories, he felt this warmth flush out of him, which faded into the wind. He wanted to cry. He wanted to scream. He wanted to throw down his weapon and give up this war. But he couldn't. He no longer had time for that. He had to act. So he cast those thoughts aside and charged.

As Logan slashed down the first two marauders, the third saw. He growled, dropped the dynamite charge, unleashed two machetes, and charged. Logan angle-blocked a lancing stab and spun around the growling marauder. The boarder slashed and cleaved wildly at Logan.

Each strike met the searing heat of a plasma blade, slowly melting it down. Logan shifted defensive poses as the boarder, almost maniacally, convulsed each strike with poor coordination.

Calis noticed Logan. A large smile grew on his face.

"Yeah! Alright Logan!" Calis cheered.

Everyone looked as Logan blocked a lower cut while leaping over the marauder. Vanis's eyes lit up, even more infatuated now. Logan slapped away a series of strikes. He then dropped to one knee, up-smacked a horizontal swing, and thrust a telekinetic blast onto the marauder's chest.

The blast sent the boarder over the edge.

Samiren narrowed his eyes at Logan. He disapproved.

Then the outcast gyrocopter lowered down to a jeep that carried marauder passengers. Two of them climbed on the gyro's wings.

"More boarders!" said Rampras while taking aim.

A mutated midget attached a mini-gun on the dune buggy chariot's steering wheel then slapped the driver's shoulder. The chariot driver blasted streams of lead onto the roofs.

Rampras floored himself in cover while bullets bounced off the transport turret's front plates, protecting Multanis. Multanis swung the turret around and fired. The bullet storm sliced the chariot in half. The two severed dune buggies swirled out of control and tumbled all over the sands.

Calis peeked out and saw the gyrocopter advance with two chain-mailed marauders hanging onto the wings. He smirked and took aim. Then he suddenly looked right. A long crane was swinging a metal pancake his way.

"Incoming!" Calis said as he dove out of the crane's trajectory.

Rampras backpedalled and landed on his back. The crane's saucer knocked a soldier off and demagnetized two plated marauders onboard. The marauders slapped onto the ground and axed at Calis. Calis batted the axes with his rifle.

A soldier ran after Calis, but was suddenly pulled into the air by the magnetic plate. The security line that hooked onto the transport snapped easily. The soldier was carried over the edge and dropped. Rampras got up. The other marauder saw and tackled Rampras to the ground.

Several harpoons stabbed onto the transport's hull. Marauders climbed up from the back seat of quads and buggies. A bolas, tied to a sandmobile below, wrapped around a soldier, ripped him off the line, and pulled him over the edge.

Samiren stood there idly waiting out the combat. Multanis tried aiming the turret to the roof, but it wouldn't bend that way. Martin kept looking over his shoulder as he blasted down the walls at the marauders crawling up.

Vanis arched her fingers at the marauders, but saw the gyrocopter coming. She took stance and lashed out a whip of lightning. The electricity whipped the wings, igniting them. The gyrocopter spun out of control. The two hanging marauders were flung off. Vanis braced as the marauders landed on top of her.

One soldier grabbed a marauder off Rampras but was slashed in the face by an axe. Rampras kicked the back of the marauder's shin. The marauder fell. Rampras grappled him and wrestled over control of the axe.

Two soldiers tried wrestling the one marauder off Calis, but the guy was a brute. He grabbed both soldiers and hurled them over the edge. The soldiers, still hooked to the transport, smacked and hung along the transport's walls, and were then bombarded with bullets, arrows, and harpoons. Calis, shocked, scampered for his gun, then saw two more marauders fly in toward the transport.

Logan watched two more marauders, cast in by the jeep's catapult mount, land on the other transport. Harpoon lines from adjacent quads supplied the invaded transport with marauders. Sandmobiles pulled soldiers off the edges with bolases, while the crane magnetized another soldier and dropped him overboard. They were about to be overrun.

Logan noticed they were not concentrating on his end. He wondered if it was because he repelled boarders so easily. But he was only one man. He could easily be overrun. Perhaps they wanted to eliminate the largest cluster first. And if that breaks, then they'd surely win this battle.

But that was a decision the impulsive would never choose. That was something the outcasts were known for, for they always took the easy path. And if taking the other transport was a conscious decision, then these outcasts were not being impulsive. That proved they were being intelligent.

The gap's distance increased after the transports maneuvered around several rock pillars. Logan saw a hatch on top of the transport's roof. He pried it open and jumped down.

Two marauders that landed on Vanis stood up disorientated. Then one grabbed Vanis by the hair as she tried to crawl away. She yelped as they pulled her to her feet. As she stood, his blade stopped just before reaching her gut when he gazed into her glowing eyes. He was unable to move. Then he suddenly stabbed himself underneath his jawline and dropped to the ground. The other marauder was shocked. Vanis smirked and blasted him off the ledge.

Calis blocked and dodged the axe all over the transport roof. The brute's strength alone cleaved through the roof's hull. Then the brute ripped Calis's gun from his hands and threw it over the edge. Calis unsheathed his boot knife and jabbed it into the brute's thigh. The brute grunted, but wasn't slowed. He hovered over Calis for one final blow when suddenly blood burst out of his head. Calis was confused. He rolled out of the way as the brute slammed to the ground. He looked toward the upper platform and saw Multanis putting away his handgun.

Rampras was on top of an axe marauder pounding on his face while pinning his axe arm to his chest. Then Rampras felt a smack at the back of his head. If it wasn't for his helmet, he would've been knocked out. Rampras turned, grabbed the marauder behind him, and threw him over his shoulder. The one on the floor axed at him. Rampras blocked it with his forearm. The axe blade struck the metal plate and was stuck. Then Rampras stepped on the marauder's neck, ending him with a bone snap.

Rampras sighed and turned around. A marauder was shot in the head and fell before him. Calis lowered his aim on his handgun then looked at Rampras shockingly.

"Cappy, are you alright?"

Rampras felt weight on his helmet. He took it off. An axe was stuck to it.

Vanis saw the crane's saucer coming at them.

She yelled, "Get down!"

Rampras and Calis floored themselves as Vanis held the crane arm with a telekinetic grip, but it was buckling fast. Vanis smacked the back of her hand with her other palm. The crane's arm warped as it reversed course. The arm swung around. It slammed into a rock pillar and toppled the crane's base truck over, smashing two dune buggies in the process.

Two motorbikes swerved around the crashing carnage and fired off crossbow bolts on top of the transport. Rampras and Calis equipped themselves with dead soldier's guns and reinforced the transport walls.

The other transport's side door slid open. A rail system slid out a hover bike with Logan on it. He throttled the acceleration.

The hover bike's ion-powered engines roared, lifted off the rail, and slapped onto the ground before hovering.

Then all kinds of small rocks bounced off the hover bike's hull. Logan looked. Two midgets on a sandmobile that were bolasing soldiers were firing rocks from a slingshot. Logan swerved to the left. The hoverbike slammed into the sandmobile and toppled it over.

The harpoon was still stuck to the hover transport's hull. Its line dragged the sandmobile and smacked it on several bumps before snapping off. Logan then unsheathed his plasma blade and decelerated back.

Two rocketed go-karts and a four-wheeler curved out of his way. Logan caught the head of the four-wheeler's driver with the edge of his blade. The four-wheeler tumbled as Logan came parallel to a motorbike with a sidecar.

The biker, wearing an executioner mask, pulled out a flail and swung it at Logan. Logan slashed off the flail head and bashed the bike with his fender. The bike's weight shifted onto the sidecar and snapped the hinge, hooking them together. The bike torpedoed into cartwheels.

Then a pair of rockets fired off from a motorbike.

"Rockets!" yelled Martin.

The rockets slammed into the transport's engines. The engines fought to breathe but then exploded. The whole transport slapped onto the ground. The whole roof hopped the squad. They slammed onto the titanium ceiling, their steel security wires straining in tension. Then the edge of the transport's front clipped a rock pillar and jackknifed it.

"Jump!" yelled Rampras as he cut his line and leapt.

Calis ripped his line off and catapulted himself off the

transport. Vanis levitated down as Samiren jumped off. Multanis fumbled with the turret chair's seatbelt.

"Come on, you bastard!" said Multanis before slashing the belt with a knife.

Martin hustled to unhook himself, but was too late. The spinning transport whipped him around circles. The line then snapped and sent Martin farther away than the rest.

Logan saw the transport jackknife as the squadron leapt off onto the sands. The transport suddenly flipped and tumbled. Sand kicked up in all directions with every slam. Logan and the outcast armada swung around the decelerating, crashing transport that exploded hull panels in its wake. One panel hacked through a go-kart driver's helmet and split his head in half.

The transport halted and the squadron was scattered all throughout the transport's debris wake. The outcast armada split up, encircling the exposed squadron like vultures while Logan tailed behind.

"Converge!" said Rampras as he ran toward the largest soldier cluster.

Multanis aided the limping Martin toward the rest. Calis blasted a short burst of fire at a closing dune buggy. The buggy veered away then smacked into a debris chunk, somersaulted all over the sands, and added itself into the metal graveyard. Parts spilled out, which drove other vehicles away while the wounded were dragged into safety.

Martin gritted his teeth as Multanis set him down within the circular barricade of junk. Vanis lifted several hull shards into place. Calis blasted a clip before ducking under a bat swing drive-by. Rampras complained to his radio while Logan sped by, chasing a flock on his hover bike.

He amplified his ventral-starboard's thrusters when the bikers hardened their right at the sight of the toppled transport. He cut through the debris grass early and fired out his hover bike's gun turrets. The bulk shells shuttered the bike with every blast. The bullet lines scaled between the turning bikes until it slammed into the metal chassis of one, slicing it apart.

The bikers glanced back, saw Logan, and split directions. Logan chased one going right, pursuing in a figure eight. After a full convolution, the squadron came to view directly ahead. Rampras saw them coming right at him.

"Logan, hard to starboard!" Rampras said on the radio.

Logan didn't want to turn. Rampras cursed, took aim, and fired a warning shot. Logan was shocked. He turned right and the biker started opposite, but was caught by a fan of bullets by the squadron. The bike tumbled out of control toward them.

"Take cover!" Rampras said as he dove behind debris.

Everyone cleared out of the way. Then the bike stopped in mid-air before Vanis who held it in kinetic grasp. She launched it to the side field at an incoming dragster, which shattered both vehicles in a nova of iron.

Logan swerved around ejected catapult parts that were mounted onto a truck. The truck guards, two go-karts, and a sandmobile made it hard for Logan to advance. SMG bullets flicked and shattered off the hover bike's hull. Then the truck itself seemingly collided with an immovable object: Samiren. The truck's front first ripped in half before an energy shield smashed the rest into smaller bits.

Seeing the handful left that they were, a driver of a dune buggy spat curses at the squadron then bolted for the east. The rest immediately followed.

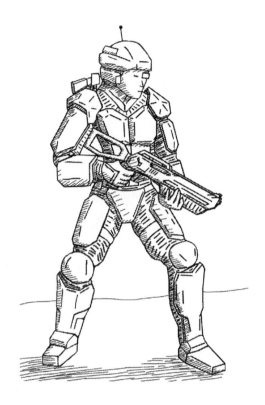

CHAPTER 10
CONUNDRUM

Calis squinted as they left, "Think that's the last of 'em."

"Bunch of daredevils, aren't they?" commented Rampras as he sat down on a bent hull panel. "Where's the rest of our squad?"

There was only the main crew plus two extras. Very little were injured.

"Think we're it, cappy," Calis said with much disappointment.

This was the second time Rampras nearly lost his whole squadron. He was not happy. "Still think this was easy?"

Calis only smirked in response.

Rampras got up and walked over to Multanis who was attending Martin. "How's he doing, mate?"

"Minor fractures. He'll be fine," Multanis said.

Then Rampras spotted Logan pulling up beside the rest of the sweating, fatigued squadron. Rampras narrowed his eyes. He got up and marched over towards Logan. Logan got off the bike. He was being cheered on by Calis.

In a rage, Rampras threw his assault rifle aside. Everyone looked at the enraged Rampras. He gripped Logan's regalia and slammed him on the ground. Multanis rushed over to them.

"What the hell were you thinking back there?" yelled Rampras. "That little action hero stunt you pulled nearly cost us our lives!"

Logan was in total shock.

Martin smirked; he saw that coming.

"You cannot just abandon your men like that!" lectured Rampras. "Especially in a world like this where the smallest mistake will get you killed!"

"He was just doing what he was trained to do," argued Multanis.

"Oh, and what's that?" Rampras ripped back with extensive venom. "By leaping off into the middle of the battlefield whenever so he damn feels like it? We needed melee support back on that platform and where was it?"

"Where were your orders?" reasoned Multanis. "You never said anything until after he jumped. He only volunteered to do something you needed done."

Rampras was already getting frustrated with him.

"You bark around all day like you were still in the military," said Multanis, "but, guess what? You're missing the fact that he isn't wearing a military uniform. He isn't trained to know these things. Neither are the rest of us with the exception of Calis. We're practically militia. Volunteers."

"If you're on my team, you better know," said Rampras.

"Why? Because if we don't, we'll get killed? Don't think we know that already?" Multanis said as he pointed to the molten core. "That damn core reminds us every day that we're close to death. Maybe we are already."

"Think that's every excuse to act any way you feel?" Rampras roared. "Well, guess what? It ain't like that. You do that in the military, you get court marshalled and sent for discipline. You resist; that's treason. You get others to help you; that's mutiny and both of those crimes are punishable by death."

"Well, obviously punishment is working with all those outcasts floating around attacking us," said Multanis. "Just how are they learning to be upright citizens when they don't even understand why they're being punished?"

"There are rules for a reason!" Rampras laid down. "Same with command structure. Same with law and following your damn orders! Don't do any of those things and you're better off dead, because that's how useful you're going to be!"

"You make it sound like harsh discipline is gonna set us straight," said Multanis. "Did you see the world around us? Have you seen how broken we all are? Trying to break in what's already broken isn't going to help anybody!"

Rampras looked around at the rest; he couldn't believe this. He shook his head then turned his back from the rest. Multanis sighed then looked down. Logan looked guilty. Multanis grabbed him up from the ground.

"I didn't mean to hurt anyone," Logan said dejectedly.

"You didn't. They did," said Multanis, "We're trained for that."

"Then what was all that about?"

"He..." Multanis left off as he analyzed Rampras, "...gets scared to lose the last of his kids."

Logan thought about that then said, "I'm not his son."

"When you're in command, everyone's your children."

"So, am I getting--"

"--Court marshalled?" said Multanis, then shook his head. "That's not the way of the new world. It was Khared-Turo's words to let everyone teach each other, but only exile those who never listen. So no courts. We have to work everything out ourselves."

"Wouldn't that make chaos?"

"Do you see chaos?"

Logan looked back at the squad. Vanis attended Martin's wounds as Calis snapped the dog tags off soldier necklaces. Logan reflected back to the settlement and didn't remember anyone stepping out of line. *What if someone did?* Logan thought. *What would they do?*

He remembered soldiers stationed all over the settlement, but if they weren't authority, what were they doing? Perhaps they all volunteered to protect the people. It would be a dangerous situation if one tried to bully the rest. But people like Rampras would never allow that to happen.

Maybe that was what Khared-Turo depended on when he spoke those words. People would naturally resist to any form of oppression anyone tried to lay upon others regardless of its scale, and it was the quality of the people's morality that policed the world. If that were the case, this world operated by mere obligation one had to another and not through the figures of authority.

He figured people were naturally peaceful regardless of what theory of selfish survival-hood was painted on humanity. He reflected back to the pre-nova world and wondered how many people walked around and did what they did either because they were ordered to or because they needed to for themselves.

There was no controller for all of these people and there was no chaos. Everyone acted inside an equilibrium in which they all created, and it was the roles they all had that held this world together.

If that were the case, did Rampras fear he would lose his power or was it a niche he wanted to protect? He was born a natural leader. There were no doubts about that. But why did everyone follow him? Because he said so or because people agreed to? He knew about combat and survival better than anyone. Perhaps that was why people followed him.

But why was he even called captain then? Did someone give him that title or did people recognize him as that after a while? What would happen if they didn't follow him if he couldn't court martial them?

He wouldn't be able to do anything about it.

Maybe that was a way to weed out terrible leaders. Nobody had to follow anyone who would get them all killed. If that were the case, then it was the performance and quality of a leader that determined who followed who and not because someone said so.

After all that thinking, Logan realized that Khared-Turo was far wiser than anyone he had ever known.

After collecting soldier dog tags, a dropship picked them up. Rampras ordered in a clean-up team in the buffer zone. Everyone was rather silent.

Then Rampras said on his radio, "Take us to the LP."

"Somethin' on yer mind, cappy?" asked Calis.

"It don't add up," said Rampras. "They were too organized."

The dropship veered a ninety-degree turn. After minutes, the dropship circled around a newly made encampment with two extra dropships parked nearby. Logan looked out the aft port and saw the listening post tower crumble with its two artillery guns melted to a stump. *Did a bunch of bandits really have that kind of power?* he thought.

The dropship landed and the squadron stepped out. There were at least fifty soldiers investigating the area. Several soldiers crowded up around an officer before the officer spotted Rampras.

The squadron walked toward the officer. Vanis suddenly stopped.

Rampras noticed her abruption, "What is it?"

Everyone stopped and gazed. Vanis clenched her gut as though sick with some bug. Logan felt emissions of fear emit from her. It felt familiar.

"Electric life gave birth within these parts," said Vanis.

"Can you be more specific?" Rampras gritted.

Vanis shook her head.

Then the officer came by Rampras's side, "Here for the show?"

"What have we got?" asked Rampras as they walked toward the site.

"The case of the murdered tower," said the officer. "It's not a pretty sight. Got dead bodies littered all over the hills. Don't understand it either. These soldiers were situated inside the post itself. Defensive procedures aside, they're not supposed to be out here especially within enemy presence."

Deceased soldiers were scattered throughout the area. All of them with their helmets melted, their heads busted open, and their brain matter everywhere. Rampras knelt down and inspected them.

"What could have caused this?" asked Rampras.

"You take a crack at it," said the officer, "I'll just be over here."

"Yeah," Rampras squeaked weakly as he became absorbed in the puzzle.

Logan felt uneasy at the gruesome sight. Vanis held his hand. Calis and Multanis showered the area with examination. Rampras touched the sand around the bodies. They looked like they were thrown.

"Judgin' by the debris scatter," said Calis, "A big ol' explosive."

"Negative," Samiren said. "Explosives imprint chemical

residual traces and cremated charring. No such traces are detected on my scanners."

Calis shuttered, "For a walkin' tank, why is it we hardly notice you?"

"Maybe it fall over," said Martin.

Rampras smirked at the thought, "Probably not. Look at the metal on those artillery. Those barrels are titanium alloy. Melts at three thousand degrees."

That got Martin going. He pulled out his mobile chalkboard and started to theorize calculations. Multanis ran his fingers along the edges of deceased soldier's wounds. Rampras walked over to him.

"What have you got?" asked Rampras.

"Blisters on open wounds," said Multanis. "Unusual blood splatter. I would've said internal explosion except for those electrical burns."

"They were electrocuted?" asked Rampras.

"Or an electrical charge caused the explosion," said Multanis. "But that wouldn't cause a body to ignite without volatile fluids, which nobody has."

"Uh, cappy," said Calis.

He was standing at the open gap of the tower. The squad hustled over. Inside there was a lot of debris, blood splatter, and short-circuited computers. But on the walls, the word "Galilea" was written in blood.

"Galilea," said Rampras.

Logan felt a shiver wash over his spine.

"Ain't this the same creep from the excavation?" asked Calis.

"The methodology is the same," said Multanis.

"So he's all ganged up with the outcasts now?" asked Calis.

"We don't even know if it's the same person, mate," said Rampras.

"It is the same person," objected Multanis, "All of the evidence points to it. Back in the facility, we got weird voices, powerful enough to nuke your brain. Dead bodies with exploding heads. Blood written on the wall over an obsession from an alternate identity called...what was it called again?"

The Determiner, Logan thought. He feared mentioning the name.

"Fine, it's the same person," admitted Rampras. "But do you think something as psychotic like that cooperates?"

Multanis fell back into thought after that point.

"What's Galilea?" asked Logan.

"A new fairy tale land people made up," said Calis. "Galilea, the eternal sanctuary. Now this lunatic's after it too."

"What do you know about him?" asked Rampras, glaring at Logan.

Everyone looked at him as though he held the key to this mystery.

"I don't..." Logan said as he thought harder.

"We need to know what you know," stressed Rampras.

Logan kept thinking, trying to force the memories out of what little he knew. All he remembered were vague images and a name. How was any of that important? What would they do if they met him down the road? Apart from the Seer's warnings, this entity seemed like a being to stay clear of.

Rampras frowned and sighed again. He wasn't going to get any answers out of Logan tonight, so he marched toward the dropships.

"Cappy, wait!" said Calis as he hustled to stop him. "Where in all the tunnels of crap they call hell do ye think yer goin'?"

"Zodia. The outcast's settlement," said Rampras.

"Are ye boardin' the plank without a life raft? Ye might as well just hang up yer pirate hat if ye wanna be doin' that crazy bizz."

"Well, you tell me how this all fits, mate."

"Y'mean how that big, long thing stickin' up from the ground fits?" asked Calis. "It's cherry popped. It ain't no virgin no more."

Rampras scoffed at him.

"Hey! It's the right shape...and it left all its little soldiers all over the floor."

"You mean that destroyed tower that created a gap in settlement defenses large enough for brigades to march through?" said Rampras. "Who do you think that benefits most?"

"How'd ya know if it was even planned?"

"Well, what do you want me to do?" Rampras said with a shrug.

"We could ask the Seer," said Multanis.

"Oh no, no, no, no," complained Calis. "We ain't addin' more lunatics to this crazy bowl of crap."

"The Seer doesn't know either," said Logan.

"How do you know that?" questioned Multanis.

"He saw him before we left," said Rampras. "The Seer's a clairvoyant who claims to see everything. That doesn't mean he knows everything even though he'd object to that opinion. That's why his messages are encoded and complex. It's a puzzle to him as it is to everyone else."

"See? Even his egg-blended head don't know," said Calis. "So, no more of them head hooligans to bring all that shenanigans."

Rampras walked around Calis and headed to the dropships.

"Did'ja have a death wish or somethin'?" yelled Calis.

Rampras turned around and backpedalled to say, "Nobody knows what's going on except those outcasts and everything's pointing to them. If they're going to attack, we need to know and I know someone in there who does."

Logan noticed how nervous Calis was when the topic of psionics came to the table. Logan wondered if it was the capabilities of a psionicist he was worried about or something about himself that he didn't want others to know.

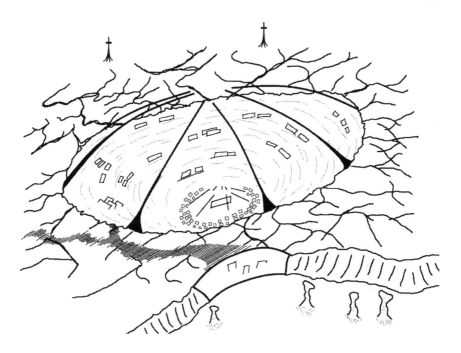

CHAPTER 11

SUBTERFUGE

Rampras had requested the dropship's pilot to deploy them at the outskirts of Zodia. The pilot had to clear it with Epsilon and so Rampras spent his time arguing with Scathers over the validity of these suspicions. Ultimately, Scathers could not stop what Rampras wanted to do. It was his team, his choice. Scathers reasoned that his skill and experience were far too valuable to be thrown away, but Rampras was adamant about his stance.

Everyone sat quietly and listened to Rampras argue in the cockpit, yet nobody said a word. Each of the core team believed in Rampras in their own way even though they didn't always see eye to eye. If they hadn't, they wouldn't have followed him into Zodia, the heart of a criminal world.

Logan felt an ever persistent powerful pain in his gut. It wanted to eat him alive. His leg shook. His hands tremored. His thoughts fled back to the transports. He wanted to take that back. He wanted to apologize for it, but he couldn't. They were dead because of him.

They would never breathe again. They would never see their families or friends. They would never be given the chance to see their young grow up, and all of the hatred that would brood into those that cared for them would hate Logan for what he did. All because of their futures ending with one quick slash of a blade — a blade held by his hand.

He felt how unnatural it was even to do that to another person. He remembered how they screamed. He didn't notice that before. Why was he thinking about that now? Everything he did then he had to do to survive or to protect others from harm. They didn't care about life. He did. Why was he sorry for their mistakes? Regardless of its reasoning, he couldn't stomach it.

Vanis felt his pain and slid out of her seatbelt. She rested his head on her shoulder as she cradled him in her arms. Logan let slip a haunting whine as tears flowed from his eyes. He couldn't help it. The pain was too excruciating to hide. Everyone watched. They knew exactly what he was going through, but didn't say a word. Vanis stroked his hair and hummed a soothing lullaby. He calmed after feeling the softness of her voice melt the pain away.

Multanis seemed worried. He clenched his chest near his heart as he breathed erratically. Calis took notice and judged his health.

"Ye don't look too well there, doc," said Calis.

"We're flying into the heart of madness," said Multanis,

"and our own Captain's commanding his own mad crusade. Should I be okay?"

"It'll be fine, doc!" Calis assured. "We'll just knock on their door, ask about this crazy idea about Galilea, get the door slammed in our faces, then we'll be goin' back home to destroy the hopes and dreams of everyone else."

"You think it's this fairy tale I'm worried about?" Multanis said, "or the fact that these criminals want our blood? What if we get caught?"

"Right, like anyone would want to hold all those weirdos over there," said Calis, nose-pointing to Vanis and Samiren. "Not that they could, either."

"Why are you so adamant on going?" asked Multanis.

"Because someone needs to save the cappy's ass," said Calis, "and why ye so adamant in not goin'?"

"Because this...I don't know what this is," said Multanis.

"Well, there's the door," Calis said as he pointed to the dropship's aft.

Multanis looked at it then sighed, "Why aren't we establishing diplomatic communications with them? Surely, these issues can be resolved peacefully."

"I don't know what world ye grew up in," said Calis, "but their zen's bullets. Your zen's bald."

Multanis was offended.

"Zen's crap and diplomacy's verbal diarrhea," Calis added, slamming Multanis even harder, "and they're gonna wonder how many facial pampers ye need before ye put a plug in it."

Multanis seemed crestfallen.

"Ye can't stop them from being how they are," said Calis,

"because they don't wanna listen. They don't care. That's just the way it is."

"Are you ready?" said Rampras as he stepped out of the cockpit.

Calis tapped Martin's shoulder as he unbuckled his seatbelt. Multanis got equipped while the rest moved to the back of the dropship.

Logan looked out of the dropship's aft. Plateau islands with cliffs and rock cuts were abundant in this area. With all the bedrock coloured textures and sand lines, it was reminiscent of a badlands area.

Logan noticed there was some actual primitive vegetation here. Moss and lichen stuck onto red rock walls. Bristle weeds sprouted in small patches. He wondered if these plants were semi-independent from atmospheric conditions.

The dropship spun its aft around, blasting up a dust storm, and aimed it toward a miles-wide plateau illuminated by a light aura of a thousand torches. There were smoke pillars and towers. It was very noticeable miles away.

Rampras's core team, with no extra soldiers, stepped out of the dropship and hid behind a rock. Calis slipped out digital binoculars and surveyed the area. Logan noticed there were many fissures subdividing the plateau and movement around the fissure's ends. People were using the rock plate's cracks and ravines as roads and walkways. *That would definitely divide an army*, he thought.

"Welp," mumbled Calis, "There's a whole whack of tradin' goin' on along them commercial gates. Their business be boomin'. Can't sneak in there."

"What about industrial routes?" asked Rampras.

"Hmmm, still guarded, but we can infiltrate," said Calis.

Then Rampras spoke on his radio, "Head back to Epsilon, refuel, and wait for a signal for extract."

The dropship lifted off.

"Alright, let's move."

The squadron got up and headed down the hillside. Their feet kicked up rocks that streamed in small rivers of pebbles as they made their way down the hill. At the base, they marched along an extensive stretch of open sand for a few miles. Logan noticed to the far right a man in desert robes ushered a flock of sheep forward.

"How did animals survive?" asked Logan.

"Some goof made an ark and stuffed a bunch of animals in it," said Calis. "Bio-farmers tapped into that, but the rest deal with Zodia's grand markets."

Just as Calis said that, Logan noticed a desert mouse nibbling on bristle leaves, then heard a shriek in the air. Logan looked up and saw a dark bird hovering above, but didn't know enough about birds to know what kind it was.

"This world's steamin' with life, popsicle," said Calis. "Hard to eyeball 'em too. They gotta be extremophiles though or mutated to live here."

The squadron jogged for several miles before getting to a boulder cluster that shielded them from sight. The boulder cluster was a hundred meters from an industrial checkpoint gate just before a great cluster of smoke pipes that towered over the rocky walls. The terrain ahead was littered with unusual potholes that were charred to black and a danger sign gave the reason why: landmines.

As the squadron got to a boulder, Logan brushed through a bristle bush that stirred up a fleet of mosquitoes. The mosquitoes attacked the squadron with irritating stings and everyone gave Logan a dirty glare.

"Ye just had to, didn't ya?" Calis remarked as he slapped his neck.

"Mosquitoes aren't supposed to live here," Logan reasoned.

"They're freaks too, like everythin' else here," remarked Calis as he stared at Vanis.

Vanis narrowed her eyes back at Calis then examined the area.

"Catalogue the patrols," said Rampras.

Rampras installed a sweeper scope on his assault rifle. Calis did that too then skimmed the horizons. Only one scouting tower watched over the area with a spotlight scanning. Logan found it a funny contrast that criminals were now doing the jobs security guards once did, except they guarded from people sneaking in instead of people breaking out.

"Logan," said Rampras, "This is a recon mission only. No frontal assaults. You're supposed to be a shock unit anyway. Hit and run guerrilla style."

Logan sighed, still guilt-burdened. It made sense though. Psi-Knights were not heavily equipped and would not last long against a constant stream of bullets. They were trained to be fast and furious, doing incredible amounts of damage in a short period of time before retreating. That they were trained to use hover-bikes made him wonder if they were the modernized cavalry.

"One patrol, then it's just the towers," said Calis.

"We'll use those holes to cover from line of sight," said Rampras.

Multanis modified his motion tracker to detect metal objects beyond them. It pulsed like sonar, which mapped out several metal blobs on his screen.

"Got them, Captain," said Multanis.

"Alright, let's move," said Rampras.

They waited for the first light interval then moved two potholes ahead before ducking again. Samiren was still standing. Rampras pulled him down from sight then sighed. The light passed overhead after which Rampras popped his head out. Two gate guards were talking.

"Can you take out those watchers by the gate?" asked Rampras.

"Let me see," Calis said.

He attached a silencer to his barrel. He aimed through his sweeper scope, adjusting its distance and focus, then fired off two muted rounds. Logan peeked out. Both guards didn't even have time to react.

"Interval," said Rampras.

They all peeked down again. The light passed over. Then they got up and hustled to another two holes ahead. The light passed over a third time and the squadron made it to the walls.

"Okay, we're here. Now what?" whispered Calis.

Rampras looked at Vanis. Vanis shut her eyes and concentrated. Then she opened them. It glowed with a bluish light. Logan noticed her retina twitched and moved as though she was viewing another location remotely.

Her view extended out of her body and scaled up the walls. Inside, there was a lookout platform underneath the higher-level scouting level of the lookout tower that served as the checkpoint's office. Vanis viewed inside the control room and saw a marauder, coated with poorly woven sheep hides, sleeping on his chair.

Then Vanis concentrated harder. Her vision shifted. It was now looking through the opening eyes of the sleeping marauder, hijacked through telepathic hypnosis. The marauder got up, walked over to the door control panel, and browsed the panels and levers. There was a number panel by a door switch.

"The doors are locked by number-crypted code," said both Vanis and the charmed marauder.

"Of course they are, ya idiot," said a voice in the next room.

The marauder's view shifted toward the sleeping quarters. Another scruffy guard gazed directly at the point of view.

Vanis snapped out a somatic motion and erupted in a blink of light. The light force blasted the squadron off their feet. Vanis emerged inside. In one combination, she jammed her heel into the neck of one, pinning him, while flicking her palm up, sending the other's belt knife into its owner's head.

She leaned over toward the pinned marauder and moaned, "Mmm, my dearest love, if you would be so kind."

The marauder grunted, tapped in the code, and hit the door button. Then she kicked the back of his head, knocking him out.

The door's gears snapped onto a cogwheel and twisted it. The system of chain links pulled tension on the doors, waking them with a loud thud.

A head popped out from the top tower, "Hey! What's going--"

--A bullet silenced him, as silent as the bullet itself.

After clearing the gates, the squad moved ahead through the ravine crack that was decorated with upper platforms, walkways, and chemical pipes. They slipped under wall guards and took out another two patrolling the base levels. They eventually snuck by an area with many twentieth-century transport trailers in front of a processing plant that converted raw materials into transportable products.

The ravine eventually led to a cavern where many crates

that boxed products were stored and distributed through a cargo bay. There, millwrights divided the packages and sent them along slide rails, while forklifts and larger machines hauled bigger packages. *Running this place requires coordination*, Logan thought. *This is too complex to be run by mere criminal minds.*

Deeper into the corridors, the squadron found themselves on the upper railways of a mechanics factory. Rampras suddenly stopped. He saw something. He was gazing in awe.

Down below, a mech warrior's arms and frontal chassis were being installed onto a metallic torso. Rampras inspected the rest of the factory. Hundreds of workers were fashioning vehicle parts in full assembly line. This was a fully industrialized centre.

"Holy jeebus," said the shocked Calis. "They producin' faster than us."

"The major benefit of a financial-based economy, mate," said Rampras.

Logan had to agree. The drive of greed was powerful enough to organize an entire world, but he wondered how many of those workers down there were reluctant of this line of work and coerced into it by currency.

They snuck deeper into a cluster of back alleys of a suburb that was somehow chiselled into the system of ravines. Houses in this area were not put together; they were carved into the walls in block shapes. It resembled an Aztec city — mazes of streets with walkways leading to other neighbourhoods.

The squadron crept between two houses when local citizens passed by. Logan glanced at them. There were two women hauling baskets on their heads with old-fashioned colts strapped to their sides. Then a dune buggy drove by, followed by camel riders hauling cargo up the streets.

The squadron moved upwards onto a platform that led to the upper streets. After the building horizon declined, a grand opening exposed everything. The whole city was chiselled along the walls of a massive asteroid crater and people travelled through a series of stairs, platforms, or inner tunnels. Every street seemed like a potential raceway for vehicles.

Suddenly, Logan heard screaming. He looked behind him two levels down and saw a lady getting beaten by a gang. Logan stood up, but Rampras pulled him down. Logan was enraged, unable to control his contempt.

"You can't do anything without risking us, mate," Rampras whispered. "This is their way of life. They chose to live this. We didn't force them."

Then several bikers appeared from around a corner. The beating gang bolted in every direction while the bikers howled maniacally and hunted them. The beaten women got up and ran away. Logan was somewhat relieved.

Later, they passed a large training facility: beer-bottle firing ranges, melee circles, obstacle courses, all of which were organized by outcast brutes shouting insults and mockery at the marauders in training.

Logan looked over the edge and down at the crater's centre. There was a large courtyard and a speaking platform in the middle. Surrounding the courtyard at the base level's ring was a large marketplace that spanned all the way around. The crater's top rims had retractable flaps that controlled lighting. The city was massive and looked to be able to house at least a million people.

The squadron made their way down to the lower market ring.

The market was a very busy place that never slept. It was decorated with colourful lights that hung off power lines scaling through the market. People of all sorts of shapes and sizes opened deals, bartered with standardized Zodian coins or other items of value. Benches, booths, and cafes were abundant, so were showmen, small mock stages, puppeteers, jugglers, and magicians.

Everyone knew who ruled; gang members walked amongst them. But much to their surprise, no one ever bullied the tradesmen around. Tradesmen were brave enough to hold their goods hostage with their lives, which forced the gangs into respecting them if they weren't left alone.

Violence and madness were an everyday thing in this world and no gang member was even capable of out-intimidating the threat of Cy-Corps or the Chimeric Infection. This created security and allowed the economy to develop.

A man with a long pimply nose and balding head chopped strange-looking mushrooms of different sizes inside an open-sided cooking tent. He looked like he was in a hurry. This was Krogani. He rolled the slices into wax packages and sealed it with a candle, but kept looking up at the booth next to him, whose cook was boiling foot-long scorpions. Another one by him cooked rat-kabobs.

Then speakers fizzled. The sound of a microphone sparked and popped. A man's amplified voice began to speak, but was indistinguishable at that distance. The crowd in the courtyard roared in cheer. Krogani gawked at all that positive energy exploding.

Suddenly, all of Krogani's mushrooms moved and tumbled around on his table. Krogani frowned at them. The mushrooms repositioned themselves and spelled out the word "RAMPRAS." Krogani looked around suspiciously.

A light blinked from a dark alley. Krogani took off his apron, messed up the mushrooms, and walked over. As he hit the darkness, someone grabbed him and slammed him onto the wall. Then a ball of fire ignited. Vanis held the flames in her hand as the light revealed the rest of the squadron.

"Rampras," Krogani hissed out in relief.

"You've been out of contact, mate," said Rampras.

"Contact?" said Krogani with a sneer, "You come in 'ere, interfere wit' my work, grab meh in the dark, and say loco tings to me? You know me! Business. Respect. Dis place? You no like. Time's changin'. Anyone got a sparky?"

"Sparky?" asked Calis.

"Yeah, y'know? A sparky," said Krogani, "A rolly. A smoke. Cigarett-ay."

"Ain't that somethin'," said Calis, "Never knew this place had 'em."

"S'okay. S'okay. I got it. I got it," said Krogani as he slipped out rolled-up smoke. He lit it with a mini-torch and sucked a few puffs from it. Vanis coughed.

"Talk to me," said Rampras. "What's been happening?"

Krogani puffed out a long one then said, "Okay. So the story goes, we had eight honchos, now we have one and eight lap dogs. This hustler, Corlance, got 'em by the balls, ya? He's got the thinkers going for him and everyone? They respect that, ya? They listen to dat cause it keeps 'em alive in the sand lands."

"How'd he manage to do that?" asked Rampras.

"This place? Full of hate," said Krogani. "And the busters? They used to whack anyone anytime they want. But this Corlance? He imposes rules, ya? Says we're smart to follow 'em. He turns out right and wins the gang lords over. Now no one steps out of line. This Corlance guy knows how to speak to the crowds, ya? And they fall for them burritos."

"I don't see how he wins 'em all over with a burrito," said Calis.

"No. No burrito," said Krogani. "He say lots of things about some promised lands. This thing called Galilea and--"

"--What? Say that again?" said Rampras.

"Galilea," repeated Krogani. "He says he gots the deeds on it. Knows where it is, ya? Someone inside the settlements. Says the guy in the settlements has proof of it, but they're hidin' it from everyone. Dunno why. Now, all the bloods want in on it."

"Who knows about Galilea?" asked Rampras.

"Hold on there, cappy," said Calis. "Don't be tellin' me yer gonna be believin' all this fairy tale crap, are ya?"

Rampras reasoned, "Mate, if these guys are willing to mobilize their entire force to move against a settlement, then we've got serious problems. We need to know who knows all about Galilea."

"It's like dis, okay?" said Krogani. "All I know is, anyone who tries to get the know-where know-hows gets cleaned by a popper named Solito. A real badass. A man hunter, ya? He's the one that helped Corlance get on the rise and nobody ain't gonna find out without him knowin'."

"Do you know which settlement they plan to move on?" asked Rampras.

"Nope! I know nada. Zilch," said Krogani.

"Alright, let's get this intel back to HQ and decide what to do from there," said Rampras. "Let's move."

The squadron hustled back through the back alleys, leaving Krogani behind.

Krogani sniffed, wrinkled his nose, and yelled, "Don'tcha be talkin' about me, ya? I don't need no bounty on me! No bounties on me, ya hear?"

Suddenly, a dark figure materialized out of thin air behind the unsuspecting Krogani. Krogani sighed in relief and worry.

"Bloody pirate," Krogani remarked.

Then the figure hooked a knife around Krogani's neck and slashed his throat open. Blood spattered out in pulses and Krogani dropped to the ground, gasping, gurgling on his own blood.

"My, my! That was a naughty thing you did," mocked the dark figure. "It's a shame your life had to end this way. But alas, it did."

"Solito..." Krogani gurgled out before drowning in his own blood. The dark figure spat on Krogani's body, then pulled out a radio.

"Oh, my dear employer, whose intellect far exceeds all," the dark figure mocked, "you would not believe who just entered your dominion."

CHAPTER 12

RETRIBUTION

"It's clear," said Vanis who just deactivated her remote viewing.

The squadron hid near the loading and distribution centre of hauling crates. The place seemed to have shut down; the slide rails were off and the forklifts abandoned. Everything seemed far too empty in there for Rampras. Multanis tracked for motion on his assault rifle's sensors.

"Nothing, Captain," confirmed Multanis.

"I don't like this," said Rampras, "Alright, let's move."

The squadron inched their way into the loading bay, their rifles aiming and covering the area. Multanis checked the tracker — nothing. Then all over the top supervision rails, outcast marauders burst out of crates, barrels, and corners, their hunting rifles, SMGs, crossbows, and shotguns aiming at the squadron. The squad aimed back, targeting lasers flashing around at them. Everyone kept cocking their guns threateningly as though to pressure the other to fire first.

"Hold!" yelled an outcast commander.

"Hold your fire!" yelled Rampras.

"Nobody shoot!" yelled the outcast commander.

"I said hold your fire, mates!" yelled Rampras.

Everybody stopped moving, invoking a suspenseful silence between the two parties. Samiren wasn't even acknowledging what was happening.

Then a dark figure decloaked in mid-flip and landed on

a forklift's roof. His dark, tattered leather clothes did not match his spikey, back-aiming red hair. But it did match the night-vision goggles he wore on his forehead, and his long, self-forged knife that emitted a field around its blade. His red, lightly glowing whip created interest over its functions. This was the assassin, Solito.

Then another man emerged from the shadows of the top rails. The man was dressed in a dark blue trench coat, narrow sunglasses, and a blue flat cap turned backwards. His face was clean but sported a chin puff, a thin moustache, long hair held back by the cap, and arching eyebrows suggesting intelligence. This was Corlance.

"Good evening," said Corlance. "And you are?"

"Captain Reginald Rampras the Fourth." said Rampras. "Commander of the hundredth and seventeenth division. Beta Squadron."

"Morgan Corlance. Speaker of the Reunion," said Corlance, "I see you've been checking up on us."

"There seems to be a great deal of checking up to do, mate. Especially after the incident at Listening Post C."

"Delinquents, I assure you. It's not strategically viable since we can provide for own resources now."

Logan frowned. He noticed a logical anomaly, but couldn't put a finger on what it was. Something was off...way off.

"I assume the factories we weren't meant to see," said Rampras.

"Oh, come now, Captain," said Corlance, "Us fighting will not help both of our communities survive longer. At least for the time being. But I wonder if you asked yourself yet why Calypso was forcing its agendas on the settlements."

"What's this guy talkin' on about, cappy?" asked Calis.

Rampras narrowed his eyes at Corlance; he's in the spotlight now.

"That argument I had with Scathers, wasn't just any argument," said Rampras. "Calypso's been slowly winning the council over with promises of rapid productivity. In order to do that, they wanted to introduce a capitalist economy to the settlements."

"That's outrageous!" said Multanis, "That'll create poverty in an already poor world. What gave them the right?"

"They have resources we need, mate," said Rampras. "Now they're slowly getting into position to call all of the shots for the settlements."

"By introducing mass production at unprecedented rates," Corlance shook his head. "They haven't changed. But they're hiding something and they're using the settlements as a shield to protect themselves from us."

"This is about Galilea, isn't it?" asked Rampras. "What is it?"

"Oh, that is so subtle, Captain," said Corlance. "It takes such exquisite, sophisticated grace and strategic articulation to reach where I am. You above all people should learn to romance the audiences with such invigorating cantons. But being the truth as it may be, I don't know. But believe me, I'm very curious."

Calis turned around, scaling his aim around the room. His rifle's computer catalogued all the marauders on his computer's targeting system.

"And you're willing to attack an entire settlement just to get to Calypso?" asked Rampras with extensive contempt.

"I'm not a monster, Captain," assured Corlance. "I will be as lenient as I can as much as honour invokes."

"Malicious spyware detected," Samiren remarked.

"Who's this?" Corlance asked.

Rampras leaned to Samiren and whispered, "He doesn't know about you."

"I'm a robot," said Samiren.

"Oh," said Corlance, waving to Samiren, "Hi, robot."

"Hi," growled Samiren.

"Because I do believe in ultimatums over violence," said Corlance, "this does alleviate me from worries of putting my former kin to death, allowing for additional lives to be saved from unnecessary disaster much to diplomatic benefit."

"Former kin?" said Rampras.

"Oh, come now, Captain," said Corlance, "How else would I know the settlement's political dynamics? I was on the council of a settlement. Not until Calypso saw fit to be rid of me."

"And they did that because..."

"Because I found a folder containing data about Galilea," said Corlance. "Imagine that. Calypso...withholding information about a fairy-tale land. I wonder what kind of impact it will have on the settlements when they realize it was real."

"Why didn't you come forward with this information?" asked Rampras.

"For the same reason I was banished," said Corlance. "Character assassination. One can do so much more damage with just words than what mere bullets can ever hope to establish."

"So this is your vengeance for what they did to you," Rampras slammed, "to plummet the entire world in war to get what you want."

Corlance looked greatly offended by that.

The outcast commander looked disgusted with the squadron, "Enough of this! Kill these dogs!"

"No!" Corlance yelled.

Bullets, bolts, pellets, and shells ripped from the outcast's barrels. They slammed into three protective bubbles guarding the squadron. Retaliatory fire streamed out of the shields. They concaved to their corresponding targets and struck several marauders dead. The squadron retreated back toward the city with Vanis and Logan protecting their aft.

"Imbeciles!" yelled Corlance, "Capture them! Don't kill them!"

Surviving marauders leapt over the top rail, landed, and pursued the squadron into the city. Corlance eyed Solito. Solito smirked and cloaked.

Distant alarms blared from hand-cranked sirens. Commotion erupted throughout the automotive factory. Then bullets snapped out from a corridor connected to the top rails. The startled workers dropped their duties and bolted for the facility's cavern exits. The squadron cleared the top door and took cover along the rails. Rampras and Calis cover fired down the path they were just in.

"I thought you scanned that room!" yelled Rampras.

"It's a motion tracker! Can't track what doesn't move!" said Multanis.

"Cappy, we can't be fightin' the whole city at every intersection," said Calis. "Our munitions'll run low in no time."

"I know, mate!" said Rampras as he thought.

Suddenly, fire erupted from the lower rails. Marauders spilled into the mechanics facility. Calis took aim and blasted. The marauders below dispersed and took cover amongst the unbuilt engine lane. They yelled down the corridors for reinforcements.

"On the east exit," said Rampras, "there's a dam that once blocked a river there that's now dehydrated. We call in for evac and get picked up at the base."

"We'd have to fight through the whole city," objected Multanis.

"It's either that or get stuck here!" said Rampras.

Then a loud gear grind boomed throughout the facility. The squadron looked. A mech warrior from the installation lane just activated.

"Go, go, go, go!" yelled Rampras.

The whole squadron stampeded along the top rails and headed toward the inner cities.

But Logan's mind wasn't in the battle. He was thinking about that anomaly in the other room. It didn't make logical sense. *How could Corlance call Telisque a mere delinquent*, he thought, *unless he was referring to the marauders*. That tower was too damaged to be done by mere raiders and no massive outcast armies were seen near the perimeters.

But how could he be referring to Telisque? He was obviously insane and seen as a serious delinquent. Yet Corlance passed his actions off as small, not acknowledging how serious a threat Telisque was. Unless he never knew. That would mean he didn't know who Telisque was or ever encountered him.

Then a flash of light awoke him from his thoughts. Inner-city towers showered the streets with spotlights. The squadron hustled through the ravine that led to the main city while being stared at by the local pedestrians walking by. Rampras led them through the back alleys that shielded their sights last time. Motor engines roared through the main streets, while yelling and hustling echoed the rumours of the settlement intruders.

The squadron climbed up a flight of stairs to get on top of the chiselled stone roofs and surveyed the area. The gangs of Zodia buzzed through all parts of the city like a swarm of wasps out to defend their nest. Gunfire was shot throughout the city, but not at them. Logan figured that gangs were taking the opportunity to assassinate their enemies and hide the blame on them.

As Rampras calculated his trajectory for his citywide navigation, Logan wondered how Corlance even knew about the listening posts. Unless the survivors arrived, beating a four-hundred-mile-per-hour dropship to Zodia with fifty-mile-per-hour desert vehicles, which didn't seem likely unless they radioed it in. So if Corlance did know, why was he confessing to something he didn't do?

Unless he thought his men destroyed the tower — a lie told to him by them. That would most likely be the case since self-praise could mean acceleration in rank and, in turn, power. This would mean Corlance was definitely not involved with Telisque. Yet Telisque wrote something that Corlance knew. So how did Telisque know it if nobody else ever encountered him?

An encounter like that alone would have spread tales rampantly like a virus. But nobody ever talked about him, not even the squadron Logan was in. Could this have been from the constriction of fear? Or did Rampras think it was not worthy of note when other pressing matters were at stake?

"Okay, let's move," whispered the worried Rampras.

He led the crew through the clothesline populated roofs. Logan worried about being in the open, but noticed the spotlights had such a massive area to cover that they probably wouldn't see the squadron passing in front of them.

The squadron dipped down a flight of stairs and stopped. The back alleys were too compressed for travel; they had to cut through the main roads. Rampras peeked out then led the squadron in open terrain. Just a few feet in, a biker gang stopped on a road ramp several decametres from their flanks. The squadron aimed their barrels at them, until hearing rapid fire from the north. Sparks littered the area. The biker gang backed away and the squadron bolted south.

"Ain't they supposed to be attackin'?" asked Calis.

"They want their rival's numbers reduced," explained Rampras.

"Is that good or bad?" Calis asked.

"Good! We don't have to fight everyone at once," said Rampras.

"Behind us!" yelled Multanis. Rampras turned around.

Three bikes and a dune buggy with a mini-gun attachment were on their tail.

"Aren't they the same ones?" asked Calis.

"Bastards! Take cover!" yelled Rampras.

Rampras blasted at the vehicle flock. Local civilians screamed and took cover indoors. The bikers roared the malice of their menace while threatening to predict their future with a twirl of a weapon. They were approaching fast: two in front and the third behind. The soldiers took cover behind walls and barrel fires, but Samiren, unaffected by crude somatic fortune-telling, stood in their path.

"Samiren!" yelled Rampras.

Samiren turned, noticing the bikers. He unveiled his laser

blade, slashed horizontally, then slammed his body onto a bike. Two heads, two bikes, and a thousand pieces of debris tumbled through the streets behind him. The dune buggy curved around Samiren and hailed a storm of bullets in its wake. The lightweight pellets of the mini-gun only resulted in mere friendly pokes at Samiren's unfriendly reactor-powered shields.

Then an electrical-charged nano-tech turret formulated on Samiren's arm. Samiren fired off a massive concussive blast. All of the crudely made fire-melted sand glass on the surrounding buildings shattered instantly. The blast bent the dune buggy inwards and shattered it apart before smashing two more buildings behind it into rubble.

"Damn, that's loud!" said Calis.

Tower spotlights shone on the wreckage, then scaled along the debris wake for its origins.

"Take cover!" yelled Rampras.

The whole squadron ducked behind the half levels of a building that ascended up from a lower platform.

"Ye think they got snipers?" asked Calis.

A spotlight shone on Samiren as he stood in the open. Distant booms echoed and sniper bullets stung his shields.

"Does that answer your question?" said Rampras.

"Probably salvaged hunting rifles," said Multanis, "Don't expect their accuracy to be great at long distance."

Bullets sliced between the squadron. Two gangs pincered them from the flanks, bypassing their cover. Multanis and Martin blasted north as Rampras and Calis blasted south. Logan and Vanis reinforced their guard with psi-shields.

"Switch to cover across the streets," said Rampras.

"But we'd be all exposin' ourselves to sniper fire," said Calis.

"Their shields will wear down in no time," reasoned Rampras. "Better with bullets that can't always hit versus close-range volleys that hit all the time."

The squadron slipped across the street to better coverage. The spotlights shone on them directly. Sparks spattered all over the walls around them in momentary intervals. Logan and Vanis were relieved. Sweat poured down their faces. They took turns predicting hits through their limited precognitive skills and blocked each confirmation with their shields. Other gangs arrived on scene at both flanks and supported them with additional suppression fire.

"I'm signalling for extract," Rampras said.

He grabbed the phone receiver on Martin's Radio pack and dialled in.

"Rampras to LP6. Come in."

But only static responded.

"Rampras to LP6!"

Again, only the snowy irritation of fizzles and pops acknowledged his voice. Multanis grabbed the receiver off Rampras and listened.

"It's a jamming signal," said Multanis. "Won't be able to make contact until we're out of the field."

As the squadron worked to clear a path south, thoughts would not let Logan go. *How could Telisque ever truly know anything*, Logan wondered as he continued to shield the squad. Telisque was obviously powerful and random, but didn't seem logical. If that were the case, how could he comprehend anything, especially something from an external source? If that were the case, how could he use any of his powers he possessed? It was like he magically knew.

Someone may have instigated his knowledge, he figured. But did he know before, during, or after the encounter at Area 77? If it was before, then the Galilea idea, place, or thing was something created before the Nova. But it was claimed that Galilea was a promised land, a salvation from the shattered world. Something like that can only be created after the Nova.

If it was after, then Telisque encountered something stronger than himself, which was hard to imagine, and that entity gave him the idea. If that were the case, why would Telisque, who was powerful enough to be completely independent of everything, would want, need, or even care about Galilea? It seemed like his own insanity alone was enough to keep him happy with his own existence, and nobody could ever offer Telisque anything he couldn't get himself.

If it was during, then something else besides Telisque was inside the facility that gave him that idea. If that was the case, that entity may have no desire for anyone to reach Galilea. But why couldn't this entity do that itself, if it was strong or tricky enough to persuade this of Telisque? No matter how he looked at it, something was definitely missing and he could not figure it out.

He wondered if Corlance, who was obviously brilliant, bumped into this anomaly too. If he had, then he was obviously putting on a face to his own men or to the squadron to hide any weakness to his confidence. That would mean he would be dishonest and, in turn, dishonourable. If he didn't, everything he said was honest and true. But Logan was more concerned with his analysis being correct.

Three pops and three whining wails squealed into the

air. The squadron looked above and around them. Then micro-explosions bloomed in eruption around them: on the roof above, a building beside them, and in the streets north of them. Dust and shards of rock and metal flooded the area around them. The squadron covered their faces from renegade shrapnel.

"The reckless S.O.B.'s usin' mortars on us!" said Calis.

"We can't stay here for long!" yelled Multanis as he backed into the wall.

Bullets sliced chunks off the corner, slowly exposing the indention. Calis peeked out and blasted a few. Sparks slashed off his armour plates, denting it and throwing Calis back into cover with only a bruise.

Then engine roars and metal clashes erupted north. Two bikers and a jeep with a repeating crossbow turret ploughed through the northern marauders. Two were trampled while one was gunned down. The crossfire intensified as two opposing gangs arriving on the scene reinforced their gang war.

Rampras grinned, seeing a good opportunity to advance, "Logan. Bust up the southern flank. Scatter them."

Logan bolted for the southern flank. Bullets reflected off his psi-shield, but could not slow his advance. He stepped up from a window ledge, leapt up to the roof edge, spun in an axel over the covering marauders, and slashed one down before landing on a kneel stance. The amazed and startled outcasts backpedalled away into the open streets, breaking their cover and firing at the shielded Logan.

"Now!" yelled Rampras.

The squadron pressed forward, unleashing a storm of bullets while stampeding toward the open marauders. Logan took cover behind a building as the exposed outcasts were gunned down in a matter of seconds. Demoralized, the rest of the gang cluster scattered through the streets.

Then a crossbow bolt bit the stone by Logan's head. A massive armada sped toward them from the north, who once were in battle. Mortar blasts painted the adjacent nearby streets and hailed the whole city's west in a warzone.

"Go, go, go!" said Rampras.

Gunfire persisted from the distant streets. Logan joined the squadron as they headed southwest. The scattered gangs poured through the streets towards the spot-lit area. Sniper bullets bit the walls with poor precision. Curious, on-looking civilians moved out of the way of the squadron. The squad was in a narrow street walk. The vehicles drove past it. The squad, however, ran into a major trading highway.

"Cappy, this ain't good," warned Calis.

Mountain goats, camels, domesticated coyotes, salvagers, miners, excavators, bio-farmers — they all populated the busy streets with a peace disturbed by the chaos beyond. Nervous people were already clearing out while viewers surveyed the chaos in the distant streets. People eyed the foreign squadron as they rushed through the crowd, looking for a path out.

Then a metal-plated marauder jumped onto a car chariot hauled by two horses. He twirled a whistle can tied to a rope in circles. The can screeched a high-pitched sound that echoed throughout the city's bowl.

"I think we been found!" said Calis.

Rampras cocked his gun and fired. The marauder's neck spewed with red. The crowd exploded in panic. They hustled and toppled over each other to reach deeper into the city or the trade entrance. The crowd blocked the vehicle armada's advances into the trade lane, but the tower lights bypassed it and honed in on the squadron.

"Take out those lights!" yelled Rampras.

Calis aimed through his sweeper scope and snapped a bullet for every light. By the time he took out the second, marauder fire blazed through the crowd. Five innocents fell to the lead shower, while the rest cleared away from sight.

Not seeing any other cover, Rampras yelled, "Drop!"

The squadron knelt or hit the floor. The marauders strafed along the streets as they fired.

"Watch out for non-combatants!" instructed Rampras.

He checked his aim, waiting for a few civilians to run past the marauders. The squadron conserved burst fire to a minimum, while marauders flooded the streets with lead. One bullet struck Rampras's chest plate and knocked him back from a kneeling position.

"Cappy!" yelled Calis.

"I'm alright," said Rampras as he got up.

"West!" Martin yelled.

Martin and Multanis blasted west. Marauders were coming in from the back alley. Bullets sliced through three charging marauders, while the rest hid behind vehicles and in homes.

The squadron kill rate far surpassed the marauder reinforcements. Marauders were seemingly throwing their lives away at a chance for single blow. Then vehicles burst through an opening in the now thinning crowd and stormed toward the crew.

"They're gonna rush us!" Rampras spotted. "Move, move, move!"

Calis got up and bashed open a nearby door. The resident's lady barked curses at them as the squadron barged through the stone house. They busted out the back and came through to a back alley with grated floors that caged a gladiator's labyrinth below.

"We should be droppin' down," suggested Calis.

"Sounds good," said Rampras.

Logan slashed the metal cage open and the squadron descended into the maze. The corridor, littered with skulls, bones, and rotting flesh, housed several prisoners shackled to the walls. Logan gazed at them, but was pulled away by Rampras who knew what he was thinking.

The squadron marched through the poorly lit maze's twists and turns until the steel door came into presence. The door could not stop the slash of a plasma blade. The squadron barged through into a watch room with two chain-mailed guards bursting from their sleep. The crew stopped and aimed. The guards reached for their guns. Rampras and Calis shot them both dead upon reaction.

The squadron went through the connecting door and came into a long underground corridor that led deeper underneath the rocks toward the east.

As they ran, Logan never realized until that moment how passionately the marauders had hated the settlements for not being accepted, forgiven, or understood. Even though their choices led them to this spot, this still pained Logan because he understood what that felt like. To be ejected and outcast from society in itself was shocking and every bullet was like a bullet of justice.

CHAPTER 13

OBSTRUCTION

The corridor shaft broke up at an intersection. Rampras
randomly selected a path and led the team into a large hangar.
Some of the steel panels held back the never-advancing rock
walls, while support beams reinforced the roof. Inside there were
salvaged and refashioned military vehicles: helicopters, tanks,
jeeps, and even a mech warrior that waited in rust. Beside the
corresponding vehicles, artillery shells, rockets, and bombs were
stacked and ready for loading.

"Ooo, bombs!" said Calis.

"You're not touching those, mate," said Rampras.

"I was thinkin' more along the lines of sabotage," said Calis.

"Do we have any explosives?" asked Rampras.

"Just proximity mines, cappy," said Calis.

"Well, that isn't going to help," said Multanis. "We should search for keys to those vehicles. If not, hotwire one."

"Damn it, doc! We're soldiers, not spies!" said Calis. "We don't be breakin' and enterin', talkin' to contacts, assassinatin' guards, and stealin' cars all fer the sole sake of escapin' an enemy base for discoverin' hidden plans now, do we?"

The sound of a metal latch detaching echoed in the room. An up-whine acceleration grinded the sound of gears. An air break release valve hissed to annoyingly high frequencies. A persistent deep electrical hum reverberated through the hangar, followed by a single heavy thump that re-drummed the heart pulses to those who heard. The nervous squadron looked around the room.

Then two powerful photon lights shone on the squadron. It came from a walking machine across the hangar. Two huge nine-cluster missile launchers were embedded on its shoulders. Anti-tank turrets were installed as arms. Its thick chassis was wrapped around its chest and legs, and was designed specifically to take powerful artillery strikes. A marauder sat inside the cockpit and fumbled with the controls. The machine was a rusting, pre-nova mech warrior.

"Cover!" yelled Rampras.

The squadron scattered for the surrounding vehicles. The mech warrior fired a pair of missiles. The missile twins split into four micro missiles each and spiralled in a clockwise-area scatter. Vanis spanned her arms in a back-slap motion. Two micro missiles dislodged its projection and swirled wildly to the walls. It creating a gap that shielded the squadron from explosion.

The other missile combustions exploded two jeeps that blasted the squadron to their backs. The explosion warped wall panels, toppled steel beams, and ignited a crate full of mini-gun rounds. The squadron braced as the bullets speared out. The rogue lead slammed into metal plates, walls, and armour as it ricocheted in zigzags.

The mech warrior switched to its arm turrets. The turrets, themselves, had five inches steel as heatsinks. The mech fired a cluster of supersonic booms. The shockwave pulses ruptured every glass window as a storm of light trails rained all around Vanis.

She x-crossed her forearms, but a bullet sliced through her psi-shield, shattered it instantly, clipped her thigh, and chiselled the ground behind her. The slice was only a nick, but it tore open her dress side and ripped her muscles nearly to the bone.

Blood splattered all over the floor. Vanis dropped and wailed in agony. Logan got up and ran toward her. He wrapped his arms around her, ripped her from the floor, and spun her around into cover, slamming his back to the wall. Vanis slid to the ground, heaved, and squealed in torment as she clenched her leg.

"You're not invincible," said Logan.

The squad took cover on both sides of the room. Each step vibrated the ground as the mech warrior advanced. On the right, Rampras and Martin moved behind an old-world Challenger IV main battle tank whose armour thickness was at least twenty inches — a suitable challenge against anti-tank cartridges.

After reloading its turrets, the mech warrior turned toward Rampras's side and fired. Each bullet penetrated the Challenger IV's armour and punched the tank toward the wall. Rampras and Martin pushed back with their backs and legs, but the blasts overpowered them. Rampras growled as he gave it his all as the tank rolled toward the final feet of space. Then the warrior depleted its volley.

"Open fire!" yelled a relieved Rampras.

The squadron popped out on both sides and blasted a clip full into the reloading mech warrior. Each lead bullet shattered upon contact with its steel casing. Even the cockpit warded off bullets with its plastic-steel windshield. After their clip was spent, Rampras and Martin hid behind another tank.

"Samiren!" yelled Rampras, but was unacknowledged.

Down at the south-western end, marauders poured in by the dozens. As they flushed between the vehicles, one slash of reddish blur sliced off the leader's head. The marauder behind him reactively caught the severed cranium and saw his executioner, Samiren, wielding a blade of laser in an crane-like stance.

The marauders panicked, backpedalled, and fired every projectile they had at him. Each bolt, rock, and bullet harmlessly fed his energized shields. With one step forward and a back-angled spin, Samiren slashed open several chests with a horizontal slice. The marauders scampered between the vehicles while some retreated back into the corridors.

As Samiren slashed down the ranks of the marauders in the south, the mech warrior up north tore into a jeep's engines with its gripping paws, crushing the metals and peeling it apart. Rampras and Martin slipped behind another armoured jeep. As the hiss of hydraulic pressure escaped its shoulder pipes, the mech warrior aimed a barrel at the armoured jeep and blasted rounds into it.

Calis and Multanis positioned behind the walking machine and loaded their assault rifle's launcher add-on with grenade canisters. They aimed at the mech warrior's back and fired. The grenade seeds exploded and speared fragments all over the machine's jet engines, gas tank, and a series of pipes, but could not penetrate its armour.

The mech warrior's jet engines pulsed a flame burst that lifted the machine and spun it around. Its hind heel, protruding behind the joint, absorbed the energy from the weight compression into a hydraulic cylinder. The hull shuttered as it distributed the residual energy. Calis and Multanis, surprised at its turning speed, fell back behind the vehicles as the walker charged its turrets.

The marauder driver laughed maniacally. The mech's bullets stabbed crazily into the vehicles. The two jeeps hiding Calis and Multanis were struck at an angle, pushing them out of alignment. The first vehicle missed them as its fender banged into the wall. The second struck between them and bent around Calis, grinding and crunching his armour as it shifted.

"Ugh! Why do them things have to be so invincible?" Calis groaned.

Logan aided Vanis's regeneration process when he heard the crashing friction of the vehicles. He looked out. Rampras blasted grenade seeds at the machine's back, while it grinded the trapped soldiers to the walls. Logan looked back. Samiren was still covering their rear. Logan sighed, knowing too well the danger of his intervention. He never fought something like that before.

Vanis sensed an intention growing in Logan. "Why forth the thinkest, Logan?" she managed to croak out sternly under her heaving.

"When humans become stronger than the machine," Logan muttered.

He unveiled his plasma blade and charged toward the machine.

Vanis felt her heart skip, "Logan! No!"

The irritated marauder turned the mech warrior toward Rampras. Rampras backed behind several armoured vehicles. He blasted into the machine's front windshield. The mech's launcher charged another missile and took aim.

Then a blur of bluish light sliced between the machine's jetpack rockets. It cleaved through several wires and circuits that were protected by six inches of aft plating. The craze of jailed sparks broke free and the bulky drone wobbled backwards.

Logan landed to a kneel nearly between the drone's two brute legs. He back-rolled away from the massive stomps, then thrust himself up into a backwards somersault. He sliced into the mech warrior's back with each rotation. The machine showered its aft with a rain of sparks and panels.

The drone wobbled into turning. The marauder inside struggled to reroute the flow of electricity around the damaged circuits on the computer console. Logan appeared in his sights. The marauder grabbed his control stick, locked on, and clenched the trigger. The large machine lanced out a missile.

Logan deflected the missile right with a thrust in midst of a side-angular axel. The missile split into four and slammed the ceiling, blasting off beams and panels. The mech warrior fired off a second missile.

Logan reacted with a side step and down chop, slicing the percussion fuse off the missile. The defused missile, still rocket-propelled, bounced off the floor and jeeps, spun wildly along the walls and burnt out at the ceiling.

Logan just realized that was a million-to-one shot he just

did. He got worried over when his luck will run out. Regardless of that, he charged in anyway. He rolled under the claws of the warrior, chopped off the left turret, and continued his striking rampage on the machine's leg plating, wearing it down.

As he hacked down at this metal colossus, Logan realized how effective Psi-Knights were when they were well placed. They were capable of eliminating anything at close range, or repelling infantry forces through guerrilla warfare. Rampras and his squad had such trouble handling this mech warrior until Logan stepped in.

But he knew their limits. They were vulnerable and limited at long distances. He could only wonder why military tactics moved away from melee implementation when it proved so effective. Perhaps historically, soldiers were undertrained, or that technology out-proved the usefulness of primitive melee weaponry. Whatever the case, his training was proving invaluable.

Samiren narrowed his eyes at Logan disapprovingly, as Logan somersaulted and struck with expert precision. Calis and Multanis watched in amazement as Logan tore chunks out of the barely unstoppable mech warrior.

"Man! I sure are glad we been defrostin' him," Calis commented.

"Aim for its missile turrets!" yelled Rampras. "Logan, get back!"

Multiple thumps expelled from the squadron. The several grenade seeds bloomed into explosion all over the missile launcher. One lucky seed splashed fragments that sliced through a rocket cylinder, disturbing the explosive warhead into ignition. Logan stepped away as the right launcher exploded. The drone staggered out of control.

Vanis stood up with a limp and stabbed her fingers at the machine. Two streams of lightning unleashed from her hands, which wove together and whipped at the hull. Metal shards scattered, sparks popped and crackled, and the ten-ton oversized drone toppled over in defeat, ending the battle with a loud crash.

"Where the hell is Samiren?" barked Rampras.

They looked toward the south. Dead, laser-burnt bodies surrounded Samiren near a corridor. Rampras glared at him, but had nothing to lecture out.

"Well, kudos for doin' somethin'!" said Calis.

Vanis limped toward the squadron. Logan rushed over and swung her arm around his shoulders. Multanis clenched his chest and heaved out whizzes. He wasn't doing too well.

"Ye better not croak on us, doc!" said Calis.

"I'm fine. Leave me alone," grunted Multanis.

"The dam's just outside. Come on," said Rampras.

"How'd ya know all 'bout that, anyhow?" asked Calis.

"This wasn't the first time I snuck in," said Rampras.

He hit the button for the hangar bay doors. A torsion-coiled tube twisted and spun the cable drums, rolling the 40-foot-wide aluminum doors up along the hinge's tracks.

CHAPTER 14

DESCENSION

Outside they saw several helipads near the edges of the dam, trucks full of barrels, a gassing station with tanks, tables with tools and engine parts, and forklifts. Several workers and mechanics had stopped a while before and were staring at the doors. Upon seeing the squadron, they fled toward a nearby cavern entrance.

Solito watched them from the roof as they hustled out of the hangar. He smirked and faded from sight. Logan stopped. He just felt eyes at the back of his head. He looked at the rooftops. Nobody was there, but he had a clear view of red lights blinking in two-second pulses from a radio tower above the hangar.

"Can that radio tower jam signals?" Logan asked.

Rampras stopped and analyzed it, "Think a couple of micro-RPGs can take it out. Calis."

Calis spun around, showing his backpack. Rampras punched numbers on a code lock and the metal backpack opened up. Inside were several tools, rifle clips that sprung out from the base, and three micro-rocket propelled grenades. Rampras detached two and handed one to Martin. They attached launcher add-ons to their rifles, slid in a rocket, and took aim.

Then marauders stormed out of the hangar and snapped out bullets. Martin squealed and, prematurely, blasted his rocket at them. The micro-missile sliced between the marauder ranks and combusted harmlessly inside the hangar. The squadron split their cover behind a forklift and a navigation pole.

"You idiot!" Rampras said.

He smacked the back of Martin's helmet. Martin pushed Rampras out into the open. Rampras landed on his back and bullets snapped all around him. Multanis ripped Rampras off the ground.

"Why in the hell of all the rotten pork chops that fell out of a pig's bee-hind did'ja do that for?!" Calis yelled at Martin. "Ye tryin' to kill the captain?!"

"Hey! Settle this business on your own time!" yelled Multanis.

Multanis kept firing toward the hangars. Martin never said a word. He just frowned and fired at the marauders. Rampras glared at Martin, wanting to smack him around for a while. He shrugged off the distracting notion and surveyed his surroundings.

"We have to go down," said Rampras. "We'll set up a single line, then transfer to another ten metres in. That way, they don't cut our journey short. On the count of three, we'll impose 'covery fire while Calis gets the first line. Vanis will launch one of those fuel barrels at 'em. My RPG can probably ignite it and hold them back while we make our retreat."

"We're wit'cha, cappy!" said Calis.

"Ready?" Rampras said to the silent squadron. "Go!"

Calis scampered to his feet and headed for the dam's edge. Logan blocked his wake with his psi-shield.

"'Covery fire!" yelled Rampras.

The squadron blasted a fury toward the hangar. The marauder took cover behind nearby obstructions.

Vanis hooked her palm toward the barrel's sight and hurled it kinetically toward the marauders. The barrel banged off the stonewall, sprayed gas, then smashed onto the ground. Rampras launched his micro-RPG. The smoke line trailed toward the hangar.

The rocket slammed at a nearby wall and exploded, stabbing shards. The shard's sparks excited the volatile gas into a burning frenzy.

The flames blocked off reinforcement from the hangar bay doors and engulfed several marauders in a fiery fury. The rest dispersed along the helipads.

Calis got to the dam's edge and looked down. The dam was several hundred meters high, partly slanted, and had several protruding platforms that were probably used as a solid foundation for construction workers.

Calis fired a small stone-biting harpoon from a rifle add-on at a nearby ledge. The harpoon uncoiled a thin metallic line as it travelled and the spearhead struck through the concrete slab. Calis ejected the line and dangled it down the dam, creating a down path to the first platform.

"Ze line iz ze ready!" said Calis.

"Logan! Vanis! Shield our rears while we slide," said Rampras.

The squadron bolted for the dam with Logan and Vanis guarding their aft. Logan looked at Vanis's cracked shield that had slowly regenerated.

"Just go. I got it," said Logan.

Vanis broke formation and hustled toward the lines. Multanis slid down to a ledge twenty meters down and established another line. Calis fired off a few rounds before going down. Vanis stepped off and levitated while Samiren and Martin slid down.

Rampras hooked the line to his girdle, swung over the ledge, then looked back. A faint visual distortion passed in front of the marauders. He frowned but dismissed it as the fire's heat.

Logan was the last on top. He turned and grabbed the

rope. Then a red glowing whip line snapped out from oblivion and constricted his neck. Logan gawked for air. The whip yanked him back and Logan stumbled toward the side, falling off a helipad's platform in the process. Logan slammed on his stomach.

Solito decloaked nearby him while introducing himself with a smirk. Logan spun his hips around, swirling his legs in the air, and flipped himself into a stand. Solito tilted his head. His keen eyes examined his form.

Marauders stampeded toward them and semi-circled around Logan. Logan charged his plasma blade and took stance.

"I hope for all of your sakes that you are not targeting my prey!" Solito growled in such a raspy voice.

The marauders backed away from Logan fearfully.

"But if you still feel the need to indulge...look down the dam."

The marauders then stormed along the dam's edge and fired down at the squadron. Logan wanted to see how they were doing, but was too nervous to take his eyes away from the seemingly cunning Solito.

"So, a Psi-Knight," Solito said. "I have not fought one of your kind in years. So graceful and elegant your training is. Tell me, dear psionicist," he purposefully hissed, "do you still train in that stone tent you call the Paradigm?"

Logan refused to give any answers to him.

"I thought so," said Solito. "I don't see the point in it when it's best to learn on the field. But you wouldn't know that. Now would you?"

Logan knew what he was talking about. He lived on the streets.

"No, you wouldn't," Solito stressed. "See. Only the best

survive these lands. It's the best that writes the history. What worth are you if you are not that?"

"The best lives alone. There's no value in that kind of living," Logan said.

Then he frowned in thought. That sounded like a harsh lesson well learned. Where did he hear that before? Was that directed toward him?

Solito gritted his teeth at him and growled. He unsheathed his curved knife. A visual distorting aura surrounded the blade. Then Solito flicked a switch on it. The blade emanated a red glow that sparkled from searing heat. Solito fidgeted toward him and Logan shuttered back. Solito chuckled and walked, encircling him like a vulture. He whisked his knife around, contemplating the type of approach he should launch.

Logan knew this was who Krogani was talking about: a killer, a man hunter, the one most feared of by the even the bravest gang lords. He had to suspect he was an assassin with a very high-quality resume for only sporting a dagger as his primary weapon.

If that were true, being able to kill hundreds armed with automatic weaponry with a mere kitchen knife can revere one's reputation to unimaginable heights. Logan was worried — very, very worried. Who was he compared to Solito? He was just a graduate from the Paradigm, someone with only the slightest sense of who he was.

Solito growled and charged in. Logan's eyes widened at the direct approach. He backpedalled away. The mirage of Solito suddenly vanished. Logan looked around nervously, unsure of how he'd attack. In a mid-air dive over Logan, Solito decloaked and jammed his dagger into Logan's shoulder blade.

Logan yelped, rolled forward, and back-slashed. His blade

didn't connect. Nobody was there. Logan concentrated on his wound; it began to close up. Not realizing why, Logan yanked his head back. From the flank, the decloaking Solito missed a throat slash and ripped a series of cuts and strikes at Logan.

Logan blocked and parried each incoming strike. He was on the defensive. How was he on the defensive against an attacker with a knife-sized weapon? His blade alone outstretched Solito's extension.

Solito had reversed the grip of his blade and used his elbow as extra torque as though to attack in parries, to draw out defensive slaps and guard them as they came. That was incredibly daring when fighting by the inch. He would have to pre-calculate every defensive slash for every attack he launched before he launched it. One slight calculation error could cut him...

...for only a master could pull off such a feat so skilfully.

*   *   *   *   *

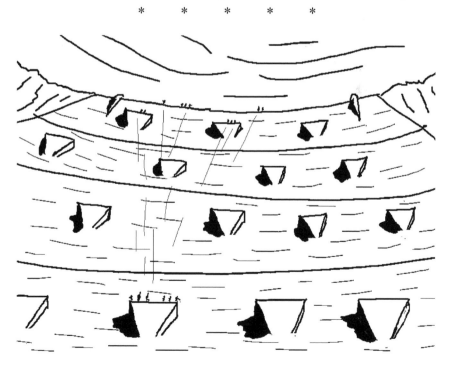

As Logan and Solito fought all over the edges, bullets blazed up and down the dam side. The squadron reached the fourth ledge down. Several marauders pursued them using the same lines, while the rest shot from above.

One crawled down the second rope line, pursuing the squadron. His legs came into a view of a circular capsule embedded underneath the platform. Its red lights activated. It exploded, blasted off the marauder's legs, and snapped the platform. The slab crashed downwards and spilled the marauders into the air.

Rampras blasted up the dam. A bullet managed to pierce one in the head. He fell over, slammed into a ledge, and spun his way down toward the bottom. Vanis blocked several incoming bullets with her crack-riddled shields. She dropped to the ground and panted heavily. Sweat poured down her face.

"The tarnished I depulsifies in fade," complained Vanis.

Calis quirked an eyebrow at her, "What?!"

"She's tired," Multanis said as he slipped out a blue vial. "Psionicists burn far more energy than we do. Here, drink this."

Vanis grabbed and gulped it down.

"What is that thang?" asked Calis as he blasted up the dam.

"Metabolizers," said Multanis. "It speeds up the metabolism by transforming fat in energy. Not recommended for weight loss."

Four marauders jumped off the dam while strapped to bungee cords. After several bounces, they stabilized and walked horizontally down the dam while lowered from above. Each pulled out a different weapon; a paintball gun that fired acid balls, a sling with steel bullets, an archer-master composite long bow, and an arm-embedded shuriken shooter. Rampras shook his head at them.

The dangling outcasts fired their cluster variety. An acid

ball splashed on Vanis's shield. With the flick of a wrist, she spat it off. The shuriken and steel pellet missed. A refined composite arrow slammed through Multanis's leg plates, piercing through to the other side. Multanis fell and wailed in agony.

"Damn! That thing got torque!" Calis said.

Calis covered Multanis, blasting the slinger in the head. Multanis snapped off the arrow's head and butt. Vanis came to his side.

"No, keep shielding the squad!" said Multanis.

Martin blasted a bullet and sliced the archer's line. The archer torpedoed past the crew. As the other marauder reloaded, the shuriken shooter spat out a wave of stars. Vanis flipped her wrists. The shurikens shot back up. The marauders braced from several shuriken stabs, but their lines could not. The bungee cords tore from the tension and plummeted the marauders to their doom.

As Rampras readied another line, the dam tremored. Gears grinded from up the dam. A side platform initiated and lowered several marauders downward.

"That thing up there would've been a whole lot easier, y'know," said Calis.

Rampras judged the platform arrangements in the area. Several ledges protruded in an awkward staircase toward the right end.

"Maybe it still can," Rampras said.

"How we getting' there with the doc wounded?" asked Calis.

Rampras noticed Multanis's wound. It was pretty bad.

"Can you heal him?" Rampras asked of Vanis.

Vanis looked up the dam, "those bullets do abolish that advice."

Rampras gave a quick look around. There was no cover at all.

"Y'know that big ol' elevator thang...that seems to be movin' things up and down?" said Calis. "Yeah...it's gonna be on us real fast if we don't be doin' sumthin',"

"He watch back while we go bye, bye," said Martin as he blasted up.

"Are ye slap-happy over the sight of bubbles now?" asked Calis. "The doc's been patchin' booboos more times than the fingers on my hands and ye jus' want to be handin' out them handkerchiefs of pure an' ultra sadness?"

Martin didn't seem to care.

"Our statistical rating will drop upon further assistance of wounded," Samiren stated.

"I don't know if y'know this or not, ye bein' a killer doomsday bot an' all," said Calis, "but we the fixin' type! We don't jus' be throwin' out broken toasters when it bakes us a pancake instead of bagels. He needs that cover and fast."

Bullets continued to blaze from above. Then, two marauders in wing suits and one in a hand glider sped off from the top. Martin and Calis blasted up the dam at the oncoming units.

Rampras gazed at the platform then stared at the wounded Multanis.

"I'm not losing anymore soldiers!" he yelled.

He picked up Multanis, weighing in at two hundred pounds of meat and one hundred pounds of metal, and slung him over his shoulder. Rampras leapt off to the next balcony and fumbled to the ground from the combined weight compression.

The platform marauders hailed down a lead armada. Two bullets slammed into Rampras's backpack. Martin cover-fired at the platform. Calis blazed a series of bullets at the hand glider circling down. Two bullets punched holes in the tarp wing, but did not destabilize it.

One of the two wing suit divers that sped quickly down the dam was caught in friendly fire by the boys on the top. The shot wing suitor bounced off the dam wall and tumbled down. The remaining wing suitor dove toward Samiren and grappled for him. He rammed head first into Samiren's shield, broke his neck and spine, and whiplashed off the ledge. Samiren turned around to see what hit him.

Rampras got up and cover-fired as Calis and Martin climbed down the platform with Vanis levitated down.

The circling hand glider dropped two of the eight brown bags that were tied to the wings. The bags exploded upon surface contact. One hit far off, while the other blasted Calis off his feet and sent him over the ledge.

"Calis!" yelled Rampras.

After passing two platforms, Calis panicked. He fired a dropline from his rifle's add-on. The harpoon head speared underneath a concrete protrusion, bounced Calis on the line, slammed him into the wall then bounced a few more times before relaxing to a hang.

"Holy crap-happy-ass automatics!" yelled Calis.

Rampras rained the madness of his bullets at the hand glider. Most torpedoed around the glider, but one lucky shot sliced off an aluminum pole. The hand glider spiralled down, unable to control itself. It sped past Calis and slammed into a ledge, igniting into flames. Rampras looked down toward Calis three ledges down. He wondered how he got to him while warding off enemies.

"Projectile threat detected," said Samiren, as he viewed the elevation platform. "A missile guidance system has locked on."

Two marauders aimed laser-guided rockets at the squadron and fired.

"Incoming!" yelled Rampras.

He carried Multanis behind Samiren. Vanis stood in front of Martin. The two missiles re-directed toward the two obvious choices. Vanis slapped the first away with a telekinetic blast. It curved around and came at her from above. She braced with her shield. The missile slammed into it, shattered it, and blasted her off her feet.

The second missile struck Samiren. His shield absorbed the full blast, scraping dust and concrete bits into the air. A thunderous blast erupted from the mist and a trail of light screamed out. The blast struck underneath the elevation platform and ravaged the gears. The platform slanted down and ejected the onboard marauders. Its weight ripped it off its hinges and the steel saucer came crashing down behind the falling passengers.

Rampras fidgeted as a concrete chunk heading in their direction, but it was far off. Rampras let out a disappointed sigh as the platform fell.

"What a mess," he said.

"Hey, cappy! What happened to our platform?" Calis yelled from below.

"Captain!" Multanis yelled, pointing to Vanis.

Rampras came to her side and examined. She was mostly dazed with a few scrapes, bruises and burnt hair.

"Carry her!" Rampras said to Martin.

Martin sneered at Rampras, but then looked at Vanis's curvy body. He lost his annoyance immediately.

"Surcease in move," said the dazed Vanis. "Locate the knightest one."

Rampras quirked a brow. He didn't even notice Logan was

gone. He scanned around at the previous ledges — nothing. Then he looked up the dam, realizing where he was.

"Damn that son of a--" Rampras cut himself short.

"What we do?" asked Martin.

Rampras analyzed the situation. Vanis and Multanis clenched their wounds. Calis still hung down below. Samiren hardly did anything, while Rampras felt Martin too incompetent. He was pretty pissed off.

"We're leaving him behind," said Rampras.

Then a blue flash sparked from Vanis's eyes.

She cried out, "Logan!"

*   *   *   *   *

On top of the dam, the vicious swordplay raged on. Solito was blinking in and out of sight, hoping to catch Logan off guard. Every attempt to undermine Logan's defenses failed completely. Solito became equally frustrated and impressed with his adversary with every failed strategy.

But Logan felt possessed. He executed movements he never knew, but used them properly as though he had known them for years. Neither Psi-Ops nor the Paradigm had this type of training. *Where did I learn this?* he thought. Their skills were nearly equal but their experiences were greatly different. It became a very irritating puzzle to him. He thought about this between short pauses in the duel.

He suddenly imagined a random cluster of images, none of which made sense to him: card tricks, miming, a janitor, ballet dancing. The list continued, but they were brief and subtle experiences that didn't connect. The only thing that did make sense was that he used to sword-fight using sticks with other homeless children in the back alleys. That alone wasn't enough.

Solito then broke his thoughts. He came at Logan with a flurry of slices. Logan worked back each attack then up-smacked the dagger, creating an opening. He palmed out a telekinetic thrust. Solito flew back, tumbled, then back-rolled to his feet. He snapped back an upswing whip crack. Logan slipped under it, but the laser-like whip clipped his regalia, burning a scar into it.

Solito casted his dagger with an underarm throw. Logan slanted a dodge and the dagger zipped by. Solito, with his arm still extended, wide-spanned his fingers, exposing an oval lens on his glove's palm. The dagger spanned out into a five-bladed star. Solito motioned a pull back and rolled out another whip crack.

Logan arched around the striking whip, but the returning star sliced his rib side. Logan yelped up and spun himself, fumbling to the ground. In one spin, Solito caught the star, ripped another whip crack, and re-launched the star.

Logan side-rolled the whip then blasted the star away with telekinesis. Solito twirled his wrists in circles. The spinning star spiralled back at him. Logan X-crossed his arms. The star slashed his psi-shield in continuous swirls. As Logan backpedalled away, Solito cloaked, leaving Logan to fend off the star.

Cracks slashed all over Logan's psi-shield. It was buckling. Logan gripped it with a telekinetic grasp and casted it into the ground. The star chopped into the concrete and was paralyzed from movement.

The red wire whisked out from oblivion as Solito emerged near the star. Logan slapped it aside and used his momentum to curve out a counter-strike, but fell far too short. Solito snatched his star that reformulated back into a searing knife and blocked Logan's incoming cleave. They muscled themselves into a weapons lock and glared into each other's eyes.

"That's quite the equipment you have," Logan grunted.

"My, my, the intuitive warrior presents itself," remarked Solito, "I'd be so obliged to bow if I weren't so binded," he said, while growling to reinforce the lock.

"Why do you need so much anyway?" asked Logan.

"The less I use, the better I am," retorted Solito, "for raw talent finds those who don't depend on petty trinkets. With you I had no choice," he said, sneering at him in disgust, "but you rely far too much on your powers. Don't be disappointed when those gifts betray you," ending the comment with a smirk.

"If talent's your goal," said Logan, "why bother when it fades with age?"

Solito snarled, hating him even more. He pulled his knife arm back, redirecting Logan's blade, and used its natural swing flow to propel his momentum into a circular down-stab. That would've been a perfect move, but Logan saw it and used the lock's release as momentum to shoulder-bash him.

After recovering, Solito came at him, but Logan kept him at bay with a wide-curving swipe, overextending Solito's reach. Solito saw through that and waited for the next diagonal up-strike. Logan launched it from a backhand. Solito stepped in, hard blocked it, guarded the next strike that came from the first deflection's momentum, and backhanded Logan in the face.

Logan stumbled back. Solito coiled for a down chop, then struck. Logan's blade came up to meet it, but Solito feinted. He shifted to a crouch, snapped a rapid thigh slash, then stabbed the other shoulder-blade as Logan dropped to one knee. Logan growled and twisted out a back slash. But Solito wasn't dumb enough to stand near a wounded foe. Logan fore-rolled to his feet.

He struck furiously in a series of X-slashes. Solito smirked at the ferocity as he knocked each one away without much effort. Then he up-blocked a down-strike, then used the recoil to throw his dagger seemingly behind his back. As the hard block recoiled Logan's arms over his head, he saw the knife, now a star, orbiting around Solito's back and nicked a cut across his chest.

Logan backed away. The star orbited Solito a few more times before he caught it. Logan cursed himself for letting his anger get the best of him. Solito was too fast and too smart to out-trick and outmaneuver. He had to find some way to use his sword's length to his advantage, he thought, but doing so would give Solito another chance to set up a defensive bypass.

This was definitely a puzzle Logan loved. It was a play of weapon strategy that needed instant decisions. No wonder he loved swords so much.

A voice amplified in sonic power scorched up the dam, "Logan!"

"I'm busy!" Logan yelled back.

Even Solito shook his head disapprovingly.

*   *   *   *   *

Vanis felt the plague of pain eat at her from his selfish response. The squad crawled down two more ledges and came across Calis swinging. Rampras towed him in and cut his line. Calis looked up. Something was off.

"I don't hear any of them guns firin'," he said.

"We're too far down," replied Rampras. "They're either going to use snipers or they'll come down after us. Come on."

Martin placed Vanis down by her request; no longer dazed and under self-power. As Martin set up another line, Vanis eased her hands on Multanis's thigh and helped accelerate his bodily regeneration process. To conserve her energy, she stopped when the wound closed up enough for use.

Then a thunderous roar boomed from twenty meters above and off to the side. A falling barrel exploded into a rosy ball of flames. The squadron looked up. A whole series of barrels with fuses burning fell from the top.

"Blast them before they reach us!" said Rampras as he loaded a clip.

"What'd ya think this is? A video game?" asked Calis.

Rampras casted a questioning brow at him.

Calis added, "Barrels don't be doin' the explodin' upon contact with leads rounds. All ya'd be doin' is pokin' holes in 'em."

Rampras frowned as he watched the barrels fall worryingly. Then he thought about the physics of it.

"What about magnesium rounds?" he asked.

The two looked at each other. The squad loaded their rifles with magnesium bullets.

Rampras blasted at a falling barrel. The muzzle flashed out glowing rounds and the searing bullets slammed into the barrel, igniting them. The squad warded off several containers. One fell directly over them. Calis took aim and fired. Liquid fire burst out of the barrel, but its burning corpse kept falling.

"Umm..." Calis mumbled.

The barrel kept growing larger as it closed in. It didn't move side to side. The squadron moved out of the way, but Calis kept his eyes locked on it with his jaw open. He cringed as it came in at the last few feet, until it stopped in mid-air before him. Calis peeked out, realizing he wasn't dead. He felt the heat of the burning barrel directly above him.

Vanis, pouring a puddle of sweat, gripped it with a telekinetic grasp. She heaved out whizzes. Her eyes slanted with exhaustion. Her arm's muscles vibrated with complaint. She casted the barrel away then dropped to a knee.

Calis gazed at her thankfully, then felt bad for her.

"I can't imagine how demandin' all that must've been," he said.

It was his way of thanking her.

The persistent slicing of chopping air echoed throughout the dam. Two gyrocopters speared from the northern rock bend. Two marauders on each copter wore parachute packs and hung onto the wings. Upon sighting the squadron, the four marauders in total detached and glided in by parachute.

The two gyros blasted the squadron with their SMGs. They polluted the ledges with clusters of dust bursts as they flew by. The squad snapped back streams of white bullet lines in retaliation.

"They just won't leave us alone, will they?" Multanis said.

"Martin. Calis. Cover our dorsal flank," said Rampras.

Martin and Calis blasted at the falling barrels while Rampras and Multanis exchanged fire with the incoming parachute gliders. The gliders circled away before getting too close. Rampras streamed out the volatile rounds at the parachute's canopy itself, shredding it and igniting it into flames.

Then a gyrocopter came around. It let loose its violence onto the ledge. The bullets speared between squadron members, some struck shields, until two lucky bullets slammed into Martin's back. Martin yelped. Sparks screamed out of his radio pack and Martin spun a 180, blasting bullets in all directions.

The squadron hit the deck, but bullets slammed into Samiren's shields. Samiren woke up from his idle state, glared at Martin, then registered the gyro threat. He formulated his arm turret and blasted at the turning copter. The marauder pilot squealed as the flying machine exploded.

The three para-marauders and the copter veered away from the intimidating firepower. Samiren stood at the edge and lanced out another ear-shattering blast. The evading gyro, shot in the back, splattered into pieces.

"Multanis!" Rampras said while pointing up.

Multanis assisted Calis in guarding the dorsal flank. Rampras ripped Martin from the ground and glared into his eyes disapprovingly. Martin, guilt-struck, didn't know what Rampras was going to say. Rampras just spun him around without a word and inspected the damage. The radio pack was totalled. Too much of its guts had melted.

"Captain, we're almost out of incendiaries," said Multanis.

"Alright, set up another line," said Rampras.

"Captain!" yelled Calis.

Rampras looked up. A full family of barrels were released close together.

"Multanis! Continue with that line! Everyone else fire at will!"

Rampras blasted his last clip of magnesium. One barrel combusted after another from the fiery stream of bullets. The squadron only managed to excite five before the barrels reached halfway. By then Multanis finished the setup.

"Everyone get down now!" yelled Rampras.

They latched themselves on with a quick click on the girdle and slid down. Rampras grabbed the line itself and slid off. He eyed a grove indention within the wall.

"Grind to the right!" yelled Rampras.

The squad kicked off the dam's wall and swung toward a grove indention.

Then the top barrel's fuse ignited. It set off a chain reaction of combustions that scaled down the dam. Rampras eyed the wave of explosions in terror as it closed in. Flaming gas sprayed all over the platforms. Cracks ripped all over the dam's walls. Then the explosive wave ended, falling short before reaching the squad. Rampras sighed as droplets of fire sprayed past them.

Complaining cracks continued to slash all over the dam. A large concrete chunk snapped off from the wall and slammed onto the platform that held the line. The ledge broke off. The line slacked and the squadron plummeted down.

Samiren slammed onto a ledge that the rest of the squad nearly struck. He saw the line sliding off. Samiren snatched it. The rope tightened and the squad bounced into a hang. Samiren held the whole squadron up with one arm.

Calis looked up. His eyes suddenly went wide, "Samiren!"

The broken concrete ledge tumbled down toward Samiren. It slammed and reflected off his shields. Samiren jolted. He narrowed his eyes, annoyed.

The ledge fell off to the side. It still had the line's pin hooked to it. Samiren reached for his laser-blade, but the rope yanked him off, plummeting him down with the squad. The crew screamed for the mercy of the gods.

Then Samiren's hand slammed through the concrete plate of another ledge and wedged his arm. The rope tightened. The crew slid to the rope's end and bounced, swinging over the suspended platform that somehow remained pinned.

The metal joints in Samiren's arm contorted and warped.

The helpless squad stared at him in mercy. Samiren narrowed his eyes at them.

"Climb...up!" Samiren grunted in irritation.

"I got me a better idea," said Calis.

He took his boot knife.

"Now, who was sayin' I was a dumb ol' dog now?"

He slashed at the other line. The knife wouldn't cut it.

"Hold on a sec, there."

Calis grabbed the other line and sawed at it. The line was made out of a metallic fabric. It wouldn't cut.

"Just a sec."

Multanis pulled his handgun and fired at the line. Calis twitched. The bullet sliced the fabric and the concrete chunk fell down to its doom.

"Holy mother of hot dogs and all the other tranny meat and bun foods that people eat!" Calis cursed.

"You do realize how quickly that gets old, right?" Multanis remarked.

*   *   *   *   *

They clashed in a fury of blows. They twisted their bodies vigorously to its maximum limit to work down the other's defenses. Each cut, each slice, curved gracefully in stellar sophistication toward its target and each guard, each block, came up to meet it in fencing conversation. The argument of blades slashed wickedly from every angle, ripping at each other as dogs would to tear each apart. But its melody, its art, was far too beautiful to be seen as violence.

Logan wasn't too worried about the minor cuts and gashes. He regenerated any wound inflicted. His worry was spending too much energy doing the unnecessary. The lack of energy meant lack of speed, coordination, reaction time, processing power. Anything that lowered his fighting performance was a concern. He had already put so much pressure on himself to keep up with Solito.

Solito was worried about something else. He couldn't regenerate like Logan. Any slashes to his muscles were rather permanent. He couldn't take reckless chances when seeing an opening in case he left himself vulnerable. For an assassin obsessed with extremism, this restriction was very upsetting, but it ensured he remained in combat. But unlike the diligently skilled Solito, Logan was the one being reckless, and Solito took advantage of that any chance he got.

Solito smacked Logan's blade to his left and saw an opening at the chest, but the gap in timing was too small. He dared not take it. Logan spun around, closing his sword arm across his chest to stab out early. Solito, seeing it coming, caught the blade coming at his chest with an up-elbow jam and pushed it outward. Logan twirled his wrist into an inside neck slice.

Again, blocked by Solito. Then Logan launched something outside of his normal repetition, swirling his blade clockwise. Solito launched a low guard. But the blade swept under his knife, into a full circle, and caught Solito's shoulder in a backhanded jab. Solito growled and sliced back, but fell short. Logan coiled back into a scorpion stance. Solito cursed his extended range.

Solito disappeared. Logan closed his eyes, listening to the faintest of sounds. He couldn't hear any footsteps, but felt disturbances of wind to his left. Logan launched a low sweep and heard a loud foot slam, landing behind it. He launched a diagonal slash upon coming up, which met a guarding knife that broke Solito's invisibility.

Solito pushed the blade away, creating distance between them, and unleashed a whip snap upon fully turning. Logan brushed it aside. Solito retracted it then slashed in rapid Xs, which backed Logan away into a pole. He didn't even realize it was there, or what was happening on the dam's summit.

Solito side-flipped and conjoined it with a spin, hoping its fanciness would mask an oncoming whip slash launched over his head. Logan barely saw it coming for his neck and slipped under it by an inch. The whip severed the pole.

Logan side-rolled away as the pole fell between them. He then blasted a thrust and pushed the pole toward Solito's trajectory. Solito side-flipped over it in a triple axel and cloaked in mid-air. Logan motioned a pull back and the pole tumbled back toward him. The pole slammed into an invisible object, causing Solito to decloak and tumble onto the ground.

"You're not the only one that can do that," Logan proudly mocked.

Then he felt a fainting spell and dropped to one knee. He clenched his chest near his pounding heart as sweat poured down his face.

Solito smirked. "What's the matter? Finally exhausting yourself? That's the problem with psionicists. They burn themselves out too quickly."

Solito got up and charged. Logan stammered to his feet and knocked a stab away with an outbound parry. Their weapons swung over their heads then crossed into a lock across their chests. Solito muscled the weapon lock upward, curved his knife around the blade then sliced down at the opening. Logan compensated for the upbound shift, but kept the weapon lock in the down slice.

Their weapon lock slid near their abdominals. Solito pushed the blade's middle down then flipped his wrists around into a neck slice. Logan barely slipped away with just an inch to spare. Logan forced him back with continuous episodes of slashes, backing him into a concrete hut that cased a flight of stairs.

Solito fended off the vicious slashes. Then he ducked under a horizontal strike, slashed Logan's sword-arm's triceps, and kicked him in the back as he turned. Logan stumbled away. Solito rolled out a whip snap, grappled Logan by the neck, and yanked him back toward a stabbing knife.

As the whip unravelled from the slack, Logan stumbled back and twisted around, seeing the knife coming for his eyes. He swept it aside, twirled his body into a full convolution, and slashed Solito's thigh. Solito groaned and stumbled to the wall. He ducked under another slash that tore a chunk off the concrete wall. Solito rolled away from the chunk, then engaged Logan again.

After another volume of slashes, their weapons halted into another lock. Solito grabbed Logan's sword-arm and threw him toward the ledge. Logan grunted from the tricep grab, then banged into the ledge's rail, nearly falling over. Solito rolled out another whip slash. The whip seared through the rail bars, but failed to strike the evading Logan.

Solito snatched up the concrete chunk with his whip and launched it toward Logan. Logan ducked under it. The rock smacked into the railing before pulling back into another whirl. Solito flushed the rock around his body in a whirlpool: over his head, around his bending back, and under his leaping legs. Logan couldn't tell when Solito was casting it in until it was too late.

The rock chunk slammed Logan in the gut and knocked him over the edge. Logan somersaulted in mid-air several times with his body wrapped around the rock. Then Logan thrust the chunk back in a telekinetic blast as he disappeared behind the ledge. The chunk dove over the ledge side and smacked Solito's shoulder, spinning him into a stumble.

Logan, with down-aiming palms, levitated up to see if he struck. Solito growled. Logan smiled then fell backwards, diving head first down the dam.

"You are not getting away that easily!" Solito yelled.

Solito bolted for the ledge, leapt off, and snapped his whip out. The whip grappled another nearby pole and swung Solito down after the gliding Logan.

Logan eased down to a ledge several deca-yards down and assessed how far away the rest of the squadron was. Then he heard screaming behind him. He turned to see Solito colliding into him. The collision's force swept them both off and slammed them onto another platform below.

They groaned and tumbled on the floor. They muscled themselves up to a stance and ripped out an exhausted display of swordplay. Logan made the mistake of launching his downward diagonal chop too slow due to his tricep wound. Solito slanted to the side, hooked his knife behind the blade, and casted the blade off into an accelerated momentum. This threw Logan off into a full spin. Solito grappled him from behind with a knife to Logan's throat side.

"You're mine!" Solito yelled as he muscled Logan toward the edge. Logan grabbed Solito's arm and leaned forward, throwing him over his back. Solito reacted with a knife jab to the ledge side, wedging it in, and tore Logan off.

Logan plummeted down the dam.

Solito heaved in total exhaustion as he watched Logan fall.

"A worthy warrior," he stated so proudly.

Then he squinted down, wondering if Logan really was defeated.

CHAPTER 15

PERSEVERANCE

Rampras detached his line and pressed his feet onto the sands. They were at the bottom. Sand, swept aside by the wind, built up along the edges of the rocky walls. The cracked clay plate underneath was exposed several meters out and made good traction for vehicles.

Rampras surveyed the area. Several huts rested nearby in front of the desert canvas. Several bikes were stationed nearby. With the debris parts welded on, Rampras couldn't tell if they were motorcycles or off-road dirt bikes.

"Convenient," Samiren remarked.

"Hey, cappy! Are ye seein' this?" Calis announced.

Rampras looked up, squinting. Something white was falling; he couldn't make out what. Vanis felt her heart skip when she realized who it was.

"Logan!"

A marauder in the open saw them, "Settlement dogs! Kill them!"

The squadron hit the floor and blasted. The hut marauders scampered out of the huts and joined the alert in retaliatory fire. Trails of light blazed back and forth between the two forces.

Up the dam, Logan couldn't slow his rapid descent. There was no floor underneath him. Ledges sped by and he was approaching terminal velocity.

Vanis didn't care that she stood in the midst of a crossfire. She held out her palms and vented out a wave of telekinesis to the furthest of her reaches. Logan felt the oncoming force and thrust downward. It was slowing his fall.

Marauders burst out of a doorway hidden by a concrete protrusion and flanked the squadron. Calis and Multanis intercepted them and held them back at bay with suppression fire.

"Where in the hell did them outcasts come from?" roared Calis.

"There was a stairwell off to the side," said Multanis.

"Ye mean we could've been takin' the stairs all this time?!"

Electrical branches slashed up and down the dam side. The visual plane between Logan and Vanis folded and warped. Vanis poured with sweat. She scraped the last of her powers from the edges of her body. A forest of lightning exploded in Logan's wake, excreting the final drops of energy.

Everyone on the battlefield watched the awe of the two lightning urchins closed in for a kiss. Logan passed through a field and bathed in Vanis's sensual aura. Vanis wailed. Her body ripped out an octopus of lightning whips. Logan growled and grinded his teeth hard enough to puncture his skull.

Then Logan reached the final feet of his fall. The two benders of reality pulsed out a final burst of energy. A sphere of visual distortions exploded onto the battlefield, blasting everyone to the ground. Vanis smiled as she saw Logan suspended in air above her. She fell to the ground and Logan fell beside her.

The two forces got up and re-engaged the fight. Multanis rushed to their sides. He administered a blue vial to both. The two were drenched in sweat. Martin interchanged between the hut and stairwell targets.

"Vanis, you can't keep taxing your body like that," said Multanis.

The harsh slicing of air chopped from above. Rampras looked up. An old-world Blackhawk military helicopter was dispatched from the dam's summit.

"Man! Them guys just don't be stoppin', do they?" Calis remarked.

"There's no way to get to Epsilon without a dropship," said Rampras, "and we can't call them in," while blasting rounds at the marauders.

"So what we doin' then, cappy?" asked Calis.

"We scale the rifts," said Rampras.

Calis gave a quick eye to the dried lake's rocky walls. It stretched for miles beyond their sight.

Rampras added, "Martin and I will advance. You and Multanis push them back to the door and nuke 'em."

Rampras and Martin paced over the sand dunes, advancing on the covering marauders. One got up and bolted. Rampras and

Martin blasted him with a burst. The other stormed toward the hut, but was gunned down. Rampras then blasted into the hut. Blood sprayed from the entrance and another marauder sped out, firing wildly. Martin mauled him down with a series of bullets.

Calis and Multanis blazed continuous small pulses, forcing the marauders into cover. Calis advanced on them in an arch, closing off their concealment. The marauders fell back into the stairwell. Calis tossed in a grenade. The marauders roared and scampered in panic. The stairway corridor huffed smoke from the interior blast. Multanis scanned with his motion tracker.

"Clear!" Multanis confirmed.

"We've got to go. Let's move!" yelled Rampras.

The squadron bolted for the bikes. Logan and Vanis wobbled to a stance. Logan took a breather, but then lost his breath when Vanis threw her arms around him. She gazed at him in sadness, then hurtfully when she saw blood and rip marks slashed all over his regalia.

"Forbid you, I, from harsh abandonment," she said.

Logan felt bad for choosing his puzzle over her. But Solito just wouldn't let him go. Turning his back meant an easy assassination for Solito, which meant Vanis would never see him again. Still, he made a choice. It was the wrong one and it pained her. He dared not make those beautiful eyes sadden, but knew he might in the future.

"Hey!" yelled Calis, "Do yer lip suckin' another time!"

A roaring crowd seeped into earshot. They were numerous and the noise came from the stairs. Logan and Vanis ran for the squadron. They each chose their bikes and sped off along the rift lanes. Logan easily handled it. They were similar to hover bikes, but with bumps and steering feedback.

The squadron passed around the rocky bend that crowned the dam. A whole cluster of vehicles was stationed around the bend. Rampras wanted to sabotage them, but the Blackhawk was in pursuit.

The marauders hustled to the vehicles and sped off. The armada consisted of eight bikes, two dune buggies, four quads, a truck with a mini-gun turret, another truck with two para-sailors attached, two rocket-propelled skateboards with tracks for wheels, an armoured vehicle with a spinning claw from its back, a self-propelled hand glider, a two wheeler with two huge wheels, and an old-world hovercraft powered by a hind wind turbine.

The squad sped along the rock wall that curved to a long right. Several rock pillars sped by. These eiffel towers eroded over the years and ribcaged the dry lake's shores. Calis had trouble handling the steering feedback.

"Ugh! These old horsin' tires are so damn prehistoric! Who chiselled out these old fossils over the hover days?"

"Communication traffic," Samiren warned. "Tanks inbound. Ten miles."

Rampras scowled, "We're going to have to--"

A loud drum roll of blasts spat bullets around them. The bullets smacked up sand in a long straight trail.

"Incoming!"

The squadron veered away from the blast line. The Blackhawk torpedoed past them then tipped its nose back to slow its speed. But the upwind wall drafts caused the helicopter to struggle for stability.

A bald marauder on the truck's mini-gun turret applied ballistic pressure. The squadron curved around rock pillars. The other outcasts shuffled their way to the front. Their lines of fire were hampered by the two trucks ahead. A hard left break was approaching. It was castled in by a series of giant stone fingers.

"Logan, on the next turn, sweep behind them!" yelled Rampras.

Logan acknowledged and moved to the front.

"Calis, how many proximities?"

"Two!" Calis yelled.

He took them, knowing Rampras's plan.

The two para-sailors glided behind the squad and took aim with their rocket launchers. They had a clear view and fired.

"Missile launch detected," Samiren alerted.

The two missiles swerved toward the crew. Samiren spun his bike around and blazed off an ear-shattering blast. The plasmatic burst tore the first missile apart. Logan turned into the second and slashed for its head. His blade caught the middle, which splashed liquids all over the sands. The two missile parts bounced over Rampras and slammed into the wall.

Another missile pair blasted off from a bike. The rockets sped between the squadron and slammed into the base of a rock pillar. The blast chipped the base apart and the rock pillar came crashing down, scraping the wall and splitting in half. The squad curved under it while the marauders curved around.

The squad turned the hard left around the stone elbow. Logan sliced between two rocky fingers and disappeared. Calis slapped a proximity mine on the last stone tower. The two trucks grinded the hard curve, vomiting sand from its tracks. Both para-sailors were thrown toward the rocks. One smacked it while the other flew between the pillars and wrapped around the rock.

The rest of the armada sped past the two trucks and pursued. The lead biker flaunted a series of nun-chuk twirls. Then a wall blast bucked him off to the side. The pillar came crashing down before the marauders. Some sped under it, but two bikes, a quad, and the armoured scorpion vehicle steered around it.

As the subdivided outcasts steered back in, a slash of a plasma blade beheaded the front biker. The startled marauders split away from the re-emerging Logan, smashing one quad into a pillar from the sudden panic.

The armoured scorpion, however, was not afraid. It's hind spinning claw dove toward Logan. Logan heard the gears grind and veered away. The claw drilled into the sand, leaving a nasty scar on the dunes. Bullets smacked off Logan's regenerating shield. Several bikers kept away and fired as Logan dealt with the armoured scorpion.

Logan knew it was catching up. He throttled down and arched around the speeding scorpion, slashing its tracks in the process. The vehicle wasn't dislodged. The hind claw swung around, missing Logan's bike by inches. Logan waited for it to use its faster speed to its advantage. The spinning claw came about and aimed for Logan as the armoured vehicle slowed down.

Every direction Logan curved, the claw compensated. He wasn't going to pass this wall of spinning bulk without sophistication. Logan then swerved from side to side in regular intervals. The spinning claw kept up with him. Logan then feinted a left. The claw took the bait and Logan curved around it, slashing off the hand. The claw bounced then spun in circles behind them.

Logan tore the armoured vehicle apart with several blade slashes. The demoralized outcasts sped away, arching toward the rest of the armada. Logan kept forward, aiming to rejoin the squad at the next turn.

As he rode forth onto the smooth dirt dunes, he watched

the squad handle the grind boarders' ambush from the walls. They used such primitive weapons: a sharpened spade and a large scissor-hand contraption. With a city that large, they could manufacture standardized rifles. Perhaps they only used what they created, not what was given to them — a world where they handled their own.

He watched the streaks of light flicker back and forth between the two forces. He couldn't believe how persistent these marauders were. They were so passionate as though their lives depended on the catch. But the squad — Rampras's squad — was as equally passionate, depending their lives on escape.

They had fought from the front gates, into the middle of the city, into a hangar guarded by a giant, outside on a summit, down a cliff side, and now in a desert chasing after something no one knew anything about. The threat, the wonder, the intrigue of the unknown Galilea empowered them all with a purpose. He couldn't believe that people would go through such extremes over that.

Then he looked at himself and realized how alive he felt.

His heart was pounding. His thoughts quieted. His subconscious was on hyper drive with tactical calculation. He was doing what he was supposed to do and he loved every second of it. He was a warrior, a guardian of the people, a holy knight blessed with the rarest gifts. He felt incredibly empowered by the force of determination, the force of wind that flowed through his hair.

To take away that zest for life would be to die in a shattered world. But in order to feel that thriving, one must struggle to survive, to feel the edges of one's life closing on them to the brink of utter doom. Only then could that will for life truly come alive. Logan felt it. He felt it all for the first time in his life. The only thing he wished was that it wouldn't end.

The next hard left was ahead. Beyond it, a forest of solar panels supplied electricity to a power station. The power lines ran toward a crystalline cavern of salt that housed the hard left, then scaled up the walls. Logan figured this was one of Zodia's many sources of electricity.

Logan re-joined the squad at the eve of the salted cave. The marauders were still shuffling for line of fire. The turret truck blasted over the biker's heads, only kicking up dust trails in the process. The squad sped fast into the cave of salted armour. Much of the outside radiosity illuminated the crystal cave with sparkles. But its dirt-white surface made the colours ugly.

The outcast armada dipped into the salted darkness while the Blackhawk curved around the cavern. The self-propelled hand glider, however, dared a hasty entrance. The glider's sides jammed into the crystal walls and grinded apart the glider's aluminum frame.

Rampras and the squad flashed on their headlights. A low-ceiling arch drooped down overhead. Logan and Calis ducked under it while the rest curved around it and a garden of salt-sicle stalagmites. Most of the armada evaded it, but the crystal arch clotheslined the turret truck, shredding off the steel chassis of the front engine, the driver's cabin, and the turret itself.

The squad sped by several technicians dodging them and raining their backs with insults. Electrical wires, embedded on the ceilings, subdivided and distributed into other caverns. Logan sliced a wire. The wire spat out electrical blood and dangled. The electric serpent crashed into the cockpit of a dune buggy. Lightning electrocuted the driver, sending the buggy crashing into the wall and into circus cartwheels for the unentertained marauders.

The squad busted through the cavern's encaging salty fingers and streamed toward a village of stone hedges. The marauders were in close pursuit. The black hawk dove over the cavern and sailed toward the village that surrounded a temple chiselled into a rock wall. Bullets and vehicles blazed between huts of tarp and the robed cultists stormed the doomsday temple for safety.

The squad roared past several cultists. The black hawk and the armada saluted them with hailing bullets, exploding terror into an already frightened cult. Rampras led the squad through the indented streets between smooth, folding hills engraved with cracks. Logan gazed at the grand temple now at their side and wondered why so many doomsday believers would put so much effort into that.

Two pops sounded from miles away, reverberated by the rocky walls.

Twin cocoons of fire sprouted into flaming trees deep within the hut village.

"Where the hell did that come from?" yelled Rampras.

"Those tanks Samiren warned us about!" Multanis pointed out. "They're out there in the dunes!"

"Are these friggen finger twiddlers that crazy?" Calis whined. "They coulda hit their own!"

"Don't think they care, mate," Rampras reasoned. "Head for those tanks!"

"I hate to be objectin' to that there, cappy," objected Calis, "but I don't be preferin' to be playin' with twenty inches of cast iron-steel plates."

"That hasn't stopped us before. Who says it will now?" Rampras asked, illustrating to the two rocket launchers embedded on the bikes.

A drum roll of bullets batted the sand and rock around them, percussing the carnage of the black hawk. The bullet line swept between the squad, only afflicting Samiren's shield with one bullet strike. Samiren retaliated with an arm blast. The blast clipped the nose of the Blackhawk and forced it into a 360 spin. The black hawk struggled for stability as the squad stormed into open desert. The marauders were hot in their tail.

The squad drove directly toward the blazing light of the Earth's core. The light masked the two twentieth-century M1 Abrams' main battle tanks. Bullets screamed from behind the squad. With the widened spread of the bullet's dust kickup, it looked like the marauders behind were greatly blinded.

"Good! They ain't gonna be seein' us in this blindin' light," said Calis.

"That means they're vulnerable," said Logan.

He spun around into a 180-degree turn and sped back toward the marauders.

"Logan!" Vanis yelled.

"I'm going to kill him!" Rampras roared, "Come about!"

The marauders saw only two humps ahead: the M1 Abrams tanks. They could not see any of the squadron in their sights. But Logan had a clear view of them. He unveiled his plasma blade, preparing to slice their lines in half. There wasn't very much of them left: six bikes, one quad, one dune buggy, a jet-powered sand glider, and the huge two-wheeler.

Then two more pops split the air. Rampras saw a long smoke trail from an artillery shell arch past them and explode between Logan and the marauders. The explosion blasted up a dust cloud. The lead marauder saw the shadow outline of a bladed bike rider charge toward them.

Logan charged through the dust and jousted for the lead marauder. The lead biker jolted and fumbled for his single shooting colt. Logan lopped off his head as he sped by. Then his blade cleaved through a gardening claw that attempted to guard a blocking marauder. But Logan ducked under a mobile band saw slicing for his neck. The marauders started to turn around.

Logan slashed down a third before coming to a stop. The Blackhawk behind them all fired off a pair of missiles. Logan sped off into a 180, attempting to hide inside the circus of marauders. The missile pair exploded in the middle of the circulating crowd, while two tank blasts added to the dusty chaos.

By the time Rampras entered the dust fog, bullets criss-crossed in all directions in chaotic calamity. Nobody could see who was firing at whom. Missiles and tank fire kept adding to the visual screen. Faint images of riders zipped by. The squad split into two directions, covering the outskirts of the dusty cloud. The riders tailed each other, circulating in a ground-based dogfight.

Martin tailed a biker along the outskirts. Two artillery shells exploded off to his starboard. The sand showered over Martin, but a dust cloud swallowed the marauder. Martin kept on his tail and speared into the cloud. He squinted, sand grains scratching his face.

He came to a fog clearing. A dune buggy sideswiped the marauder's bike. Metal parts splashed about. The biker toppled over the buggy, but the bike slid under it, tearing off the front axle from the buggy's vehicle frame. Martin swerved around the tumbling wreckage, nearly scraping his face from the buggy's hind fender. He was in total shock from its suddenness.

Vanis curved a long left. The two-wheeler appeared on her tail. She curved between two exploding sand geysers. The two-wheeler's driver whipped out a nail gun and blasted the steel pins at her. Each pin slammed into Vanis's regenerated shield. Then she disappeared into a subsiding fog.

Vanis came out the other end and saw a biker with a mobile band saw slicing for her head. She barely skimmed under it. The band saw sliced a few threads on her black gown. Then her eyes flashed white. The band saw biker's eyes became hijacked with a white glow. He steered at Vanis's tail and rammed his bike head on. The tailor screamed, but such a screech could not stop a bike.

Samiren was tailing a bike through a series of dunes, artificially created by explosion blasts. They went uphill. The marauder veered right. Samiren was about to pursue. The Blackhawk launched another missile pair directly at him. Samiren tried to swerve away but the missiles collided.

Smoke and dust swept in an out-roll. Bike parts showered the area. Samiren emerged from the smoke and dust, rolling to his feet. His arm's cannon formulated and aimed at the Blackhawk, blazing off a sonic boom that could cause avalanches in a thirty-mile radius. The blast shredded the Blackhawk apart and pieces of the once-mighty machine dropped down in flames.

"That coulda saved us a lot of that trouble if ye did that before," Calis yelled out, zooming by. "I'm jus' sayin'!"

Calis and Multanis tailed the jet powered sand glider. They kept out of the propeller's wake as it would slow them down or dislodge their traction. Bullets exchanged in rapid fire between them. The sand glider's gunner blasted coins from a wide barrel shotgun. Multanis cringed. The coins showered all over his bike and armour, slicing into the metals by a half inch.

Calis blasted a series into the propeller's central turbine itself. The bullets punctured the rotator and jammed lead into its gears. The propellers halted. Calis and Multanis sped around it, peppering the whole sand glider with lead. The gunner and driver took several in the chest.

Rampras saw Logan gaining on a biker ahead, one of the final few. He came to Logan's port, yelling over the engines.

"We're running out of decoys. We have to take out those tanks."

Logan sighed his frustrations but agreed.

They saw Samiren slicing up a bike ahead. The biker in front of Logan wanted vengeance. He slammed his foot on the petal and charged in full force. Samiren saw him coming. Logan kept up with the biker, trying to beat him to the punch. The biker pulled out an antler-axe and whipped around, closing in.

The biker tried to slash him, but his antler-axe shattered onto Samiren's shield. Samiren, simultaneously, just grabbed the bike itself, spinning from the excessive momentum. The force bucked the biker off. Logan swerved away from the spinning chaos, but slashed the biker as he landed. Samiren sat the bike down, got on, and rode again.

The squadron's seven bikes stormed toward the oncoming tanks. They gunned down the final biker during a curving crescent to get on their tail. They were free from further interceptors, but those tanks had at least a two-mile reach. The squadron each turned on and armed their bike's integrated rockets, aligning their bikes in formation.

"Make ready!" Rampras yelled.

Logan could see the tank barrels aiming at them. Their images were taking full shape.

"Aim!" yelled Rampras.

Logan could see the barrel's black holes now. He got scared over Rampras's dramatic delay, but dared not anger him further. But Rampras knew what he was doing. outcast technology was not known for its accuracy. Rampras didn't want to take any chances, but waiting was risky.

"Fire!"

Seven pairs of rockets launched simultaneously from the bikes. They left a contorting cloud of dust in their wake, blinding the vision of two tank blasts. But its sound gave it away. The tank shells crossed paths with the missile fire. Each left behind a comet tail of smoke.

One tank shell blasted far off but the other exploded just before Rampras and Calis. Their bikes banged into the explosion cave and both of them were sent flying in the air.

The missile pairs took turns slamming into both tanks. Each explosive bite ripped metal fragments from its chassis. The tanks caught fire and halted to a stop. Two drivers opened the top hatch and scampered out of the flaming metal beasts. But their burning selves spelled their futures with doom.

CHAPTER 16

SOJOURN

Rampras fumbled onto the sands. Calis landed on his ass, sitting up, and slid a few meters toward the burning carnage.

"Ah! Front-row seats!" Calis remarked.

The squad circulated around and stopped before Rampras.

"Captain!" yelled Multanis.

He got off his bike and gave him a quick assessment. The metal-plated armour cushioned most of the blow, while the softness of the sand did the rest. Rampras was just sore.

Rampras grunted but got up. He stared toward the horizon back at Zodia. It was so far away now. But hundreds of shimmering surfaces were moving along the cliff sides.

Rampras took out his binoculars and gauged them. There were hundreds of vehicles scaling the cliff base, transporting at least several thousand marauders.

"Corlance's army," Rampras said. "They're going to attack."

"Where?" Calis questioned, "There's at least three of our

settlements along this side of the sand lands...and Epsilon's right smack in the middle."

"They're not going to attack Epsilon," Rampras assured, "Corlance said he was part of a settlement council once and I know it's not ours, mate. Chronos is southwest, but we headed north and apparently that army did too. That means they're heading to Aquarius."

"Aw hell," said Calis, "Aquarius took more beatings from them chimeras than any of the western settlements. Corlance don't stand any chance."

"Corlance is a strategist, mate," Rampras reasoned. "He knows how they operate. He knows their defenses and can exploit their own tactics against them. That makes him the perfect enemy to take down Aquarius. If he has enough man and fire power, he just might. We've got to get a hold of a radio tower and warn them of the oncoming threat."

"How we doin' that without bein' seen?"

Rampras looked around. Up north, blinks of light flickered from the horizon — the very blinks of light that warned of an electromagnetic storm. The dark clouds at the base of the second fragment's magnetic pull proved just that. Their magnetic polarities caused friction and disturbed the atmospheric balance.

The whole squadron sped toward the electromagnetic storm. Rampras instructed them to turn off all copper-wire machinery. Logan was concerned about Samiren, but he was a machine of fibre-optic wiring. He was well insulated. Their bikes themselves were ancient and motorized, and were not affected by the EM pulses that would've disabled them.

"YEEEEHAAAAAAWWWW!" Calis screamed as they reached the outskirts of the storm. The squad dipped into the thick cloud walls. It was loud. It was windy. It sounded as though trains were wrestling with each other.

Logan felt his head pound from the difference of atmospheric pressure. Multanis explained that psionicists were pressure-sensitive.

They soon came into a clearing. Blue rays showered the fields. Electrical surges sparked from cloud to cloud. Huge rocks, once mighty stone pillars, populated the air with spiralling, floating rocks. All the while, Logan watched in awe as several tornadoes twisted and danced within the eye of the storm.

The squadron kept within the outskirts of the eye. Logan was mesmerized with the subdividing and combining of these airy monstrosities. They warped. They changed. They never stayed the same shape as though the nostrils of the gods sucked and destroyed the world around them.

They came out the other end of the storm and bolted for a tower at a rocky corner. As they drew in closer to the tower, Logan noticed it wasn't a tower at all: it was a base or a mansion suspended above ground by four arching legs. He couldn't tell if anybody was alive in there, but did notice a diagonal elevation shaft that took those to the summit.

Calis called it the Monocle Citadel because it spied on an excavation site under it that once quarried the rock sides. Nobody knew what happened to the inhabitants, but they knew it took thousands of man-hours to build. Logan figured the outcasts kept it as a visual landmark because it could be seen from miles away.

They sped between a roadway that took them deep into the quarry. Many aluminum scaffolds were set up along the clay walls braced by metal beams. Many of the mining equipment was left behind, but Logan saw skeletons of humans and different beasts in the area.

They passed the quarry and sped up a long path along the hillside that took them into a series of ravine cracks similar to Zodia's. Logan figured this was used as a maze of some kind to lose chasing intruders. But hardened sand gave away the path of the most travelled areas.

After several twists and turns, they saw a bridge of steel ahead. Dozens of vehicles were driving across it. That was Corlance's army. They were moving fairly slow for a massive armada. Logan saw why. The M1 Abrams only sped to fifty miles an hour and were bulky things to turn. Plus they had transports hauling several Blackhawk helicopters and rocket-launch pads.

They slipped under the army with very little notice. Seeing seven bikers was like seeing everyday traffic that travelled the low roads. The squadron passed several excavators travelling on foot and hauling steel utensil ware.

The ravine walls eventually faded into a wall full of mushrooms. Soon the mushrooms were getting larger the farther they went until eventually, the ravine itself flowed into a forest of brown-spotted mushrooms reaching as high as fifteen stories tall. Logan was amazed with the sheer mass of the forest.

Calis explained that radioactive alterations caused these mushrooms to balloon in size — that and survival necessities. But that didn't stop Calis from grabbing a mushroom and eating it. Logan gawked at the sight. Calis gave it to him to try. Logan declined, fearing poison would enter his system. But Calis insisted and so Logan gave it a try. It was like meat and celery.

He was surprised it was edible.

The squad sped out of the now size-decreasing mushroom forest and came to a plain, watched by a massive floating mountain. It wasn't just any mountain. The mountain was upside-down and only tethered by two mountain tips touching each other as though a mirror reflection. Several large rocks floated and orbited this mountain-of-physics insanity.

Multanis said this was Bytopia. *He should have called it limbo*, Logan thought. He saw a town within the Bytopian Mountain that was upside-down and opposite from their gravitational pull. He figured that people walked up the mountain, then sideways up the touching tips, then upside-down to get to the mountain.

How strategic it was against enemies, Logan didn't know.

After three hours of travelling, they came adjacent to a very large plain full of desert plant life, but it was far from barren. Plants sprouted everywhere but in moderate patches. It wasn't enough to fill the whole field with grass. But it supplied hundreds of mutated animals migrating to other sections of the fragment.

Logan couldn't believe his eyes when seeing herd after herd of animals. There were goats, rabbits, rats, and coyotes at first. Then he saw the long extinct mastodons that supposedly grew hair during times of cold weather.

Cockroaches, mosquitoes, ants, earthworms, spiders, and scorpions were of heavy abundance too. They seemed to supply the hungry falcons, vultures, and hawks that flew overhead. Even salamanders were seen. But Logan couldn't believe his eyes when he saw a variation of prehistoric life walking before him.

There were four brontosaurus-like creatures migrating ahead of the pack, with a family of velociraptors travelling with them. He wondered why those raptors didn't hunt the brontos. He did remember a story of a backpacker who once travelled the arctic and told of how wolves travelled with caribou herds.

The zest for life filled each of these creatures. They all survived by their own means and their intelligence proved it so.

Logan couldn't help but feel the power behind these creatures' will for life. Being able to survive these harsh lands proved almost an impossible feat especially with no visible water for miles. But these animals somehow flourished and developed their own ecosystem.

He could only wonder how they did it every day.

An hour later, they came by another doomsday cult, but with a circus show in addition. Logan wondered if it was the same cult or a different one altogether. He couldn't help but think of where they were going, what they were planning to do, or how many cults had perished for being so objective-less. He couldn't understand why these people of morbid mentality would just outright give up.

He, himself, was a survivor and would never give up. Life treated him too harshly just to lay himself down in defeat. The only way to go was forward. He knew that. He always knew that. Perhaps his years on the streets hardened him into discovering that the only defeat possible was one defeating oneself into submission. Beyond that, there was only the option of moving forward.

He quickly dismissed these thoughts when he saw a visual intrigue. The squad passed a town of trinkets and experimental technology. The squad could not stop for gas because they had no method of exchange, so they continued on. Logan saw that mutants and cyborgs were of population abundance here. Perhaps they felt outcasted by regular society and founded themselves a home.

Logan felt warm inside, knowing that no matter how screwed up a person was in this world, there was always a place to belong. He watched the town of pipes, wind farms, and gizmos disappear in his rear-view mirror and planned to go back someday to see any innovations useful for survival. To him, this was only his first adventure, but one he would never forget.

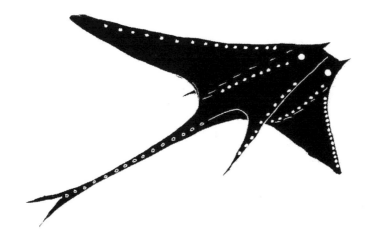

CHAPTER 17

COLLISION

They heard an inhuman screech, a screaming of a thousand voices binding together. It was as though each voice synchronized in perfect harmony but octaves apart, but it was only one screech from one monstrous voice.

This haunted the squadron to a stop. They stared at the northern hills. Lines of laser fire, plasmatic charges, and bursts of glowing acid sprayed above a ridgeline. Screaming, roaring, and mechanic grinding were all of sonic abundance. Fire blazed and highlighted the horizon with a faint red glow. Smoke of black and brown infected the skies.

Logan couldn't tell what was happening. But he recognized the stylistic configurations of a vessel, protected with plasmatic plates, fly over the ridgeline.

With the added sight of tentacles curling and diving over the hills, he knew this was a grand Cy-Corps-chimera battle zone — the two very oppressors of humanity.

"How badly y'all want to be doin' hero thang?" asked Calis.

"Corlance would be stupid if he came anywhere near," said Rampras.

"That don't mean we should be them dumb ol' goats," said Calis.

"Calis's right. This is too risky," said Multanis.

"The periled we unhazards jeopardy," Vanis stated, "and not for any's sake a risker takes."

"Samiren, what's our survival rate?" Rampras asked.

"Slim," Samiren announced.

"Ye call that statistics? Where's all of that ultra bot number crunchithon show?" Calis complained.

"Captain, I really advise against going through those lines," said Multanis.

"I know, mate," said Rampras, "But that battle can halt Corlance's advance. We're a small force. We won't be perceived as a threat, and if we make it through, we can beat Corlance to Aquarius."

Just as Rampras said that, a loud growl erupted. A serpent-like tail with red glowing spots whipped over the ridgeline, crashing into something hard. Logan was very nervous from approaching that war zone.

"And what if they do that super scanner thang and see us lil' wee measles scoopin' up under their eyes...eye...eye things?" asked Calis.

"Be us too small to be important things," Vanis reasoned.

"Until both forces detect a psionicist," said Samiren. "Cy-Corps and BioDyne fully acknowledge the threat of mental utilization since Khared-Turo."

"And ye the freak that killed our hero, ye bastard!" Calis spat at him.

Samiren didn't seem offended or showed any signs of caring. Logan never thought of that before. He did find it odd that the squad accepted Samiren as one of their own. He figured he was a neutral subject for being a reprogrammable machine capable of instant change. Blaming him was like blaming nature.

"We'll scale the ridge side around the battlefield," said Rampras, "If we have to, there's a BioFarm nearby we could take shelter in. Their force fields were designed to ward off enemy attacks. Sound good?"

No one else had anything to add. They gazed at the carnage ahead. Only a maniac would dare go near that savage battle, but it was something they were about to do. They saw a cluster of explosions go off. A Y-shaped Cy-Corps aerial unit bombarded the area with plasmatic blasts. Several flying manta ray-like creatures with red glowing spots were hot in pursuit. Seeing that didn't help.

"Ready?" Rampras asked.

But no one had to respond to give the okay. They sped off between lumps of rock, patches of sand and desert weed, and into remnants of debris. The grand ridge had most of the battlefield in a bowl. The northeast housed a grand glowing bubble on top of a hill. The one-mile diameter bubble shield looked like it could space enough growth for a small farm.

But Logan was more interested in what was going on over the ridge. He saw the Manta Ray fliers bombard the battlefield with drops of glowing red acid. Several laser beams from battle below sliced in the fliers' wake. He saw several tentacles wrap around a Cy-Corps sentinel and pulled it down, despite the many objections fired from its weapon ports.

The squad came to the base of the ridge and scaled alongside the up-slope's base. Logan wanted to drive right in there and see everything. He couldn't believe how much both of these forces evolved since their newscasts on pre-nova Earth. But when he saw a mutated whale suspended in air above the battlefield, he knew that these things only evolved because of each other.

They couldn't have been mere people, he figured. *They must have been animals once. Some may have merged together,* he thought, *or DNA taken from dead fossils and were used to create specific beasts.* Logan realized how powerful this chimera virus was as a biological tool. He thought of all this as he watched blast fire, acid streams, and explosions erupt over the ridge.

He figured BioDyne scientists probably tried to use this to amplify regular soldiers and got out of hand. Then the chimera agent merged people together to create monstrosities or infected other animals. But how did they get loose? Rampras never said that part. Maybe he didn't know. Whatever the case may be, he couldn't help but feel how out of this world all of it was.

Perhaps that was why Cy-Corps created their defense platform. He remembered a series of discussions concerning both companies before the nova, but could never decipher the political jargon. But he got the feeling both companies perceived the other as a threat. Now their internal cold war became an outright total war through the artificial offspring they left behind.

Logan felt unusually grateful that there were two forces instead of one. One force dominating the other meant they could wipe out the last of humanity. But since there were two and of equal strength, this allowed them to be busy just enough for humanity to survive.

What an uncanny stroke of luck, he thought.

Until the ground tremored, shaking off loose dust. Bulges

and humps formed on the sandy surface. Then a massive tentacle spiked up from the ground.

"Mytus worm!" Calis yelled, swerving around the tentacle.

Several tentacles speared through the surface barrier. Each tentacle sported the trademark of the chimera's red glowing spots. Their black scales protected against intruding bullets. Yet each tentacle acted independently as though it had its own mind. The squadron curved out of their reach.

The glaive-headed tentacles arched and stabbed. Each strike slammed near, creating archways to pass under, while more tentacles harpooned through the floor. Logan struggled to turn and swerve. These tentacles reacted as though lightning. His bike clipped the scaly wall of a tentacle, nearly dislodging him.

A large funnel sprouted up from the ground, blocking their path. The scales lightened around its rippling neck muscles. Two carapace plates unfolded and exposed the worm's flytrap face. Huge finger-like teeth unwrapped around its mouth, fashioning three sets of grinding jaws. The squad halted before it and gazed up in awe at the four-story-high Mytus worm.

The Mytus worm jerked its neck back, its tentacles behind them sucked underground. The worm spat out large balls of mucus from its throat glands. The mucus egg-spores slapped onto the ground and unballed from their mucus cocoons into humanoids. Their red spots gave away the shape of sophisticated stalkers that Logan had not seen before.

"Go, go, go!" Rampras yelled.

The squad hammered on their petals. Tentacles speared up from the ground. Rampras blasted rounds at the worm's neck, but clipped his bike on a tentacle. A tentacle spearhead stabbed Multanis's bike and threw him off. Calis halted and blasted as the others dodged hooking arches, fishing for movement.

"Get back here!" Calis yelled.

Rampras and Multanis got up and blasted wildly in all directions. Bullets smashed into tentacles and the circulating stalkers that looked for a clean opening to take them down. Calis kept the self-conscious stalkers at bay with suppression fire, while the rest of the squad curved a 180 back.

A stalker leapt between tentacles and landed on top of Rampras who blasted a clip load in the stomach of the flailing stalker then bucked him off. Black puss sprayed all over his armour.

Multanis saw, "Captain!" and tossed him a hydro-can kit.

Rampras blasted away in one hand and sprayed himself with steam with the hydro-kit with the other. The steam ate the black puss away with boiling temperatures, easily and quickly disinfecting himself.

Logan took lead and slashed an opening back toward Rampras. Vanis noticed the Mytus worm jerking its head back a second time. She slanted her bike and slid to a turn-stop. The bike jetted away as Vanis hooked a foot onto the sand. She took stance and palmed a stream of kinetic force.

The Mytus worm's red spots flickered in glowing waves along its neck and toward its mouth. Then it squeezed out two narrow pillars of glowing acid from its glands. The acid pulse sprayed toward Rampras and Multanis until a wave of telekinesis dislodged its path.

"Psionic force detected," Samiren informed. "Cy-Corps units engaging."

The Mytus worm growled at Vanis, then a line of tentacles speared up simultaneously toward her. Vanis gazed at the oncoming line.

"Move toward the tentacles," Rampras yelled.

Logan thought he was nuts to suggest that. Vanis ran toward the closest tentacle that hooked over her, stabbing at her last position. The tentacle could not curve on itself. But another oncoming tentacle could. It curved around the one hiding Vanis. She blasted a stream of lightning at it, frying its nervous system into twitching jerks.

Logan cut his way through the garden of tentacles toward the cased-in Rampras and Multanis, while Martin guarded his back. Rampras and Multanis backed into a wall of appendages that hooked over them. They fired mercilessly at the strafing stalkers.

A tentacle swept across the sandy dunes in front of Logan. Logan slapped his bike on the ground and slid under. The tentacle caught Martin's front tire, crumpling his bike and tossing him over the tentacle.

A half-dozen stalkers took notice and broke off from circulating Rampras. They charged and leapt at the fallen Logan and Martin. Logan saw them coming as he stood. He slashed down

two before they landed. Logan kept them at bay as the bruised
Martin rolled around on the sands in agony.

Samiren watched from afar as several tentacles dipped
underground, repositioning themselves for assault. The squad
looked like they were about to be overrun. He didn't seem like
he was going to do anything. But that didn't matter. His motor
sputtered and choked until it quit altogether. The gas in his motor
ran out. He couldn't do anything anyway.

Logan twisted in circles, sweeping wide strikes at the
evading stalkers. He noticed Samiren still far north along the
slopes. Samiren suddenly quirked his view toward the slopes.
Logan glanced in reaction.

A dark machine, cased in plasmatic plates with six spider
legs and a large hind abdomen, fired a pair of streaming lasers
from its nano-tech-formulated turrets. The lasers sliced through
the tentacles, creating an opening that roofed over Rampras and
Multanis.

The Mytus worm wailed in pain. The stalkers responded
and charged after the enforcing spider droid, the tentacles slithering
back into their holes.

"Go while they're distracted!" Rampras yelled.

"What about the bikes?" asked Multanis.

"They're low on fuel! Forget them!" Rampras instructed.

Calis grabbed Martin and helped him make a run for it.
Two AT units landed by the droid enforcer and supported it in
warding off the stalkers. The stalkers crashed in melee combat with
the Cy-Corps units.

The squad ran past a fuel-less bike and caught up to
Samiren along the eastern slopes of the battlefield. The bio-farm
and its protective shield was hundreds of meters ahead. But

something was changing. The explosions, roaring, and blast fires were getting closer.

"What's happening?" Rampras asked.

"Cy-Corps detected a psionic presence and sent units to intercept," Samiren explained. "Upon occurrence, the battlelines shifted. Cy-Corps forces are being overrun and are retreating toward the east."

"Y'mean, where we all are right now?!" Calis yelled.

The grinding of tank tracks shook the ground. A dark, massive tower, armoured with plasmatic light and an array of missile turrets, was backing up ahead of them. Its one-story-high hind tank tracks grinded the sandy slopes into powder.

"It's a bloody arbalest!" Rampras yelled.

They watched in horror as balls of glowing acid slammed onto the arbalest's plasmatic plates. The arbalest retaliated fire with a cluster of missiles. A line of explosions swept over the slope. A.T. units flew backwards, firing at the stalkers flooding over the slopes.

"They're gonna be too busy with each other. Just go!" Rampras yelled.

The squad bolted for the bio-farm. They ran and watched the clash of lines all around them. Plasmatic plates and carapaces smashed into each other. Claws, jaws, and stabbing legs ravaged through plates of light, while lasers and balls of plasma blasted back.

Logan was horrified at the sight. His mind struggled to comprehend all the shapes and sizes that were being presented before him. He saw a massive mech warrior with huge plasmatic claws reigning devastation on a horde of three-legged spawnlings.

He saw a half-dozen A.T. units land in front of the flooding stalkers, halting their advances with twin-beamed laser blades. These weren't just any all-terrain droids. They had far thicker plasmatic plates. They slashed and cleaved through the stalker lines, slowing the line-breaking rush. Logan stopped and watched. He couldn't help but notice how much they resembled Samiren.

"Proto-Warriors. An unelaborated version of my model," Samiren explained, then grabbed Logan, forcing him into a run. Logan watched as he ran.

He saw several X-shaped probes floating and firing streams of orange lasers at damaged droid units. These lasers did not burn, but instead suspended parts in low gravity and snapped them back together. These must have been the Langolier repair probes that Rampras mentioned before.

The squad ran under the feet of two retreating sentinels. Logan saw two mind flayers dislodging and redirecting missiles back at the massive tripod. He clenched his ears as the loud crash smashed through a sentinel's plasmatic plates. Debris and plates of glowing light shrapnelled onto the field.

Then he realized why they called them chimeric as he watched several mind flayers slam together. Their liquid bodies formulated into one large abomination of a thousand tentacles. The combined mind flayers each growled from faces positioned all over the body. They then let out a combined wail, which flushed a wave of visual distortions. The wave exploded everything around it off its feet and crashed the other sentinel's plasmatic plates in the process.

Several manta-fliers flew past, delivering payloads of glowing acid into AT unit ranks. The acid overpowered the protective plasma, devouring the droids fully. Two huge hydra-shaped snakes further decimated the retreating lines with streams of acid, while a four-legged behemoth of the size of a factory stormed over the slope and crushed Cy-Corps droids with massive incisory tusks.

None of these things noticed the squadron running between their feet. Logan figured these two forces saw their enemy so great a threat they ignored two psionicists running between their ranks. The squadron curved and bent around every debris chunk, foot slam, and corpse tumbling they came across. Logan was so glad the squadron reached the up slope toward the bio farm.

They ran past a Langolier probe as it opened up a fissure of blue with retreating droids stepping into them. Logan figured these were portals or wormholes. He was taught never to seek them out or use them for they could damage the fabric of space in one's wake. He watched several stalkers be sliced apart from the fissure's tentacle distortions and realized it was an effective strategy when fleeing.

They left the battle behind and came up to the doors of the bio-farm. Logan looked back. The chimeric forces were still overrunning the Cy-Corps retreat into open field, leaving behind a wake of explosions and corpses.

Calis narrowed his eyes in total exhaustion. He panted and heaved as he watched the battle diminish.

"That was the craziest ring-ding-a-ling thing we've ever done!" he said, panting. "Can we do that again?"

CHAPTER 18

INCISSION

Calis accessed the door's computer and overrode the lockout with emergency settlement codes. The door opened. The squadron rushed inside away from the continuing devastation of retreating drones.

Two large arches criss-crossed at the centre. They served as the dome's structural beams. The bubble itself was a force field that could ward off artillery strikes. What supported the two crossing arches were five steel pillars: one in the centre, four on the sides. Steel walkways were attached to the pillars, suspending them above ground by twelve feet.

The base of the central pillar sported a large shield generator. It fed power to the force field through a series of thick cables. It also fed power to a metal house made of silicon-steel because of its electrical resistance. The house looked as though it could crunch in a family of four.

Logan found this place impressive. It was one mile in diameter and looked like it could feed at least a hundred people a week. He figured thousands of these had to be made in order to sustain human life and an army of construction workers to build them all.

"Secure the perimeter," Rampras ordered, "Multanis and I will search for radio controls."

"If this big ol' pimple can ward off missile clusters, where's all of them inhabitants?" Calis asked.

They paused and looked around. This place was lifeless.

There was an indoor ranch next to the eastern doors, but no signs of cattle. The only signs of life were the fields of wheat and potatoes, the ultraviolet lights warming them, and the series of wind turbines outside of the dome.

Logan didn't like this. Either enemy had penetrated their defenses or the inhabitants thought they were going to be and abandoned the place. If either were the case, then the structure itself had a strategic flaw. But he couldn't tell when looking around. Of course, he was no military strategist or an architect. He wouldn't be able to spot it if he saw it.

Then a loud static fizz screeched the ears. The squad gazed at the eastern shield facet. Several stalkers smacked onto the force field.

"Do we need to be worried?" Logan asked nervously.

The stalkers burrowed underground. Logan looked at the ground inside the dome. It was sand and soil, connected to the outside.

"Yes!" Rampras growled. "Everyone! Topside! Now! Go, go, go!"

"Radio's on the east side!" Multanis pointed out.

The squad climbed up a circulating stairwell on the eastern supporting pillar and fanned out along all four arms of the pillar. Suddenly, several sand geysers burst out amidst the potato fields. The squad blasted at the holes. But nothing squealed, bled, or came out.

"Cappy! They camouflagin'!" Calis yelled out from his spot.

"Use your infrared specs!" Rampras yelled back.

"But, captain! The EM Storm!" said Multanis.

"I thought they were protected if we turned them off!" Rampras said.

"They're sophisticated instruments!" Multanis explained. "An EM pulse does a great deal of damage to electronics! More so to ones connected to power lines!"

"Motion sensors?" Calis asked.

"They're down too! We're fighting in the blind!" said Multanis.

The snickering of creeps echoed throughout the dome. The squad aimed in all directions, but could not spot the invisible stalkers. The squad kept quiet while listening to the faintest sounds.

Logan was heaving really hard. He was worried he wouldn't be able to hear them, which made it even worse. *Why are you worried?* he thought. *This is just like fighting Solito.*

Then some leaves rustled in the potato fields.

"There!" Rampras said while firing a single shot. It struck nothing. Another bush rustled underneath Rampras's spot.

"Captain!" Calis yelled while firing. Again nothing.

"They're toying with us," Rampras said. "Conserve your ammo."

Again, the silent war continued. No one moved from their spot while being pinned in a open field stalemate. Logan just wanted to charge out on the field to draw them out of hiding, but he didn't know what he would run into.

Multanis thought for a moment and said, "The radios!"

"Ye jus' said the EM Storm got to it," said Calis.

"I know, but the chimera agent!" Multanis said. "The EM Spectrum! Mitosis! The radios freak out when they're close!"

"Great! Find us some tin cups and a string so we can talk about it!" mocked Calis.

"You don't get it! These radios don't have microprocessors on them or batteries! There's nothing to fry!" Multanis said.

He turned on his radio. It was working. Though it spattered and squealed as though damaged, it was functional enough for capturing waves.

"What about the rest of our trinkets?" Calis asked.

The radio suddenly squealed wildly into cacophony. The walkway near Multanis tremored from disturbance. Multanis turned around and blasted wildly along the rail lane. Bullets sprayed all over, hitting nothing.

Then one lucky shot slammed into an invisible object. It tore open a wound of a stalker climbing up and splashed black puss outlining another. Multanis gunned the other down, then blasted a few rounds on the dead corpse, spilling puss on the walkway, hoping to reveal anything through footprints.

Martin's radio scaled wildly. Leaves rustled underneath him in the potato fields. He blasted in small bursts near the leaf movements until black puss contaminated the garden.

Calis flicked on his infrared micro-monitor. It wasn't working. He flicked it off then saw red glowing spots in front of him suspended in midair. Calis booted at it, kicking a stalker out of camouflage, and ended its life with a bullet.

After his fight with Solito, Logan's mind had honed in on fighting invisible enemies. He felt subtle vibrations travel down the walkway. He glanced down the walkway and saw a visual distortion. He flicked his wrist into a simple slash, which struck nothing.

Then wind flowed upward through his hair. Something just jumped over him. He launched a blinding slash behind him, which grazed the steel railings. Sparks bounced off an invisible object and a blur of bluish light slashed it.

Vanis kept her fingers arched and arms nearly in an X

cross, in stance for a quick electrical burst. She was nervous. She wasn't as keen as Logan or the others. She didn't know what to look for.

She motioned her hands into an orbital, spiralling flow. Wind stirred up in the dome, shaking off loose leaves from their sockets. Martin and Rampras got her plan and kept an eye on anything that disrupted the current. The leaves suddenly bounced and flowed around three invisible humps.

"There!" Rampras yelled.

He fired a burst at the humps, splashing black mucus. Two stalkers screeched and bolted for Rampras, irritating their camouflage into a noticeable visual anomaly. Martin saw the humps and fired. The bullet trails scaled behind the stalkers' wake until they climbed up on the rail after Rampras.

Rampras unleashed a full clip load at the oncoming stalkers. His rifle kicked off. He switched clips, only to hear a thud behind him. He turned around. A visual distortion flirted with his eyes. The figure swiped at him, breaking its camouflage.

Rampras guarded with his rifle, but the swipe's force slammed him onto the ground. He loaded one bullet into the chamber itself and blasted up at it.

The bullet slashed through the stalker's head and struck a pipe above them, which he didn't even notice before. The pipe's fissure splashed out water. It quenched the thirsty potato fields below and smeared water, outlining a stalker.

"Multanis! Turn on the water systems!" Rampras yelled as he gunned down the other noticeable stalker. "And get that radio going!"

Multanis bolted for the pillar and followed a satellite cable along the pillar's walls that was connected to a dish embedded above. The wire led to a circuit breaker. He found a switch indicating water and switched it on. Water piped in through the aluminum tubes and sprayed out.

The water outlined dozens of stalkers slowly creeping up on the squadron from all directions. The startled squadron reacted with bullet fire.

"Holy hell and all the demon heavens that twinned it!" Calis cursed.

The squadron worked to flush back the stalkers. Bullets slashed into the stalkers' ranks that easily outreached the stalkers' arm-length attacks. The stalkers fled back under the railing, using its ceiling to cloud them from the sprinklers.

Multanis looked through the control panels. There were so many foreign controls. He couldn't tell what century the technology was made from.

"Calis, what kind of tech is this?" Multanis asked.

"Tech?! Thought ye were the apple-thumped, finger twiddler of white coat insanity!" Calis said before giving it a quick look. "Analog!"

Vanis stood on the walkway between Martin and the pillar. She had been sweating. The water diluted the sweat and flushed down to the floor. As each droplet slammed into the ground, breaking apart into smaller drops before evaporating, it added to a powerful odour — odour that was released into the air.

It was an odour that smelled awfully sweet for sweat.

Martin sniffed, "What's that smell?"

Then a whole crowd of squealing came into hearing. They caught wind of it. Leaves rustled like crazy. Radios scaled wildly. The horde of invisibility made itself known. Bushes rustled and water splashed, leaving dozens of trails crashing toward Vanis.

"My odour's wake," Vanis gasped. "They come for me to mate!"

"Get that radio up now!" Rampras said.

He blasted into the stalker crowd. Calis supported while Martin covered Vanis. Logan leapt off the walkway and stormed toward Martin and Vanis's position. His keen senses rapidly snatched clues from rustling leaves and moving water bodies. His swirling blade met them in a cleaving arrest. His mind and body whisked away into a series of fluent slashes that engulfed him into melody.

He felt so bewitched. He still didn't know where this skill was coming from, but he couldn't stop his blade from spiralling out of control. It made him feel like the master of music in motion. Everything around him faded from his attention as his blade — his instrument of art — tornadoed away, cleaving down unfortunate stalkers that happened on its path.

Stalkers kept decloaking underneath Vanis, attacking each other, clawing at each other, leaping for the railing, while others leaped on top of them, sabotaging their chances.

Vanis felt so incredibly aroused by the amount of stalkers coming for her, fighting for her, seeking any chance they could just to touch her. A powerful high flushed through her body, intoxicating her into a drunken state of lust. Her eyes slanted. Her mind spun wildly. She heaved incredibly, while her skin glimmered with excessive sweat.

But she fought it. She resisted it. She couldn't do that with any person other than Logan. She couldn't even understand why so many stalkers would be after her since she couldn't even attract men.

But she couldn't think anymore. Something was taking

over her. She was in extreme heat and had this powerful craving to mate with thousands. She ran her hands up and down her body, preparing herself to be taken...even if it meant by force. Even if it meant death.

Multanis kept flicking switches until a recording played on the radio's intercom. It was an emergency beacon.

"To whom this may reach," said a woman on the recording. "We're stranded in this BioFarm and the creeps are trying to get in. We can't escape."

Calis kept firing into the stalker ranks as he listened in. Multanis finally found the right control set and synchronized the radio frequency.

"She's ready, captain!" Multanis yelled.

"Cover me!" Rampras said as he ran to switch spots with Multanis.

Rampras got to the radio and grabbed the receiver.

"Rampras to Settlement Epsilon. Come in!" Rampras said.

"Rampras. This is Epsilon Communications," said the operator. "Scathers is furious with you."

"That can wait! I need Aquarius's frequency code and priority clearance. There's going to be an attack."

"An attack?" the operator objected in doubt. "Hold on. Bringing it up."

The emergency beacon kept playing. With each word spoken, it sunk into Calis's ears, disturbing something from its peace.

"I don't know why we even try," the woman's voice continued. "This world is doomed and we're all just waiting to die."

Suddenly, Calis's expression changed. He lowered his rifle. He froze suddenly and stared blankly into nothingness. His eyes gave off an expression of extreme dread, like the woman's voice just hit a pause button.

"There is no life beyond this place," the worried woman spoke. "This world can't sustain itself for much longer. We're all going to die!"

Then screaming was heard on the radio and a loud growl became responsible for its end. The radio beacon cut out and Calis's dread built up in his eyes. Suddenly, Calis started scratching himself, vigorously, wildly behind his neck. He was about to snap.

Martin kept firing into the stalker crowd. He didn't even notice Vanis and her awkward episode of lust. Suddenly, Martin stopped firing and looked at the formation in which the stalkers were gathering. They were all crowding and bunching underneath her. There was something about that formation.

He was inspired, fascinated. His mind raced with possibilities. Possibilities that could solve many problems. Problems that had outcasted him from the in-crowds of military intelligence.

Martin reached for his portable chalkboard and bolted for another walkway bridge to work. He wanted no distraction, but left Vanis unprotected.

A stalker dropped onto the steel walkway before Vanis. She heaved in fear and lust as she pinned her back to the railing submissively. The massive bulk of muscle, armoured with a blackened carapace, towered over her, dominating her with its presence.

It gritted its teeth inches from Vanis's face, threatening her from movement. Vanis closed her eyes, panting uncontrollably. She slowly lifted up her dress, exposing the skin of her parting legs.

Deep inside, she was screaming. Screaming for herself

to stop. Screaming at herself to act. But her mind was in a storm of chaos that no psionicist could ever penetrate. It broke down language, thought, and idea at its core process and distorted it into nothingness.

It was like she took a backseat from her body's actions.

Her eyes caught a glimpse of Logan, her desire, her love. She saw how he got so swept away with his own skill. Nothing else in the world mattered. But he mattered to her. It broke her heart that she didn't matter that much to him.

Multanis kept firing at the loose ranks. The stalkers had re-circulated its crowd of bodies, which piled up under Vanis.

Then Multanis's aim was getting worse. His hands began to shake. His face sweated the fountain of his youth away. His breathing heaved from the tightness in his lungs.

Multanis dropped to one knee. His heart was pounding, pounding far harder than it was capable of. It wanted to give up. It wanted to peel over and die. It wanted to rest from the stresses of its life.

Multanis fell to the ground, immobilized in health. He reached for the ceiling and his chest, gasping for air.

"We're all gonna die," Calis muttered in whispered tension.

He held back a flood of fear that wanted to burst through his dam of courage. Tears built up in his eyes and his breath gasped in rapidity.

"We're all gonna die!" Calis screamed out in terror.

He exploded into action. He laughed crazily. He cried psychotically. His rifle's bullets filled the air in a ricochet of chaos. He fired in all directions, hitting nothing, hitting everything, hitting anything still a stranger to himself.

He had totally lost it.

Rampras fumbled with a piece of paper and redialled the radio channels.

"Rampras to Settlement Aquarius. Come in," said Rampras. "This is a priority one message. Come in."

The radio fizzled with complaint until it honed in on a stable frequency.

"Rampras. This is Aquarius Prime. We read you."

"Aquarius. There's going to be an attack--"

A stray bullet smashed into the radio's base.

"Damn it! Where the hell are you shooting?!" Rampras cursed.

Then he turned around and saw the non-existent battle. Rampras couldn't believe his eyes.

"What the hell is going on?!"

Logan got carried away. Multanis was on the ground. Vanis was being seduced. Calis was on a rampage. Martin was nowhere to be seen and Samiren had been standing idly by. He didn't even notice Samiren all that time. All this happened while the stalkers were so busy destroying themselves.

Rampras was stupefied with the situation. He wasn't sure what to do. His squadron broke and he was redheaded with fury. But he sucked up his anger and forced himself to think strategically. Logan and Samiren were capable. Multanis was down and needed help. Rampras had no idea what the hell Vanis was doing, but Calis and Martin needed some sense slapped into them.

"Samiren!" Rampras yelled.

Samiren awoke from an idle state. Rampras pointed to Calis. Samiren gave a quick assessment of the situation then walked toward Calis.

"Logan!" Rampras called out.

Logan looked up. Rampras pointed to Vanis. Logan finally noticed and his jaw dropped in disbelief. The stalker slithered its tongue all over Vanis's neck, absorbing her scent, and she was enjoying its slimy touch.

It was on the brink of entering her.

Logan couldn't move. He was in shock, in pain. He wanted to freak out at the freakish sight he was seeing.

Then Vanis's eyes met his. She saw him gazing back. Her eyes widened. It snapped her out of her lustful spell. She gazed at the stalker and quivered out frightened breaths. The stalker noticed the pheromone change and growled at Vanis. She heaved and whined in total terror.

"Help me. Please," Vanis managed to squeak out.

But Logan couldn't. He was still in shock and memories of loss flooded in him that even Vanis sensed. Memories of the lost Cherise.

"Please...help," Vanis mouthed at him.

The stalker let loose a ribcage-shaking growl. Tears of extreme fear flooded her cheeks as she locked her desperate eyes on Logan, begging for help.

"Please..." Vanis whispered.

Her mouth concaved into the most sorrowful, painful arch.

Logan couldn't bare it. He couldn't bear to lose her as he lost Cherise. He couldn't bear to see her in so much pain, when all her loveliness came out in her smile — a smile he put on her face for accepting her into his life.

He gripped his plasma blade with all his might and stormed up the stairs, leaving a wake of stalker bodies slashed up in his path.

The rejected Stalker flashed a gaze of hatred at her, a stare that could burn a hole in her head. Vanis glanced back with the saddest apologetic look.

"I am so sorry," she quivered.

A violent roar slipped into hearing and a blur of light beheaded the rejected stalker. As the stalker's body toppled to the ground, Vanis threw her arms around Logan and let out a devastating cry.

"I couldn't help it!" she bawled out. "I couldn't stop myself."

"It's okay. It's okay," he comforted, swaying her in his arms.

"I'm so sorry," she managed to squeak.

She sobbed so hard it threatened to soak his whole regalia with moisture. Logan felt relieved, then realized how much Vanis sounded like a normal person just then. A claw swipe to the side railing dispelled their moment. Vanis squealed. Logan assessed their surroundings.

"We'll have time for that later," Logan said, "Multanis needs help."

Calis screamed chaotically and barraged the dome's shields with reckless scatter fire. Bullets harpooned and scattered all over. As the clip ran out, he quickly interchanged clips as though his life depended on it. Then he fired again.

Samiren came up behind him and unveiled twin blades of laser. Bullets reflected harmlessly off his shield. He grabbed Calis by the shoulder and spun him around. Calis went wide-eyed to the tip of the laser blade in front of his face.

"Sentient being," Samiren growled. "Function properly...or else."

Calis nodded frantically. He was petrified, far more terrified of Samiren than his own paranoia.

Rampras searched the walkways for Martin. The scratching

of chalk gave away his position. Rampras honed in on it and found him near another pillar. He was drafting mathematical equations obsessively.

Rampras ran over to him and kicked away his chalkboard.

"Put that junk away, you idiot!" Rampras roared. "Your men are dying on you! They need you out there, right now!"

Then Rampras came eye to eye with Martin's handgun. Rampras immediately calmed down, coiling up his rage and contempt like a cobra. Martin stood up, casting a cold gaze at the enemy he saw in Rampras.

"The hell do you think you're doing?" Rampras hissed at him.

"I had nough you, Rampras!" Martin spattered as he glared at Rampras with so much hatred. Hatred that leaked out, twitching on his face.

"You yell at me. You call me name. You say I stupid. You no know me. I know me. I KNOW ME!" Martin screamed into his face.

Rampras was hardly affected by the outburst.

"Who you, huh? Who you?" Martin questioned. "You old captain. Old captain! Gonna die soon, captain. That old captain! You yell at me lots! All the time! For what? For why? Because you big tough guy? Huh? Big tough guy?!"

Rampras wondered where this was going.

Vanis came to Multanis's side.

"Just...go..." Multanis squirmed out. "I'm too old...too old."

"Too old to age in here, oh wisest one," Vanis toyed.

She pressed her hands on his chest and concentrated. Logan guarded her from oncoming stalkers while she worked her magic.

"Oh, breathe with me," Vanis spoke with her softest tone. "Let flow the fearest streams."

Her voice suddenly affected Multanis. His facial muscles relaxed from a anxious state, as though a flood of warmth suddenly washed over him.

"Un-dwell those doors and feel oneself renewed," Vanis said.

She gave Logan a look, letting him know he would be fine. Logan was relieved. But the stalkers were still busy fighting with each other. Logan wondered how long before they realized Vanis was gone.

"You think big tough yelling make little guy tough, huh?" Martin cast a questioning gaze at him. "Let see how big tough guy be tough with big tough bullet in head! Maybe tough guy will have big tough funeral!"

That didn't surprise Rampras. He expected this somehow.

Logan saw Calis and Samiren hustle along the walkway. He led Vanis and the crippled Multanis there. Logan looked around. Rampras and Martin were still nowhere to be seen. The two teams met between the two pillars.

"Oh, you're back," Logan said snidely.

"Go suck on an egg, popsicle," Calis retorted. "Where's Rampras?"

Samiren pointed. They saw Martin pointing a gun to Rampras's head.

"Oh crap," Calis let out.

"You treat me like I no matter," Martin whimpered. "I matter! You no see me like I no exist. I exist! Then, you see me... like I no important. I important!"

"Martin, I need you," Rampras assured with such assertion.

"You no need me. You have squad. I better than squad. I smarter than squad. Me! Squad! I squad!" trailing into a whimper.

"I squad. Everybody hate me...because I so smart. But no one need me. No one want me. No one care me! NO ONE!"

Martin pointed his gun to his temple.

"Martin! Don't!" Calis yelled.

Martin lashed out amidst the sobbing, "I hate stupid war. I hate stupid world! I hate stupid life! But most of all...Rampras..."

He aimed the gun to Rampras's head.

Everyone gasped. Martin suddenly went calm.

"I...hate...you."

His finger squeezed the trigger tighter.

Rampras narrowed his eyes, keeping his rage encaged.

Everyone watched with jaws dropped.

Vanis hid her face in Logan's chest.

Suddenly, there was a loud pierce. Then total silence as the piercing sound reverberated around the room. Martin, disorientated, looked down to his stomach. A bone tentacle pierced through his steel body armour.

He looked up. Doom was in his eyes.

The tentacle lifted Martin in the air. His weight forced him to slide down the tentacle. The tentacle's bony sides tore the wound wider. Martin screeched in excruciating pain, so terrible it would haunt dreams for months.

"MARTIN! NO!" Calis yelled.

"MARTIN!" yelled Vanis.

The tentacle split at its end, slicing Martin's body in half. Blood splattered everywhere, painting the area with Martin's fate. The two halves of the lonely soldier fell from the sky and the enraged Rampras growled.

His fiery eyes followed the tentacle to the base of the

perpetrator. It was a Mytus worm. It was still unburrowing into the dome.

Rampras heaved with acid rage and drool flung out of his mouth like lava. His eyes reddened far more than blood itself, as though to redefine its color. Oh, he was so going to destroy that worm.

But the Mytus worm struck first. It let out a bone-rattling squeal that alerted the stalkers. The leftover stalkers halted their in-fighting and saw the worm. They shrieked at the squadron over their humiliation and charged.

"Uh, cappy?" Calis said.

"Weapons free!" Rampras growled.

The squadron blasted a full volley at them, slicing their ranks thinner with a tsunami of bullets. Stalkers pounced and climbed up side railings, but were intercepted by the intruding glows of Samiren and Logan's weaponry.

Within seconds, the stalker ranks dwindled to a half dozen. The demoralized retreated into the canals they came from and the Mytus worm shrieked at their cowardice. Rampras smirked.

The worm speared several tentacles near its base, using them for defense. Rampras saw two or three of these appendages were headless. It was the same damaged one from before. It had come back for revenge.

"Eye for an eye, is it?" Rampras commented with disgust.

"What we doin', cappy?" Calis asked.

"Tentacles first, then its base." Rampras ordered. "If you mates flip out on me, you're useless, and I'm gonna shoot you if you do. Got it?"

Everyone went silent.

"Weapons hot," Rampras said.

The whole squadron readied. The worm coiled up several tentacles for assault. But Rampras wasn't scared. He had taken many beasts down during his years. This worm was no different. But Rampras was determined to cause it pain before it died. Rampras gave it one last look, then readied his weapon.

"For Martin," Rampras whispered. "Open fire!"

The squad unleashed its blast of rounds. Tentacles curved around the worm's base, shielding it from bullet fire. Samiren and Logan leapt off the walkway and charged in.

Tentacles speared up from the ground and wrapped themselves around the nearest walkway, tugging at it, tearing off a bridge section. Steel wires sprung off the torn bridge and whipped around the dome. Metal fragments ricocheted off the walkway's railing. The whole bridge system quaked from the sudden slack.

The squad backpedalled away from the broken bridge and centered around the eastern pillar. Several tentacles whipped at them. The three soldiers ducked under the swipe as tentacles wrapped around the eastern pillar, muscling it to warp. Metal screeched as it was crunched. Vanis and the three soldiers fanned out to the other bridges.

"It's destabilizing!" said Rampras. "Logan! Samiren! Cut them down!"

Logan and Samiren ran through the forest of tentacles. They came to three of the offending tongues slithering around the pillar. Logan hacked at a base, cleaving a massive scar into one. The tentacle flinched, let go, and concaved toward Logan. Samiren slashed through another, then saw Logan tumbling by him, followed by a crash of dirt behind.

Vanis flashed a blaze of lightning at a tentacle reaching for a bridge farthest from the worm. Electricity showered all over its carapace, frying its nerves. A tentacle brother swept at her, seeking vengeance for its brethren's limb.

Vanis posed and a flash of light engulfed her whole. The tentacle crashed onto the bridge, snapping it in half, but missed the teleporting Vanis. The crash rippled through the system even more and the eastern pillar shuttered. The bridge system shifted balance and the squadron tumbled along the railing.

Rampras and Multanis got off the floor and blasted a full clip load onto a tentacle wrapped around the pillar. Black puss spewed in constant streams until the appendage was sliced in half. The tongue of muscle sank back into the ground. One more was still wrapped around the pillar.

"Calis, use your sweeper scope," Rampras said. "Take out its neck!"

Calis attached his sweeper scope on and waited for an opening in the tentacle wall. He saw one. Tentacles adjusted its muscles. He took aim and blasted. The round speared between two tentacles and struck a red glowing spot on the worm's neck.

The worm uncrossed its boneless arms and uncoiled its neck back. Its neck's red spots pulsated in waves. Calis went wide-eyed and leapt off the walkway. The worm blasted a geyser of glowing acid, which flooded the metal bridge in seconds and incinerated it into puss.

Calis landed on the ground and saw the geyser spraying over him. The acid also struck a portion of the arch, eating away at it. Metal whined with complaining warps. It was bending.

It would have remained stable regardless of the amount of bridges lost. But since the eastern arch was damaged, the last bridge tethered to it caused tension and started to bend the arch inward. Light fluctuated across the dome's force field. It was on the verge of collapse.

"Cappy! Get off the railing!"

Rampras glanced. "Vanis! Cover that arch. Don't let it fall." He then blasted a bullet cluster before jumping off the walkway.

Logan and Samiren launched a series of slashes on the last tentacle gripping at the pillar. The appendage twitched and convulsed as it held onto the pillar with the last of its life. Samiren's blade of laser cleaved the last inch and the outraged worm reacted.

The worm shifted and a tentacle slapped at them. The tentacle's force slammed through Logan's psi-shield, smacking him across a potato field, but deflected off Samiren's. The soft soil cushioned Logan as Samiren sliced up the tentacle that annoyed him.

Vanis saw it all. Her heart skipped when his shield shattered. But she remained focused on her lightning fencing with these monstrous whips, warding them from the eastern arch.

The shield cushioned most of the energy, but Logan was still aching from the impressive slam. He got up off the ground and viewed the battle.

Rampras, Calis, and Multanis were warding off tentacles from ground level. Samiren kept several tentacles busy by being an immovable object, while Vanis guarded with eastern arch. The worm concentrated on keeping the squad busy with its boneless fingers.

The tentacles outnumbered them. Logan had to find some way to shift the battle otherwise that octopus would eventually overwhelm them. He didn't see any critical advantage until he looked at Vanis. She was defending the arch.

He narrowed his eyes in thought. The arch itself was only a long arm. The dome's force field had no mass at all. If the arch fell, the debris would only be limited to the perpendicular line it could cover. Same with the pillar. Small units could easily evade it.

But large tentacles would get trapped.

The worm blasted another glowing geyser. Vanis dammed it with telekinetic force, but she was sweating. Her sweat did nothing to the worm, but her energy was running low. As acid droplets sprayed onto the potato fields, leaving only a smoke of dissolved plants, the geyser finally expired. Vanis panted. She mustered up reserve energy as much as she could, until she saw Logan running toward her.

"Vanis! Get away from the arch!" Logan yelled.

"No! Stay at your post!" the enraged Rampras rebuked.

"We need to let it fall!" Logan explained.

"Are you insane?!" Rampras argued. "That arch will crush us if it fell!"

Vanis wasn't sure what to do. She wanted to listen, but listening involved reprimanding Rampras's wishes. She knew she didn't need to follow him. Yet he was the one responsible for keeping the squadron alive many times in tight situations. She knew Logan was very intuitive. For him to contradict an order outright meant he had a plan, and it didn't seem like a selfish one either.

Logan thrust himself onto the walkway. Vanis sensed Logan's confidence immediately as he drew near.

"You know how parents say 'don't stick your fingers where they don't belong?'" Logan explained as he pointed up the arch.

Vanis gazed up at it, then looked at the long tentacles. She got it.

Then she glanced at Rampras. He was growing angrier

by the second. She saw a tentacle concaving toward him with his back turned. Vanis gasped then blasted out a beam of light from her forehead. The psi-blast spearheaded onto the tentacle's head, throwing it back into a convulsing jerk. Rampras turned around and saw the dazed tentacle flopping around.

Rampras was shocked. That was a deathblow and he didn't even see it coming. That wouldn't have happened if he was paying attention, which made him angry. But Vanis's act let him know that she was an ally no matter what, even if it meant she didn't follow him. Rampras only gave Logan a dirty look over his shoulder, then went back into battle.

To Logan it was a reluctant look of approval. He was relieved.

"Guys! When the arch falls, run past it!" Logan announced.

"Why? What's happenin'?" Calis asked.

Logan was already hacking at the arch.

"Holy crap balls!"

Calis bolted underneath the last bridge and across the potato fields. Multanis ran second while Rampras covered their rears. The worm saw the retreat and launched several tentacles at them, diving in and out of the ground. Samiren intercepted two with a slash of a blade as he retreated with the squad. Two tentacles dove for Logan. Vanis slapped them aside with a blast of a telekinetic sphere.

The blade of searing plasma left red blotches of melted puss on the steel beams with every slash. The beam creaked as it shuttered inward until finally the top shaft sprang off fragments from its cleaved areas. It slid down the molten puss and the dome's shield fluttered. Logan leapt off the walkway followed by a gliding Vanis.

The arch fragment's foot slammed onto the last walkway bridge, crushing it. The inner bow arm of the arch remained intact. But the outer bow swung toward the pillar itself, collapsing into pieces. Metal chunks slammed into the pillar's base and bent it east. The pillar's top ripped off its hinges, which brought the inner bow down with it.

Dust swept across the potato fields and debris flung through the air. The worm squealed in pain as the rattling of fallen metal stung the ears. Rampras and the squad backed away from the controlled wreckage, but quickly gained sight of the catastrophe.

The dome's force field fought to stay alive as a gap in its defense was now evident. But the fallen bridge crashed down on top of two tentacles while the arch trapped several others.

Rampras finally understood the plan. Most of the tentacles were disabled. The base itself was left defenseless with the exception of two wounded appendages, while the rest tried to tug themselves free.

Rampras uttered a glory-filled roar, "Open fire!"

Then he blasted at the worm. The squadron blazed out a fury of bullets. Vanis pulsed out a psi-blast. Samiren and Logan cut down the two guarding tentacles with a series of slashes before attacking at its base.

The Mytus worm tried to ward off the attackers with a blast of glowing acid. But Vanis dislodged its course and the worm was left defenseless. It took every bullet, every slash, every blast into its body as it squealed for its life. As the barrage of violent vengeance left its body mangled, the worm let out one last growl before crashing to the ground.

That one single crash quaked the ground and rattled the debris again. The puss of blackest futures spewed out of every wound like a thick avalanche of snow. Rampras gawked at it in disgust and ignited a flare. He threw it into the puss, which engulfed the worm in flames.

It was defeated. Rampras was glad. But loss quickly filled his eyes as his thoughts turned to Martin. Then something gurgled.

"Help...me..."

"Martin?"

CHAPTER 19

COALESCENCE

Blood had stained the sands. The very blood that once boiled with hate now pumped his veins with terror. His heart skipped beats, squishing out thick pulses as though his strength faded with every pump. His chest weighed heavier with every breath, stinging his lungs with acid.

He felt the flames of hell searing down on his lower half. He tried to move, but only felt the phantom essence of his lower limbs echo beyond his body. His fingers gripped onto the sands with all his might as his muscles tensed with boa constriction.

He was dying, his horrifying screams rumbling through the area with haunt. His nerves felt the burn of electricity surge through him with fear, with panic, with a devastated blaze of agony.

He couldn't do anything. He was helpless. Hopeless, with only minutes left in his future. He couldn't believe it. It was going to be the end. He didn't want it to be the end. He didn't even begin.

He gazed up at the sky in total plea. There was a massive hole in the dome's force fields. The shields around it fluctuated, but there was a clear view of an asteroid field. It glimmered teasingly into Martin's eyes.

This was the last sight he was going to see. A dread filled him and he let out a devastating scream.

"Martin!" Rampras yelled.

Martin lay in wreckage between pillar and arch chunks. Snapped metal wires were everywhere. The squad muscled through the debris and then came to Martin's side. They paused in total shock. They took in the horrible, dreadful sight of gore. Blood was everywhere. It kept squirting out of torn arteries.

His intestines had spilled out onto the sands. Logan couldn't even look at his body as it all looked red with clots and chunky stew. He didn't even mean to get a glimpse of his spine, which stuck out through the gore.

"We're here, Martin! We're here!" Multanis said with worry.

Calis unlocked Multanis's metal pack and unloaded a med kit. Martin was so pale. He quivered and sobbed with compressed pain and fear. Sweat flushed out of his body, which made the naked eye see its own reflection.

"Gonna have to clamp those arteries. Move!" Multanis said.

Everyone backed away while Multanis worked his magic. Vanis held his hand, which gave him little comfort. Martin let out an ill-fated whine that trailed their hearts with sadness.

"He needs morphine," Rampras asked.

"No, it'll lower his heart rate," said Multanis.

"His body's energy depletes with speed," said Vanis. "Not I who can replenish it to mend."

Multanis had trouble clamping his arteries. Too much blood gushed out, which flooded the veins from sight. Multanis grunted with frustration.

"Just cauterize it, doc!" Calis said.

"Next to lacerated intestines?" Multanis retorted. "There's methane and hydrogen there. I'll ignite him in flames if I do."

"You no let me die, right?" said the sobbing Martin.

"No. I won't let you die, Martin," said Multanis.

"Yer gonna be alright there, buddy!" said Calis. "Just hang in there!"

"Please, no let me die," whimpered Martin. "No let me die. No let me die," he kept repeating as his voice led into a haunting sob.

"Need a clean piece of cloth," said Multanis.

"Don't have any," said Calis.

"Then give me a dirty one!" Multanis roared.

"Won't that infect him?" asked Calis.

"There's a piece of fat there and don't want him to have an embolism!" said Multanis.

Calis handed him a handkerchief. Multanis ripped it from his grasp and stuck it in the gore. He used it to grab the fat while the clamp held another artery closed. He pulled it out along with a thick blood clot. Blood gushed out more as the clot was removed.

"Crap!" Multanis said as he hustled to close it off.

Martin hocked as he felt the weirdest pressure changes in his body.

"Noooooo..." Martin cowered into a whimper.

"Listen to me, Martin!" said Multanis as he worked. "You're going to make it, okay? You're going to make it! You're going to go home, have a nice long rest, then you'll be back to do the awesome work you love."

But Martin only replied with cries.

"It pisses me off how good you are, you know that?" said Multanis. "And I went through nineteen years of university. Worked at the most acclaimed laboratories. Even worked for the government. Then here you came in, not even half my age, and just blew everyone right out of the water. Makes me so fricken mad!"

Martin didn't care about that. Extreme agony engulfed his reality.

"We can't lose you, Martin. Not now," Multanis said. "Not now."

His breaths were getting lighter. His skin kept getting whiter. Eyes around him kept getting sadder, as it seemed like Multanis fought with the inevitable. Then Martin whimpered something that crushed their hopeless hearts.

"Mom...."

"You're losing him!" said Rampras.

"No, Martin," said Multanis, working even faster to sew the arteries shut.

"Mom!" Martin barely uttered out in a desperate whine.

His eyelashes began to flutter. His arms whipped about wildly in convulsion. His breath hissed as it fought with the last ounce of strength it had to sip the air. Then an image of a woman holding a newborn flooded Logan's mind.

"No! Logan! Close your mind!" Vanis yelled.

But Logan felt it all. She was happy, but cried instead. The baby cried because it was so scared. She held the child. Swayed it in her arms. She was so in love with the beauty of her creation.

Logan was pained. He was in agony. He stood up and backed away from the failing Martin. Memories exploded out of him and flushed into Logan whole, burning into him the person that was now a history.

Logan fell on his back and scampered away from the sudden rush of sadness. Vanis came to his side and cradled him in her arms. But Logan couldn't take it. He didn't want Martin to be history, the history that bombarded into his mind. The history of little Martin being surrounded with toys but with no friends to play with. And the lonely birthday cake that was celebrated in an empty house.

Logan saw the eyes of a sad Chinese woman and how she wished she could give little Martin a better life. He saw how she pushed school so hard in Martin so that his intelligence brought riches to end their poverty. And the hopeful butterflies in Martin being crushed upon sighting his first crush.

Memories of sadness, failure echoed on repeatedly as though without end: kids teasing, bullies beating, girls laughing at him, and the constant nightmare of reaching out to his mother as he was dragged into a bunker.

He cried a lot. He cried so much when he lost her to the nova. He had been alone for so many years without a single friend to offer him belonging. But one memory stood out for Logan that caused him so much dread.

He saw himself fighting the outcast marauders during the transport battle and felt how much in awe Martin was when seeing the skilful display of swordsmanship. Nothing had surprised Martin more.

The waves of memories receded. Logan felt the dread of knowing Martin's fate. He was gone after suffering such a horrible death and no amount of tears would ever bring him back.

Vanis held him as tears flooded out.

Multanis closed his eyes and sat back in defeat. Calis was teary-eyed and Rampras felt that blow. There was a sorrowful silence as thoughts began to flow. Thoughts of their dearest friend, whom they wished had more time, faded in the deep and dearest parts of them.

The squad sat quietly for an hour. Memories still lingered. The only one unaffected was the distant-souled Samiren. But guilt plagued into Logan. He kept thinking of Vanis's words and how right she was:

The needs of others far exceed our own, for who are we without their greatest aid? To see one self-divine then be alone, for lonely souls cry out the greatest creed.

"Think not those thoughts that burn you so engraved," Vanis said.

"But I killed him," Logan whimpered. "I killed him. I could've saved him. I was only thinking about myself. I was only thinking about...me."

She swayed him back and forth, humming a soothing melody. Logan took comfort in Vanis as the guilt flushed through him.

The Earth's core shifted slightly since then. It beamed in a ray of light that passed between two distant hills and shone onto the grave. Rampras, Martin, and Multanis sat nearby. All were lost in thought until Calis spoke.

"So what we doin' from here, cappy?"

Rampras looked through the debris fields. Small blinks of light flickered along the horizon. Rampras figured the once great Cy-Corps-BioDyne battle shifted into a scavenger hunt for retreating drones. Even a few hunting stalkers could be a serious menace to an entire army. One swipe of a claw could infect them all. Rampras figured Corlance wasn't stupid enough to go near the war remnants, which bought them more time.

Rampras was worried about how to get a warning back to Settlement Aquarius. Their bikes ran out of gas and all of the radios were shot. Walking would take at least two days, but on open fields, it was dangerous.

Rampras didn't want to think anymore. He was beaten and bruised from the breaking of his squad.

"I don't know," he said simply.

But Calis knew there was more to it. "What'd ya mean ye don't know? Ye the captain. Ye always draftin' up blueprints to tear the walls of Alcatraz."

"So all the ideas have to be mine?!" Rampras growled at him. "While you were poking the shield with bullets out of sheer fun, I was bust my ass off making sure that you mates live!"

"Captain!" Multanis injected.

"What?!" Rampras snapped.

"We're tired," Multanis said. "We're all tired."

Rampras glanced around. Fatigue was in their eyes. They had barely rested and it was no wonder they were exhausted.

They had no holidays, no weekends, no days off. They had no pay, no pension, no insurance that secured their well-beings. It was like they spent their entire lives giving without reward and got nothing but food and a bed in return. Their entire lives became the fight for survival and now they were tired.

"And so are you," said Multanis. "It's like this world's sapping the life out of us. I mean, what do we do? Where do we go from here? Do we just keep fighting until we die? Every single one of us? I mean, what kind of life is that?"

Rampras looked overwhelmed. He quickly sat down and kneaded his face with his palms. He had no answers.

Suddenly, something sparked in him, in Logan. He felt that feeling before. He had been in that spot so many times without end. He felt that pain, that despair, that hopelessness without a future. He knew nothing but agony and solitude his entire life. It had never let him go.

"It's like a vampire," Logan let slip. "Feeding off you every day. Always constant. Never-ending, as though one's whole life was in forever pain."

He remembered the days he was dirty and in tattered clothes, grieving over the loss Cherise. He was living in a ventilation shaft in the old world, staring out at all the happy families and all their lives he so greatly craved.

"It's in there with you every day, following you everywhere you go, burning inside of you, feeding off you, wearing you down to your last breath...like...it's never going to end."

He struck dead on and the evidence was in their eyes. They all felt every word he spoke as though it had been true for years.

"I remember this story someone told," Logan said. "It changed my life."

*   *   *   *   *

A blind guy had lived his entire life in the dark. He couldn't see. He had no eyes. He never saw until one day he did. He saw this light, this powerful light, on the horizon up on a hill. He followed it, climbing up that slope, then walked over it and wandered. Until he bumped into this woman.

She was broken, in tears, in agony over her shattered life.

So he said to her, "I saw you. Saw you from over the hill. You were crying. Why were you crying?"

She said, "That's impossible. How could you see if you have no eyes?"

"I saw a light. I followed it and I found you," he said.

"I don't understand. How can you see?"

"When a soul cries, I can see it. It gives off this glow because it wants to be seen. It wants to be heard after all the pain that it's been through. But when I walked over that hill, I was blinded by that light. I was blinded by how powerful it was."

"But I'm broken. It's not powerful. It's not powerful at all," she replied.

"You don't understand. That light wasn't a beacon of pain. What you don't realize was that the light that I saw...was really... strength."

*   *   *   *   *

They felt it. They all felt the power of that story. It drew something out of them from the power of Logan's words.

"And since that day," he said. "I continued on...no matter how hard life was for me. No matter how much pain tore me down, no matter how much agony this world struck upon me, it gave me fuel. It gave me strength."

Then his voice gave off this powerful quiver.

"It burns within me. It fuels inside of me, igniting the world with this blazeful awe. It will never let me stop. It will never let me go. It's forever eternal like the shine of the stars."

He stood up and gazed out of the dome, viewing the shattered Earth.

"This world, this shattered world..." said Logan, "...has never been about one person. One person's pains or glories, dreams of light or nightmares of despair. No. It's about the people, the people that wanna live. They wanna live...for each other. It's all the connections that they have that bind this world together. Not the fractured dirt spilling out into the sky."

They all gazed out of the dome at the fractured world.

"And that's what we have to protect," said Logan with a fierce rumble. "The memories, the laughter, the tears. It's all they have. And I will not stand idly by and let my comrades fall. I will not stop as this world shatters itself apart. For that light, that glow within us all, is constant...like the force of the storm...dancing to the wail of the banshee...and letting its blaze scream with war."

And so their eyes lit up with life, with strength, with divine power they never knew they had. They stood up from the ground, with years of inner flames powering their very souls.

"Yeah! YEAH!" said Calis. "I'm with ya all the way, buddy!"

"Hell yeah!" said Multanis.

"This facility should have a vehicle," said Calis. "Let's search for it."

Calis and Multanis grabbed their gear and took off.

But Vanis was in tears. She was in love with the radiance within him, inside Logan's soul. He was coming to life. He was becoming something so powerful no one ever dreamed would happen: a beacon of light, of hope. An archon of power that flourished in the depths of despair.

It was a power that this world needed, a power that would move the world, uniting it together under one breath of emotion. It was streaming through him. It spiraled around him and it would infect all of those who came in contact with it.

It was a power that would change the world.

She saw it. She saw it all and she was in love with it. She wrapped her arms around him as though threatening never to let go, wanting to be with it, wanting to forever bond with this glow.

"My dearest glow," she said. "I give myself to you."

He never knew he had that in him. He was so proud.

But as his eyes happened upon Rampras, he saw a strange look on his face. Rampras looked sad like he just lost something so significant. Something he could never do on his own that Logan had swirling around him.

Anger was his life. Anger was his fuel and taking that away left him with nothing. Rampras had carried his team on his back for so many years until that moment when they finally broke. And when they did, he didn't know how to piece them together again. Until Logan rose them from the ashes.

To Rampras, it was a significant loss. Brute force had its limits.

So Rampras left for the front doors as a truck started up from someplace. Samiren stood outside on the outskirts of the dome's wreckage. He was staring out in the horizon lost in thought. So Logan came to his side.

"Ironic," said Samiren, sensing Logan's presence, "People were shattered in a united world, but it was human emotion that united people together in a shattered world. Now that same emotion shattered that unity...causing two human armies...to war."

"Don't deny something we all know you have," said Logan.

"Don't mistaken denial for reluctance," said Samiren. "Humanity is flawed. I want no part of it."

"Imperfection is perfect in an imperfect world," said Logan. "And it's not supposed to be any other way. That's what makes the world go round."

Samiren gave him a dirty look. Logan let out a weak smile. Then a jeep horn disrupted their moment. A twentieth-century armoured jeep sped toward them then spiralled to a stop.

"Hey, you two! Look what I found!" said an excited Calis. "How 'bout we do some hotdoggin' on this wild stallion? YEEHAWW!"

They all got in the jeep, but Rampras was still quiet.

"Where to, Cappy?" Calis asked.

Rampras had drifted, until he realized Calis was talking to him.

"Aquarius."

And so they left, speeding off to the north, leaving a wake of dust behind their path. They left behind their sorrows, their pains, and the grave of Martin that united their shattered selves.

Every one of them had a glowing memory of him. Memories that finally became important. Memories that they would forever cherish.

CHAPTER 20

FRONTIER

They followed the BioFarm's locomotive tracks, which were usually used to transport food into Settlement territory. The tracks led between clusters of asteroid craters until coming to a rock cut with a pathway slit in between. A listening post was situated above it. Its long turret surveyed the horizons.

Because the jeep had a transponder, indicating it to be Settlement-friendly, the listening post's defendants did not respond to them. But that concerned Logan. He wondered how easily it was to penetrate Settlement territories if anyone got hold of those transponders.

The rock slit led them into a grand valley, a half-pipe of rock that stretched north for miles that was populated by sand, rocks, and desert weeds. The tracks were parallel with the main roads.

Logan saw many hoof tracks migrating in both directions. These roads were used frequently, either by traders on camels or neo-animal hordes. But he couldn't see any vehicle tracks. That puzzled him until he realized settlement vehicles hover and leave no tracks.

Rampras looked over the window and onto the ground. "Good! Corlance didn't make through here yet."

"How can ye be tellin' that?" Calis asked.

"No tire tracks and that LP's still up," Rampras said. "That would've surely gave them away to Aquarius."

"They all could've just travelled through Epsilon's breach," said Calis. "It's on the same path anyhow."

Rampras didn't think about that. He finally realized why they were attacking now. If that were the case, they didn't follow the path the squad took and used the much longer path, the valley inside Settlement territory.

Rampras got worried that it was too late. He couldn't predict who was ahead of whom. But if they took the longer path, it meant they had already penetrated through the investigative team at the damaged LP.

Seeing a massive outcast army would've surely made Epsilon nervous enough not to attack. But as long as Corlance kept out of range of their settlement defenses and kept in between the valley of listening posts, he could march in the clear toward Aquarius without resistance.

But Scathers would've easily responded with a bombardment of missiles. A few of their Tomahawks could easily level a football field. The only reason they wouldn't is because of low ammunition reserves, which had been a constant complaint recently. As long as Corlance made it look like they were just passing through, that would've fooled Scathers into letting them go.

Unless they didn't know the investigation was eliminated. Then Epsilon wouldn't have had a clue about the outcast army. That one valley was a visual pocket capable of hiding an army. All of the listening posts surveyed outside of the valley. Not inside, which Rampras always thought was idiotic. But it wouldn't have done any harm if no one knew. Only traders used that path.

But Corlance knew and now Aquarius wouldn't see them coming.

The only way they would be spotted is if they used aerial

units. That would surely be noticed on radar. But the squad saw them being hauled on transports, on ground level and under radar detection.

Rampras growled. Either Corlance was a brilliant bastard for knowing all of that or took advantage of an awkward stroke of luck. Either way, Rampras didn't know what was happening beyond his sight. He had to get to Aquarius.

Suddenly, Logan felt eyes on the back of his head.

* * * * *

eye SEES them! eye SEES them ALL!

* * * * *

"Wait! Wait! Stop!" Logan yelled.

Calis slammed on the breaks. Logan stood up through the armoured jeep's top hatch and surveyed the landscape behind them. He saw nothing.

"What's happenin', popsicle?" Calis asked.

"Nothing. Just go," Logan said.

They sped off toward a distant hill that looked like it had houses chiselled onto it. But if Logan had waited a few seconds more, he would've noticed something moving in the sands.

Aquarius was the north-eastern tip of Settlement territory. Its main base resided along an upslope of a hill and guarded the rock wall that gated the grand valley. Anything north led into Cy-Corps territory.

Houses were put together by stone slabs and a stone wall to block the south winds. Outside of those walls, a great town of tents was set up in open fields. Only a primitive fence marked the edges of town.

Rampras gazed up a silvery building deep inside Aquarius's

base. It was the only building that had a flashy sign: "CALYPSO." Rampras narrowed his eyes and let slip a disgusted grunt.

The squad's jeep sped toward the southern checkpoint. The gate guard waved at them to slow down. Calis slammed on the breaks again.

"Whoa! Hold on there!" said the checkpoint guard. "What can I--"

"--Captain Reginald Rampras. Beta Squadron," Rampras said. "Contact the officer in charge. Marauder forces are coming!"

"Captain?" the guard questioned.

"Evacuate these people to the bunkers!" said Rampras as the jeep drove deep into the tent town.

Logan watched the town's civilians. They kept looking at the jeep. The squad was attracting a lot of attention. Soldiers were talking on radios then started moving people to the main base.

Logan suddenly felt an irritating ring in his ear and Vanis clenched her gut. She groaned in agony and disgust.

"You okay?" Logan asked.

"A distant storm shall come for water hauled," Vanis said.

Most people would've passed that off, but Logan was becoming an expert in Vanis's use of words. He knew what was coming.

The base's walls were guarded by several towers, each with its own turret. The jeep drove up the hill into the main base's south courtyard. Logan saw many chiselled streets made up of hardened sand, resembling the Middle East.

A tall man, in his mid-fifties, already wearing battle armour, marched over to the oncoming jeep. His white buzz-cut hair mismatched his darker stubble. But his sharp features, wrinkles and dehydrated skin signified his experience.

"Colonel Bowle. Gamma Squadron," said Colonel Bowle. "You better have good reason for arming my forces, Rampras."

"A massive outcast army is heading this way," said Rampras. "Led by Corlance."

"You don't say," said Bowle. He took a moment to take it in. "That dirt-eating terd. I always knew his banishment would be the death of us."

"We need to contact Settlement Epsilon," said Rampras as he and the squad got out of the jeep. "We'll need the reinforcements."

"Well, hold on there, son," said Bowle. "How massive are we talkin'?"

"Enough to punch a hole in any settlement defenses, mate," said Rampras. "He's using an entire Zodian gang to do it. Armed with a full armada of excavated old-world technology."

Bowle didn't like that. He understood the threat very well. He gestured the squad to follow him as he led them toward communications.

"What can you tell me about him?" Rampras asked.

"Intellectually assertive," said Bowle. "He's a politician, but a brilliant strategist. We found evidence of him selling information to the marauders."

"He suggested that Calypso set him up," said Rampras. "Now he's coming back to get revenge."

"Aye, probably," said Bowle. "But don't lose sight that he banished himself for the faulty appeal from the likes of Calypso."

"Are you saying he left on his own?"

Bowle stopped and sharpened his gaze at Rampras. "What I'm saying is, if he didn't step one foot into Zodia, he would still have political allies in Aquarius. But now he burned all of his bridges and it's beyond delegation."

Bowle's gaze drifted, reflecting back. "Those were strange times. But there is one thing we can depend on that we can use against him in battle. This man has a conscience...somewhat."

They came into a building with a lot of electronics running. Logan couldn't tell what these machines did, but it looked like an entire network of communications. Monitors surveyed many areas in the dune lands, while others made security passes inside Aquarius.

Bowle led them to a room with a huge fifty-inch plasma LCD screen. He dismissed the communication officers and let the squad wait outside. But Logan had to peek in. He was too curious.

Bowle took manual control and dialled in. A communications operator came on the screen. Bowle requested for the commanding officer of Epsilon and the officer patched him through.

Then the screen fizzled, but another face came into the screen. It wasn't Scathers. It was an overweight man in his mid-sixties. He was decorated with many old-world awards and had features of strict discipline.

"This is General Wes Zintlaris. Alpha Squadron," said Zintlaris.

"Zintlaris?" Rampras said with much disgust. "Where's Scathers?"

"Don't you be dissing me, boy," Zintlaris sneered. "Scathers is in Grid Zone Thirteen."

"We need backup at Settlement Aquarius," said Rampras. "We have marauder forces inbound."

"Marauders?" Zintlaris nearly laughed. "That hardly calls the attention for Alpha forces."

"We've got people here!" Rampras argued. "And the marauders are very well organized! We need reinforcements to help ward off the attack!"

Zintlaris rolled his eyes. "So many lives at stake, Captain. So many preposterous pleas for help. We set the training margins. We set the performance standards and we've been counting on our officers to utilize their own resources to their maximum capacity! If you cannot handle the defenses of Aquarius, what makes you think you deserve to wear that uniform?"

Rampras was dumbfounded by his response.

Then Zintlaris glared at Rampras, strickened by a point of the finger. "If Aquarius is lost, I would hold you personally accountable for its downfall!"

Rampras couldn't believe his ears.

"General," Bowle interrupted. "I understand that many--"

"--Get out of my face, maggot!" Zintlaris slammed.

"Sorry, sir," Bowle said, backing off.

Logan wondered why the hell this Zintlaris character was even in command. Who would follow him? Why would they follow him? Something was definitely off with all of this.

But Rampras didn't know how to respond. Then some part of him told him that maybe Corlance was right...about everything. So he dared a question.

"General," said Rampras. "What's the Galilea file?"

Bowle snapped a gaze at Rampras, wondering what the hell he was talking about. Zintlaris tilted his head back in full realization. He knew exactly what was going on, or so he thought.

Rampras caught his reaction, realizing Zintlaris knew, but wouldn't dare say. There was a long silence between them.

Zintlaris spoke out, "We're sending an air strike..."

Rampras was relieved.

"...on Settlement Aquarius."

"WHAT?!" Rampras roared.

"Sir, you can't do that!" Bowle raged.

"Did and done. Zintlaris out." Then the screen cut out.

They both went silent, until Bowle asked, "What's Epsilon's best response time from six hundred clicks?"

"Including ready time?" asked Rampras. "Twenty minutes."

Bowle casted a gaze of doom at Rampras. "Why do I get the feeling this file is going to plunge the settlements into civil war?"

Rampras didn't know how to respond.

"I'm surprised you didn't know, mate," said Rampras. "That was the reason Corlance was banished."

"Oh good lord," Bowle was appalled, finally understanding.

Rampras and Bowle quickly exchanged stories to close off information gaps, then decided on a course of action. They came out of the private conference room and walked toward the exit. The squad scampered to catch up.

"Aquarius has a running standard when dealing with chimeras," said Bowle. "That and the fact we're at the edge of Cy-Corps territory, he's gonna have a hell of a time penetrating our defenses."

"But he knows those defenses, mate," Rampras reminded. "He knows how this place operates and he'll surely take advantage of it."

"What's goin' on, cappy?" Calis slipped in.

"We're seizing control of the Calypso building," Rampras said.

"Y'mean to tell me that crazy fantasy land is real?" asked Calis.

"If it is what they say it is," said Rampras.

"Heh. Wow. I guess that be makin' Corlance our ally now," Calis said.

Both Rampras and Bowle stopped.

Then Rampras turned to him and said, "Would you trust the same people who just banished you for hiding the truth?"

"Maybe," said Multanis. "If we all sat down and talked about it."

"We don't know what he wants, mate," said Rampras. "And until he gets here, him leading a massive army of criminals sure isn't worthy of trust."

They marched down to the industrial ward. There were many factories here. Pipes pumped out carbon gasses. Black stains painted the walls and the people working within. Workers took part in constructive lines along side tread rails to dismantle parts from vehicles and other old-world electronics. Metalsmiths, engineers, and electronic technicians made armour, weapons, vehicles, devices, and other things. It was a war-driven industry.

And all the products made sported the "CALYPSO" trademark.

Logan finally understood how tender an issue like this was. Calypso was powering almost all of its military armour. If they were eliminated, the Settlements would eventually exhaust all of their assets and would be left defenseless. This gave Calypso incredible leverage over the Settlements to start making outrageous demands.

But Logan wondered if the people working for Calypso were volunteering or being coerced with currency. They all had acquired the skills and the knowledge to do many of these things themselves. But when he reflected back to the days on the streets, he understood the powerful lure of cash.

It could make anyone do anything they wanted. That, and without Khared-Turo's influence, the Settlements became vulnerable to coercion.

But the Settlements still had the capacity to defend itself, even without Calypso. They had the people, the knowledge, the skills, and the resources. The only thing left that people didn't have was security. If Calypso could promise that — no BioDyne, no Cy-Corps, no worries — people would surely fall in line.

Logan figured that was where Galilea stepped in. In a world like this, something like that was far more valuable than gold. But that was only assuming the rumour was true and Calypso would have to admit to it. But that didn't happen, at least not to his knowledge. And if that were the case, he wondered how Calypso even gained power in the first place.

CHAPTER 21

ANIMOSITY

They came to a silvery building made of marble walls. It stood at least ten stories high with a helipad on top. Massive reflective windows skinned it, while small scanning devices extended out of it. This was a Calypso HQ. They had one for every Settlement to manage local operations. It stood as a monument of what is achievable, but was only glorified to the eyes of the fascinated. To practical people, it was a waste of resources.

Bowle and Rampras's squad marched to the main entrance. It was guarded by two Calypso guards. They wore bulky, silver-plated gear that resembled small mechs as opposed to pieces of armour. Their suit's generators supplied energy to its own personal shielding and to their massive pulse rifles.

The two guards saw the squadron coming, charged their weapons, and aimed their barrels at them. The barrels glimmered with a white glow and screeched with rising energy.

"Halt!" stated the radioed voice of a Calypso guard. "Nobody enters without proper authorization."

"Son, do you realize what you're doing?" Bowle asked. "You are aiming your pea shooter at a colonel, first class, commanding officer of Gamma Squadron and sworn defender of Settlement Aquarius."

The two Calypso guards fidgeted, but didn't move.

"By order vested in me by the council of Aquarius," said Bowle, "I am hereby ceasing operations in Calypso Headquarters for pending investigation."

"Under what charges?" the Calypso guard challenged.

"Treason. Conspiracy to Corrupt Public Morals," said Bowle. "Both are serious statutory offenses. If you resist, that's Assaulting a military official, Murder in the First Degree, Obstruction of Justice--"

"--Nobody...gets in...without authorization," stated the Calypso guard.

He was shaking in his boots, but called Bowle's bluff. Or was it a bluff? Logan was getting confused. Were there laws or weren't there? He heard they discussed infractions in the hall of speakers, but only if both parties couldn't settle it themselves. Maybe there were laws, but only in the back burners of society.

Then Rampras took Bowle aside, "You forget this is the new world, mate. They can shoot you and only get banishment."

"I'm aware of that," Bowle said sternly. "But all things concluded by public consensus can be deemed admittance as law... which...they will be violating. Believe you me, if they ever hear about Galilea, they will consent."

"But taking action before consensus, that's vigilantism," said Rampras. "They won't like that."

"Unless they back down and cooperate first," Bowle said with a clever smile. Rampras laughed. He liked that.

Logan was pre-occupied. He watched the Calypso guard talk on radio. Then jet-powered engines roared from above. A Calypso dropship lifted off the Calypso helipad. It caught everyone's attention. They were running out of time. So Bowle went at it again.

"This is your final warning!" Bowle stressed. "By order of the council of Aquarius, stand down and--"

The dropship above suddenly exploded. A missile trail traced back from the southern horizon. The settlement's siren sounded.

"Colonel!" a soldier on the radio said, "Outcast forces are breaking through the domestic parameter!"

*   *   *   *   *

Civilians were cluttering up at Aquarius's base gates.

Suddenly, vehicles ploughed over the fences. There were hundreds of them: tanks, armoured jeeps, dune buggies, motorbikes — vehicles of all shapes and sizes. Dozens of mech warriors and missile launch pads were hauled on transport trailers. All the while, Corlance stood through the top hatch of an armoured SUV leading the armada into the tent town.

*   *   *   *   *

Rampras looked at the horizon, then at the Calypso building. He couldn't decide what to do.

"If we doin' somethin', we better do it now, Cappy!" Calis said.

"I need you on the field, Rampras," Bowle said.

"But we ain't gonna get another chance at this!" Calis said.

"If we don't do something about those marauders..." Bowle argued.

"Ugh! Can't do both, mate! Come on!" Rampras said as he bolted for the settlement's gates.

They ran across the industrial ward and into the upper plaza inside the main base. Civilians were still pouring into the base. Several soldiers led them down into bunker hatches underneath buildings. Most soldiers were on standby near the barracks, until Bowle fired off orders on his radio.

"Front line infantry, gate side. Auxiliary at back. Psi-Ops units, roof side. Artillery units, man the turrets. Recovery units, assist evacuees to the bunkers. Move radio traffic to a secure channel."

Rampras pointed to Multanis then to the recovery units.

Multanis bolted for them, while Logan, Vanis, and Samiren headed up for the roofs. Calis ran for the front gates.

"Initiate settlement force field," Bowle said.

Logan watched a glowing blue hue flush over the settlement in a bubble. Rampras ran for the nearest elevated platform to survey the oppressors of the settlement. He was shocked. There were so many. They flooded the entire edge of the tent towns with reflective metal. They rattled every piece of metal they got hold of and taunted the entire settlement with psychotic screams.

"Visual confirmation on the armada," Rampras said on radio.

"Relay the info to intel," Bowle said. "Warrant Officer in charge of mobile forces. Inventory report on vehicle units. We need to know our cards."

"Twelve dropships. Two executioner class main battle tanks. Six armoured SUVs in the hangar, sir," said a warrant officer.

"Recall all on-field units and converge at grid zone five," Bowle said. "Fire up those dropships and main battle tanks. Keep them on standby."

Logan and Vanis got on top of the roofs where other Psi-Ops units had positioned themselves. They were near the front gates that branched into two main streets leading deeper into the base. This would've been a perfect ambush site if it wasn't for the open view in front of them. Logan was concerned about sniper fire, but remembered he had psionic shielding.

Several soldiers climbed up the wall stairs and manned the turrets, while soldiers below him were setting up barricades on both sides of the gate. Logan heard several machines powering up. He looked up-slope onto the higher buildings in the base. Several missile launchers were powering up.

Then chatter polluted the radio channel.

"Forward batteries online."

"Activating missile launch pads."

"Fire up the anti-aircraft silos," Bowle said. "We're gonna need them to repel a high-speed air strike."

"We need activation clearance for the missile silos."

"Affirmative. Alpha. Tango. Uniform. Niner. Sierra. Foxtrot."

"That's a confirmation. Anti-aircraft silos are going hot."

"Evac status," Bowle asked.

"Civilians still coming in, but bunkers are filling up fast."

After being lost in the radio chatter, Logan became dizzy. This was all so surreal. He was entering his first major battle, the first of many in an all-out civil war. This was all becoming very real to him. Too real. He heard the roar of thousands of engines, the crazed screams of the outcasts, and the anxious rumours flooding the settlement. He even smelled the gasoline fumes blowing in his direction. All of this was extremely real.

Anxiety flushed through him. His heart pounded. His breathing heaved. His mind couldn't stop thinking about how many people were going to die today, how much blood he'd be seeing. Somewhere deep inside of him he felt guilty. Guilty for waking up. Guilty for knowing. Guilty...for everything.

Vanis gripped his hand. Logan gazed at her. She was scared too.

"All systems check."

"Frontlines ready."

"Auxiliary ready."

"Psi-Ops ready."

"Forward batteries standing by."

"Missile launch units standing by."

"Anti-aircraft silos standing by."

"All units are combat-ready, sir."

"What's the status of the air strike?" Rampras asked on the radio.

"They hit an EM storm, Rampras," said Bowle. "That'll buy us some time while my Coms Officer works 'em down. But don't press your luck."

Vanis suddenly clasped her stomach again. Logan came to her side.

"The closers tread the rims of liquid's lift," Vanis said.

"Colonel. Intel reports several missile launch pads in the enemy ranks."

*   *   *   *   *

Corlance slid off his binoculars and squinted his eyes.

"Hmm. Looks like we have an old-fashioned archery contest," he said. Then he turned to the transports. "Load up the scatterers!"

Marauders unbuckled missiles strapped to the transport trailers, while one got on the computer station. He tapped a few buttons and the missile launchers came to life. The launchers swung around and aimed at the settlements. Missiles were divided into two color codes: red and blue. The marauders loaded up mostly blue-striped missiles, while the rest were red.

Behind the armada of missiles was a convoy of transport helicopters. Propellers started spinning. Strike teams were being loaded on, while others armed the flying machines with rockets.

*   *   *   *   *

The helicopters were in Bowle's view. Bowle was on the balcony of the base's central command, populated with soldiers and analysts. They kept settlement schematics handy while a hologram of the battlegrounds was being displayed. Bowle slid off his binoculars and spoke on his radio.

"I see them, Rampras," Bowle said. "They're going after our turrets. I highly doubt they'll break through our aerial firepower."

"Corlance isn't stupid, mate," Rampras said on the radio. "He will definitely have a plan."

"Good!" Bowle mocked. "I haven't lost a battle in nine years. Let's see what this chess champion can do. All batteries fire at will!"

The ground shook. Smoke flashed from all over the settlement. Dozens of missile volleys blasted toward the sky. The missiles passed through the settlement's shields and continued onwards toward their targets.

*   *   *   *   *

Corlance watched the hundreds of blinking lights erupt from the settlement. Smoke trails sliced up into the air and started arching toward them.

"Launch all charges!" Corlance yelled. "Fire the scatterers behind them!"

A full volley of blue-striped missiles blasted into the air. A few seconds later, the red-striped missiles ignited and fired off, followed by another cluster of the blue. The helicopters lifted off the ground and sped toward the settlement.

*　　*　　*　　*　　*

Logan glanced up into the sky.

The missiles continued to scale up and were about to meet their opponents. As the missiles closed in from both sides, they turned and collided with one another. Explosions scorched the sky in a garden of fire. Then Logan saw a cluster of missiles passing through.

"They're using anti-missiles," Rampras alerted on radio. "And they have a line incoming!"

"The shields will hold, Rampras," Bowle assured. "Don't you worry."

Logan started backing away as the missile line closed in.

"Hold your ground," Samiren said.

But the red missiles overshot the settlement. It exploded in mid-air above them, spilling clusters of fire-cracking sparklers that spun in circles.

"Colonel! We can't get a lock on anything!" said a soldier on the radio. "There's too many targets on radar!"

Then Logan saw a full line of helicopters closing in.

"That clever bastard," Bowle grunted. "Mobilize auxiliary units up front! Intercept those choppers!"

Echoes of footsteps filled the streets. Logan saw dozens of soldiers carrying rocket launchers on their shoulders moving to suitable locations.

*　　*　　*　　*　　*

Corlance watched the line of helicopters on his binoculars. The helicopters suddenly blasted off a missile line at the settlement.

"No! Don't fire!" Corlance said on the radio.

The whole missile line smashed into the settlement's shields, splashing a blue wave along its surface.

"Just land the task units and get the hell out of there," Corlance said. "We need to conserve our firepower."

*   *   *   *   *

The helicopters pressed forward and flushed through the settlement's shields. As they divided and flew toward the vulnerable turrets, rockets blasted off shoulder launchers from all over the base's streets. Smoke trails speared up and torpedoed after the metal dragonflies.

Logan saw it first hand as a helicopter flew not even two stories above him. Rockets chased it beyond his line of sight and a loud explosion reverberated through the streets. Pillars of smoke swept into the air as metal parts flew.

Several helicopters were struck and spiralled down to their doom. Other rockets missed and speared toward the heavens. Gunfire blazed up and down from the helicopter's wake, until the choppers disappeared behind buildings.

Logan kept looking around. He couldn't get sight of anything. Then he heard low-pitched echoes of gunfire reflecting off the walls. Then screaming. Then indecipherable radio traffic. It sounded like heavy fighting.

"What's going on up there?" Rampras asked on the radio.

"Don't know, cappy! Can't see a thing!" Calis responded.

"They're crazy! They have TNT strapped on them--"

Suddenly, a pillar of fire puffed into the air from Logan's left. The explosion rumbled the grounds that he felt on his feet.

Then another fire pillar exploded. He saw only a few helicopters retreating back to the marauders, while the settlement was bombarded with a forest of mushroomed fire.

"Report!" Bowle demanded on the radio.

But there was no answer. Logan saw smoke and debris scatter throughout the settlement. He couldn't see the result, but knew it was bad.

"Yeah, I can see it," said Calis. "They got us, Colonel. All artillery units have been immobilized."

Then another explosion ripped into hearing. It was louder than the others. Suddenly, the blue glow surrounding the settlement dissolved from sight.

"Colonel! The shields!"

Logan felt his security and safety lower as the shields diminished. He gazed out to the horizon at the outcast army. They were winning easily.

"That dirt-eating terd," Bowle said in total awe. "He just got control of the air in five minutes."

Logan suddenly felt even more vulnerable. The outcasts could bombard the whole settlement and the squadron wouldn't be able to resist. He watched the whole outcast army advance on the settlement. Somewhere in those legions of criminals, he knew Corlance was smiling with immense pride.

CHAPTER 22
DERELICTION

There was a civilian traffic jam. People kept crowding around the bunker entrances but nobody could squeeze in. Soldiers kept dividing people and positioning them between buildings. Others took to their homes and began boarding up their windows.

Logan watched them all wander helplessly. He saw a mother holding a newborn in her arms, hiding behind a garbage bin. He heard the child's cries from where he was. The child was scared, hungry, and wanted the mother to make it all go away. The mother cradled the child and swayed it in her arms.

Logan glanced out onto the field. They were in a tight spot. The outcast forces had pushed all the way to the front of the main slope. Any artillery fire would be nearly instantaneous from that range. Then radio chatter flared up.

"Routine status update. All units."

"Auxiliary munitions fifty percent depleted."

"No movement on the enemy front."

"Colonel, the bunkers are full. Repeat. The bunkers are full."

"We should exit them from the north side, mate," said Rampras on the radio.

"Negative," Bowle replied. "North side's heavily fortified. Land mines on field. Meant to ward off frontier invasions."

"What about the dropships?" Rampras asked.

"They were using anti-aircraft missiles, Rampras," said Bowle. "Dropship extractions are a no-go."

Vanis clenched her gut again. Logan rested a supporting

hand on her shoulder. She moaned in discomfort, louder than before. That concerned him. He could only imagine how close it was to coming over the horizons.

"Movement. Front and centre."

Logan took a look. Someone in the marauder ranks used a dirty white t-shirt to stick on a pole. They waved the flag wide enough to see.

"We have a white flag. Repeat. We have a white flag."

"That's a visual confirmation."

"Rampras. Meet me up front," said Bowle.

*　　*　　*　　*　　*

Corlance jumped out of the armoured SUV and glanced at the vulnerable settlement. He let out a one-sided smirk, thinking. Then he adjusted his sunglasses and dug in the backseat.

A muscular figure stood behind him. His skin was ebony, revealed mostly from the lack of coverage his leather vest exposed. Handmade jewellery decorated him, as well as facial studs and iron teeth. He had many scars and had a stained impression of being on the verge of violence. His name was Virgil.

"Ye really banged up those peace kissahs, C.L," Virgil said with a husky voice. "Think ye jus' proved to my brothahs ye ain't an alley cat."

"Was I ever?" Corlance chuckled as he pulled out a black tattered scarf.

"So, whatcha doin' then?" Virgil asked. "Why ain't ya finishin' it?"

Corlance stopped and let out a deep sigh.

"I say we lay the smack down on dem with a couple of bangers, or jus' march our asses in there," Virgil added.

"Maybe they're just waiting for us to waste all of our artillery. Did you think of that?" Corlance stabbed at him.

Virgil went silent. Hatred grew on his face. He hated how Corlance kept making him look stupid. Then Corlance pointed at the settlement.

"That compound was designed from the ground up to withstand micro-nuclear blasts. Okay? It has bunkers!" Corlance said. "And there's a reason why seven of theirs were able to break into our city, cut through our ranks, killing a hundred men...and ran out the other side. Seven of them. Seven!"

Corlance waited for it to sink in. Virgil just stared at the settlement.

"That settlement has four hundred. Armoured and well trained," Corlance said, then shook his head. "No. We step in there, we're dead. But if we can bring them out here...on the field...with artillery support..."

Corlance trailed off with an optimistic brow. Virgil finally got it.

"As long as we remain conservative..." Corlance said, then tugged on his sleeve, "...cards up the sleeve and they're doing the same. Just wondering when it'll show itself."

Virgil looked like he just got his brain beat up. Corlance adjusted his glasses, spat on the ground, then tossed the scarf around his shoulder.

"You may know how to survive on the streets, Virgil," Corlance said. "But out here, if you don't do what I say, then I'm sorry I can't help you."

Corlance walked toward the settlement.

Virgil kept behind him, like a reluctant lap dog.

*　　*　　*　　*　　*

Logan watched as soldiers surrounded Rampras, helping to attach new plates on his armour. They buckled and strapped him in. Bowle was attaching a wire and mic inside his armour plates.

"He's as manipulative as politicians are," Bowle warned. "Don't you trust him."

"I know, mate," Rampras said. "Why you sending me?"

"Because you're a hard head," Bowle said. "You don't budge."

"We can't give him what he wants. Why we even bothering with this, mate?" Rampras asked.

"Courtesy," said Bowle. "And to find out what he might slip. But don't give him any more information than you have to... and don't tell him about the air strike. We've been monitoring, and so far they're running the slowest blast record. Malfunctions to EM Storms. Something...is on our side."

Rampras went silent. He wondered how much of that luck would hold up. After he was prepared, he walked out the front gates unarmed.

Corlance saw him emerge. His eyebrows rose. He was surprised to see him. Virgil was uneasy. Rampras met them at the halfway point.

"Good evening," Corlance said with unburdened delight. "We were just talking about you."

Rampras kept quiet. He glanced around at the outcast army.

"Ugh, where are my manners?" Corlance said. "This is my associate, Virgil. I was just telling him how Squadrons abide by proper military etiquette when it comes to truce meetings. He was worried that the settlement would be....," he quirked his cheek into a half-smirk. "...dishonourable."

Rampras did wish he had a rifle but kept his silence. Corlance noticed it. He remembered Rampras being chattier than that.

"How wrong he was, wasn't he?" Corlance said, still trying to get a response out of him. "I've always trusted the squadrons to maintain their reputation for being the gentlemen of war."

"What do you want, mate?" Rampras asked with haste. "I'm sure it's something we can't give you."

He was trying to hurry it up. Corlance noticed that. He noticed Rampras was pressed for time, but Corlance was giving him a lot, taking the war at a slow pace. That concerned him, but hid it from expression.

"Speaking of gifts," Corlance grabbed the black scarf. "Here."

He handed the scarf to Rampras. Rampras snatched it and looked at the tattered thing, confused.

"That...is for Colonel Bowle," Corlance said with a smile. "It's something he spoke of before I left."

Rampras didn't get it, nor did he care. Then Corlance clapped.

"Now! My wants," Corlance said. "I'll just say Calypso. You'll say no. We'll exchange blank promises and be on our way."

Corlance was about to turn around. Rampras was relieved.

"Oh...there is...just...one more thing, Captain," Corlance said with a smile. Rampras was getting annoyed. "This is pretty much an automatic 'no,' but I wanted you to hear it from the horse's mouth. Just...so you realize the differences in characters conflicting within our ranks. Virgil?"

The spotlight shone on Virgil. He was getting angry at Corlance, but then stepped up to Rampras.

"We want all yer weapons, yer armour, yer women, and yer food," Virgil said bluntly with spit droplets spraying. "Give it up. Give it all up and yer boyz can walk free outta dis hell hole."

Corlance laughed silently at Virgil. He flashed his hands at Virgil with a big smile, gesturing his formal introduction. Then he pointed to himself.

"I...was just thinking Calypso," said Corlance. "They... wanted something else. You see...the whole point of that was...when you rise up the ranks of any hierarchy, the wants of others conflict with yours."

That caught Rampras's attention. Corlance noticed it.

"If you are within their sphere of influence," Corlance added, "and if they hold all the cards, they will stop at nothing to destroy you unless you give them what they want."

That affected Rampras on so many levels. He couldn't tell who exactly he was talking about. Corlance preyed on it, honing in on him.

"And I can tell by your reaction that Calypso has moved against you," Corlance noted openly. Rampras was getting weary. "First in small steps. Then they'll build a compound around you, aligning you up for that one...final...nail...and then they will finish you off...from every aspect...from every corner...and you wouldn't have any idea what just hit you...until they were done."

It was like Corlance just told Rampras's near future. That got Rampras worried about the consequences of asking about Galilea.

"Why did you leave?" Rampras deflected.

"To avoid that final nail," Corlance said. "Calypso can touch you, Rampras. But they can't...touch...me. I'm outside of their influence," he said with a smile, which quickly melted away with a finger nod, "You guys...don't know what you're defending."

Corlance turned around and started walking away.

"Neither do you," said Rampras.

Corlance turned around, backpedalling while saying, "Perhaps I say I don't, but really I do. You will never know, will you?" ending it with a smile.

Rampras narrowed his eyes in disgust at Corlance. Virgil casted a dark glare at Rampras. Rampras retaliated the gaze of death. Then both parties headed back to their sides.

Rampras walked through the base's doors, handed the scarf to Bowle, then ripped off the wire. He was obviously frustrated like he just got played in some way, but couldn't say how. Bowle looked at the scarf then chuckled.

"That dirt-eating terd," said Bowle.

"What?" Rampras asked.

"He's trying to tell us..." Bowle said, "...that we're not his enemy. Only that...we're making him...ours." He dropped the scarf. "The courtesy of war."

*   *   *   *   *

Corlance leaned against the armoured SUV and stroked his chin puff, staring at the settlement. He was lost in thought.

"Da hell was dat about, C.L.?" Virgil asked. "Cause, I tink I missed it."

"They're hiding something," Corlance theorized. "They're worried. Time is not on their side for some reason and Calypso's got the hammer on them. This one attack...is going to set off a chain of events."

Virgil was confused. How the hell could he tell that? Then he got right into Corlance's face. Corlance was startled by his sudden advancement.

"We have the air," Virgil hissed out. "Bomb them. Kill'em all."

Corlance was reluctant. But Virgil pressed on, intimidating

Corlance with his violent presence. His maddening eyes pierced at him. His raspy voice spoke the whispered tone of death.

"They...deserve...to die," Virgil hissed.

And though Corlance's eyes were hidden behind his sunglasses, there was never a time his eyes weren't filled with disgust with these outcasts...

...especially at that moment.

*   *   *   *   *

Rampras walked the streets of Aquarius. He walked past the worried soldiers, looking up to him for confidence. But none came from him. He was worried too and was lost in the deepest thoughts.

The outcasts outnumbered the settlements ten to one. There were more criminals than there were peaceful people. What were they doing wrong? Was it so easy to fall into savagery when seeing the death of their world? Did they think it didn't matter anymore, then just unleashed chaos everywhere they went?

Everyone felt the doom every day they lived. They could feel it. They could see it in the sky. They saw it on the lands: the destroyed cities, the corrupted people, the war that could shatter them all. It made them want to give up, give up and die because it didn't matter anymore. Life was fading every second and that their struggle was useless.

He kept thinking if it was reason enough to lose control, or a reason to fight for life. Who deserved to survive? Those who fought for it or the ones who suffered far too much from it? But he had no answers.

He kept wondering why they were really attacking. Weapons. Armour. Women and food. These things kept contradicting Multanis's pacifist thoughts. But weapons and armour gave a feeling of security. He knew that because he had them. Woman for company, for pleasure. Food for survival.

All of these were things everyone craved. Security, company, pleasure, and survival. If they were given anything they wanted, they wouldn't as destructive as they were now. Something in Rampras began to believe Multanis.

But that didn't mean it was right. They would get from someone else's expense and they didn't care who it hurt. Plus they were so violent. They loved it. They craved it. They lived for the feeling of overpowering someone, dominating them. It was a disease that had been infecting people for eons.

But could such desires eventually be quenched over time? Or prevent them from being started? He didn't know. He only knew the world of combat and survival. He knew nothing of peacemaking, except from a bullet.

Rampras had long-lasting wishes of everything coming to an end, where he would be at peace, but saw them so far out of sight that they were impossible. Even during the days of Khared-Turo's rise, he never believed it.

But he heard so many stories about Khared-Turo talking about how criminals came to be, criminals created by one's own doing, society's doing, and it was everyone's responsibility to lead them away from that.

He kept thinking if that were true, then it was the settlement that made them savages for outcasting them, for cutting them out of their world. Now they were back for revenge, their savage revenge. The price...for order.

Rampras gazed up at the Calypso building and let out a burdened sigh. He couldn't help but have this dreadful feeling...that it was the beginning of the end.

CHAPTER 23

CONTRARIETY

Logan watched the outcast army from the roofs. He was weary. The whole battle halted for that meeting. Even after it ended, he kept wondering when the whole marauder battalion would attack.

The frontline squadron soldiers remained inside. The roads from the main gates split into two directions. Each side, the squadron set up barricades from junk around the plaza, readying to pincer any force barging through. Even though they were a few streets ahead, that made Logan feel a bit safer.

Then in perfect synchronicity, the whole frontline of the outcast army charged. Logan's security collapsed. Flashes of light flickered throughout the marauder ranks. Smoke trails scaled into the sky.

"Movement. All sides."

"Multiple launches detected," Samiren said.

Just as the settlement wall turrets opened fire, the outcast missiles arched toward the wall. Logan braced. The missiles exploded ten meters above and erupted a powerful clap. The clap smashed glass in a powerful spherical shockwave across the settlement, colliding with psionic shields.

But the frontlines took the brunt of it. Their ears stabbed with searing pain. Their bones rattled through their plated armour. Their brains tremored like Jell-O, which left their vision spinning into limbo. The blast immobilized them, leaving them disoriented with an irritating ring.

Calis dropped to the ground, clenched his ears, and screamed. But he could not hear himself. The ringing wouldn't stop. It was so painful. His eyes caught glimpses of blood coming out of people's ears, but he didn't care at that moment. Only the excruciating pain was important.

He did not see the front gates being blasted open or the soldiers operating the wall turrets being sniped out. He did not see the hordes of marauders pouring in, kicking the agonized Squadron soldiers to the ground. Nor did he see their lives end with a bullet to their faces, until the ringing stopped.

He heard footsteps at the edges of hearing, then gunfire. He looked up. Half of his company was already down. He mouthed something. Nobody heard, nor did he even hear himself. He grabbed his rifle off the ground, staggered to his feet, and mouthed out again to the deafened crowd.

"Fire! All Fire!"

Calis blasted wildly. His bullets swept into the marauder ranks, smashing into armours of leather, plastic, and steel. Other soldiers took cue and fired. Marauders were dropping like flies. They fired back with a series of bullets, arrows, knives, and other throwables. Most reflected harmless off the reinforced steel of Squadron armour. But a few lucky rounds met the faces hidden inside helmets that threw the soldiers back.

The lightning exchange engulfed the main street whole. The squadron kept pincering the suicidal maniacs, but marauders just kept pouring in. They stepped over the dead and filled in the gaps with a density of muscle. Each marauder forced his way forward even when being struck with bullets until the lead brought them down. But even that wouldn't stop their advance.

Logan watched as the main streets flooded with blood and the thunder of screams and bullets. He was horrified at the sight.

"Psi-Ops units. Advance. Skirmish them," Bowle ordered on the radio.

Psionicists leapt and levitated toward the main gates. Logan was reluctant to go, but kept at the back ranks of the advance. The traffic jam of bodies kept hammering at the squadron ranks, inching their way deeper into the settlement streets, until beams of light struck down from the rooftops.

Blasts speared into the marauder, leaving explosive wakes that split their ranks apart. Dust cast into the air. Bodies flew about. Limbs slammed onto the gate walls, all of which attributed to the breaking morale of the marauders.

*   *   *   *   *

Corlance watched the front from behind the armoured SUV. He narrowed his eyes as he saw body parts fly over the main walls.

"Ugh, that's right. They have psionicists," Corlance said.

"Da hell do ya tink yer doin', boy?" Virgil said.

Corlance turned and hammered into his face, "You only got the air because of me! We do this my way or you are going to be facing a lot of that!"

He pointed to the meat-grinding battlefront. Virgil went silent. He squinted, registering the horrendous sight as a blocker of strategic thought.

Corlance snatched the SUV's radio. "Tank fire. Rooftops. Ground forces. Plant the charges and fall back."

*   *   *   *   *

Rapid fire at the main gates kicked up a dust storm. Stone houses chipped from bullet slams and bodies polluted the roads. Bullet streams had sliced up the outcast ranks, but psionic charges forced them to the gates. Logan kept shielding Vanis from retaliatory fire. He saw that outcast forces fought to step through the gates to get a shot off before being hammered.

Then several loud bangs rumbled from the armada. Tank blasts speared into the settlement and struck the roofs. Explosions tore the building tops off, perfuming the battle zone with the aroma of debris and dust.

One explosion slammed through Logan's shields and blew him and Vanis off the roof. They landed in a nearby alley, with cuts, bruises, and char marks from the flames. They were fine, but many dead psionicists became their lifeless neighbours. Even the house they stood on bled debris.

After the sudden barrage of flame and dust, the frontlines shifted. Squadron soldiers kept firing blindly into the brown mist, while medics hauled the wounded away.

Then a wall of handcrafted tower shields barged out of the dusty clouds. Outcast shieldbearers were pushing the fire lines farther into the streets, while demolition hobbyists hid behind. Lead bullets fought to puncture holes through the thick alloys. Some succeeded but met the metal slabs soldered on jackets.

The shield bearers held off near the squadron's barricades while the demolitionists set up laser trip lines along the walls. The power behind the shower of bullets fired at point-blank range became far too much to handle for the shield bearers. Their muscles were buckling.

Then lumps of metal acorns landed beside them. The firing stopped and the shield bearers looked at the lumps. They were grenades. They reacted for only a split second until several blasts swallowed the shield lines with dust. The demolitionists braced from the shrapnel, but the shield lines were broken.

The squadron raged the roads with lead and the demoralized marauders started falling back. Several demolitionists barely finished setting charges before being shot down, but the chaos clouded their actions. The marauders stormed out as fast as they could, which created a chase for eager soldiers.

"We got'em, partners! We going all out now!" yelled a Gamma sergeant.

"Hold your ground!" Rampras yelled on the radio.

"Screw that! I ain't missing out on all the glory!" yelled a Gamma soldier.

"Ye heard the cappy! Get yer raggedy asses back in line!" Calis yelled.

"Let's get these outcast dogs!" yelled the Gamma sergeant.

"No, no, no, no, no, No, No, NO!" Calis roared.

The excited soldiers stormed toward the front gates until the foot of one ended the feet of others. The laser trigger squeaked with excitement and a fiery blaze ripped across the streets. The blaze set off others and consumed the streets with fire and shrapnel. A dozen Squadron soldiers laid dead while several dozen were wounded.

Calis rushed to the wounded's side. So many of them were charred black.

"We need recovery units. Gate side," Calis said into his radio. "We got heavy losses. Repeat. We got heavy losses."

Just as Calis said that, he heard the squealing of small gears. He looked up. He saw a fleet of remote-controlled toy trucks barging through the main gates. They dodged debris and drove over dead bodies. Calis kept staring at them, puzzled, wondering what kind of trickery this was about.

As the trucks closed in, sweeping in between Squadron

ranks, Calis finally saw it. There were dynamite charges strapped
to their back loading boxes.

He yelled out to his team, "Fall--"

--But the trucks ignited. A series of explosions blasted
within Squadron ranks, sending soldiers to the walls.

*　　*　　*　　*　　*

Corlance smirked as he saw the explosions in his
binoculars. His guerrilla war play was smashing their ranks
effectively. But he was never one to become arrogant and stupid at
such a critical time. He knew far too well that war changes quickly.
Corlance grabbed an old-world tablet computer and entered in keys.

"Send two stompers in on both sides and one tank shell at
each of these coordinates," Corlance said into his radio. "Uploading
the data now."

He sent out the data with a final tap. Then he added, "Send
in the second lines behind them. Blitzkrieg."

*　　*　　*　　*　　*

Calis groaned as he got up. Burn marks scorched the
side of his face and parts of his armour plates dented inward.
He was wounded but mobile. He took a quick assessment of his
surroundings. More dead and wounded flooded their ranks, but
they had enough numbers to ward off attacks.

Then the ground rumbled. Calis's eyebrows pricked up.
Broken glass shook loose off their skeleton windows. Then another
tremor. It was louder and heavier. Then another one, which began
to beat in consistency, louder and heavier. Calis looked at the walls
directly, the source of the sound.

He heard metallic gear grinding. It sounded familiar.
Then blurs of bullet lines flashed through the stone walls and the
brigade of stacked bricks blasted apart. The stone blocks smashed

into everything, walls, houses, debris chunks, and helmets, which splashed a mist of blood.

Not before long, a monstrous, bulky mech warrior stepped into the breached walls. Its colossal foot crushed a garbage bin into pulp from the sheer weight of its protective armour. Its hind pipes let out an irritating hiss, which made people want to rip their ears out. The sight nearly gave Calis a heart attack.

He screamed out, "Fall back now!"

The squadrons broke cover and bolted for the deeper settlement. The mech warrior stormed after them, letting loose a storm of anti-tank bullets. Each bullet rattled the bones of everyone in a one-hundred-meter diameter and each stomp shook the ground.

Squadron soldiers turned and cover-fired until their buddies ran past. But the bullets weren't penetrating its armour. The steel titan crashed through the barricades and crushed stone debris under its feet.

Civilians watched from between houses the carnage it left behind. Then they saw marauders creeping behind the mech warrior, keeping behind the walking steel block. The marauders cackled and screamed wildly at the mech warrior's rampage. People shivered in fear as their homes and streets were invaded by the people they once outcasted ages ago.

Logan was in the alley still healing Vanis's wounds. He heard the commotion and took a quick glance down the alley. Squadron soldiers were backpedalling and firing. Many of their bodies were then sliced apart by the thunderous blasts of anti-tank bullets. He then saw the mech warrior walk past, followed by marauders. Then radio traffic responded.

"The mech's armour's too strong! We need auxiliary support!"

"Negative," Bowle replied on the radio. "Auxiliary munitions are already low. Use battery fire from grenade launchers."

"Them explodin' coconuts ain't gonna be beatin' the senses outta these thumpin' gorillas!" said Calis. "We need that auxiliary support! Now!"

Logan gauged the marauder forces. Vanis knew what he was thinking and stood up beside him. Logan unveiled his plasma blade and charged.

Calis led the retreat to a curve. A weakened structure landmarked it until a spear of smoke struck the building. The tank strike smashed through a frontal pillar before wrecking the insides. The front deck's weight lost support and collapsed. It ripped half of the second floor down with it and spilled onto the road, crushing two soldiers. The debris hill impeded on their path.

"Calis to HQ. They got us blocked off!"

Then stomps rumbled into the spines of the soldiers. Calis turned around. The mech warrior was almost upon them.

"What in all the toilet bowl hells y'all still doin' on open grounds?!" Calis yelled.

The soldiers just started splitting up as a volley of bullets rained in. One soldier's head split open from the bullet's velocity while the rest of the soldiers evaded. Bullets ripped apart buildings behind them. The soldiers returned fire in futility, leaving with a dazzle of sparks reflecting off the mech's armour.

A scream erupted behind the mech warrior. Marauders looked up to their left. Logan crashed down in the middle of their ranks, slicing a marauder in half. He swirled his blade in circular strikes, slashing down four more in the process. The outcast backed away in a circle, then blasted at him.

Logan dropped to one knee and palmed out to the ground

an omni-directional psi-shield. Bullets smashed into the shield, which was buckling after seconds. Then a flash of light engulfed him. A spherical force crunched the concrete floor beneath his feet and bullets started to orbit around him.

Logan looked up and let out a relieving sigh. Vanis was by his side, gesturing spherical motions, which caused the bullets to orbit. The awestruck marauders halted and gazed up at the hundreds of light trails speeding around her.

She spanned her arms outward, which expanded the orbital ring. The ring of bullets sliced into the marauder ranks, passing through more than one body. The marauders backpedalled and fired but only added to the ring.

Vanis kept launching continuous artistic somatic motions, then noticed Logan wasn't moving, "The metal giant halts not for but a blade."

Logan wanted to stay, but took cue and stormed north. He slid under the ring of bullets, seeing the blurs of light pass in front of his face, then charged after the mech warrior.

The walking machine was devastating the squadron numbers. Soldiers holed up in nearby houses and behind building parts. The anti-tank rounds wrecked holes in them, slicing bodies up even behind metal cover.

Amidst the carnage, the mech suddenly blasted skyward, falling on its back with bullets slicing to the clouds. Logan emerged behind it, side-rolling out of the devastating crash when the mech hit the floor. Its knee joint was glowing red from a plasmatic slash. It wobbled and squirmed like a beetle on its back.

Calis jumped out of cover and bolted for the fallen mech.

"Logan! Move yer gassy brown factory outta the way!"

Calis reached into his pack and pulled out a brick-sized

explosive charge. He quickly armed it and threw it onto the mech's front view port. Then he bolted away as the mech thrashed around, alerted by the charge. The charge exploded, blowing through the windshield and setting the mech ablaze.

*　　　*　　　*　　　*　　　*

Corlance saw the blaze from his binoculars. He checked on the other mech and saw psionicists taking it down. Then he lowered his binoculars and cast a smug smirk at Virgil.

"They didn't last long now, did they?" Corlance said. "I wonder what would've happened if we sent everybody in, hmm?"

Virgil did nothing but glared at Corlance. His eyes easily revealed how many times he contemplated killing Corlance. But he knew enough to know there would be serious consequences to the battle if he did.

"But their ranks are still dense. This will not do," Corlance said while stroking his chin puff.

*　　　*　　　*　　　*　　　*

Bullets and projectiles blazed up and down the road. Squadron soldiers fired from debris cover. Marauders were firing through windows and rooftops. Other gunfire echoed through the back alleys. Logan and Vanis took refuge with the soldiers near the collapsed building.

Calis kept bursts to a minimum, until one brave marauder went commando on the streets. The commando marauder rolled into the middle of the road and blasted wildly at the soldiers. The soldiers all turned, targeting the easy prey. Bullets sliced up the brave marauder, making him a foolish hero to the outcasts.

"Calis. What's your status?" Bowle asked on the radio.

"Status?! I'm a man of low calibre!" Calis yelled. "And we gonna be needin' some extra calibre rifles real fast!"

"I'm sending in reserves. Push them back to the front gate," Bowle said.

"Why?" Calis asked. "Them gates are totally FUBAR. And by FUBAR, I mean it's now a three-sided a-hole that can brown spray it in three directions!"

"We need time to set up a counter strike. Get to those gates!"

Calis closed his eyes and sighed. He didn't like that. He wondered how he was going to advance with a street full of marauders. Just as he got up, another wall of shield bearers rushed toward them. Marauders got out of their covers and charged behind the walking tanks. They were coming at full force.

Calis roared out, "Frag 'em!"

Squadron soldiers let loose a fan of bullets. Light trails speared into marauder ranks but met only the shield walls protecting the advance. Each soldier ripped the pin off a grenade with their teeth and threw onto the roads not even ten meters ahead. The shield bearers, knowing their doom, tucked their heads behind their primitive shields as they charged into the farm of grenades.

Explosions sprouted. Geysers of smoke sliced into the midst of marauder ranks. It blasted two shield bearers off their feet while a third jumped onto a grenade, meat shielding the others. One halted and attempted to back away, but was pushed into an explosion by the flood of charging bodies.

Bullets sliced into the shield wall opening. But their lines were just too dense. It could not stop the advance. Marauders charged right at them and tackled several soldiers to the ground. Squadron soldiers blasted them and bashed at them with the butts of their rifles.

Logan stood behind the street riot, wondering how to get in. The roaring, screaming, and smashing of bone was intense. To him, it was full-blown chaos. Vanis kept pummelling the left side of their ranks with telekinetic thrusts, but all of the gaps they made were quickly filled in like fluid water.

"I know yer front-row seats to yer popcorn newscast is all interestin' and all, popsicle," Calis said while hauling a soldier away from the carnage, "but ye mind namin' a few goons with death with that super cool hot poker of yers?"

Logan let out a nervous sigh and unveiled his plasma blade. He pulled a soldier back and stepped in his place with a slash of a blade.

The Squadron was easily being pushed to the rims of the collapsed building. Several soldiers emerged from the roof sides and aided the pinned soldiers with covery fire. But that wasn't enough.

Logan was losing maneuverability in the dense crowd. Then in the midst of battle, he noticed marauders kept trying to peel armour parts off soldiers.

He took a quick glance around. He saw a soldier being carried away into the marauder crowd. They were clawing at the soldier's armour plates. Then he saw a marauder slap armour pieces onto themselves before being shot down. He also saw several soldiers fighting back with half their armour on.

A loud whistle squealed, quivering an irritating rattle. The marauders backed off, storming down the streets they came from, some even grabbing the dented barrier shields for cover as they withdrew. Squadron soldiers fired in their wake, blasting down a few before they disappeared around corners.

"Calis to HQ. We need a back alley clean-up crew. Have them reserves rendezvous with us at--"

"--Corlance to A-team. Proceed to sector five and plant wall charges."

They scanned around confused, honing in on the source of the voice. It was coming from one of their own. A soldier with half his armour on had a radio receiver strapped onto his belt. Then they noticed dead marauders with squadron plates on them.

"Infiltrators!" a Gamma Corporal yelled.

Soldiers aimed their guns at their half-armoured crew. The shocked soldiers stared at the gun barrels in confusion.

"Hey man! We're with you!"

"Don't you recognize us?!"

"Weapons on the ground! Now!" said the Gamma Corporal.

"What in all the premarital hells do ya think yer doin'?!" Calis asked.

"A-team! Where the hell are you?" Corlance radioed in.

"Put your weapons down, now!" the Gamma Corporal yelled.

"How the hell can you guys not recognize us?!"

"They're infiltrators!" yelled an outraged soldier.

"It's a damn trick, ye damn fools!" Calis reasoned.

"Screw these bastards! Blast 'em!" the Gamma Corporal yelled.

The corporal aimed and fired. The bullet slammed through a half armoured soldier's head. The other targeted crew fired back and the debris hill exploded into crossfire. Logan and Vanis shielded themselves while Calis took cover.

*   *   *   *   *

Solito watched it all from the rooftops. He watched soldiers gun their own in the back, trying to flee down the street. He smiled with much delight. He dragged a dead soldier away from the roof's ledge and glanced toward the settlement's upper slope. There was commotion.

He saw two bulky blocks of metal roll up onto the upper platform ledges in the settlement's base. They were tanks. Then he saw a flock of dropships speeding out of their hangars. They were heading for the outcast armada.

*   *   *   *   *

Corlance laughed as he watched the circus unfold onto the streets.

"Feeling the pleasures of immense pride, are you now?" Solito radioed in. "Look deep in the settlement."

Corlance adjusted his binocular's view. He saw the dropships. They were still in the settlement but in the air. He frowned at Virgil and pointed to them.

"If we had bombarded the entire settlement, we would've expired all of our resources...for that!"

Virgil's mouth slacked open as he watched the dropships.

*   *   *   *   *

The in-fighting had died off when all of the alleged perpetrators were killed. Bodies littered the main streets. Bullet holes and flame sprouts domesticated the neighbourhood. The mech warrior was still burning. Calis gave them hell about military protocol before radioing in.

"Ye ain't gonna believe what's been happenin'," Calis said on the radio. "Corlance sacrificed half a division to make some turncoats."

"Because we outclass them, mate," Rampras replied. "Corlance knows we can repel any ground forces he sends in, so he's using war games and artillery to break our ranks."

Then a roaring burst erupted overhead. Calis looked up.

The dropship flock flew by. They flew toward the settlement walls in a single-line formation.

"We got rogue birds, Colonel," said Calis. "They abandonin' us!"

"Relax, Calis," Bowle radioed. "We're sending a strike against their artillery. Clean up the streets then proceed to the front gates."

"We could've used those dropships for emergency escape, mate."

"Aquarius is my darling, Rampras," Bowle said. "I ain't abandoning her during her time of need."

*   *   *   *   *

A decot siren sounded off. Missiles blasted off launch pads and fired toward the dropships. Several rockets smashed into the head shuttle, smashing it and engulfing it in flames. The single-line formation was shielding the others.

"Solito, sabotage anything you can!" Corlance said to his radio before ducking behind his armoured SUV. "No! Point all launch pads south!"

The dropships dove in at relatively low altitudes. Missiles speared overhead without a lock on. The shuttle fleet spread out throughout the armada and opened their hind bay doors. A turret was mounted on the back.

The shuttles dropped a payload of cluster bombs. Explosions spiked out in lines throughout the armada. Mech warriors, tanks, and missile launch pads were consumed in a fiery blaze. The heat set off munitions rounds and an array of sparks snapped in the air. Marauders scampered away from the explosions.

After the dropships flew by, their hind turrets blasted off a drum roll of mini-gun rounds. Bullet lines sliced into armoured vehicles, busting tires and engines. The fleet left behind carnage in its wake.

Corlance saw an opportunity after the dropships flew by. They were heading south and were curving around for another assault. But they had created enough distance for their targeting systems. He grabbed his radio.

"They're coming about. Launch missile charges now!"

Several launch pads, which managed to shift south, each fired off a missile. Smoke lines slashed across and over the armada. The projectiles tailed behind the dropships, curving into them, striking several dropships. The struck metal birds spiralled down to their doom.

Two missiles slammed against a dropship's engines. The engines fluttered and blew. The dropship dove. Marauders scampered away. The shuttle smashed into several vehicles before exploding sparks and searing crackers.

Several harpoon heads slammed into a shuttle's hull. Thin metallic wires were tied to them. The cord tensed then ripped the spool off a dune buggy. The wire whiplashed and slashed the face of a marauder.

The shuttle fleet were half their number and were heading back, leaving a wake of bullet streams hammering into marauder ranks. Just as Corlance grabbed the radio, a smoke line speared into the armada, stabbing into a dense vehicle cluster. The blast swept smoke and debris across a fourth of the field. Corlance gazed at the colossal mushroom of fire it left behind. He didn't like that.

"Did you get its trajectory?" Corlance asked into the radio.
"Yes!"

"All tank units return fire!" Corlance said.

Several tank barrels spun around. They aimed toward the

upper slope of the settlement and fired. Blast lines harpooned back into the settlement.

*   *   *   *   *

The tungsten rounds slammed into the 30-inch thick hull of the executioner class main battle tank. The tank nudged back with every strike, causing its double track sets on each side to re-grip its traction. But the rounds did not penetrate. The tank shifted its massive, reinforced heatsinked barrel over and blasted a round before a lucky tungsten round stung it on the canopy neck.

The round set off a chain reaction of fire bursts that erupted inside the executioner tank. Huffs of fire eventually led to a full-out explosion that engulfed the metal block whole.

*   *   *   *   *

The second tank strike tore into a mech warrior. The strike exploded into a storm that washed trailers, missile launch pads, and vehicles in flames. Debris scattered and ricocheted off the ground and other machines.

Corlance frowned at the devastation from behind his SUV. He relaxed his eyebrows when he saw a distant explosion in the settlement. But he knew the second tank was still out there.

"Solito, do you have the second tank in sight?" Corlance asked on the radio.

"Getting to it, now," Solito replied.

A moment later, a second explosion marked the location of the other tank. Corlance let out a sigh. He glanced around at the carnage in the armada.

Launch pads were on fire. Mech warriors were wrecked. Buggies, motorbikes, and other smaller vehicles were still functioning. They withstood heavy losses, but they still had a great number of bombardments available.

He glanced at the disapproving Virgil, wondering if he was right.

"This is getting to be far more costly than I had anticipated," Corlance commented. Then he spoke to his radio, "Solito. Get out of there. We're gonna hit them with everything we've got."

Virgil smirked. *Finally!*

*   *   *   *   *

During the dropship barrage, the battle took to the back alleys. Debris and bullet holes filled the streets. Houses were stormed. Some had collapsed. Fires burnt rampantly. Blood stained the walls. Bullet shells made home on every street corner and back alley as the Squadron repelled outcast forces to the front.

It was a vicious blood bath.

But the terror of rapid fire echoing throughout the settlement did not terrorize Samiren. He stood on the eastern alleys a fair ways from Calis. A small satellite antenna sunk into his metallic head and he began to walk.

Squadron soldiers used a destroyed mech as fortification to ward off the attack. They fired into dust clouds made from battle chaos. Return fire blazed out from the fog.

Samiren walked right toward the fog itself. Bullets reflected off his shields. His confusing action puzzled the gamma squadron soldiers, so their Lance Corporal radioed it in.

Logan was clearing a path for squadron soldiers in the back alleys to get to the front gates. He slashed a marauder down then saw Samiren pass by at the alley's end. Marauders just watched Samiren walk by. Samiren didn't even acknowledge them. Logan ran down the alley and Vanis followed.

He got to the alley's end. Marauders kept soldiers

suppressed from squadron barricades. Logan stormed toward them. The marauders saw him flanking and backpedalled away from cover. Bullets slashed all over their now exposed bodies and the survivors fled toward the front gates.

As the squadron advanced for the gates, Logan came to Samiren's side.

"Samiren. What are you doing?"

"Engaging the enemy," Samiren said.

"By yourself? Are you mad?!"

"Statistics report a thirty-seven percent chance of the settlement's defendants surviving. I intend to alter those statistics."

He was mad, or so Logan thought. He had never seen the full potential of Samiren's power, nor had anyone else since the time of Khared-Turo. Was he bluffing...or was he really going to engage a full armada of vehicles?

Then Samiren stopped.

"Sentient being," he said. "Bring plenty of water."

Rampras was on a suspended balcony shielded by an embattled parapet. The balcony was tucked inside an indention of a crossroads. He kept ambushing marauders turning the corner with bullet fire, until the radio kicked in.

"Colonel! Samiren's heading for the front gates!"

"What the hell is he doing?" Rampras roared.

He stormed up a walkway that connected to a rooftop. He saw Samiren heading for the front gates. He knew exactly what Samiren was planning.

"No! Samiren! You don't have your heat sinks on!"

But Samiren did not listen.

Instead, he formulated a bulky nano-tech turret on his left arm. It flickered with blue lights and an electrical pulse pitched out a sizzling whine. Three lights radiated in a triangle on his chest, which indicated rising power. He walked out of the front gates and stood before the armada.

*   *   *   *   *

Missile launch pads were being reloaded and turned for the settlement. Tanks armed and were in firing position. Helicopters were powering up, while mech warriors stood up from slumber. Corlance had just finished armaments when someone pointed up to the settlement.

"Someone's emerging!"

Corlance feared his plan was made. He rushed for his binoculars and took a quick view of the gates. He saw a black figure with three orange lights on his chest. Corlance gasped and dropped his binoculars. He was absolutely petrified. He knew what that was. He barely managed to grab the radio receiver.

"It's a Samiren drone! Everyone! Fire everything!"

*   *   *   *   *

And as Samiren channelled into his reserves, his three chest lights flared like stars. Energy flushed through his circuitry and into his turret, reddening from searing heat. The heat spread onto the nearby rocks and blazed them into a reddish glow. A field of vapour hazed around him, distorting sight.

He was ready; ready for the family of twinkling lights flickering from the metal crowd. Ready for a cluster of missile cousins spilling smoke in their wake. Ready for the doom of lives arching over the battlefield.

And they all watched in morbid suspense from their rooftops, homes, bunkers, and vehicles at the thousand aerial lances jousting for a single being. The fan of missiles arched over the retreating marauders, like a barrage of arrows leaving the empty nests of archer hands. As they closed in, they clenched together like a metal fist, crushing for Samiren.

Then they slammed and a bright light cloaked the eyes. Debris chunks blasted over houses and ricocheted into a stampede throughout the streets. Dust swept all over, enough to fill the lungs with sand. Soldiers and civilians took cover inside alleyways and buildings, even though it seemed so futile at the time.

*　　*　　*　　*　　*

Explosions bloomed all over the front gates, overlapping constantly like popcorn in fast motion. Thousands of thunderous claps blended together into a near constant ring. Portions of the slope deformed and wall segments collapsed. Rocket fire and artillery shells rained heavily at the front entrance.

Corlance persisted on the missile fire and tank-blast assists. The bombardment lasted a full minute before complaining clicks from artillery machinery whined.

"We're out. All missiles depleted."

But the nervous Corlance peered into the parting mists of fate. He was determined to know Samiren's state before deciding his next action. Of all the stories he heard about these ridiculously powerful drones, he wondered if he was the lucky one — to confront a dysfunctional machine.

"My turn," radioed the voice of death.

A horrendous wave of needles flushed through Corlance's body.

*　　*　　*　　*　　*

Yet deep within the midst of carnage and debris and in the mists of exhaling flames, the two red eyes of Samiren pierced through. He was angry. He was annoyed. Not one of these missiles with kilojoules of combustive power even penetrated his shields.

With that ill-threat in mind, Samiren added into mockery.

*   *   *   *   *

A blast line sliced out. The ground shook from the drumbeat of the gods. An explosion struck marauder ranks out front, spilling flaming bodies onto the field. The flames were massive. Nearly seven stories high. It towered down on the helpless eyes of the marauders gazing up at it in doom.

The abuse continued with a second blast strike smashing into machines. By then, the front-rank marauders scampered into disarray.

Corlance barked out, "Take cover now!"

Some listened. Others fled for the horizons. The whole front ranks were scattered about, undeciding on whether to cover or flee. Corlance kept behind his armoured SUV, hoping his presence wasn't in the targeting eyes of the machine.

But the two strikes alone shook up the ranks. The third slandered their bravery even more, igniting a transport trailer full of ammunition. Sparks flashed out, painting the sky with comets, while masking a fourth attack.

Corlance could see the mushroom of fire over the SUV's roof. It was close. Far too close for his liking. Tanks, mech warriors, and transports, along with an army of debris, flew over the SUV and rained from the sky. Corlance was in awe. A gust of flames slipped under the SUV that nudged the vehicle whole.

He wasn't sure how he was going to get out of this one. He still couldn't gauge how badly damaged the drone was, assuming it was damaged. But what he knew of physics, sustaining that kind of power on the assault would be impossible without serious metallic cushioning to redistribute the residual energy.

And from what he saw of that drone, it was tall but scrawny.

*   *   *   *   *

And so Samiren blasted off a fifth. Pebbles skipped the sands as the ground tremored like the quake upon a saviour's death. The blast struck out into the horde of fleas. The flames laid siege upon their ranks and even though their numbers were still great, the marauders were at a knife's edge of defeat.

But the heat all around Samiren was too excruciating for mortal skins, even for himself. Portions of his body glimmered with red and puss of melting plastic slipped through the gears. Inner circuitry finally gave away with the jail breaking of sparks.

Small flashes of blue flickered within his torso, and Samiren shuttered in response. The sparkling paparazzi tickled the final images of the animated Samiren before he shut down in full.

He halted in position, frozen into a metal statue, land marking the front gates as an icon of his guardianship. With the final red glow dimming out of his eyes, nothing was left to stop the advance of marauder horde.

CHAPTER 24
RELINQUISH

Smoke hissed from the flickering flames in the icebergs of sand. Metal poles protruded from the graveyard of houses. Electrical wires cackled with menacing delight from the broken hydro poles.

It was a sight of devastation; a rough coarse surface as though a painter dashed in a couple of strokes. Touches of red, blue, white, and other brownish variants populated the city of rubble.

He saw it all and his mouth gaped into disbelief. He gazed at the once front gates and surrounding plazas. There were utensils in the rubble; cups, broken clay plates, tools, and pieces of torn clothing. He never thought to see how detailed such carnage makes.

But all of the artistic wonder died with the view of burnt bodies sticking out from the rocks. He didn't want to look.

Soldiers began to emerge from their gambled hiding spots. Some came from the stone houses while others came from basement bunkers. The back alleys puked out soldiers, wounded and scratched from the debris.

After surveying his surroundings, Logan glanced ahead. Samiren was there. He was frozen in firing pose. Two fractured pillars of the once gate hinges seared with glowing heat.

He managed to get a look at the outcast armada from his line of sight. They didn't look so well. Smoke titans reigned supreme in the armada of melted vehicles. But they looked like they were reformulating.

Yet something else caught Vanis's eye. She was painted

with years of war stains. Anything catching her attention was noteworthy. So Logan had to look.

It was a distant storm. Electrical in nature. At first, Logan thought it was an EM storm, which would've gave Corlance an edge. But from the dread in Vanis's gaze, he knew it was something else.

It was coming and their time was running out.

*   *   *   *   *

Time, however, was not Corlance's main concern.

Tanks were burning. Jeeps were ablaze. The marauder forces were suffering from abandonment and in-looting. Crates of supplies were raided and left open. Horses and dune buggies were navigating through the wreckage for escape, while the horizons were slowly populated with those who fled.

Corlance and Virgil were in the midst of a vicious argument when several looters jumped into his SUV. With one smack, the SUV's windows busted open and un-sneaky hands dove in and felt around.

"What did I say about unity as a force?" Corlance lectured. "If you want something done, you can't have these men be cowards! Abandonment is an ensured method of defeat!"

"Yo! Whatchu talkin' about, C.L.?" Virgil retorted. "Deez ain't yer boyz! Deez are my brothahs here! We ain't no SWAT team seekin' to feed the maggots!"

"If it wasn't for my lead, all of these men would already be dead!"

"Like ye da one that stopped tin-man from going AWOL!"

Corlance didn't know what he was talking about. There was so much chaos within the ranks that he didn't even notice the blasting stopped. He glanced toward the front gates. Smoke still deluded all sight, until a fortunate gust exposed the metal gargoyle. Samiren wasn't moving.

Corlance saw an opportunity. He ignored the looters of his SUV and reached for the radio head and spoke.

"He's down! All units advance!"

Some ignored him and kept running for the hills. Others stopped and glanced at Corlance like he was the elephant in the room. Corlance was confused with the reaction.

"The drone is down! Repeat! The drone is down! Advance now!"

They all glanced at the front gates. The smoke had cleared from the bombarded area and Samiren's inanimated self was easily seen. The unthreatening sight spawned an eruption of remoralizing roars. It was like the whole outcast army had just awoken. They stampeded for the front gates and Corlance let out a sigh of relief.

Virgil gave Corlance a dirty glare, disapproving of his momentary loss of grip. But Corlance only ushered him to go with a shrug. With that, Virgil merely snatched up his handmade flintlock with a tightened grip before going.

Corlance shuttered to the gripping crunch.

*   *   *   *   *

The once explosion of disbanding brigands now horded for the settlement. Calis watched them from the debris. He saw the shift of disarray combining toward them, so he leapt to his feet.

"Cappy! We got incomin'!"

Rampras casted a glance at the armada from the survivor extraction area. The marauders were climbing the slopes and met the bullets of the gate watchers. Rampras threw his hands, pointing directions while he barked out orders.

"Extract! Back to the bunkers! Rampras to all available ground units! Converge at the front gates! Don't let them in!"

Their numbers had dwindled to less than half. Their clips were slowly getting empty. The one-minute calm gave them time for a quick salvage, but now they were going back to a full-on firefight.

Rampras was aware of these concerns. He wanted to keep the pincer advantage at the main steps. Breaking the lines with street fighting was like fighting a battle blind from every direction. With Corlancian strategies focusing primarily on exploiting those advantages, Rampras knew how crucial it was for the settlement to hold the front gates.

He hustled over the debris and in between medic teams. He found a suitable vantage point in the rubble neighbouring the other soldier gophers. He was at least thankful that the landscape change threw off the enemy's knowledge of the battlefield. But with the settlement's forces dwindling in number, he didn't think that was enough.

The marauders curved around the still-hot Samiren and poured over the lip of the slope. Bullets blazed out from the debris hills and sliced into their oncoming ranks. The frontline marauders hustled for cover and shielded the second lines with bullet retaliation.

Trails of light threaded both ways across the debris, sewing the unlucky fates with death. Logan witnessed it all from a crevice in the debris: the strobing lights, the lightning stabs, and the constant screams of death. He was used to it by now. He was just waiting for an opportunity to strike.

But his eye caught the sight of a civilian straggler hiding between two crumbled houses. It was a woman. She was holding a baby. They were caught between two fronts of the settlement soldiers.

Logan was worried. She was scared. He had to get them out of there, but didn't know how. He knew he wouldn't last long in a stream of bullets and the marauders were slowly gaining ground. He looked around for back alley passages but the bombardment closed them all off.

She was stuck there. She was going to have to wait. As long as she stayed there and kept hidden, no attention would be drawn to her.

Then he heard the baby's crying. It tugged at his heart. He had to defend them no matter what. This was a newly born being, a new entity full of flesh and blood. It had never experienced laughter and joy or the fruits of life so enjoyable even in the harshest of days. He had to protect that life.

He had to protect that future.

As he waited in those rocks watching the hordes of outcasts throwing their lives away in the heaps of streaming bullets, he realized something. He was anxious. Not for his own life, but for another's. He was never like that before.

He just wanted to bolt through that battlefield and carry that woman away regardless of how many of those lead bugs had bit him. But he didn't even know if he would make it. There were a lot of bullets firing on the field. He would have to wait for an opportunity.

The firing intensified. Marauder bodies built up at the entrance. Then after moments, exploded onto the courtyard.

They stepped over the uneven grounds of the debris, through the mists of discharged sulphur, and stormed for the soldiers. They dropped like flies, splashing blood into a battlefield drizzle. The bullet storm was not even slowing them. They intended to break the squadrons.

Logan felt the opportunity arise. If the lines clashed, the main focus would be on melee and he could slice his way to that woman.

As the lines drew closer, Rampras knew this was going to be an all-or-nothing fight. He shifted his legs to ready himself for a spring and waited.

The army of dark silhouettes hopped through the debris floors, seemingly snickering in their grievous ways. Shot figures dropped to the ground as though targets in a carnival game.

They weren't even registered as lives anymore. Only enemies that had to be stopped. It made things easier for a rifleman to sleep at night unless they thrived on death.

Then the lines collided. Bodies smacked together. Rifle ends and metal plates smashed into an orchestra of melee. The waltz of the warrior ballet consumed the frontlines and war screams were the only audience.

Rampras sprinted into action and thrashed his rifle around, taking down two nearing his rubble grove. Logan dove into the melee circus and hacked his way through the forest of flesh with his machete of light.

He had to hurry. The marauders were just crashing into anyone willing to fight. He cut through several bodies and ignored the expressions on their faces. He did not want to be plagued by the burdens of their fate. So he shielded his mind from their psychi explosions upon their deaths.

Rampras kept bashing his bent rifle around until he caught a glimpse of Logan. He was ploughing deep into marauder ranks. Rampras was outraged. He stopped. But just as he was about to yell, he heard a pierce and his gut felt warm.

Logan stopped. He felt something was wrong.

Rampras looked to his stomach. A bayonet had stabbed through his armour, through missing plates damaged by the earlier barrage. The blade was attached to a musket held by a smirking marauder.

Logan turned around. He saw Rampras. The blade reached through to the other side. Dread washed over Logan and he nearly dropped his blade.

But Rampras let out a furious roar and stomped in the marauder's chest. The blade snapped off and the marauder flew back, disappearing into marauder ranks. Then Rampras fell to the ground, clenching his wound.

But just as Logan was to react, a snap echoed in his ears. It was a bullet blast; a foreign sound fired deep within the stage of melee. More dread washed over him as the cries of a woman engulfed his heart.

He turned around. He saw a gun on the ground. It had automatically discharged on drop. Two guys were on the ground. They were fighting near it but stopped. They were staring at the woman.

Blood was all over her as she held her lifeless child in her hands. The sight, that very horrendous view, tore into him and sliced deep within his soul. The sight of a mother losing her child.

Then all sound receded and the cries of the fallen angel became the dominant sound as she held her broken cupid. Tears of that heart fell from her eyes and her quivering lips tremored.

No words or thoughts came to him, only shock and disbelief. But he felt it, that horrible pain, emitting from her soul. That stabbing blow, that bodily scream, the shock coursing through her whole body. It blazed so brightly that his legs began to buckle.

The death of a goddess losing her little star.

Then he noticed another was watching. It was a marauder, affected by the god-slaying wails. Logan glanced around. Everyone was watching. The whole battle had stopped to that view, and guilt and pain tattooed the faces of all.

But he didn't understand. Many children died in wars before. Some even as young as newborns. Why was this one special? Then he remembered where he was. He was in a shattered world where even the darkest light mattered.

This was one life, one brand-new soul, the future of a broken world that was lost to devastation. This one life mattered to them all.

There was nothing he could do for that woman now. So after one final glance, he turned and came to Rampras's side. Rampras was on the ground, holding his torso up with an elbow. There was blood, but his wound seemed clean. There should've been more.

He figured it was internal bleeding, so he knelt down and held his hands out. Rampras smacked it away. Logan was taken back. He didn't understand, but Rampras didn't bother to explain. Instead, he crawled to the nearest marauder corpse and ripped the radio from the belt.

"Corlance!" Rampras roared. "Is this what you want?!"

*   *   *   *   *

"Her baby...is dead."

Corlance finally understood the sudden battlefield silence and he too was still. The woman's weeps filtered through the radio and guilt washed into his face. He didn't know what to say.

Even though he was a minister of death, the respect for life remained. He glanced around the emptied tent towns, looking for inspiration to break the silence. Only the muse of debris from damaged motors filled his sight.

But it was muse enough for his words.

"All forces...pull back for now," he said so solemnly.

*　　*　　*　　*　　*

There was a pause before his command was done. The battlefield of eyes had laid siege upon the woman. Her dam of tears had given away and fed their sights with a flowing of tears. It was a wake-up call, even through their malice.

One pried his eyes away forcefully...knowing all too well that those quivering wails would echo in his mind for days. Another took cue and ripped his glance from her. Then another... and another.

As they took turns tearing themselves from thought and gaze, Multanis came to the woman's side and eased her up to her feet.

"Up you go," he said calmly.

Her legs were shaky. She didn't want to stand. She was lost of strength and the will to live. But Multanis managed to lend her the will with an ushering of his comforting arms. He led her toward the bunkers, leaving behind the shocked soldiers burdened by the thought.

Rampras watched her leave then glanced at the conditions of battle. Everyone was getting tired and there were too many pauses in this oddity of war. But he realized Bowle was right. Corlance did have somewhat of a conscience. Rampras wondered how many more lives he could save through this example.

So he spoke into the radio, "What now, Corlance?"

*　　*　　*　　*　　*

Those words spoke more than what was said. Corlance

knew that but didn't know what to say. He was put into the spotlight in an awkward position. He had given into compassion and cursed himself for it. It was a weapon that could be exploited and used against him. He didn't like that. Still, he knew Bowle and Rampras to be honourable and would not compromise their integrity for a simple gain.

"Rampras...I, uh..." he managed to spill out, but trailed off into thought.

He watched the marauders walk out of the settlement courtyard, some with hanging heads. Then he gazed up at the asteroids orbiting the molten core. Somewhere in those rocks, the lords of war were laughing at him, laughing at his stupidity.

But this wasn't about intelligence. It was about humanity and he wanted to preserve it as much as he could in this crusade of debatable sin. But he wasn't about to give it up. He knew what he wanted so he had to be flexible.

"You have two minutes," he decided, "to evacuate the people."

*   *   *   *   *

That was a very small timeframe, not enough to exploit. But it was time enough to cherish a miracle. Rampras was relieved. He nodded to Calis and Calis forwarded it through.

"Y'all heard the man! Let's move! Move! Move!"

Soldiers bolted for the bunkers that were hidden in the aqueducts and nearby basements. They cracked open the two-foot thick rusty steel doors and ushered the people out in a rush.

Civilians from all over the settlement grabbed their gear from bunker bunk beds, debris piles, and shattered buildings. Water canisters, stored dry foods, and other canned goods were taken in a rush. They hustled down the streets, over the piles of rubble, and hurried their way through the crater that was once the gates.

Rampras watched them, watched them all, passing him by and toward a better place. He was glad. They were leaving it all behind: all their worries and troubles of safety; the battlefield that would otherwise kill them.

And even though his breathing became harsh and heavy, he felt a blessing in that moment. A blessing that no other battle in the history of mankind had allowed such an action to take place, save for a few.

But he knew that they, these outcasts, would not change their ways. It was a shock to the system, but hardly enough to change who they were. So he waved Logan over while there was still time.

"Logan, come here," said Rampras.

Logan pried his watch over the people and knelt down beside him. Rampras hacked and coughed. His lung muscles were getting weaker. Logan helped him lean against a nearby boulder. He wanted to do more, but he understood Rampras was too stubborn to accept help.

"I knew it," Rampras heaved, "from the moment...you spoke those words in that farm...that...you were going to replace me."

Logan was taken aback. He wouldn't dare do that. He hardly had the experience to be a human being, let alone a squad leader.

Then Rampras continued, "I've been a renegade...to the claws of death...too many times. I'm tired now. Tired of this war. Tired of this broken world. Tired of seeing sad faces."

Logan drifted, imagining his words; imagining a world of sadness living in the settlements. Then Rampras gripped his shoulder. Logan was startled. His eyes locked onto Rampras's. Rampras gazed at him sternly.

"These people need a champion. You can give them that."

Logan shook his head instinctually.

"I've seen it. I have seen it. That force of persuasion that can move entire crowds. You gave me that moment. You gave me a miracle that could set the world free. How?"

Logan didn't know what to say. He could only reflect back to the harshness of living off the streets, but didn't say a word. Rampras understood that it wasn't easy to talk about. Not easy to live it every day.

"What ever happened to you, it gave you a voice. You can make miracles that the world needs to hear. So make it happen. Make it happen."

Logan didn't know how. He had no idea how or where to start, let alone if he would even succeed. But Rampras looked at him as if he had complete faith in his abilities to do so. A faith he wished he had in himself.

Then a glorious ray caught Rampras's eye. A soft light had pierced through the clouds of this sullen rock. He glanced and his eyes lit up with wonder. Logan had to look.

Puffy rose petals clouded the skies, pillowing in the warm purple haze that spread along the horizon. Eyelashes of light blazed in over the sky's misty cheeks and gazed back at him. It was a glorious sight.

So glorious that Rampras's one single eye began to twinkle as though witnessing heaven for the first time.

"Wow. It's gorgeous, mate. Gorgeous. Something greater than ourselves."

Logan had never seen him like this before.

"It's my home. My...home..."

And with that, a rift of wonder opened in Logan's mind.

*   *   *   *   *

He saw light. He saw vision. He saw the glimmer of silver paint coating a vehicle. It was a Volve 95XT, a survivor in the automotive design wars. He loved this car. Loved it so much he repaired and cleaned it for low cost.

But it was not his. It was someone else's. A customer's who brought it into his shop before the nova of the world.

He saw in a mirror a face that was not his. It was Rampras with two eyes. Younger and with a smile. He was happy then.

He saw how Rampras struggled to put his oldest in college, his daughter into rehab, and his youngest into disability. Making ends meet was his worry.

He saw how he worked hard to keep the auto shop afloat in the harshest of economic climates. Those were not good days.

He saw how his wife's eyes worried with their mortgage nightmare, but hid it from his view. He always knew.

And how he was trapped in a bunker, frozen by a faulty pipeline before the nova explosion. And the devastation he felt when he was left alone on this world.

There were millions of memories overlapping with emotion. Memories of joy, sadness, and sorrow. Memories that could fill up a heart with a lifetime of experience. But the fondest of them all bubbled to the surface.

A memory of how he sat on a bench on his back porch with his wife. They were drinking tea and watching the glorious sun set over the trees.

"My home...my home..."

And as those thoughts echoed on, trailing into infinity and

oblivion, so did the vision of him and the moment he wanted to live in forever.

*   *   *   *   *

Thus he smiled. Then he was gone and Logan was sad. He closed Rampras's one eye, letting the last of that one glorious sight be his final view.

And with that, he stood up, weighing in on the legacy that was left behind. He didn't know how to start, but he knew it would not be this day. This was a time of battle in a world he hardly knew.

It was not his battle. Not yet anyhow.

*   *   *   *   *

Corlance watched the civilians trail out of the settlement's broken gates. He had waited far longer than two minutes in hopes that they were all clear, clearing his conscience of guilt to attack.

Virgil was by his side. He greatly disapproved. Many of those bodies carried away desires that he had lingered up. Desires he wanted to express. But he did not speak. Instead, he waited. Waited for the signal to attack, for other things could be salvaged in that wreckage of a town.

As the last of the people left the settlement, Corlance signalled for assault. The army of outcasts roared with delight and charged for the gates.

*   *   *   *   *

Logan saw them coming, coming for their lives. Coming up the slopes of the war-torn town that depended on his defense. One blade could not do it all or the cluster of bullet-less soldiers watching them come. The settlement was going to be overrun. They all knew it and there was nothing they could do.

The outcasts ran past the deactivated Samiren and onto the crumbled streets. Calis signalled a full retreat, but Logan just watched. He saw the roads fill up with the menace of sin as soldiers withdrew to the north. There were so many of them. He didn't know what to do.

Vanis grabbed him by the arm and pulled him as she ran. And so he did too, running through the streets, over the chunks of rocks and bodies of char. He ran through the back alleys, dodging a building that landslided onto the road.

As he caught up to the squadron, outcasts poured out onto the roads from every gap way that connected to the streets. The lines clashed. Soldiers fired off the last of their clips, covering for the withdrawing lines.

But they could not stop them. The marauders were too many. Too stubborn. Too angry with the judgments that made them to be, and so they charged. They forced their way through the streams of bullets, ignoring the painful slams of lead entering their bodies and continued their chase for the squadron.

The soldiers were being hunted down like cattle. The wounded were slashed down. Their helpers were beaten and trampled on the rush. Those that turned to fire were tackled to the ground. Thus they were being pecked off by their tails and the rest could only run.

They ran up the upward slope of the domestic ward and adjacent to the hall of speakers that was nearly crumbled from shock.

And as the soldiers fled for their lives toward the building of Calypso, a curious sight came into Logan's view. A dead Colonel Bowle lay on the concrete with his throat sliced open. Solito stood over his body with a mischievous smile and a detonator in hand.

But before Logan could react, Solito triggered the detonator and faded from sight. Fire erupted from the nearby facilities. The hall of speakers behind them collapsed to the ground. Barracks and hangers were ignited in a blaze. The whole of the northern settlement was populated with fire mushrooms and the demoralized soldiers trudged through the sandy showers of dust and debris.

Logan was terrified. He didn't know how it was going to end, whether through battle or captured as a prisoner and executed as an example of vengeance. He hated the hate. He hated the reasons for this war. He hated greed and tyranny. And most of all, he hated the violence. There was too much.

His head was pounding. His heart was racing. The only sound he heard was the pounding of his own blood rushing past his eardrums. His lungs stung with acid and his eyes teared from the dust. His hands got rough with calluses from all the fighting he did in the last two days. It was all too real.

And he was tired. So tired, while still only being a newborn to this horrible world. He wished he could wake up. But he couldn't. The dream was a reality and the only dream he thought of was the reality that was left behind.

He slashed down several marauders ranging too close. He aided a few that were wounded by lead but could only watch other soldiers and psionicists being trampled by the horde. There was nothing he could do.

So he looked ahead. The Calypso building was near. Maybe there was a chance to know what they were fighting for. At least, or so he thought.

*　　*　　*　　*　　*

As the last of the marauder lines filled the streets with pillagers and salvagers, a faint light flickered in the eyes of Samiren.

Corlance was too far away to notice that light. He stood by

his SUV watching his army in the siege. He was nearing his win. But it did not seem so. Not to him. Somewhere during that battle, he lost something. He couldn't figure it out.

As the roars of the wild savages claimed victory in takeover, he heard it from outside. Then he heard a rumble in the sky. It sounded like jet engines. He looked to the west and saw two fighters approaching from the distance.

He finally understood why Rampras was in a hurry and it was far too late to recall his forces. They were done. They were destroyed against a final tactic hidden from his view. He admired the cleverness and deceit.

But just as he resigned his battlefield throne, he noticed something else. Daylight was darkening. Unusual for this hour. He looked up. Thick clouds were rolling in. Echoes of lightning flashes hiccupped between the rolls.

It was huge. It was fast. It was an oncoming storm.

CHAPTER 25

DETERMINATION

Squadron soldiers stormed into the industrial ward of the settlement, but they were vastly reduced in number. No more than three dozen of them remained including Logan and the remnants of Rampras's squad.

The ward was mostly abandoned, but many supplies and tools were left behind in a rush. The silvery mirror-like building of Calypso, now cracked from sonic blasts, was landmarked near the edge of the ward.

Calis ordered the squad to fire off single-round suppression fire since ammunitions were running low. Extra clips were pulled off the dead, while wounded were carried to a blacksmith's forge. They kept cover in nearby market stalls and open-building indentions while the marauders were returning fire.

Logan didn't want to leave their side, but was very curious about the Calypso building. He wanted in.

"What're we doing, Calis?" Multanis asked.

"Uh...jus' lemme think!" Calis said.

Marauders were wailing wildly and popping in and out of cover from the ward's entrance. They hopped from cover to cover like gophers as though toying with the remaining squad.

"We're not gonna last much longer under this pressure," said Multanis.

"Don'tcha be thinkin' I didn't know the textbook tactics on that there, doc?" Calis retorted. "Why don't ye be tryin' some of yer diplomatic hocus pocus on 'em?"

Multanis knew the situation was beyond delegation. There was no bartering torque in a situation like this.

"There's still shuttles in the hangars," said Multanis.

"Get wit' the news, doc!" said Calis. "They gots the sabotage written all o'er 'em and that Corlance fella' prolly has the air." Then he paused in thought. "But they no have the north on their sides."

"Y'mean, the landmine fields?"

"Yeppers. We can skid-addle all our bee-hinds behind the bee's hind!"

"That's crazy! That field will wipe us all out!"

"Unless ye can pull a magic rabbit out of a top hat that covers the hairless hot and smoothness of yers, we don't have much of a choice if we wanna be countin' our next 'oh-it's-not-a-period' days!"

Multanis didn't have much of an argument on that.

"What about the Calypso building?" Logan asked while staring at it.

Calis took a quick glance at it then went back to shooting.

"Yes. It's a very nice building, popsicle."

"If we want to know what they're after, now's the chance to go see."

"Oh, did'ja have a plan on how to keep our dead men walkin' not so dead in a field of the big kabooms?"

"Get one of the locals to navigate. They should know the terrain."

Calis didn't have any other arguments to add. So he turned to one of the Gamma Squadron soldiers.

"Hey, happy pants!" Calis said. "Get yer men across the your's field?"

"My field?"

"Yes, the your's field! That field ye be callin' the minefield! And don'tcha be stoppin' for tea and doughnuts either, ye hear?"

The assigned Gamma soldier moved out. The squadron remnants followed. Calis and Multanis backpedalled and fired while Logan and Vanis shielded them from bullets.

After moments, they made their way to the base of the Calypso building. Marauders were still in pursuit, threading the streets with streams of lead. A sonic blast sliced through the sky. They looked up to the Western skies. Only the oncoming storm was seen.

"Aw, crappin' hell. They here!" Calis said. He bolted for the building. "We gotta be doin' this, right now! Go, go, go!"

They ran for the main glass doors. Logan slashed into the glass, then busted through with his body. Multanis and Calis jumped through the hole, but Vanis stopped at the doorway, clenched her gut, and groaned.

"Be him, the fieriest one, approaches high," she uttered.

Logan took a quick glance at the sky. He could only see the fast-moving storm. Then he grabbed her hand and pulled her in.

As the marauders pursued, one suddenly turned around. The others, alerted, halted with him. The one that stopped was listening to something. Bullets were being fired deep within the settlement. It confused him.

Then he saw something. He took aim...and fired.

*   *   *   *   *

Two fighter jets curved around a rocky bend and flew under the storm of webbing lightning. They came to the final valley stretch that led to Aquarius. The two jets were Blackbird 5s. They were slow but held many heavy-duty drop bombs in their hangar nests.

The captain of the two fighters dialled in trajectory calculations into the fighter's computer. Then he radioed in a response.

"Tango Alpha One to Epsilon Prime. We have our target on sight and are commencing our assault."

"Good!" Zintlaris responded. "Exterminate them all! They're traitors to--"

The radio fizzled out. Popping static and buzzing wailed on the channel.

"General. Please repeat. You're breaking up."

*　　*　　*　　*　　*

Inside the Calypso building, the floors of the main lobby were decorated with ceramic tiles. Marble walls and pillars were also decorated with reflective tile squares, giving the presentation a professional feel.

The word "CALYPSO" was engraved on the first few steps of coming in and footing around the front desks was carpeted. Many monitors around the lobby played videos advertising Calypso propaganda of grandeur, while a central computer terminal was between two side elevators behind the pillars. It displayed Calypso's layout, forefront criteria, and industry statements.

It was a very clean world.

"How we gonna be findin' it, popsicle?" Calis asked sternly.

But Logan had no response.

*　　*　　*　　*　　*

Nor did response come to the controls of the fighter jets. Sparks and electrical streaks surged through the main panels. Dials went wild. Arrows inside instruments spun chaotically. And the nervous alarm system screeched in terror.

"What in the world?" blurted the pilot.

He grabbed the main sticks, but it fed back a downward shift. The jet's nose dipped downward, aiming for the settlement head on.

"Tango Alpha to Epsilon Prime. We're going down. Repeat. We're--"

--A loud hum drummed into his ears. The pilot clenched his ears, trying to shut out the noise. He screamed wildly. He trashed around in his cockpit. The pain was excruciating. It was tearing into his head. The chaos of radio screeches drilled into his mind, clawing into his memories, his thoughts, scrambling everything he once knew, and distorted it into cacophony.

He opened his eyes. A vibrant colourful rainbow was in everything he saw. And the shakes of the jet shifted the hue. He was seeing sound.

Then he heard the whispers. Those horrible whispers.

*   *   *   *   *

Sounds of a jet engine roaring in pitch whispered through the marble walls of the Calypso building. They all stopped and listened. The pitch heightened. Then a loud slam and a rumble from an explosion.

"Was that the..." Calis said, then paused in thought.

They all looked at each other, shocked and alerted. Their mysterious assailant had arrived in the area. They took guard behind pillars and desks. Guns were loaded with the last of their rounds. Logan unveiled his blade while Vanis took stance. They were ready...ready for their final stand.

And thus they waited, staring at the broken glass doors of

the building. Only sand and the chiselled steps to the doors were seen. But gunfire was abundant. It was distant. It confused them.

They were so used to those sounds that they dismissed it for ambiance. But now the only thing on their minds was who were they shooting at. The Gamma soldiers supposedly retreating? Or something else they could not see?

None of them spoke. All of them listened. They heard the psychotic screams erupting from the marauders. They were distant but getting closer. They sounded like they were firing wildly, chaotically, and without care.

It was making them nervous. Then they felt it, that tingling scratching within their guts. Like a sudden plummet that causes the butterflies. But this one felt awful, like a sickness infection, a wave of fear, horror, and dread washing ashore within them whole.

Then the whispers came. Those horrible whispers coming into hearing. But they couldn't understand a single thing that was said. It was only a sound emitted as whisper. But something they couldn't hear with their ears. A sound emerging within their heads. A sound of malice indistinguishable with words.

It was the sound of randomness, the sound of chaos.

"I-I-I d-d-don't l-l-like t-t-this," Calis tremored.

His hands were shaking. His knees were weak. His heart was pulsing so hard that he was about to black out. He was breathing so hard. The others were too. Multanis was sweating and a puddle of urine formed around his feet. Logan was locked in dread and Vanis shed a stream of tears as she gazed at the entrance.

Then the sands around the building's entrance began to brighten, highlighted by an unseen force. Wind blew dust inside in a constant stream. The gun-fighting and wild screaming closed in on the building and the whispers intensified in their minds.

A vacuum of white light absorbed the doorway whole. Windows flared with flashes and the grounds tremored from its wrath.

"It's him," said Vanis. "He comes...the pinnacle of light."

The one who was there before you. The one who was there after you. The one who will be there...long after you had died.

"Telisque," Logan uttered.

Just as he said that, a powerful light blazed through the door and a marauder burst in, firing wildly in all directions. The squad didn't move. They couldn't move. They were frozen in fear from what was behind him.

More marauders bled inside, screaming and clawing at their heads. One screamed as he was sawing his skull open with a knife. Another was shooting bullets along the skin of his own face, slicing his head open.

Then the core of the light's source invaded the building. Sight distorted in their eyes, corrupting their very views. An irritating ring hammered into their ears as streaks of lightning spilled onto the walls.

The ground shook heavily, threatening to dislodge the pillars. Pieces of glass bounced along the floor as everyone else wobbled for balance.

But they did not pay attention to that. They all stared at the core, at the brightest bonfire of white they had ever seen. And deep within those white flames, a dark figure of a man floated in.

Then an echo of psionic power erupted from his body. Their ribcages and lungs rattled from the force. But the force that spilled was the force of words.

Determiner. DETERMINER. Where ARE you? HAVE you FORGOTTEN me? the psionic voice of Telisque spoke.

But there was no response. Only the electrical hums emitted from his body were heard. Not even the crazy wails from psychos were paid attention to.

WHAT is YOUR will, DETERMINER? Telisque said.

Then the deepest, most horrid voice of death hammered into their minds: *DeSTRoY THeM! DeSTRoY THeM aLL!!*

Calis collapsed to his knees. Tears were pouring down his face.

"N-n-no...P-p-please! N-n-no!"

I'm SORRY, Christopher, Telisque emitted. *SO, so SORRY! But NOT sorry. BUT yes NO yes NO maybe MORE or LESS not YES!*

Telisque cackled psychotically, which made Calis burst into a cry. Telisque floated toward them and all of the light and electrical charges followed.

Suddenly, Logan snapped out of it. He shook his head, but was confused as to why he was suddenly shielded from fear. He didn't have time to think. He grabbed his psi-blade and charged at Telisque.

He smashed his blade into him, but was blocked by a solid bubble of light. He kept hacking. Not even a single crack formulated on his shield and Telisque didn't even bother to notice him.

Eye FEEL the TWISTIES in ME! Telisque emitted out. *Quarrelly WHY the PING may TWO?!*

Telisque let out a wail. It sounded like multiple voices, octaves apart, screaming. It blended into an irritating ring, drilling ears onto a crucifix that was far more painful than claws on a chalkboard. Logan dropped to his knees and clenched his head. Blood was dripping out of his ears.

The others squirmed onto the ground, screaming their heads off from the agony of the psionic burst. The earlier affected Marauders suddenly bled from their eyes and ears. Then, the head of one exploded, while brain matter spilled out of the eye sockets of another.

Logan felt it was the end. There was no way he could combat a force so powerful and not even make a scratch. Thoughts fluttered and overlapped with memories. Memories of the streets, of buildings filled with light, and the lost Cherish he so craved to have saved.

But just as his mind filtered through the recent moments, thoughts of the Seer escaped and the Determiner spoke out:

WaiT! HiM! He KNoWS THe SeeR!

The ringing eased up. Telisque turned around and Logan suddenly flew toward the wall. His body slammed onto the marble cement and was pinned there by an invisible force.

THE seer...the SEER! WHERE is GALILEA?! We MUST have IT!

"Let...him...go."

Logan didn't know who said that. He instinctively looked at the doorway. Samiren was there. All of his black bandages were charred to shreds and his internal gears were exposed. His arm's turret had already formulated and the central micro-reactors were feeding power to it.

A low threatening growl erupted from the Determiner. He wasn't gonna let go without a fight.

And a fight Samiren intended as he charged up his turret. The charging whined in upward scale. His three chest lights brightened in intensity.

Telisque eyed him up, studying his dynamics. Samiren

was definitely a threat, a threat Telisque never felt before until that moment. He was proceeding with unusual caution, while Samiren powered with force.

Just as Samiren reached the summit of his power, heating the marble walls around him, Telisque thrust a hand at him, which let out a burst. The burst smashed through the southern building's walls and Samiren's shields shattered instantly. The blast sent him and the southern walls torpedoing into the sky, far past the compounds of the settlement, and into the distant horizon.

Logan was in total disbelief. He had never seen such a powerful force be cast away like an insect. So he gazed at Telisque in total submission.

But Telisque totally forgot about them. He floated to the lobby's terminal and smashed his hand into the internal gears. His electrical surges forced power into the machine and the screen flickered with images.

WE must HAVE it! Telisque said. *GALILEA is OURS!*

Logan tried to see, but the images were flickering by so fast, he couldn't make out what Telisque was grabbing.

Suddenly, a red hue flushed into the room. Everything was engulfed in that colour, except Telisque who fought against it. The terminal shattered into pieces and so did every other device: guns, radios, and all.

Tentacles burst through the floor panels and wrapped around Telisque's body. Redness was infecting his aura and Telisque fought hard to repel it. He squealed wildly, until the redness absorbed him whole.

His powers diminished quickly and Logan dropped to the floor. The tentacles pulled Telisque into the hole and he left behind screams in his wake.

As the red hue faded, Logan and the others ran for the hole, but only saw a red light diminishing. Whatever that was, it only wanted Telisque and not the others. Logan felt relief.

He looked around the room. A trail of dead bodies littered all the way to the front doors. Every electronic circuit and gadgetry was shredded to bits. And debris now redecorated this once fine hall.

Whatever chance they had in finding Galilea faded into nothingness.

There was nothing more they could do there, so they took a moment to absorb what just happened and left.

*   *   *   *   *

Miles away from Settlement Aquarius, a huge scar in the dunes led to a crater. A figure in black stood at its edge. It was Samiren. He was heavily damaged, but his fists were trembling. And a growl slipped out of him.

He was angry. Very angry.

EPILOGUE

Logan stood before an endless plate of sand. A thousand adventures and a thousand experiences could be had beyond that horizon. But his eyes weighed too heavily on his own experiences. He was scarred. Too deeply scarred that he needed time to absorb it all. And so he thought.

This all started because of me. When they pulled me out from the cages of a mad man, they woke him up...and all it took for him is to write one word.

One word...to plunge this world into chaos.

Galilea...galilea.

What is it?

...

How can we survive in a shattered world when all there is... is death? A world where the only enemies there are...are the ones we create?

How can we live...if we can't even unite?

...

I don't know. I don't know what to do. I wish I had the answers.

But I will not stand idly by and watch this world be destroyed.

Not again...never again.

This is my home. Our home.

And I...will do what I must to protect it.

We must rebuild.

We must survive.

With that, he felt charged with a purpose. He walked toward the horizon, waiting to meet up with that purpose. And so the survivors of Aquarius followed, following him toward the edges of those sands and toward a better place...

...toward a better home.

Printed in the United States
By Bookmasters